A LAND OF MIRRORS

D1331943

A LAND
OF
MIRRORS

Alfred Coppel

IVY BOOKS • NEW YORK

Ivy Books
Published by Ballantine Books
Copyright © 1988 by Alfred Coppel

Excerpt from "Rhapsody on a Windy Night" in Collected Poems 1909–
1962 by T. S. Eliot, copyright 1936 by Harcourt Brace Jovanovich,
Inc.; copyright © 1963, 1964 by T. S. Eliot. Reprinted by permission
of the publishers and Faber and Faber Ltd.

Excerpts from "Diaspora" in W. H. Auden: Collected Poems edited
by Edward Mendelson, copyright 1945 by W. H. Auden, and "Songs
and Other Musical Pieces" in The Collected Poetry of W. H. Auden,
published by Random House, Inc. and reprinted with their permission.

Excerpts by V. I. Ivanov from Modern Russian Poetry edited by Vla-
dimir Markov and Merrill Sparks, published by Bobbs-Merrill Company, Inc., 1967.

Library of Congress Catalog Card Number: 88-2147

ISBN 0-8041-0502-2

This edition published by arrangement with Harcourt Brace Jovanovich, Inc.

Manufactured in the United States of America

First Ballantine Books Edition: December 1989

Design by Camilla Filancia

For JULIAN MULLER,

editor, critic, advocate, and friend,

with friendship and profound admiration

PART ONE

March 12

the first day . . .

Cruelty has a Human Heart,
And Jealousy a Human Face;
Terror the Human Form Divine,
And Secrecy the Human Dress.

—William Blake,
  "A Divine Image"

1. ROME

She left the steps of the Hotel Gregoriana with a swinging, American stride. A child of privilege, heedless and filled with the vitality and curiosity of youth, the two watchers thought.

The rain bothered her not a bit. The rose-pink ski parka kept her warm and dry. The designer jeans hugged her slim hips and long legs. She answered to the name of Denny—for Denise. Her dark hair, long, straight, parted in the middle, glowed with good health and care.

The two men in the black Fiat watched her as she strode up Via Gregoriana in the direction of the Spanish Steps, as she had done every morning since she and her friends had arrived in Rome. Despite her almost sixteen years, she was a person of disciplined habits, and for this the watchers were grateful.

She paused for a moment to look through the rain-smeared glass into L'Isola Art Gallery. The exhibit there had been changed since the day before, and she stood, weight on one leg, foot extended, chewing childishly on the bow of her sunglasses. The pictures did not please her. She had seen better in Carmel-by-the-Sea, California's quaint town of art and tourists, eight thousand miles from Rome.

Denny Wells was a young woman of unafraid opinions. Sister Immelda, the art mistress at Dominican, had written in her yearbook: "Be tolerant of the Masters, Denise. They did not have your advantages."

Whenever Denny remembered, she smiled. Sister Immelda had also written glowingly of her to the department of art history at Yale, where Denny planned to start studying in the summer.

She thrust the sunglasses into a deep pocket of her parka and walked on past the *haute couture* establishment of Valentino. Not, she had been told, for the timid. But she had risked the

5

price of a scarf there, paying for it with her new American Express Card, a bon-voyage token from Megan.

She enjoyed calling her mother by her given name, though she suspected Megan would have preferred she did not. But Denny had long ago decided that to be too respectful of her elders would be to deny her heritage. The first Denise, her grandmother, had run off to join the French Resistance when she was younger than Denny was now. Her great-uncle Jack had nurtured her on tales of Grandfather Matthew Wells and Denise de Lattre.

The black Fiat rolled slowly along Via Gregoriana. The watchers were grateful for the girl's habit of making this walk fairly early in the morning, before traffic would make it necessary to follow her on foot.

The younger of the two men looked hungrily at the slender girl. He was fresh from a small town in the home country and unaccustomed to young women who looked like Denny Wells. When he was off duty, he fantasized about her, imagining her lascivious and naked. He hoped his superior had no suspicion of this. He liked Rome, though Italians' lack of discipline made him uneasy. And sensitive tasks were not given to libidinous men of no culture. The instructors at the training school had been very clear about that. Still, the American girl had a most provocative way of swinging her ass as she walked.

Denny glanced at her watch. It was not yet ten. Debbie and Liz were probably not even dressed yet. They would be having breakfast in the hotel room, playing at being sophisticated ladies. Wasn't there a song with that title? Something from Uncle Jack's day.

Thinking about her great-uncle made her smile. He was, of course, very old. Sixty this year, she thought. She could never understand why there was always a hint of estrangement between him and her mother. He had raised Megan Wells and treated her like a goddess. In expiation, Denny wondered, for some ancient guilt? Liz said that she was romanticizing, and maybe she was. But I come from a long line of adventurers, Denny told herself with inner joy, so who has a better right?

Via Gregoriana joined Via Sistina at the Palazzo Zuccari in a kind of narrow piazza. From there Denny could see the obelisk that stood at the head of the Spanish Steps. The guidebooks said that it had originally stood in the Sallust Gardens and that it had been moved to its present location in 1788. It was a Roman copy of an Egyptian original. In other words, Denny had told Debbie, "an early art fake." Debbie, who was entranced by being allowed to roam Europe in the company of two schoolmates and no chaperone, was shocked. As though, Denny had thought with a smile, such irreverence would bring the Dean of Dominican down on them in a black cloud of disapproval.

Denny raised her Minox—a gift from Uncle Jack—and aimed it at the obelisk. The colors in the tiny range-finder aperture were dulled by the lowering sky and the misting rain. But she had promised Uncle Jack that she would send him pictures. He had meant of herself, of course, but she had been neglecting her tourist photography recently. She had undeveloped pictures of Grand-mère and Grand-père de Lattre on the roll in the camera, and pictures of the gravestones marked "Thierry" taken during her top-secret visit to the churchyard in Thierry-sur-Saône. She must have the roll developed before driving up to see Mary Quinn at Santo Stefano.

The black Fiat had stopped. "Now," the driver said. "We will not have a better opportunity."

"There are people on the street," the younger man said.

"There are always people on the street. Do your job right and no one will notice." The driver put the Fiat in motion and swung past the American girl.

The car interfered with her field of vision, and Denny lowered the minicamera. A rear door opened, and a gross young man in a badly cut suit got out, leaving the door ajar.

In badly accented Italian, he said, *"Ah, signorina, prego—"* What followed was incomprehensible. He seemed to be asking for something. Perhaps directions.

Denny was completely bilingual in English and French, but her Italian left something to be desired. Yet she was too polite simply to ignore the man.

"I'm sorry," she said in English. "I don't understand you."

The man moved swiftly, pinning her arms and shoving her toward the car. The camera clattered on the street. A passerby stared. Denny said angrily, "Just a minute! What do you think you're doing?" She was unaccustomed to being afraid, and there had not yet been time to learn.

She found herself thrust into the rear of the Fiat, pushed to the floor. The door was slammed, and the car squealed away from the curb and through the traffic.

Now Denny began to react. She struggled to rise, but suddenly there was a cold, hard weight against the back of her neck. She could smell the acrid odor of sweat.

7

She half turned her head and sucked in a gasp. She had never seen a pistol held at such close range. Beyond and above it was a pale face, light-blue eyes that were bright with fear. This frightened her. Instinct told her that fearful men did foolish things.

"Don't shoot me," she said. "Please."

"Be still," the man said. In his free hand was something black. He slipped it over Denny's head, pulling her hair painfully. Now there was only darkness.

"Who are you? Why are you doing this?"

From the other man came a sharp, harsh order in a Slavic-sounding language. The man holding the pistol translated. "Don't talk!"

Denny shivered. She was beginning to understand about fear.

2. PORZA-LUGANO, SWITZERLAND

The man had once been handsome, but time had taken a toll and so had physical violence. The scars were old; the face had been battered and carelessly left to heal without medical treatment. The result was both frightening and deeply melancholy: a defaced statue of a man, brutalized by persons who had spent a lifetime learning casual cruelty. He sat at the wheel of a black Nissan at the *Kursaal*. There were few others in the parking lot. The restaurant was open, but there were few tourists. It was too early in the year, and the weather was fitful, with cold bursts of wind blowing off Lake Lugano and clouds racing across the sky to dapple the town and the lake with light and shadow alternately. From time to time the clouds would establish a temporary dominance over the day and there would be sharp little showers of rain with drops as cold as the ice that clung to the distant mountaintops.

The trees along the lakefront were still gaunt and bare of leaves. More trucks than cars rumbled along the cobbled esplanade, on the road to Gravedona, Chiavenna, and Saint Moritz. The tourists would come later. For the moment, the town of Lugano was Swiss, and attending to its business.

The man waiting in the Nissan approved. Not that the presence of tourists had ever interrupted his work or even caused a change in his sometimes elaborate plans. But it was better if his presence was taken to be a natural thing, a presence so ordinary—despite his ruined looks—that it would not be remembered.

He was by nature a precise and measured man. This seemed a denial of his French blood, but he was by now so far removed from his heritage that he thought of himself, sardonically, to be sure, as a citizen of the world.

From time to time there came particular duties he relished performing. When the object was an Englishman, it gave him pleasure. He had never liked the English, with their airs of superiority. Germans and Europeans of all kinds he regarded without preference. But when the object was an American, he worked with real, cold joy.

And now, on this day of sun and shadow, his pleasure almost showed amid the ruins of his shattered face. Today was more than business.

Today was retribution.

The parking lot occupied a corner where Via Rezzonico came to a dead end against the esplanade along the lakefront. The man in the Nissan had a view of the piers where the steamers docked in season, empty now, and of the distant breakwater of Campione d'Itália, across the lake. He also had a clear view of the faded pink façade of the Municipal Medical Clinic, into which the American had vanished forty minutes ago.

Across the street stood a kiosk containing racks of Swiss and foreign newspapers and a coin box. From time to time one of the orderly Italian Swiss stopped, selected a periodical, and placed the requisite number of francs in the slot. The man in the Nissan noted with contemptuous amusement that in the time he had been watching not one Luganese had neglected to pay. The American, however, had taken a paper without paying for it. The journal had been stolen with the ease of long practice. Even if there had been a doubt about the client's identification after all these years, the petty theft would have settled it. Dishonesty was bred into the man's blood and bone, the waiting man thought, as were treachery and treason.

9

He flexed his gloved hands on the steering wheel as the minutes slowly passed. Church bells struck the quarter-hour. Next to the newspaper kiosk stood a stone-and-wood shelter where passengers could wait for the omnibus. An old woman sat there with a string bag of groceries on her lap. She huddled in her gray loden coat, obviously resenting the wet cold. Patients and others came and went through the chrome-and-glass door of the clinic: a heavy-legged nursing sister in a cap and blue cape; a prosperous medico wearing a fur-collared greatcoat and homburg and carrying a medical bag; a man in a wheelchair attended by a gaunt, sad-faced woman drained of hope.

The man watched them empty-eyed. Most of them would be better off dead, he thought. Except for the prosperous doctor, who probably regarded them in much the same way they were being evaluated now. But the others? The cripple in the wheelchair and his melancholy wife? daughter? What did it matter, after all? She was as lost as the man to whom she was tied. The fat-calved nurse? What kind of life could she call her own? And the shivering, resentful old woman in the shelter? None of them elicited even a shadow of compassion. The world was filled with human wreckage better cleaned away.

At three minutes after eleven, while the echoes of the bells still reverberated in the stone church towers all over town, the American reappeared. He walked with pain; one could see that. He leaned heavily on a cane and dragged one foot. The man in the Nissan remembered him otherwise: always heavily fleshed, but oddly graceful on his feet, like a dancer. So what they said of him was true: He not only had cancer, but he was dying of it.

The man watched while the American, who might have been fat or thin under the heavy gray overcoat he wore, made his way across the street, following his routine exactly.

He sat down on the bench in the shelter as far from the old woman as he could contrive. Still misanthropic, the man in the car thought. Well, why not? Had anything happened to change that?

The American opened his stolen newspaper and began to read. The headlines were visible, even from across the street. The West Europeans were happy that all was going to be well with the world. The leaders of the great powers were going to clap their hands, and, once again, some few more of the weapons of nuclear war were going to vanish. The editors of *Corriere della*

10

Sera were calling it the Great Summit, to distinguish it from all the others. Yesterday, the date had been agreed upon. Today, it was not so sure. Less than three weeks ago, the U.S. Secretary of State and his entire traveling staff had been killed in the crash of their airplane as it returned from a Moscow planning session. A shock had moved through the sensitive political nervous systems of East and West. Things were still in limbo, though there were the usual rumors. Where would the world press be without rumors?

At ten minutes after the hour precisely, the bus appeared at the shelter. Public transport in Lugano was the responsibility of the federal government, and it was as exact as a digital watch. Both the old woman and the American stood.

The man in the Nissan started his engine. The old woman and the limping American boarded the bus.

The black Nissan stayed a discreet distance behind it as it climbed the hill and took the road to the village of Porza.

The Nissan followed for fifteen minutes as the bus negotiated a number of steep switchbacks and climbed into the wooded terraces overlooking the lake and the town of Lugano. At one particularly dangerous section of road was a shrine, erected by the family of some long-ago road fatality. Dead flowers lay on the altar before the statue of the Virgin.

As the road approached the village, the nature of the terrain changed. The swales were broader and there were chalets and cottages built into the mountainside. Dark pines stood in narrow groves between the houses. Gardens of rock and flowering plants made near vertical parklands where the chalets stood.

In the village square, in front of the church, the bus sighed to a stop, and the American descended. The man in the Nissan watched from a distance. The American seemed ill at ease. Instinct? Tradecraft? Would he remember it after so long?

He turned and started up a street out of the square. The bus moved on and vanished behind the stone-and-plaster buildings at the head of the square. Presently it reappeared as it negotiated the start of the narrow road to Bogno, three kilometers farther up the mountain.

On the way from Lugano it had begun to rain. The man in the Nissan parked the car, locked it, and started up the street the limping American had taken.

Rain dripping from the pines struck the scarred man's coarse graying hair. He wore a plastic raincoat that made soft whispering sounds as he walked.

He was not a large man, though he looked large. In fact, he was not six feet tall. His hands, hanging like objects from the sleeves of his raincoat, flexed slowly, unconsciously, as he walked.

A single bicyclist rolling down the mountain passed him. He waited until he had disappeared down the road to Lugano. Two women hurried across the square adjusting scarfs over their heads. They vanished into the church.

The man walked deliberately and without haste to the end of the steep street. There were stone steps leading down into a neglected garden. The stone-and-wooden cottage stood beyond that. A once-thatched roof had been replaced with plastic shingles. *Naturally*, and how typically American! the man thought as he walked the path to the door.

There was a tiny stained-glass window. He looked for a surveillance camera, but found none. Such things were expensive, and it had been a very long time since the American had had anything of value to sell.

He knocked softly at the door.

It was many minutes before he heard the rattle of a safety chain.

The door opened an inch. A pale eye and a sallow cheek appeared in the gap between door and jamb.

"*Che cosa?* Who are you? What do you want?" The voice was not as remembered. It was old and sick.

There was anger in the man outside the door, a consuming fire that made his flesh feel hot. He had not imagined it would be like this.

"What do you want?" the American said again, petulantly, still in Italian.

It felt like a bursting in his chest, all heat and red anger. "*You!*" the man said. "I want *you.*"

The American tried to close the door, but all his strength had been eaten away by age and disease. A single blow tore the safety chain from the wood. The American retreated across a dark room. Somewhere, he must have a gun hidden, the intruder thought. But there isn't time. His days have run out.

Suddenly there was recognition on the American's sunken face, and his voice clotted with fear. "*I saved your life,*" he said in English.

"I never had a chance to thank you."

The visitor moved slowly, deliberately. He was good at inflicting pain. The older man stumbled and fell. The visitor ground a heel into his genitals. "They used to do this often at Bung Kan," he said. The sick man screamed. His eyes protruded with terror. A blow broke teeth and mashed flesh. "Stand up," the assassin said.

The old man staggered to his feet. There was a blow, delivered with the heel of the right hand. It smashed the old man's nose, driving the splintered bones upward into the frontal lobes of his brain. He crashed backward, his face a bloody mask, to lie amid a rubble of smashed shabby furniture, twitching with the reflexes of the dying.

The killer stood for a moment, remembering. How good that felt, how very good!

He walked around the body of his victim into the bedroom. He searched the chamber with the efficiency of long practice, found nothing of value. Cancer and old age had drained the American. There was a certain luxurious justice in that, he thought.

There was a chest. He opened it. It was half-filled with books and old newspapers. He lifted the body easily, as if it were weightless, dropped it in the chest, and closed the lid.

He abandoned the bedroom and returned to the front door. He had stepped in blood and left a trail of rusty prints on the wooden floor. Let it mystify the dull Swiss.

He stepped outside and pulled the door closed. Still without haste, he walked up the path to the street.

A postman pedaled up on a spidery bicycle. He touched his hat and paused momentarily, balancing the bicycle with a foot on the ground.

The stranger's hand in his raincoat pocket closed on the grip of a 9mm Makarov automatic pistol.

"Have you been calling on Signor Blaisdell? Is he well?"

"Quite well. Considering." A pause. "Have you some mail for Signor Blaisdell? I would be happy to take it to him. He is resting, you see."

"Ah," the postman said, with a shrug. "Signor Blaisdell never gets letters. A pity. Everyone should get a letter now and again." He rolled the bicycle forward and remounted. *"Ciao, Signor."*

The hand on the Makarov uncurled. *"Buona sera, Signor Postino."*

As he watched the postman go, the village church struck the

half-hour with a booming of bells that reverberated through the trees. He froze, listening. Each time he heard church bells, he remembered his youth, and how he always wondered if the bells still sounded the same in France.

In time he came to know that it did not matter. It did not matter at all.

He went on down the steep street to the square, retrieved his car, and started back down the mountain toward Lugano.

He did not stop in the town. Instead, he drove on to the *autostrada*, turned south, and crossed the border into Italy at Varese.

March 13

the second day . . .

And the bullet he has made will
  whistle
Over the Dvina—gray-haired with
  foam.
Seeking out my heart, that very
  bullet
Cast by him will come and find
  its home.

—Nikolai Stepanovich Gumilev,
  ''The Worker''

3. SAN FRANCISCO

The ringing of the telephone woke Megan Wells degree by painful degree. She was not a light sleeper. Once she had fought her way past her chronic insomnia, she could sleep like a teen-ager. Work helped, and so last night she had read briefs—the kind of hopeless briefs a public defender got—until after two.

Lewis Baird had troubled her for an hour after dinner at the Spinnaker, trying his well-bred best to talk himself into her bed. But she had put him out on Green Street at midnight, pleading an overload of work, which was true enough but not the real reason she chose not to sleep with him. Her associates were certain she had lovers. Lewis ("separated" but not divorced) wanted desperately to be one of them.

The telephone bell insisted. She opened her eyes and looked at the illuminated numbers of the digital clock on the bedside table. Five after five in the morning? She tried to imagine which of her desperate clients would be likely to call at this hour. She could think of none. The people she represented were more likely to telephone a bail bondsman than a lawyer.

Sudden apprehension—not yet fear—started in her chest. Early-morning telephone calls were unwelcome when your only child is roaming foot-loose through Europe with her friends.

She groped for the phone, brushed a fall of hair from her ear, and said, "Yes?"

A thin, accented woman's voice: "Mrs. Megan Wells Thierry?"

Shock flashed through her. No one had called her *Thierry* for years.

She sat up and snapped on the light. The room around her sprang into existence—the bedroom of an affluent, successful professional. To a degree, the image was accurate. But her suc-

17

cess was unconnected to her affluence. Her money was family money, guarded and enhanced by Uncle Jack. Her salary from the city barely met the mortgage payments on this handsome apartment.

Her cat, Robert, named by Denny for Robert Redford, awoke, stood, stretched. He looked at her reproachfully and jumped from the bed. His panache of a tail stood erect as he marched out of the bedroom.

"Are you there, Mrs. Thierry?"

"Who is this?" Her voice was still thick with sleep, but she was fully awake, her heart pounding.

"This is the overseas operator. There is a call for you. Please wait."

Megan did not know why she was sure the woman was lying, but she was. "Who is this?" she demanded.

"Please wait."

Megan reached across the telephone recorder and snapped it on.

The woman said thinly, "You may record if you wish."

"Tell me who is calling." There was an edge of desperation in her voice that had been mercifully absent for many years.

The strap of her nightgown slipped down her arm, exposing her breast. Megan was in her late thirties and had an athletic body turning, at last, voluptuous. Her hair was the color called "auburn"—not blond, not brunette. It curled softly about a sensitive, mobile face. She still had some of last year's tan, a deep saltwater tan from hours of sailing on the *Denise*.

"Hello? Is anybody on the line?"

The numbers on the face of the clock-radio changed to five-eleven.

The voice, when it came, spoke in French.

And it was the voice of a man who had died in the jungles of Cambodia in 1972.

4. LANGLEY, VIRGINIA

The office of Director of Central Intelligence Daniel Street overlooked a broad forest of slender eastern pines, their ruddy trunks and pale-green needles glowing in the brightness of approaching spring. The sky was a thin, pale blue, a color to which Frank Traina, the Director of Operations, had never, in all his years at Langley, become accustomed. He had come east from Wyoming a long time ago, and he still missed the vibrant light of those mountain skies. "The East Coast," he had once said disdainfully, "always has a ceiling over it."

He stood for a moment at the window before turning back to face his superior, the man who held the job he might one day have—if he lived by all the rules.

Judge Street had served for twelve years on the federal bench before being dragooned by the President to take over the headman's desk at CIA. He had not sought the job, nor did he particularly like it. But he, like many others, owed a circumspect loyalty to the embattled man in the White House, and so he took Central Intelligence and had spent the last two years running it with almost virginal delicacy. Clandestine operations were down, co-operation with the Congress was at an all-time high. And the basic mission of the Agency was, thought Traina, being changed. The President's secret army was becoming Congress's department of foreign-policy research.

Now, suddenly, a ghost from the Agency's distant past was arising from an unquiet grave. And in spite of Street's disinclination to action, something had to be done about it.

Traina returned to his seat, a deep leather chair that left him regarding Street, at his desk, the way defendants must have looked at him in a court of law. Traina could not blame the Judge for the setting. The man longed to put on his black robes again. He had dreamed of an appointment to the Supreme Court one day, and his dealings with the Congress reflected this hope. It was a measure of the man's patience that he remained at his

19

post in intelligence, a specialty he had always found distasteful. It was said of Judge Street that he would have been happiest in a time when, as Secretary of War Henry Stimson once said, "gentlemen did not read one another's mail."

"I realize that it is going to create problems, Judge," Traina said. "But you are simply going to have to demand that the President step away from the Wells nomination. If he insists he must have Wells, at least prevail upon him to keep his intentions secret and his options open for another week or ten days. Until we can resolve this situation."

Daniel Street, a spare, balding man with the build of a long-distance runner and the look of a Sunday-school teacher, regarded his operations chief steadily. "I always thought you were Wells's friend, Frank. Didn't you two serve together here?"

"In Germany. We go way back. I met him at Stanford just after the war. I was a kid from Laramie and he was a big man on campus. The Wells family was important in California. There just weren't very many of them. But to answer your question, yes, I am a friend of Jack Wells and proud of it."

"Then you know how much he wants to be Secretary of State."

Traina pulled a brier pipe from the pocket of his coat and put it in his mouth without lighting it. Hillary had prevailed upon him to give up smoking after his last physical, and there would be hell to pay if he started again. But God damn, how he longed for a good deep belt of mixed nicotine, carbon monoxide, and coal tars. Hillary, who had once been a nurse, made certain all the latest literature of dread was available in the Traina house.

"I do know. And what's more, I'm sure he would do a hell of a job. Jack never wore a uniform, but he's a fighter, and don't ever forget it. We lost a great spook when he resigned from the Agency." He fondled the old pipe and then returned it to his coat pocket. "He has the three warrior virtues."

Street smiled bleakly. "Enlighten me, Frank."

"All right. Courage. *Toujours le courage.* That's one. Two, a need to protect the innocent. And that's something we had better think about. I'll have to approach Jack very carefully. His family means everything to him. And three—which is the only thing we can count on to keep him under control—loyalty to the king. Without that, any warrior is a loose cannon."

"You are quite a philosopher, Frank."

"For an old ranch hand, sure. But I need time to deal with Jack." He put a hand on the red file of intercepts delivered to

20

him that morning by armed messenger from the National Security Agency.

"How is he going to take it?"

"Jack worshiped his brother, Matt, and he fell in love with Denise de Lattre, Matt's wife, the first time he saw her, when he was eighteen. Their daughter, Meg, and Denny, their granddaughter . . ." Traina shook his head. "Judge, I really don't know *how* he is going to react. All I can say is, I'll talk to him. You'll have to authorize surveillance. Restraint, if necessary."

Street stared at Traina over steepled fingers. "I can't do that, Frank. You know I can't. The Congress would eat us alive if it came out that CIA was operating inside the country again."

"Goddamn it, we *owe* Jack Wells."

"Maybe we do and maybe we don't, Frank. But I was put in charge of the Agency to care for it, not to start the old troubles over again. If you feel so strongly about keeping Wells from doing something stupid, I will do this much: I will initiate a request *through channels* to Warren Kelleher at the Bureau. If he approves it, the FBI can handle Wells."

Traina's eyes turned steely cold. What could you expect, he thought, from one who had never stood on the barricades, who had never fought the good fight? He had said it himself. He had been made director to keep the Agency from ever doing anything that might embarrass the administration. But he was dead wrong if he thought Wells was going to do anything stupid. Jack wouldn't.

Street saw Traina's expression and raised his hands in mock defense. "Don't look at me like that, Frank. So Wells is your friend. Hell, he's the *President's* friend, and in this town that counts for a bit more. I will do what you asked about a postponement of the announcement. Not that it will scotch the leaks and rumors that are already flying. I met the Soviet Ambassador at a reception last night, and he asked me how soon the Senate would vote on Wells's confirmation. You know the Soviets have hated John Wells for twenty-five years, but the General Secretary wants the summit to proceed smoothly. So I will ask the President not to make an announcement about Wells. But he is going to want to know why."

"Tell him you are still reviewing some of the operations he ran in Germany. That should be good for ten or twelve days."

"You underestimate the President, Frank."

"As a matter of fact, I don't, Judge. He is a man who knows

21

when to ask questions and when not to." Traina reached for the red file.

"Don't take that outside the gate, Frank."

"Jesus, Judge! I need hard evidence. I have to convince the man. As far as Jack knows right now, Thierry is leaf mold on the Thai-Cambodian border. I won't be able to hold him when he hears that his grandniece is missing and so is her mother."

"Play the tape for him on a secure line. We can't let the Soviets know we have penetrated their communications in the San Francisco consulate. It's their favorite station for sending off the material they steal in Silicon Valley."

"They would never have tapped Megan Wells's telephone if it hadn't been for all the rumors about her uncle. We have the press to thank for that."

Street said, "Well, some you win and some you lose. Just play the tape for him and impress upon him that we are handling it on the European end."

"Good luck to us, Judge. Jack hasn't been in the field for years, but I'll bet you his tradecraft is as good as it ever was."

"How good was that?"

"Damn good. In a time when spies still got shot for doing their thing, he walked around East Berlin like he had a lease on the place. He knew the East German Secret Service like one of their own. I could tell you stories, Judge."

"What a pity we lost him."

Traina thought: He would have had your job and he would have done it better. But what good did it do to dream old dreams? "He had personal reasons for leaving us," he said. "You never met his niece."

"No. I understand she's a *pro bono* attorney."

"Almost the same thing. A public defender in San Francisco," Traina said.

"How do you think she is reacting?"

"The way you or I would if one of our children had been snatched. I sent someone to her apartment as soon as I read the NSA transcript, but she was not there. She wasn't in her office, either. My guess is that she is going to do exactly what Thierry instructed her to do."

"If it *was* Thierry."

"You heard the tape, Judge. *She* thought it was Thierry. That's what is important. He set up a message drop. Rome Station will have to black-bag it."

"A break-in, Frank? Is that wise?"

"What choice do we have? We have to know where and when he plans to meet her."

"Who will Herrick put on it?"

"Probably Ashburn. The actual black-bagging—well, Herrick has plenty of locals who are good at that. But I'll have to warn him about security. The Russkies don't know NSA's getting everything they have at the consulate in San Francisco." He took the pipe from his pocket again and rubbed the bowl with his thumb. "Did you know the White House had ordered protection for Jack and his family *three days ago*?"

"And Miss Wells just walked by them and left the country?"

"They weren't there yet, Judge. The people at Treasury told me they were going to start 'protecting' today."

The Director pursed his lips. His eyes were leaden. "How much of this does the White House know?"

Traina stared hard at his superior. "I would never, under any circumstances I can envision now, go over your head to the White House. I resent the inference."

"Calm down. I wasn't suggesting you would break protocol. Good Lord, Frank, this town would be a shambles without it. I was thinking more about what must be happening over at Treasury. Are they just going to knock on Megan Wells's door and ask the housekeeper if she is out of town, or what? For that matter, what are *we* going to do about the Secret Service people who will be descending on Wells?"

"Ask the President to hold off on the protection until the announcement is made. If he won't, we will have to hope that they keep their mouths shut when Jack makes monkeys of them and takes off after his niece and grandniece."

"Is that what he will do?"

"That's what the old Jack Wells would have done."

"If he leaves the country, we can legally take a hand, Frank."

And be a step behind for as long as the rabbit runs, Traina thought. He looked up at the wall clock showing Eastern standard time. "It's eleven-thirty, Judge. I had better go back to my office and make that call."

"Yes. Impress upon him that we are doing everything necessary."

Traina stood, picked up the file. "I'll tell him, Judge." And he thought: Will Jack believe it? Would I? Thank God I do not have to.

5. JOHN F. KENNEDY AIRPORT, NEW YORK

The man calling himself Dr. James Wylie stepped through the metal detector and picked up his carry-on case. He was a tall man, with regular features gone craggy and eyes of an astonishing, piercing blue. His passport stated his age as sixty, which was nearly correct, although it was the only thing about him it reported accurately.

The Glock pistol rested comfortably in a holster under his left arm. He was concerned about the plastic weapon. One could never be certain a piece of equipment would perform as promised. It had slipped past the metal detector as advertised. Whether it would fulfill its more lethal function as easily remained to be seen.

He could readily have acquired a weapon in Europe, but his connections there—of the darker sort—were no longer totally reliable. He preferred to deal with the retired spooks he knew at home, romantics who still longed for action.

Sam Sontag, the weapons maven, was one of the best. His sources were Israeli, all secret soldiers with good memories of Sontag from the days when he ran with Mossad and Shin Beth.

If Sontag had a fault, it was greed. Well, he was not the only ex-Agency man with that failing.

The Glock had cost two thousand dollars. To be fair, Sontag would have charged anyone else twice that. And, for the price, one bought not only a weapon, but Sontag's absolute silence.

Wells walked swiftly through the littered airport to the crowded Alitalia section. For a man who had been able all his life to afford the best, Jack Wells had an abiding regard for ordinary people. He was capable of awesome fury, yet his anger was always controlled and reserved for those who, like himself, lived extraordinary lives.

He found an empty seat next to a harried young Italian woman with two small children. The seats in the waiting area were hard and none too clean. He had considered, but only briefly, catching the Paris-bound Concorde from Dulles. But that would have been the first place Frank Traina would have Kelleher's FBI agents cover. Frank had been open about it. Judge Street insisted that he make no attempt to leave the country, no attempt to follow Megan, no attempt to recover Denny.

"You are one of the President's men now, Jack," Traina said. "You are platinum-plated. You are to let us handle all of this. *All.* Am I making myself understood?"

The infamous Wells temper had come close to bursting its bonds at that moment. But tradecraft came to the rescue. One did not bluster at bureaucrats. One acted. Swiftly and with purpose. So within minutes of terminating his conversation with Traina, Wells was on the move, within an hour he was armed, and within two he was on the New York shuttle. If one wished to become anonymous, New York City was the only place in North America from which to start.

One of the children, a boy of perhaps five with ice-cream traces on his chin, came near to tripping on an untied shoelace. The young mother, face damp with perspiration and weariness, shifted the sleeping two-year-old on her lap.

Wells said, *"Con permesso, signora,"* and put the boy on his lap and tied the shoe. The young woman thanked him and sat the boy on a piece of luggage at her feet.

Wells had been preparing to leave his downtown Washington offices for a lunch meeting with a client at the Madison when Frank called.

Joan Clement, Wells's executive secretary, had been slightly shocked to announce that Traina was on the secure line.

How like Frank it was, he thought, to know the codes. At the White House it was assumed that only the President's men knew how to reach Wells on the encoder-decoder, the KL-43.

Because it was Frank, Wells took the call, despite the fact that he, a compulsively punctual man, was running behind schedule this March day. Politics were thick in the air. The President had spoken to him privately only ten days ago, and already the rumors were flying.

A secret in Washington was like a naked virgin at an orgy. It was not a question of whether; it was only a question of how soon and by how many.

An hour later, his appointment canceled, Wells was still listening to a National Security Agency intercept of a Soviet wiretap on the telephone of Megan's San Francisco apartment. The blessings of modern communications and the new intelligence technology had combined to create a nightmare.

Frank asked if the voice was, in fact, Jean Thierry's. But Wells had no way of knowing. He had never spoken to the man. All of his business in Southeast Asia had been transacted through Blaisdell.

The sound of Megan's voice told him *she* thought it was Thierry. Wells heard her shock, then her anger, and finally her terror. But he heard no uncertainty. Damnable Lazarus was risen.

And with him had risen memories of Feliks Plakhanov, the old, almost forgotten shadow enemy.

Thierry had told Megan that he had taken Denny, and held her now, hostage to Megan's behavior. His words, spoken in the French they had customarily used together, had been as bald and as cruel as that. Since her return from Vietnam, Megan had become stoical. But Wells had heard the mingled fury and anguish in her cry of protest. His own pain echoed hers. Did she hate as much as he did? All those years ago, when Jean Thierry was only a file in the Langley counterintelligence computer, Wells had loathed him in an abstract way, as an enemy of the United States, as one of Plakhanov's trained killers. But when he learned that Thierry had found Megan and seduced and married her—used her to play his fetid Cold War game—he had succumbed to an icy, killing rage.

Now the nightmare had returned, the dead were suddenly the quick. And not only Megan, but also Denny was at risk. What sort of man, Wells asked himself, used his own daughter to extort concessions from the woman who bore her?

That was a foolish question, he told himself. He looked dispassionately at the people in the crowded holding area. There were as many bad fathers as good, and using a child to control a parent was nothing new under the sun. We are all capable of astonishing evil.

What is different, he thought, is that it is *you*, Jean Thierry. I was promised that you lay dead in the bloody clutter of an ambushed Khmer Rouge patrol.

Before this was finished, Blaisdell would have to be seen to. The Glock was for him.

It had been many years since John Wells had killed an enemy, but it was a skill one never completely lost.

The Company used to have bureaucratic euphemisms. "Terminate with extreme prejudice" was one of the best. Never "murder." But I am capable of murder, capable of cold-blooded execution, he thought.

He had known it for years, even as the softer life covered over, layer by layer, the reality. How ironic that it was the very same reality Matt had tried to share with him when he told his stories of life and death among the French Resistance fighters.

What Matt had tried to tell him was that life was a war that never ended. The alliances changed, and the weapons. But the intent never altered: Life for me and mine; oblivion for you and yours.

The passenger agents appeared and opened the doors to the boarding tunnel. Through the soot-smeared windows of the bay, Wells could see the big Douglas jet dressed in Italian livery shining in the fading light of the March evening.

As the waiting passengers for Geneva and Rome began to move through the gate, Wells tried to think what Megan would do first.

She would follow Thierry's instructions. That was a given. The man said he had Denny, and there was no reason whatever to doubt it. Megan had spent the entire morning yesterday trying to reach the families of the girls with whom Denny had been traveling. She had finally reached the girls themselves, and they were badly shaken. Denny was, indeed, missing. She had left the Hotel Gregoriana at nine, Rome time, and had failed to return. The police had a report of what appeared to be an abduction in the area of the Spanish Steps. Descriptions had been sketchy. A Fiat—no, perhaps a Volvo, or even a Toyota. It was astonishing that in a country as much in love with the automobile as Italy, descriptions of a single car could vary so.

Dealing with the Italian police was certain to be a problem. There were the national police, the Carabinieri, a kind of National Guard force with authority everywhere in the country. Then there were the Polizia Stradale, comparable to U.S. highway patrolmen. And there were the Vigili, the city police, descended from the police cohorts of ancient Rome, who "watched" the peace. The Carabinieri Captain to whom Megan had spoken, one Eustacio Guindani, had muttered darkly about *brigatisti*, the members of terrorist Red Brigades. It appeared that there had been a heavy infiltration of terrorists into the city of Rome in the last few weeks. The terrorists had not been active, but there were rumors of an important operation in the wind. And was the *signora* planning to come to Rome at once? The Captain would be honored to obtain accommodations for her.

Thierry had specified where he wanted Megan to stay. She had not passed the information on to Guindani. She intended to play it straight with Thierry. And she had been warned not to "contact Wells." That warning had been most specific and chilling. There had been a definite threat to Denny. Wells let the cold anger build in him as he walked into the crowded airplane.

But wouldn't Megan make one small variation from her instructions? She had some time in hand. Wells was almost certain that she would go first to Mary Quinn, at Santo Stefano.

The place was near Rome, and Mary was as familiar with Rome and Italy as any American was likely to be. She had retired there after returning from Southeast Asia, two years after writing her bestseller about the Bulgarian and KGB attempt on the life of the Pope. Megan trusted Mary Quinn. And Mary had made a study of underground and underworld life in Italy.

Yes, almost certainly Megan would seek out her friend first, Wells thought, sinking down into his aisle seat. She will be safe there while I look for Blaisdell and Thierry.

He closed his eyes and thought about his grandniece. Her face seemed to blur into his image of the portrait of the first Denise that hung in the living room of his Washington apartment.

He thought about Matthew and Denise as they were when he last saw them, boarding Matt's Cessna Twin so many years ago. A short flight to Squaw Valley for a weekend of skiing. A day so sharp and winter bright it made the heart ache. Denise de Lattre Wells was the most beautiful woman in the world; and Matt, the most handsome hero. A day, Wells remembered, just six days from his twenty-fourth birthday, the year he graduated from law school, the year Megan entered Miss Porter's.

He heard a child whisper, "Mama, the man is crying."

Across the aisle, the dark-eyed young Italian woman and her children sat. She said, in Italian, "Are you well, sir?"

Jack Wells loosened his tie and fastened his seat belt. "No trouble, *signora*." Then, because that seemed somehow inadequate, he added: "I thank you for asking. It has been a very long day, and I am not a young man."

6. MOSCOW

The thought was like a breath of icy air: *The Frenchman is running.*

General Feliks Ivanovich Plakhanov, commander of the First Chief Directorate—the foreign-intelligence branch—of the KGB stood at the tall window with his back to the long narrow office. He hid his tension with practiced ease.

The empty square two stories below was dusted with a late-winter snowfall. It gleamed glare-white in the floodlights. In the center stood the statue of Feliks Edmundovich Dzerzhinsky, a giant glaring sternly at the nineteenth-century façade of Number 2 Dzerzhinsky Square and the Lubyanka prison.

Plakhanov's father, Ivan—an angry and disappointed man—had named the young Feliks for Dzerzhinsky. Before vanishing into the fog of the Great Patriotic War, he had given his teen-aged son an admonition to revere the Revolution and the men who made it, the founder of the Cheka—the first version of the Soviet secret police—foremost.

The Cheka, became, through many metamorphoses, the *Komitet Gosudarstvennoi Bezopasnosti*. In spirit and discipline, the KGB was still the same as the Cheka, an organization symbolized by the escutcheon on the wall of Plakhanov's gloomy office: the sword and shield of the Revolution. But to Plakhanov, the KGB was more than a secret-police army. It was *the* instrument of Soviet power, never forgetting, never forgiving the enemies of the Soviet Union and its people.

Plakhanov stood with his back to the room's other occupant, his aide, Captain Valentin Ekimov. Plakhanov had once been an awkward boy, but in his sixties he was a graceful and impressive man. His lower-class origin was far behind him. All that remained was the memory of a brutal, scornful father, no mother, and a series of coarse women who shared his father's bed. Sometimes they fondled young Feliks, and laughed at his humiliation.

The elder Plakhanov had been a warrant officer of the secret police, the NKVD. During the war, he commanded a death squad operating behind German lines. The unit was to harass the Hitlerites, but never to engage them in open combat. Its primary mission was to find and kill Russian deserters and collaborators.

With such an assignment, Ivan Plakhanov's survival was destined to be brief. After an accidental skirmish with an SS unit on the outskirts of the village of Safonovo, he was captured while hiding in a cellar and hanged by evening of the same day.

Marshal Stalin heard of the execution on a day when heroes were being made. Ivan Plakhanov was made a *zampolitpolkovnik*, a political officer and a colonel, and posthumously awarded the star of a Hero of the Soviet Union and educational preferment for his son.

Of his father's honors, the last was the most useful to Feliks. After graduation from Moscow University and the foreign-intelligence school at Yurlova, Feliks Ivanovich Plakhanov became an officer of the KGB. Three decades later, he was a general and commander of the First Chief Directorate.

Though he had loathed and feared his father, Plakhanov had taken to heart the admonition to emulate his namesake, Feliks Edmundovich Dzerzhinsky. It was, he thought sardonically, the least he could do for the memory of a Hero of the Soviet Union.

Now, he looked down at the great bronze figure in the square. Dzerzhinsky had never failed in his mission. At Stalin's side, he held the Soviet Union in his fist. A cold man, but loyal to the death.

If there was one virtue Plakhanov valued above all others, it was loyalty.

Again the thought was like icy air, blowing across a darkened steppe: *The Frenchman is running.*

Strange sexual images ran through Plakhanov's mind, as they always did when he was under stress. He remembered Natasha, the sweat-smelling waitress who lived with his father during the early days of the war. Once, she had taken young Feliks's penis in her mouth, and when he failed to respond, bared her teeth, laughed, and threatened to bite it off, making him scream in terror.

What a sick and ludicrous thing to remember! It dishonors Peter's memory, he thought. And for a moment he remembered instead the play of pale sun on Peter's young back, his slender legs, the elegant curve of his brows, and the silver-gold of his hair. . . .

Captain Ekimov waited discreetly for a reply to his last question, and got none. The General, he thought, was a strange one. He appeared to be younger than he was. He had a smooth, narrow-cheeked face and a long boyar's nose. It seemed to Ekimov that the longer one lived like an aristocrat, the more one came to resemble one. It was easy to imagine Comrade General Plakhanov dancing at a tsarist ball.

Ekimov was never able to relax around the General. His manner was too cold. He was a shut-in personality. When the Captain's wife, Yelena Petrovna, met him for the first time, she'd said, "Valushka, he frightens me." He does not frighten me, Ekimov thought, but he does make me uneasy. His cold, quiet manner, his deeply set eyes, and, above all, his silence made Ekimov wish for other employment. It was a thought he had never spoken aloud, not even to Yelena. But she would understand if he did.

He cleared his throat and murmured, "You were saying, Comrade General?" It was late, and he had promised to drive Yelena and the children to the dacha tonight, to start the holiday weekend early. Now it appeared he would be staying in Moscow. The General was waiting for a telephone call from Comrade Kalganin in the Kremlin. At least, that was what Ekimov had been told by the last secretary to leave the office.

There were lights in the Lubyanka. Even though its primary functions had been taken over by the prison at Lefortovo, there was always activity in the old jail, no matter the hour. But the administrative offices of Number 2 were now almost deserted, except for the alert staff and the duty officers.

Comrade General Plakhanov liked the isolation of these old buildings, liked their dark history. Why else had he moved his personal headquarters out of the shiny new steel-and-glass complex at Teplyy Stan, twenty miles back to central Moscow?

Ekimov sat upright, military in every way, his pad and pen poised to continue making notes.

Plakhanov spoke without turning. "You have the dacha for the weekend." A statement, not a question.

"I do, Comrade General." The dacha was for the use of the junior officers and their families. But since it was nearer and more convenient to the complex at Teplyy Stan than it was to Dzerzhinsky Square, the people at Teplyy Stan tended to monopolize the bookings of the river cabin. Ekimov had been look-

31

ing forward to taking the children there. Now he would not be getting drunk, making love to Yelena Petrovna, or building snowmen with his children this weekend.

"I want you prepared to travel. I will inform you tomorrow or Sunday," Plakhanov said. "Does this interfere with personal plans?"

"Certainly not, Comrade General." Yelena would be furious, but what could be done about that?

Plakhanov heard the tone of voice and half smiled at his reflection on the heavy glass of the window. "Good. I will want you to make the arrangements. The women are inefficient."

Plakhanov never worked with the women in the personnel pool, and he had stripped his staff of all females. His contempt for women in intelligence work was legendary.

The General looked through the window at the lights of his native city. They were few at this hour. Moscow was not a city given to nighttime display. Only the monuments and the official buildings were kept illuminated.

Like a specter over the city, Valentin Ekimov's reflected image appeared to float in the darkness. The Captain was blond, good-looking, very correct. In some ways he reminded Plakhanov of Peter Arendt. But then, every handsome young man reminded him of Peter.

Valentin was tougher than Peter, and not so clever. And without Peter's joy and sweetness of manner. Of course, Valentin was married, to a dull wife, and had three small children.

Plakhanov said, "Notify Tikhonov in Rome that he is to cooperate with the Frenchman if asked to do so. It is not likely to happen. Thierry works with his own assets. But tell Tikhonov that if a request is made, it is to be honored."

"Are there limits, Comrade General?"

"There are always limits. But we do not spell them out for senior officers. Tikhonov will understand."

Ekimov absorbed the rebuke with disciplined passivity.

"Transport, weapons, personnel?"

"Unnecessary. The Frenchman has his own." But nothing, Plakhanov thought, will be demanded. Thierry prided himself on being an independent force. In the two-dozen missions between then and now, Thierry had worked silently and alone. The man had a genius for active measures. His contacts with Department V were so infrequent that Colonel Ryumin, the current head of Executive Action, did not even know the Frenchman by name. What a pity Thierry was not a Russian.

But, thought Plakhanov, we share a Russian sense of crime and retribution.

Ekimov said, "I will send the messages in the morning."

"Tonight, Ekimov."

"Yes, Comrade General."

"Now one thing more."

"Comrade General?"

"Notify Tikhonov that I will be in Rome myself, probably on Monday. I do not want to surprise him."

Surprise him? The man will shit in his trousers. As who would not? General Plakhanov had moved up to command the First Chief Directorate only six months ago. He was still the new broom, and bureaucrats feared new brooms with a passion. With reason. Already the General had shaken up KGB headquarters in Warsaw, Budapest, and Sofia. Agents of the Second Directorate's 11th Department, the so-called Sluzhba, which investigates economic crime, had all but eviscerated the KGB staff of the Kabul, Herat, and Kandahar *rezidenturas*, arresting members of State Security suspected of trafficking in drugs, selling military exemptions, or dealing in the black market.

Plakhanov, about whom there had been whispers for years, was developing a fearsome reputation as a puritan.

Tikhonov could be getting one hell of a jolt, unless he was a good deal cleaner than most chief residents on foreign service. Living in the West tended to corrupt men. For Tikhonov, who was serving out his last few years before retirement, to receive an unscheduled visit from the head of the First Chief Directorate was indeed going to be a shock. And Tikhonov was a friend of Yelena Petrovna's father, the Party Secretary for the city of Kirov. The old man would want to know why Plakhanov descended on his old comrade unannounced, and he would expect Valentin to tell him. But Ekimov had no idea whatever why this austere chief did the things he did. If pressed, he would have to improvise. He was getting good at that.

But he remained curious. Why *was* the General slipping off to Rome? Fantastic notions raced through his head.

There was a rumor that Plakhanov was ill with leukemia, and that was why he was so thin and white. Could he be going to seek medical attention in the West? That seemed impossible. The man was too much the patriot to look for medical help outside the Soviet Union.

Was it remotely possible the General planned to defect? That notion died even before it was fully formed. A quarter of the

33

members of the Politburo would be likely to defect before Feliks Plakhanov.

Ekimov considered the operation Plakhanov was running with the Frenchman in Italy.

He knew nothing about it, really, except that Plakhanov was taking an intimate and personal interest in it. Ekimov had never met the Frenchman, of course. Officers destined for high political offices (as he hoped he was) never met the bloody-handed mechanics of death who served in Department V. But the Frenchman was legendary. He had performed some of the most delicate and dangerous removals required by the KGB. And Feliks Plakhanov always ran him. Always. They had a history of working together that went back almost to the days when Plakhanov was chairman of the Intelligence Board of the KGB residence in East Berlin, at the time when the Wall and the Cold War were still new. Or so it was said. Ekimov had been a schoolboy in those days.

"Did you hear what I said, Ekimov?" Plakhanov had not turned from his scrutiny of the city beyond the window, but his tone had grown sharp. "I asked you if your father-in-law's friend in Rome has any reason to fear a visit from me?"

"I heard you, Comrade General. No, there is no reason Colonel Tikhonov should fear a visit from his commander and comrade. Even an unannounced one."

Plakhanov's thin lips sketched a smile. "You have no idea of why I am going to Rome, have you. Good. Keep it that way. In our work it is burdensome enough to know what one *needs* to know. You will advance more swiftly and farther by judicious ignorance than by being too eager to know too many things. Learn the art of sloth. If you cannot manage that, learn to dissemble."

"Comrade General, I assure you—"

"Do not assure me, Comrade Captain. Only send my messages."

"*Sir!*"

"You should have been a soldier, Ekimov," Plakhanov said. "You have the military manner." He turned and regarded his blond young associate with hooded eyes. "Go home."

Ekimov was instantly on his feet and putting his notebook into its case. No, Plakhanov thought, he does not really resemble Peter Arendt. Peter hadn't that slight coarseness of features that marked Valentin Ilarionovich Ekimov as a Great Russian Slav.

34

Ekimov finished with his papers and came to attention, clicking his boot heels like an officer cadet.

I wonder why we do that, Plakhanov thought. It was a tradition in Russia that wearers of a uniform be as military as Prussians. From the rifle-balancing, goose-stepping guards at Lenin's Tomb to the pouter-pigeon marching of the Young Communists on May Day, the citizens of the USSR were branded with the mark of the starchy old Germans imported by Peter the Great and the Empress Catherine to teach the Russians to be soldiers and to whip the Motherland forward into the modern world.

He nodded dismissively to his aide and turned back to the window, barely aware of the sound of Ekimov's boots on the polished floor and the closing of the office door thirty feet away.

Go, Valentin Ilarionovich, Plakhanov thought. Go to your damp-skinned wife and your sour-smelling children. The tragedy is that the future of the greatest nation on earth belongs to you and to them.

He opened a single pane of the window and breathed in the cold air. There was a slightly fetid tang of river bottom in the wind. He closed his eyes and tried to imagine what it must have been like, on an icy night not unlike this one, to have been one of the tsarist officers who got Rasputin drunk, stabbed him, shot him, and finally had to drag him, kicking, screaming, and cursing to the river, which finally put paid to the old monster.

What an incredible history this city has! he thought.

Across the square stood the Detsky Mir, its windows laden with luxury goods no Soviet family could afford and no Soviet child would ever wear.

Peter had never understood that luxuries were unimportant. He would look, first puzzled and then amused and finally tolerant. And he would say, "If you believe it, Feli, it must be so."

Do you believe it, Feliks Ivanovich? he asked himself. You certainly believed it then. But now?

He frowned at the empty square and at the illuminated domes of the Kremlin just visible across the roofs of the buildings beyond the Detsky Mir.

It was beginning to snow again, very lightly. Flakes fell spiraling out of the darkness and came to rest in the white square.

Peter had loved snow. He loved the unbroken white on a winter morning. The way trees stood leafless, black and stark against the snow.

Plakhanov became aware that he had himself under enormously tight control. His hands resting on the window frame trembled from the effort he was making to keep them from trembling. Paradoxes within paradoxes. The dagger was drawn in the name of one of the most peaceable and loving creatures he had ever known. What would Peter Arendt have thought about the Frenchman and the Wells woman and her daughter? The girl was not yet twenty—Peter's age.

Wasn't it fitting, after all? Wasn't that the meaning of revenge?

The gold telephone, the one that kept him connected to Gregor Borisovich Kalganin, the fat fool the frantic General Secretary had appointed to be chairman of the Committee for State Security, flashed a light and made its distinctive whirring call.

Plakhanov picked it up and said, "Yes?"

"Feliks Ivanovich," said Kalganin, "the meeting is over. I have a message for you from the General Secretary."

"I am ready, Comrade Chairman."

"He instructs me to tell you that you are to undertake no—repeat *no*—new initiatives *anywhere* until the matter of the summit is resolved. Is that understood?"

"It is, Comrade Chairman."

The man in the Kremlin paused suspiciously. "Whenever you are so politely acquiescent you make me uneasy."

Plakhanov remained silent.

"Did you hear what I said?"

"I did, Comrade Chairman."

"The day of the Stalinist is done, Comrade General. It may come again, but not now. Is that clear to you? We *must* have a rapprochement with the Americans. The General Secretary has met John Wells. He feels he can work with him. Operation Paladin is *rejected*. Is that clear, Comrade General?"

"Quite clear, Comrade Chairman."

"Then I bid you good night."

"I shall be leaving Moscow for another short inspection trip, Comrade Chairman. Do you wish me to give you my itinerary?"

"Leave it with my deputy." And then, as an afterthought and in a relieved voice, "Have a pleasant journey, Feli."

The use of the intimate nickname by Kalganin was like the screech of a fingernail on a blackboard. No one had been allowed to call him Feli since Peter Arendt.

Plakhanov hung up the gold telephone. The writing was clear on the wall. The decision to move aggressively against the West before the Americans could recover from the death of their Secretary of State had been rejected. Within a matter of a month, at the most two, there would be another man sitting at the desk of the commander of the First Chief Directorate. Plakhanov would have been retired to some threadbare dacha on the bank of some distant river. Ends came just as suddenly as that. To careers. To lives.

A crisis arose in the West. An aircraft crashed, and a man died. Decisions had to be made. That was understandable.

But when the Americans began to talk of Wells—of *John Wells*—as the most likely man to fill the dead man's post, Feliks Plakhanov felt fury.

In all the world, there was no man Plakhanov hated more than Wells.

In all the world, there was no man who had inflicted more grievous injury on Plakhanov than had Wells.

In this, the Frenchman and Plakhanov were united.

The General had had the Frenchman airlifted out of Pakistan, where he was on the trail of a troublesome Afghan mullah. Thierry had needed no convincing. He had been glad to come. And, moreover, Plakhanov had been running Thierry for the last eighteen years. The Frenchman was near retirement. It was one last act of love.

Plakhanov thought of Chairman Kalganin and the General Secretary. They had slipped into a never-never world of *glasnost* and *perestroika*, openness and restructuring. They had envied the West for one long season too many. They had visited too many foreign capitals, prowled in state and splendor through too many stores overflowing with useless luxuries.

He turned and looked again at the city. Moscow was not a city of nighttime gaiety. Its pleasures were hidden in clubs and cellars where young Muscovites danced the West's degenerate dances and listened to the West's ugly music and smoked the kilograms of opium brought home from Afghanistan by weary, frightened soldiers. Moscow streets were supposed to have been swept clean of drunkards. So they had been. The city's ancient vices had been gross and straightforward. Now they were sophisticated and degenerate.

This is your Moscow, Comrade General Secretary, Plakhanov thought, no longer mine.

He watched the lights used to illuminate the domes and walls of the Kremlin turn the underside of the low clouds to the color of tarnished brass.

He thought about the long night meeting at the Kremlin. They had talked and talked there, he thought, just as if they, and not I, controlled tomorrow.

They were planning an agenda to present to Secretary of State John Wells. I am planning his descent into hell.

The Frenchman is running. At last. At long, long last.

March 14

the third day . . .

The memory throws up high and dry
A crowd of twisted things;
A twisted branch upon the beach
Eaten smooth, and polished
As if the world gave up
The secret of its skeleton,
Stiff and white.

—T. S. Eliot,
  "Rhapsody on a Windy Night"

7. ROME

Denny awoke shivering with cold and afraid of the darkness. There was a strip of surgical tape across her mouth, another over her eyes. Her arms ached. Her hands felt numb, dead. She could not understand why they had done this to her. Did two men and possibly others fear she was going to attack them?

They had taken her clothes. She lay in a closet or a room as small. There was a thin pad or mattress on the floor. She could not see it, but before her hands went numb she had felt it by groping behind, straining against the wire wound around her wrists.

She was in bra and bikini briefs. The briefs were wet and fouled, and so was the mattress. They had given her water but no opportunity to relieve herself. She was humiliated and terrified that such things could happen to her.

Her nakedness made her vulnerable in a way she had never before experienced: helpless, unable to repel, or even resist, assault. She felt open, her most intimate parts undefended, indefensible. The horror of it was that the sexual fear she felt congealed in her loins and brought her to the edge of orgasm.

Yet the people who had taken her from near the Spanish Steps and thrust her into this loathsome place had made no move to trouble her sexually. They appeared to have stripped her to heighten her sense of powerlessness. She remembered reading long ago something Bruno Bettelheim had written about the Nazi death camps: that on arrival at places like Sobibor and Treblinka, prisoners had been paraded naked before the SS guards, and the woman were made to run so that their flesh bounced and jiggled with a nightmarish vulnerability. There was no record of any of those women ever resisting, even when all hope was gone. It was not the nearness of death that held them, but the conviction of their own helplessness.

In the acrid darkness, Denny fought back the spasms that had in the last twenty-four hours—or longer—drained her of tears.

There were steel cuffs around her ankles. Her bare feet were icy. Her briefs had ridden high between her buttocks, and she could not free them.

She had begun to remember some of the stories Uncle Jack used to tell her about her grandmother, that she had risked this, and more, fighting with the French Resistance during the war. They had never captured Denise de Lattre, but if they had, Denny told herself, she would have felt as she did now.

But she would not have surrendered. The steel core Uncle Jack always said was inside a truly brave man or woman would have held her together, made her resist in any way she could, until death released her.

Death . . .

It was a concept unfamiliar to a teen-ager. Oh, there was death in the films, death in the back alleys of a TV Miami or Chicago, even death in the war stories Uncle Jack used to tell. But nothing in her life had ever prepared her to encounter death in a closet that stank of her own urine. Death while clad in strips of soiled silk that exposed more than they concealed. Death without explanation, without reason . . .

Without dignity.

She strained to ease the ache in her arms. Her hands tingled as though being attacked with pins when she flexed her fingers.

She could lean against the bare wall. Or she could lie on her side on the wet mattress. She could do neither for very long.

She tried to remember what she had read of the case of Patty Hearst. Not much. But the girl had been held in a foul place like this one, and it had broken her. She had joined her tormentors. It had been a long time ago, when Denny was barely aware that such things happened in real life.

She began to wonder why she had been taken. Why Denny Wells? Why *me*?

And, for the first time, she began to think of herself as though she were one of the players in Uncle Jack's stories. Long ago he had told her that prisoners, some who faced years of confinement, kept themselves sane by reviewing the things residing in their memories unknown until the moment of need. A woman agent held for years by the East Germans had mentally transcribed all the Beethoven piano literature. A scientist in the

42

gulag had remembered and reviewed the entire New Testament. Less intellectually gifted prisoners had found something, anything, remaining from their previous life with which to keep themselves sane, and resisting.

But I'm only a girl. . . . The tendency to whimper and look for sympathy was overwhelming.

And from whom should she ask sympathy? From the two thugs who had kidnapped her? From the owners of the other voices she heard through the walls of her evil-smelling hole? Uncle Jack had always said that the prisoner must find a way to escape prison intellectually, when there could be no physical escape. Try to understand what had happened and why. When one knew the reason for events, one might just possibly be able to influence them.

Then why had she, Denny Wells, been abducted on a Roman street? Her mother was a reasonably affluent woman, but both of the girls Denny had traveled to Europe with came from families wealthier than hers.

Her breath caught and shuddered in her throat as she thought about her mother. God, how was Megan taking it? By this time—and how long had it been? what did it matter?—she must be frantic.

But this had not been done because of Megan Wells. That simple fact became clear. Even if it was the only thing that did.

No. She had been taken because Uncle Jack might become the Secretary of State.

There could be no other reason. The act was political. And that both frightened her further and relieved her at the same time.

She probably need not face any but impersonal cruelty, the hatred of foreigners for Americans. Was that a reasonable assumption? She thought it was.

She tried to think of what Jack Wells's response to the abduction of his grandniece was likely to be.

Uncle Jack had been in the CIA many years ago. He was a friend of the President. He was an important man.

Surely there were forces being mobilized to find her by now. How could there not be? Hadn't the Italian police rescued an American general once? Hadn't they crippled the terrorists who once ran rampant in Italy? How often did one hear about the Red Brigades nowadays?

Her shoulder, resting against the splintery wall of the dark box in which she lay, began to ache. She struggled to take her

43

weight off it and fell against what felt to her naked arm like a door.

From outside came a booming, banging on the wall and a command to be silent. In German.

She did not recognize the language immediately. For one terrible moment she imagined she might be hearing Farsi or Arabic—which would mean that she was in the hands of fanatics, people who were appallingly willing to kill in the name of a merciful and compassionate God.

Suddenly the door was opened, and Denny felt an icy blast of air on her bare shoulders and belly. She had been sweating. Not from warmth, but from fear. The cold air on her skin racked her with shivering. She squeezed her thighs together to hide her pudenda.

A man's voice said in that Low German dialect, "Has she been fed?"

Another said, "Not yet."

"Once a day is enough." The crude one again. She listened for the voices and Slavic accents of the men who had abducted her, but she did not hear them. Had they done their part and gone?

A woman's voice said, in Italian. "She's shivering."

A German said, "Wouldn't you be?"

She felt a hand on her barely covered breast. Fingers pinched her nipple, and she recoiled violently, kicking out at nothing with her chained feet.

"Pig," said the woman. "Be careful. She is valuable."

Denny, shuddering, tried to curl in upon herself, like a spider pierced with a needle.

But she was "valuable." Bastards.

Probably they assumed that, like most Americans, she spoke only English. That gave her one tiny advantage. She could understand things she was not expected to understand. When Uncle Jack came for her, she could give him snippets of information about her abductors. She could help him—do what? Punish them.

I am Denise de Lattre's granddaughter, she thought. I will not be afraid of these people.

There were tears smeared on her cheeks where they had leaked out under the tape on her face.

A woman's hand, small and hard, pushed her down in the closet, the box, whatever it was, the hateful stinking place of her confinement.

The woman addressed her in a kind of Euro-English. "Behave yourself, American bitch. Tomorrow may be better."

Tomorrow, Denny thought. When is tomorrow?

Not too many years ago, in Tehran, Americans were held for 444 tomorrows in their own embassy. In Lebanon, Americans, Germans, Frenchmen had disappeared years ago and lived only in taped images cruelly sent to their grieving families.

How long will I be here? she thought. How long?

She had a strange connected flash of memory. Sister Marcia was reading Shakespeare to a sixth-grade class. *King Henry VIII*. Somewhere in the third act. One of the old churchmen, Cardinal Wolsey, or perhaps Sir Thomas More—it was difficult to remember after so many years—was complaining of his king:

> *Had I but served my God with half the zeal*
> *I served my King, he would not in mine age*
> *Have left me naked to mine enemies.*

And a roomful of little girls had tittered and giggled.

If the fear would not retreat, perhaps she might keep it at bay with the bitter wand of irony.

8. LANGLEY, VIRGINIA

Technology, Frank Traina thought, how we have come to rely on it. There was once a time when the high-tech communications console in his office would have been considered a miracle. Now he sat face to face with Reuben Herrick, the Rome Station chief, as though they occupied the same cubicle in the subbasement. Herrick, his stretched New England face as dour as ever, regarded him out of a television monitor so refined that the unshaven spots on his hollow cheeks (missed, no doubt, because it was six in the morning in Rome) were revealed in three-dimensional detail.

At nine o'clock last night, Washington time, Langley had been able to inform Herrick that Wells, traveling with one of several false passports, had left New York aboard an Alitalia flight.

Now, at midnight, the word had gone out that Wells was carrying a passport in the name of James Wylie, a medical doctor. An addendum had warned Herrick's station that it was not likely the passport would be used again, but a check with Italian Customs might be useful.

It was typical of Herrick that, though he had been awake most of the night, he had still managed to put on a clean shirt and a tie and to shave before his television meeting with the Director of Operations.

Herrick would have made a fine eighteenth-century preacher, Traina thought. He had the face and manner for it. And, in fact, an ancestor of his had served in the Continental Army as a military chaplain. Traina's own people had come to the United States only in 1907. It took all kinds to run a circus. Traina had learned that long ago from Jack Wells.

Herrick said, "All right, here's a sitrep."

Times did change, though. No Valley Forge preacher trying to keep the troops loyal would ever have used a word like that one.

The Rome Station chief proceeded to give his situation report. "I had to pull Ashburn off his present assignment, but it's done and he's on the way to Mary Quinn's place at Santo Stefano. She's not very happy about that, by the way. Her journalistic purity is at stake."

"Bullshit, Reuben. Every terrorist in Europe knows Mary has a private line to the Company. It was her choice to use the stuff we gave her. Now that it's been published, she can't grow another hymen." Quinn's book, *Blood in Saint Peter's Square*, on the attempted assassination of the Pope by the Bulgarians and the KGB, had changed her from a retired foreign correspondent to a best-selling author. In the last six years she had developed contacts inside every Western intelligence service and had become an authority on political terrorism in Europe. Traina was certain that Megan Wells, who had known her in Vietnam, would not go to Italy without turning to Quinn for help.

The watch CIA had put on Leonardo da Vinci Airport had located Megan as she deplaned, hollow-eyed with worry and exhausted from her transpolar flight from the West Coast.

Herrick reported that she had rented a car and headed northeast toward the mountains of the Abruzzi.

He said now, "We broke into the Sword and Scabbard and

46

fiddled the message drop. Thank God for the computer hackers at NSA. The meet is set up for 2200 next Tuesday. The Vatican Museums.''

"Ashburn is not to tell what we know or how we know it. That comes from the Judge," Traina said.

"You seem to be suggesting he might be difficult. Why?"

"He knew Megan Wells in law school. I don't know what there was between them. Something. But he's probably the only man she'll accept as a baby-sitter in her present state of mind.''

Herrick's face grew even longer. "The police found Denise Wells's Minox. They developed the film. There is one shot she must have taken just before she was abducted. There are two Moscow hoods in the picture. We put their faces on the circuit with Bonn and Paris and London, and the Brits came up with a make on them. Low-rank muscle, but new to Rome. My guess is that they were just moved in to snatch the girl.''

Traina reached into his desk for an antacid tablet. "Thanks, I really needed that. The pressure is on, Reuben. Wells is a Cold Warrior, and the bad guys are scared he is going to take over at State." He frowned. "What I don't understand is why they are taking such a chance. Wells is a buddy of the President. They could end up with a Defcon Three on their hands. What the hell could they be thinking of?"

"Something is brewing here, Frank," Herrick said. "The antiterrorist police units are on alert. They won't say they've had any warning, but no one is heading for the seashore, either. I wish . . ." He broke off abruptly.

Traina knew exactly what he wished: that the American intelligence community was still trusted, as it once had been. But the oversight laws voted by a leaky Congress eager to micro-manage foreign policy had made American intelligence a pariah among the spy services of the West. They are afraid of us, Traina thought bitterly, and I'm damned if I blame them.

"If Megan Wells is on the way to Santo Stefano, how long will it take her?" he asked.

"It's rough country, Frank. The roads are goat paths. She must be worn out from her flight. I'd say she should get to Quinn's about seven-thirty or eight. She won't be able to make any sort of time in that country." He hesitated, but there was no way he could avoid saying what he had to say. "We lost Wells." There was no point in attempting to deceive the home office. A storm of spears was falling on his station, and there was no way it could be avoided.

47

"You *lost* him?"

"He remembers, Frank. Keep that in mind. Tradecraft. He's still pretty good."

"Pretty good?"

"All right. Damned good. We thought we were on top of the situation. We had Alitalia contact the flight. What we didn't realize until then was that it made a stop in Geneva. We didn't cover it. Sorry, Frank. What can I say?" Herrick looked chagrined.

"I suppose we should have been sharper on this side," Traina said. "I should have spoken to you personally."

"Rome Station thanks you. But I am assuming you want him found. How much manpower am I to allocate to Wells?"

He means, Traina thought, to a potential Secretary of State on a rampage.

"None, Reuben," he said.

"*None?*"

"That's what I said. Leave him alone. He has a Glock 17 with him. He might use it on anyone who tries to stop him."

"Holy Jesus."

"Do you blame him? The opposition is targeting his niece and his grandniece. I'm the one who set him off. I let him hear the tape the Russians made of Thierry and Megan. I knew he was going to go ballistic, but I couldn't keep the information from him. He had a right to know."

Herrick's image stared out of the television screen, hard as a prosecuting attorney's. "There's something I don't understand, Frank. Enlighten me. What is the Frenchman to Megan Wells? Or to Jack Wells, for that matter?"

"It's a long story, Reuben. I suggest you drop it."

"No need to know?"

"Someday. Not now."

"All right," Herrick said. "But you should copy this, Frank: General Plakhanov runs the Frenchman. Personally."

"I'm aware of that, Reuben," Traina said.

"You had better tell the President to pick himself another guy to run State. The odds on Wells aren't all that great."

"You're out of line, Reuben."

"If I am, I apologize. But if we don't do something about protecting Wells, he's dog meat."

"Your comment is noted, Reuben."

"He's an old man, Frank."

"He could surprise you."

48

"Is the Secret Service on his case?"

"I appreciate your concern."

"So fuck off, is that it?"

"Keep an eye on Megan Wells. Cooperate with the police on the girl's kidnapping, I'll be in touch with you regularly."

"Can I at least have a copy of the tape NSA stole from the Russians?"

"It is on its way to you by diplomatic pouch. You should have it by the morning courier." Traina managed a rueful sketch of a smile for Herrick. He understood the station chief's feelings exactly. It was thoroughly unpleasant to have your territory invaded by both friendlies and hostiles without ever being told the whole story. It was even worse to know, with gut-wrenching certainty, that before events ran their course, there would be bloodshed.

Reuben Herrick knew John Wells only by reputation, but that was enough to impress him. Wells was not a man one challenged without an explosive response. Perhaps, he thought, what that old fox Plakhanov had in mind was to discredit Wells, goad him to violence—even murder—and so make him useless to the administration.

No, he thought, no. That rang false. He stared at Traina's image on his screen.

The Director of Operations knew. He had served with Wells in Berlin. Whatever it was, he knew it all.

Traina said, "All right, Reuben. I want hourly reports until all the cattle are back in the barn."

"Yes, sir."

"Have a nice day," Traina said, and broke the satellite link.

He picked up the telephone on his desk and said, "Get me the duty officer." Then he stared at the dark forest beyond his windows as he waited. The almost-empty parking lot below gleamed in a thin, drizzling, almost-spring rain.

The duty officer said, "Cannaday, sir. I have the duty."

Traina's mind worked automatically. Cannaday: ex-Naval Investigative Service; before that, Seals. We could have used a dozen like him in Berlin in the fifties. But we had Jack Wells. *Tyger! Tyger! burning bright . . . Did he who made the Lamb make thee?* Not likely, but He actually had. Made him out of images of his elder brother, Matthew Wells, hero of the OSS, of the French Resistance. Lord, thought Traina, that must have been a hard act to follow.

"Sir?"

"Cannaday, ask the computer for the present telephone number of Charles Morgan Blaisdell. He is a retired intelligence officer living somewhere in Switzerland. Get the number and get him on a secure line for me."

"Yes, sir."

Traina replaced the receiver and waited. The unpopulated offices around him had an almost palpable emptiness. Echoing spaces under cold fluorescent light.

The telephone blinked. Traina lifted the receiver.

Cannaday said, "There is no answer, Mr. Traina."

Traina stared, unseeing, at the night beyond the windows.

"Mr. Traina?"

"Where did the computer say he was living?"

"Porza-Lugano, sir. Do you know where that is?"

"Yes, I do. Thank you, Cannaday."

"Shall I try again later?"

"No. And, Cannaday, since the call did not go through, there is no need for you to log it."

There was a long pause on the line. Then, "Yes, sir."

9. THE ABRUZZI

From Rome to L'Aquila there was a high-speed expressway, and Megan used it, fast. She knew European driving, and the Alfetta she had rented at Leonardo da Vinci had been designed with Italian roads in mind.

She had left the airport at five o'clock, and by six she was in the mountain town named for the eagles of Rome. But as the dawn began to lighten the sky to the east of the bare mountains, she found herself on secondary roads that were both narrow and twisting as they wound through steep valleys and clung to the flanks of terraced hills.

Life in the Abruzzi had never been easy. The land was beautiful, but in a hard, austere way that previewed the stony landscapes of the south. It was said that even Christ had stopped at Eboli. The Abruzzi lay north of that place, but, as the natives took pride in saying, it escaped Christ's dismissal by accident and the devoutness of its people.

Megan had visited Mary and Zachary Quinn with fair regularity. She had seen their hillside villa grow from a stone mountain farmhouse into a quite respectable home for a pair of expatriate Americans past middle-age and ready to enjoy comfort, mountain silence, and the lunar vistas of the Abruzzi.

Even at this early hour of the morning in the last month of winter there were a number of people walking the roads. The farmers had grown few in the Abruzzi, and villages lay deserted on the higher slopes of the mountains, stone ruins unable to sustain a working farming population and not yet discovered by the smart set who would almost certainly, in time, turn the area into a resort where millions of lira would be made by future entrepreneurs.

In the last hours of true darkness, Megan, gravel-eyed with fatigue (she had not truly slept since receiving Jean Thierry's terrible telephone call), had clung to the steering wheel of the Alfetta with aching hands. She had hardly slackened her pace since leaving the expressway. From time to time, weariness would play tricks on her, and she would imagine that small animals were snapping out of the darkness of the roadsides and under the wheels of her car. But after the first few dangerous avoiding swerves, she gritted her teeth and drove straight through the darting shadows, and discovered that they were products of her tired eyes and brain.

But now that there was a morning twilight to drive by, and long stretches of road between villages empty of traffic, she found herself driving even faster. She dare not think too clearly about Denny. Jean had, at least, as much as promised that she would not be harmed. For the moment, that was all she had to cling to.

There was movement by the roadside, and this time she reacted, sending the Alfetta into a long, tire-screeching skid that nearly ended against a kilometer stone. A man and woman shouted abuse and shook their fists. The woman carried a rake, the man a sickle. The woman's hair was tied up in a kerchief; her thin legs were in black stockings under a black skirt. Both of them wore heavy boots. They were like blackbirds cawing their anger at the driver who had nearly struck them. Megan, her heart pounding, considered waiting for them so that she could apologize, even, perhaps, offer them a ride to wherever they might be going.

She decided against it. There was no time. She needed desperately to speak to Mary.

She caught a forward gear and spun the rear wheels on the loose gravel coating the road as she accelerated up the valley.

Ten minutes later she was swinging from one switchback to the next as the narrow road wound up the sheer mountain topped by the village of Santo Stefano. The Quinn villa was a hillside establishment on the crest of the mountain beyond the village proper. She heard a church bell ring in the valley and then another and another. Presently the bell began to ring in the stone tower of the church in the town above her. The remaining villagers were being summoned to late Mass. Early Mass in these hills was at five. Yet since almost striking the blackbird couple down in the valley, Megan had seen no one.

She thought about Mary. Did she really have the right to descend upon her like this, arriving in the dawn and bringing nothing but her terrors and her demands for assistance?

Mary would accept the burden. She did not doubt that. In Saigon, Mary had made the difference between self-destruction and survival. No one but Mary knew that. And perhaps Uncle Jack.

Megan's fine-featured face was drawn, etched in light and shadow as she drove up the mountain and into the first light of the sun breaking over the eastern ridge of the Gran Sasso.

What was this dawn like for her daughter? She uttered a sobbing cry, grateful that there was no one to hear it. She hated animal wails of grief. She was finished with all that, long ago, when she was told that her husband, the father of the child in her belly, had died at the hands of a squad of Thai soldiers.

God, she thought bitterly, was there no end to betrayal, no finish to lying and deceit? Hadn't it been to get away from such things that she had held herself aloof from the one man in all the world she was certain loved and valued her?

She pressed harder on the accelerator and shifted the Alfetta down into first gear to negotiate the last tight switchback before the arch leading through the wall into the precariously situated village.

The cobbled streets, most of them no more than footpaths, were deserted. A few dark shadows flickered into the open maw of the village church. A thin dog loped across the square as the Alfetta rumbled past, its exhaust note echoing from the stone buildings. A young carabiniere, resplendent in white crossbelts and patent-leather hat—no more than a boy—stood in the corner of the square and saluted her as she drove by. Italian police were always entranced by Alfa Romeos.

She drove straight through the village and under the medieval archway over the hillside road. A half-kilometer farther on stood the leaning pillars that marked the entrance to Mary Quinn's property. A name had been painted on the stucco facing of a gatepost: VILLA STEFANO. That had been Zachary's idea. "A country house should have a name," he'd said, "and Stefano is as good as any." To the old radical, the villa was a fortress.

Mary squandered money on the place. "We have no one but ourselves to spend my royalties on," she said. "And Zachary does love the house."

Since his retirement and Mary's success, Zachary Quinn had devoted himself exclusively to working on the house and to learning how to cook like a native of the Abruzzi. "I always hated writing," he often said. "Now I don't have to."

Mary kept strict working hours. From six until noon and from two until five she stayed in her study on the second floor and worked. Zachary was the host of Villa Stefano. He ran the house, kept the garden, and resolutely refused to add another line to the monumental biography of Eugene Debs he had abandoned on the day Mary's *Blood in Saint Peter's Square* reached number one on the *New York Times* best-seller list. He had published only one slim volume, anecdotes about the Spanish Civil War. In 1940, the year it appeared, sixteen hundred copies were sold. "Most to my friends," Zachary said. "And a few to my enemies." The following year, the publisher's surplus of nine hundred copies was remaindered. Mary bought half of them, and in the cellar of the Villa Stefano, a few dozen copies of *¡No Pasaran¡*—its title the Loyalist battle cry, "They shall not pass!"—still moldered among the wine racks.

In Spain, Zachary had known Hemingway, Dos Passos, and Malraux. He had fought alongside the best and brightest—at least as they were defined in that time. But he had come home disappointed by the cynical behavior of both the Spanish Marxists and the Russian officers sent by Stalin to stiffen the Loyalist forces. Through the Second World War and for some time afterward, he had remained silent about the Communist influences and failures that had contributed to the crumbling of the Spanish Republic.

Zachary had also returned with a hip so badly shattered he would never again serve as a soldier. Mary nursed him until he was once more established as a teacher of political science, this time at Michigan State.

That done, in the summer of 1943 Mary got a job as a war correspondent and reported on the Italian campaign, from Messina to Florence. She returned home an established correspondent.

It was after she had covered Korea that Zachary's record was discovered by Senator Joe McCarthy's staff, including the fact that both he and Mary had, in their youth, been dedicated members of the Young Communist League. They stood side by side and fought the Wisconsin Senator, Zach with his integrity, Mary with her acid pen and Irish eloquence.

She later realized that they had emerged from the witch hunt relatively unwounded because McCarthy had been hunting bigger game. Zachary imagined that it had been because Mary's name as a war correspondent and journalist made them too dangerous to pursue.

If there was a realist in Villa Stefano, it was not Zachary Quinn.

Mary's last grand fling as a correspondent took her to Southeast Asia, first with the French and later with the Americans.

It was in Saigon that fifty-six-year-old Mary Quinn and nineteen-year-old Megan Wells had become friends.

Megan drove the Alfetta up the last stretch of road—gravel-surfaced now—to Villa Stefano. She was disappointed to see a BMW motorbike on its stand in the carport, between Mary's Porsche and Zachary's old Fiat 500. The Quinns were not alone; there was a visitor in the house. Megan, tight-lipped and aching with fatigue, wished him gone. Anywhere. But gone.

10. VILLA STEFANO

"You aren't going to get any work done today, so stop pretending and tell me what the hell is going on here."

Zachary Quinn leaned against the window seat in Mary's

study. He wore bib overalls and rubber boots. They were the mainstays of his wardrobe at the Villa Stefano, which, in recent years, was where he spent most of his time. He had given up traveling with Mary. He hated New York and barely tolerated London, where her two principal publishers were. And over time he and Mary had learned to deal with separations.

Mary busied herself with cleaning the type of her ancient Underwood. It was what she did when she was experiencing difficulty with a phrase, a paragraph, or a difficult piece of reportage. She liked to say that getting ink on her fingers helped her to think more clearly. Zachary contended that it was he who gave her lines like that to use during interviews.

The Quinns, quarrelsome and argumentative with their friends and each other, were unable, however, to conceive of any life but the one built of their own peculiar version of togetherness.

Zachary's face, lean as a greyhound's, bristled with white whiskers. He shaved only every third day at Santo Stefano.

"Why is that beach boy asleep in our living room?" he demanded.

"Reuben Herrick asked us to take him in. You listened in on the call," Mary said, removing the worn ribbon from the typewriter and dropping it in the wastebasket under her writing table.

"As a matter of fact, I didn't eavesdrop on your call from Herrick. I didn't have to. I know David. No one believes he's a political officer."

Mary shrugged. She was a large woman, robust and strong. Her straight hair was streaked with gray. Her eyes were large and a luminous green. She was Irish, she said, "by birth as well as by marriage"; her maiden name had been Malone. Zachary always rejoined with "Mary was born a Malone from County Cork—but she was never a maiden."

"You have something going with Herrick," Zachary said. "That's all right with me. I just want to know how rough it is likely to be. Do I have to call Rome for reinforcements?"

Since Mary's exposé of the attempt to kill the Pope, she was periodically targeted for attention by East European intelligence services and terrorist groups. The local police maintained a watch over Villa Stefano, as did the Rome Station of the CIA and, from time to time, the local representatives of Interpol.

Mary was accustomed to this sort of attention and she tended to ignore it. "Alive, I am only a journalist. Dead, I would be a martyr. The KGB or the Red Brigades would need a hell of an important reason to kill me," she had told a *Time* feature writer who had journeyed to Santo Stefano to interview her. She believed it. Zachary did not. He kept an extensive list of Roman and Neapolitan toughs he hired, from time to time, as guards for the villa.

"Stop fretting, old man. Nothing is going to happen."

"That's what you said when you told Frank Traina that Abou Abbas was mixed up in the *Achille Lauro* business. Traina probably got a medal for being smart. We got our insurance canceled when Arab shits tried to burn this house down."

Mary regarded her husband fondly. Ever since his return from Spain he had limped through his academic life and retirement, never complaining, allowing her to carry on doing the work that he so silently and so fervently wished he could do.

"Look, old woman, *why* do we have one of Herrick's spooks sleeping on our living-room couch? I'm going to keep asking until I get an answer."

"Let's go for a walk," Mary said. "Get my sheepskin coat. It's in my bedroom."

Clearly she would get very little done today. She had first been distracted from her work—a book on the workings of international terrorism—by Megan Wells's call from San Francisco.

The idea of a still-living Jean Thierry was one to which she was finding it difficult to become accustomed. She remembered the dashing Frenchman from her days in Saigon. She had mistrusted and disliked him then, and she had not been sorry to hear that he had been killed in a skirmish.

She had tried to help Megan through what turned out to be a very bad patch, but she had privately concluded that in the long run a dead war hero would be better for Megan than a living French correspondent of uncertain antecedents, shadowy connections, and alley-cat morals. For all her thirties bohemianism, Mary Quinn was a lifelong hostage to her Roman Catholic upbringing.

Thierry had appeared in Saigon within days of Megan's arrival. He had made an immediate set for her, and because she was nineteen and rebelling against authority and he was thirtyish and sexy as Yves Montand, she had fallen hard. It had troubled Mary, and others in Saigon, because Megan was the niece of John Wells, then Deputy Director of Operations of the CIA.

Mary stood on the stone piazza Zachary had tacked onto the house. At this hour of the morning, the sun was still well below the Gran Sasso mountains to the north and east. The sky was clear, dusky blue fading steadily as the day advanced. To the south and west, Mary could look down toward Santo Stefano, the steep mountain road leading up from the still-shadowed valley, and the valley itself. Far down the terraced mountain, she could see the lights of a single car.

She hugged herself against the morning chill and watched the sky. A flock of crows wheeled and darted above the ridgeline. "Enjoy yourselves, you ugly little bastards," she murmured. By noon there would be hunting hawks soaring on the rising currents of air that came up the valley and cascaded in reverse falls into the high reaches of the sky above the steep hills of the Abruzzi.

Zachary appeared from the house carrying her sheepskin coat and wearing the fancy Eddie Bauer arctic parka she had bought for him on her last trip to California.

He helped her on with the well-worn coat. She also wore an old fisherman's sweater, a heavy tweed skirt, Irish knee socks, and cloddish, but marvelously comfortable, English walking shoes.

In companionable silence they walked down the drive, surfaced with sharp stones and bits of slate, to the gateposts. Zachary poked at the ground with a stick he carried, also a gift from Mary, bought in New Bond Street, London.

"Is David still asleep?"

"The sleep of the innocent," Zachary said. "How can that be, I wonder? Have you seen the edges of his hands? They're like stone. You don't get that way unless you've been a black belt for years."

They turned up the empty, narrow road, away from the village.

Mary said, "Reuben asked me to let him be here when Megan arrives."

"You think that's a good idea?"

"I do. She is terrified something more will happen to Denny. She is going to need all the help she can get. . . ."

"The French bastard said 'come alone.' "

"They always do, old man."

Zachary limped along in silence, frowning at the bare mountains across the valley. In this morning half-light they seemed made of pure slate, the same blue slate that lay scattered all around them as they walked.

"Terrorists," he said darkly.

"Meg didn't say it first. *He* did. Thierry."

Zachary glanced at her sidelong. "Why are you getting involved, Irish?"

Mary thrust her hands deep into the pockets of her coat. "I feel responsible. I should have tried harder to keep her from marrying Thierry. I was there. I saw it happening."

"I didn't know you felt that way."

"I never wanted to talk about it. I'm too old to start having conscience pangs. But I knew the son of a bitch was no good. We all did. The Saigon press corps was like a private club in those days. We were all against the army, against the government, against Johnson and Westmoreland, Henry Bloody Kissinger, and Tricky Dick Nixon. Most of all, we were dead set against everything the CIA did, and we hated the people they had working there. Charlie Blaisdell, for instance."

She had found a pack of Gauloises in her coat pocket, and though she was in the throes of one of her frequent attempts to stop smoking, she put one of the fat cigarettes in her mouth and demanded a light from her disapproving husband. She sucked the bitter tobacco smoke into her lungs and held it there with guilty pleasure.

"Meg wasn't twenty years old when she showed up at the AID office with a GS-10 classification and a personal letter of recommendation from the AID Director in Washington.

"By the way, two-thirds of the working press in Saigon were convinced the Agency for International Development was just another CIA front. I'm still not certain it wasn't. I don't believe Meg could have walked into a job at AID in Saigon unless Jack Wells had pulled some wires in Washington. Hell, Military Intelligence had her penciled in as a potentially dangerous student radical. Of course, once it became common knowledge that she was the DDO's niece, the soldiers changed their attitude."

Zachary swung his heavy stick at a piece of shale and sent it spinning and bouncing along the road. Overhead the sky was turning white as the winter sun, still below the peaks of the Gran Sasso, climbed higher. "I haven't heard one word that makes me think you're responsible for anything," he said.

"She was a kid. A baby. A sweet girl. You know how she is. She was trying to be tough in Saigon, but she couldn't make herself into something she wasn't. The fact is, she never really got on well with Jack. She had the idea he compared her unfavorably with her mother."

"Did he? Does he?"

"I don't know, Zach. I don't think so. He resigned from the Company because of Megan. It was work he loved. He was born to be a spook. Something in the Wells genes. But he resigned and brought her home and put her through law school and helped her raise her daughter. Of course, Thierry was out of the picture then. He was reported killed in May, and Meg went home to the States in June." Mary broke off, shaking her head in anger and disgust. "Jesus wept! What kind of a man *is* Jean Thierry? Denny Wells is his *daughter*."

"I'm a bit surprised at you, Irish," Zachary said.

"Why?"

"You are jumping to a hell of a conclusion on damned little evidence. How can you be sure whoever called Megan actually *was* Lazarus risen? After how long? Fifteen years?"

"*Megan* thought it was Thierry. She should know."

"Maybe. Maybe not. Can Thierry just disappear for all those years and then materialize out of thin air?"

"If he was what some of us in Saigon thought he was, yes, he could."

"Let's stop for a bit," Zachary said, and eased his shortened leg up onto a stone road marker. Mary sat beside him and smoked her Gaulois.

Zachary asked, "How sure were any of you that Thierry was a Communist?"

Mary laid a hand on his knee. "No one knew whether or not he was a Communist, old man. People in Saigon didn't think in those terms. It wasn't like New York in the nineteen-thirties. People like Thierry didn't sit in the press bar and argue dialectical materialism. They didn't have to. The press hated the whole war effort. The army was more the enemy than the Vietcong were. Don't ask me to explain it. You were still teaching when the kids were trashing everything in sight. It was like that in Saigon. We used to go to press briefings at the Military Assistance Command headquarters just so we could laugh at the lies we figured we were being told. The fact that Thierry was rumored to be a North Vietnamese agent just made him interesting to the media people. I don't know if this is true, but I heard that one of the major networks offered to interview him, in silhouette, as a VC spokesman. He refused, of course, and denied he was anything but a journalist. But he didn't run. He was that confident, the arrogant bastard."

"That was before he married Meg?"

"Around the same time. Thierry was accredited to about a

dozen small French and Belgian journals. He made no bones about being a leftist. He liked to sound like the Lincoln Brigade people we used to know. Charlie said he was part Vietnamese. It's possible. He was supposed to have gone to the Sorbonne, and that's possible, too. According to the records he signed in Saigon when he and Meg were married, he had French nationality. Charlie claimed he had attended a PLO course in Syria and a KGB-run Spetsnaz school in Cuba. But no one paid any mind to Charlie. He was a Saigon Cold Warrior. We all thought he had gone Asiatic. He used to say himself that he had got too involved with the Vietnamese.''

Mary drew the last of the bitter smoke in and exhaled it reluctantly. She squinted at the brightening sky. ''We ought to get back to the house. I'd better be there to ease the strain when Meg and David meet.''

''I thought they knew one another.''

''They were in law school together. I think David was taken with her then, but nothing came of it. He flew a helicopter gunship in the war. It was Jack who recruited David for the Agency. And Meg has hated spooks all her life. An overdose of heroism in childhood, old man. It can sour you. I know. I feel the same way every time I wander by mistake into a church.''

''Sure,'' Zachary said, heaving himself to his feet and leaning on his gnarled stick. ''I've seen you curtsy to the statues.''

''Genuflect, you old atheist.''

''Whichever. All I know is, show you a plaster Virgin and you're young Mary Malone all over again.'' Zachary started back down the road, Mary keeping pace at his side.

He asked, ''Everyone knew he was an enemy agent, and no one did anything about it?''

''No one *knew*, Zach. The press people *thought* he might be an agent, that he probably was. They thought it was funny that within a few months of arriving in Saigon he was married to the niece of the CIA's DDO. Funny, Zach. Funny ha-ha.''

''Not you, Irish.''

''No, Zach. Not me. But, despite what the Wisconsin prick thought about us, we've dealt with the comrades, you and I. We have a different perspective. We know what they're like. And besides that, I just didn't like Thierry.''

''Woman's intuition.''

''Someday Molly Yard is going to put you up against the wall, old man,'' Mary said wryly. ''But if you want to say it was intuition, I won't argue. He was a wrong one, Thierry. I could feel it." She fished for another cigarette, and when she found it, Zachary took it from her and shredded it on the slate-and-gravel road. She sighed and thrust her fists back into the pockets of her coat. "The South Vietnamese wanted to arrest Thierry. Throw him in a cell. But by that time they were afraid of the press. They had a right to be. After the Tet offensive everything the Army of the Republic of Vietnam did was dismissed as incompetent or corrupt. The Thieu government wasn't about to throw a journalist into a tiger cage. There would have been hell to pay."

Zachary frowned, remembering the television war—the one with the immolated bonzes, or barbecued priests, as Madame Nhu called them; and the wounded infantry grunts and the burning hootches and weeping peasants—the war America lost in her own living room between six and seven every weeknight. When I was a member of the Young Communist League, he thought, we talked a lot about agitprop. It had taken fifty years and four wars to show what it could do.

They descended the road in silence. When they reached the gateposts, they saw an Alfetta with rental plates standing in the drive.

"Shit," Mary said. "I hope the Vietnam War isn't starting all over again. Let's go break it up, old man."

11. TEPLYY STAN

Valentin Ekimov sat at attention on the first three centimeters of an uncomfortable chair. He was attempting to maintain a military bearing, but his surroundings and his inquisitor made him very nervous.

A staff captain in the KGB was of no importance whatever in the Soviet cosmos—even one who was married to the daughter of a mid-rank Communist Party official. But the man for whom this particular captain labored, the man who controlled the power of the First Chief Directorate, *was* of importance, not only to Captain Ekimov, but also to persons far more exalted. General

Plakhanov's doings were of intense interest to the Politburo and to the men who controlled the future of the Soviet state.

Plakhanov had instructed Ekimov to make the arrangements necessary for a journey to Rome. He had also informed him that he, Ekimov, would be making the trip, too. And in a sudden, distressing change of plan—or was it really a change?—he had instructed Ekimov to schedule their departure for tomorrow, Sunday, and not for Monday. Usually, when Soviet generals traveled, they went by military aircraft and were surrounded by security. After all, that was what rank and privilege meant, did they not? But Plakhanov's instructions called for neither military aircraft nor KGB bodyguards. He intended to travel by Aeroflot and Lufthansa. He also intended to appear in Rome as a civilian, a minor Soviet trade official accompanied by only a single aide and secretary. Ekimov was made distinctly uncomfortable by the prospect. *He*, Valentin Ilarionovich Ekimov, uxorious father of three small Soviet citizens and son-in-law of the Party Secretary for Kirov, was to go to Rome with an incognito KGB general on Sunday.

As a result, Ekimov found himself in Teplyy Stan, where he least wanted to be, in the enormous office of Gregor Borisovich Kalganin, the Chairman—the Soviet Union was awash in chairmen, but some were more important than others—of the KGB, the chief Soviet secret policeman.

Ekimov sat in an echoing stadium of a room, one that would have accommodated a soccer match, he thought fearfully. It was a vast cave of steel, glass, and burnished-tile floor that could have been designed by some American.

In fact, it had been copied from the design of the CIA's Langley, Virginia, headquarters. Some Moscow wag had so taken advantage of *glasnost* as to write in *Pravda* that the KGB's Teplyy Stan facility resembled the box that Number 2 Dzerzhinsky Square had come in.

Perhaps it did, Ekimov thought. But it also resembled the realm of machines, not men; a headquarters without any of the nineteenth-century ornateness of Number 2, with none of the older building's makeshift, revolutionary improvisation. There were no "temporary" offices dating back to 1917, no shabby mementos of the Great Patriotic War.

At Teplyy Stan one sensed the vast underground caverns where thousands of Japanese computers filed and organized the immense data bank on which the KGB relied to maintain both security from aggressors and domestic tranquillity.

And here, thought Ekimov, if one required the traditional "neck shot" with which traitors to the Motherland were dispatched, a robot would bring the revolver.

He watched Kalganin circling, a huge carnivore in a British business suit. The Chairman of the KGB seldom wore a uniform now. It was part of the policy of openness with which the Soviet Union had been wooing the West. The man looked as though he could swallow Ekimov in a single morsel. In the KGB, the Chairman was sometimes called "the General Secretary's Dancing Bear." Well, he was not dancing now, Ekimov thought; he was stalking.

Kalganin was immensely fat, with 240 pounds distributed over a six-foot four-inch frame. In the 1950s, he had won a gold medal lifting weights for the Soviet Union in the Olympics. Now in his late sixties, he was an intimidating figure. What made him really fearsome was that he had come to his present high position primarily as a specialist in internal security. He had been a policeman since middle-school days.

Kalganin frightened most of the people who encountered him. Captain Ekimov was certainly no exception.

And suddenly there was the question of loyalty to Plakhanov.

Somehow, it seemed, in some manner that persons of Ekimov's rank would never be able to discover, Feliks Plakhanov had drifted into the appearance of disaffection. How this had happened, and when, Ekimov had no way of knowing. Until this moment, he had not even considered the possibility that so exalted a person as Plakhanov could ever fall from grace. It was especially strange because the General had only recently been given command of the First Chief Directorate.

But the change in the atmosphere was unmistakable. Kalganin lumbered around Ekimov with ursine hunger. As he moved, the Captain could catch the mingled scent of Western after-shave lotion and acrid body odor.

"I want you to concentrate, Captain Ekimov," Kalganin said. He had the high-pitched voice of many large men. "What projects have absorbed most of General Plakhanov's time over the last few months? Think carefully. Take your time."

This question had been asked, in one form or another, no fewer than a dozen times in the last forty minutes. Ekimov wished he dared say simply: For God's sake, Comrade Chairman, why don't you ask *him*?

But no junior officer responded to the Dancing Bear in such

a manner. Kalganin had both the authority and the means to extract whatever answers he wanted from whomever he chose.

Ekimov was not a man of tested bravery, but he was essentially a decent person, or assumed himself to be. He was an officer in the service of the *Rodina*, the Soviet Motherland, and there could be no more honorable service than that.

Yet it frightened him to be questioned with such vigor about the doings of a superior. Feliks Plakhanov was not a man who attracted affection. He was, in Ekimov's opinion, a cold, distant, overly fastidious man. He never relaxed, never unbuttoned his tunic to sit and drink with his men. He had all the attributes and most of the disadvantages of an aristocratic personality—though the personnel files, which Ekimov had read carefully, assured the inquisitive that Plakhanov was from worker stock and the son of a war hero officer of the NKVD. "The secret police," Ekimov once said to Yelena Petrovna, "is a family business to General Plakhanov."

The Captain's wife understood terms such as "family business" because her family descended from petit-bourgeois forebears who had had the good sense to join the Revolution early.

Now, suddenly, here in the frigid maze of Teplyy Stan, alone in this vast unpleasant room with Kalganin, Ekimov felt his fear growing. He had seen interrogations. They were not his department, but he had seen them. And heard them. And smelled them. The knout in the hands of a questioner was a very Russian image. Long before there was a Soviet Union, even before there was a Russia, there had been an interrogator with a lash in his fist.

Chairman Kalganin had no whip. He needed none. Ekimov had been in the cold steel-and-concrete levels below the computer rooms at Teplyy Stan. He knew what was done there and why. He did not for one moment doubt the KGB's authority to do what it wished with both its prisoners and its own officers. The sword of the Revolution was never wrong.

He heard himself babbling about Operation Paladin, stretching what little he knew of it, expanding each line he remembered into a paragraph of little fact well fattened with supposition.

The Dancing Bear stood before him. Very close. He loomed like a fleshy mountain. His fingers were thick as sausages. He could crush my skull with his hands, Ekimov thought, dry-mouthed.

Kalganin turned suddenly and pressed a button on his slab of a desk. "Send me the Kirov file."

Petrov Orlov, father-in-law, Ekimov thought, what have you done?

Kalganin said in that high, thin voice, "Your wife is Yelena Petrovna Orlova. Am I correct?"

"Yes, Comrade Chairman."

"You have three children: Irina, Yelena, and Piotr."

Ekimov suddenly yearned for a glass of water. There was none in sight. He nodded.

There was a rap at the door, and Kalganin opened it, accepted a file, whispered some instructions, and closed the door again.

He stood again in front of Ekimov. His foreign-made trousers touched Ekimov's knees, so that the Captain had to look sharply up to see past Kalganin's great belly and chest. The Chairman dropped the file in his lap. "Read it," he said.

The file was fat with papers. It bore a SECRET stamp and the legend GIVEN NAME: PETROV. PATRONYMIC: YUREIVICH. SURNAME: ORLOV. And his political rank, PARTY GENERAL SECRETARY, KIROV.

With sinking heart and many misgivings, Ekimov began to read.

In five minutes, he knew most of the worst. The agents of the Sluzhba, members of the KGB who rooted out "economic crime," had been busy with his father-in-law. Orlov had been selling scarce materials. Ekimov read down the list of articles: paper stock, machine-tool parts, fuel, clothing coupons. Name of God, what could Petrov Yureivich have been thinking? Did he think "openness" and "restructuring" meant a return to bourgeois capitalism?

Farther down the paper, Ekimov encountered worse. His father-in-law had been conducting a thriving business of lending money at interest. A drop of sweat trickled down his spine. The money he had been lending, according to the Sluzhba ferrets, belonged to the Kirov Party. And he had been lending it to soldiers to finance the importation of hashish from Afghanistan.

With an enormous amount of luck, Yelena Petrovna's beloved—and unbelievably stupid—father could expect thirty years in prison camp, severe regime. With a bit less good fortune, a neck shot was a better-than-average possibility.

He wiped his damp palms on his trousers and carefully closed the file. He looked bleakly at the dark figure of the Dancing Bear silhouetted against the cold light streaming into the room through the glass window wall.

His voice sounded as thin and high as Kalganin's.
"How can I serve you, Comrade Chairman?"

12. VILLA STEFANO

The glass doors to the piazza stood open despite the morning chill that hung in the air. Megan remembered from previous visits that Zachary and Mary followed their own variation of the old European method of using the house heat. It went on the fifteenth of November and off the fifteenth of March, regardless of the weather.

Zachary once said, "In a relativistic world a cold ass is something one can count on."

She walked into the living room and dropped her airline carry-on on a chair. The house was still. Through the open doors came the faint sound of crows cawing in the distance.

"Mary? Zach?" Megan's voice was ragged with fatigue and shaky with anxiety. "Is anyone home?"

There was a couch facing the cold fireplace. The leather creaked, and a man rose into view.

"Hello," he said.

Megan regarded him dubiously. He unfolded what turned out to be a six-foot frame inadequately draped in an old blue terry-cloth robe of Zachary's. His hair was uncombed, longish, and the same auburn color as Megan's. His features were regular, the facial bones prominent. The ascetic effect was somehow familiar. The eyes were blue-gray and they seemed to undress her. It was unsuitable. It made her angry. "Who are *you*?" she asked.

The question elicited an oddly melancholy smile. "You don't remember me."

"*David?* David Ashburn?"

He took a pack of Swiss cigarettes from his pocket and lit one. There was a Fifth Special Forces crest on his steel Zippo.

It was Uncle Jack who had first brought David to the house. Uncle Jack had recruited him for Frank Traina. And in those days she wanted to forget everything that reminded her of Vietnam. David did, even though they had never met in Southeast Asia.

"Right on. David," Ashburn said.

"God! I'm sorry. I'm not thinking straight," she said, sitting down abruptly.

"You look beat. I'll make some coffee."

"Where are Mary and Zach?"

"I don't know." He essayed a smile, and it softened the harsh planes of his face. He looked younger when he smiled. She recalled that smiles used to come hard to him. He had spent fifteen months in the Montagnard highlands, where the North Vietnamese had behaved savagely. So, she thought, had David Ashburn and his men. He had told her once how it was. She didn't like it.

"Why are you here?" she said.

He leaned against the marble mantelpiece and smoked his cigarette. "You know why."

She drew a deep, shuddering breath. She was afraid for Denny. Somehow Uncle Jack's friends had discovered what had happened. Given who they were, it was not surprising. But Jean's instructions had been so coldly, menacingly explicit.

"How did my uncle find out?" she asked.

"I don't know."

"I don't believe you," she said.

"I had *no need to know*. You didn't live all those years with Jack Wells without knowing what that means," Ashburn said dryly.

He walked, barefooted, across the terrazzo floor to the hallway. Megan followed him into the villa's large country kitchen, where he busied himself with the coffee-maker. "Zach and Mary must be out walking," he said. "They might have had things to talk about they didn't want me to hear."

"Mary hasn't called the embassy, has she?"

"Not if you asked her not to."

"Oh, God, what a mess," Megan whispered, and hugged herself, shivering.

David watched her, his expression unreadable. A spook, she thought. I wanted to remember him, but I was so sick of heroes and heroines and liars and cheaters and killers. And now here was David again—older, thinner, tougher, and less pliable, but David.

"You've stayed," Megan said. With the Agency, she meant,

and he understood it. They had always been able to converse in a kind of shorthand, as though there was an unspoken rapport between them.

"It's a living," David said, and plugged in the coffee-maker.

"Uncle Jack knew you would love it," she said thinly.

"He was right. About most of it. Not all."

"Any is too much."

"I'm sorry you still feel that way," he said. He studied her as she sat in a straight wooden chair. He compared what he saw with what he remembered. She had aged well. The thought brought a twinge of amusement.

We're older now, he thought, nearly forty. And what do I see before me? A female just as attractive, just as enigmatic as she was before.

Had she any idea, he wondered, how in love with her he had been? Probably not. God knew he had done his best to be cool, not to press. When you find one you really want, the conventional wisdom about women went, you let her have her head; you held the reins lightly.

I did that, he thought. And she simply broke free and ran off. Left me.

Summer-blue eyes, auburn hair, a small firm-breasted body. Yes, how little she had actually changed. Yet Denny—he wondered if she remembered the "friend of Mother's" who used to play ball with her on the lawn of the house in Atherton—Denny must be about sixteen by now.

He poured a cup of steaming bitter coffee and handed it to Megan. She did not drink it, but sat with both hands around the cup with her eyes closed.

She touched his heart. Still.

"We'll get your girl back," he said.

She opened her eyes and stared at him in fear. Suddenly he wanted to kill Thierry.

What sort of man reappeared after years and stole his own daughter to use as a hostage?

"Don't play with my daughter's life, David. Just *don't*."

"Meg," he said gently, "we can't let it go. Denny isn't just anyone's daughter. She's *your* daughter, and you're Jack Wells's niece. I'm sorry, but it's that simple. That's the way it is."

"Damn you," she whispered, her eyes hot with tears. "Who asked you for help? Who sent you here?"

David straddled another of the chairs around the large oak table that dominated Zachary's great Italian kitchen. "You remember Reuben Herrick? He sent me. Last night. In great haste.''

She was pale with weariness. How long had it been since she had slept, he wondered. He took the coffee cup from her and set it on the table. Then he sat facing her, her icy hands in his.

"How did the Agency find out?" she asked.

"*You* have no need to know. That's the truth."

She only repeated the word. "Truth . . ."

"You rest. Then we can talk."

Her voice was growing progressively threadier, thinner, closer to the edge of hysteria. "If Jean finds out about you, he'll kill her."

"He won't. We will find her first."

There was a sound of boots in the house. Megan half rose, startled. It was Zachary. Behind him stood Mary.

Zachary looked from Megan to David and back again.

"I see you've met," he said dryly. "I'll make her some breakfast and some proper coffee, David. I suggest you go put your pants on."

David smiled grimly and left the kitchen.

Megan said to Mary, "How could you? I asked you not to tell anyone I was coming here."

"Easy, Meg," Zachary said. "Those people aren't stupid, you know."

"Reuben Herrick called me last night," Mary said. "He told me he was sending David. He also said he would rather do it with my permission than without, but that he was going to do it."

"You can't keep them out, Meg," Zachary said. "They have too big a stake in this game."

Megan's eyes flashed angrily. "*Game?* We are talking about *my daughter.*"

"His daughter, too," Mary said. "If it was really Jean who called you."

"You don't need to remind me of that," Megan said bitterly. "It *was* Jean. Do you think I could forget that voice?"

Zachary broke eggs into a pan. In another skillet, thick bacon crackled, filling the kitchen with its savory smell. Astonishing, Megan thought, suddenly I'm starving. I'm sick with worry, but I'm fainting from hunger.

Soon Zachary put a plate of American-style bacon and eggs in front of her with toast made from thick slices of Italian bread

69

on an open burner. For himself and Mary there was *caffe filtro* and *panettoni*.

Megan ate like a refugee.

Mary said, "Tell me exactly what Jean said."

"Let her eat first," Zachary said.

David came into the room. He wore faded blue jeans and a cable-stitch cotton sweater. He looks like a prep-school master, Megan decided. Deceitful man. He sat down and helped himself to coffee. Mary offered him the plate of *panettoni*. She likes him, Megan thought. For some reason this did not disturb her. She needed to be among people who could be kind to one another.

"Now tell me what he said. Exactly," Mary repeated. It seemed right that she should take the lead. She had been an investigative reporter for a quarter of a century before the term became trendy.

Megan put down her knife and fork and held the warm coffee cup in her hands. She said, "In French. It was all in French. Somehow that made it all believable. Jean hated to speak English. Remember?"

Mary found herself remembering that her first impression had been that Thierry spoke no English. She had mentioned it to Blaisdell, and Charlie had said, in that sneering way he had, "He talks better American than you do, Irish." Charlie had already known a great deal about Thierry.

Megan said, "He told me . . ." She stopped and began again. "First there was a woman on the line. I thought it was an operator, but now I don't think so. She had a German accent. Not heavy, but identifiable. Then he came on the line. He said he was calling from Rome and that he had Denny. He gave me instructions about finding a *trattoria* and hotel here in Rome. La Spada e Fodero. He gave me the address. Number 17 Via Sforzesca." She looked at the others. "What does it mean? I'm not as good with languages as Denny."

"It means the Sword and Scabbard. Probably one of those Trastevere ripoffs," Zachary said. He looked at David as though challenging him to make his presence—his unwanted presence—worth the price of breakfast. "Rome is your territory. Do you know it?"

"I know it. A bar. Rooms and girls upstairs."

Mary said, "It will be a drop. Jean won't be there."

David said, "He'll have help."

"How can you be so sure?" Megan asked.

70

"He's already had help. We found Denny's Minox." He took two prints from an envelope, handed the photographs to Mary. "Anyone you know?"

Mary studied the faces in the pictures. She shook her head. Then she said, directly to David, "How do you know these two had anything to do with Denny's abduction?"

"Because we know them. Or at least the computer does."

"Let me look," Megan demanded.

Mary glanced at David, who nodded almost imperceptibly.

Megan examined the men in the photographs, frowning. "You know these people?"

"We know who they are. Their names don't mean anything, but they're Russians. Low-grade Soviet muscle. KGB. Active measures."

Megan looked bewildered. Fatigue was clogging her brain. In her circle of friends in San Francisco, references to the KGB people in the Soviet consulate on Green Street, with its crown of microwave antennae, were camp theater, not to be taken seriously.

"What have the Russians to do with me?" she asked.

"Not you. Your Uncle Jack." David's voice had turned icy.

Mary threw herself into the breach. She saw how suddenly contemptuous David was in danger of becoming. He was not a man who could sympathize with the silent battle Megan had fought all her life to be free, to be something different from what she was born to be, what Jack Wells had expected her to be.

Naïveté was one defense. Against an activist like David Ashburn, it was not a good one.

"Enough for now. You need some rest. Come upstairs. I mean now, girl." Mary rose from the table and put her arm around Megan.

"Just a minute," David said. "When did he say for you to be at the Sword and Scabbard?"

"He didn't specify a time."

"God damn it, *don't lie.*"

"Then don't make me lie," Megan shouted. "Leave it alone, David."

"I'm sorry," David said, "I wish I could. But there's no way."

"Enough," Mary said, and guided Megan up the narrow stairs to the second floor.

David gave a hard glance toward Zachary and stood. "I really am sorry, Zach. But we can't play by Moscow rules."

71

"It's her daughter, for God's sake," Zachary said.

"I know. That makes no difference."

"Spoken like a fascist, David."

David smiled bleakly. "Just remember that inside every liberal there is a fascist struggling to get out and run things *his* way in the name of compassion and democracy."

Zachary said angrily, "What a cynical bastard you are. At least watch what you say to her."

David said, "We *are* going to get her daughter back."

"I hope so. You had better."

David turned and walked through the house to the piazza. He stood looking up at the shelves of gray slate and limestone bordering the road to Santo Stefano Pass and on into the Gran Sasso.

It was past nine now, and the sun had topped the eastern ridges and was climbing up the stepped terraces and rockfalls above the villa.

David frowned, looking upward. A thin wisp of smoke seemed to materialize against the dark gray of a slide of tumbled fragments of slate. It was gone so quickly that he thought for a moment he had imagined it. Then he saw the momentary flash of sun on glass.

He took a pair of compact binoculars from his pocket and raised them to study the steep mountainside above the house.

Presently he walked back to the door and called to Zachary. "I'm out of cigarettes. I'm going into Santo Stefano for some."

Zachary's reply from the kitchen was, "Mary's got a trunkful of cigarettes."

"No, thanks. I can't handle Gaulois. Back directly."

He hurried out to his motorbike, kicked the flat-four into life, and roared out through the gateposts and onto the road toward the pass.

Two hundred meters from the summit he stopped and shut down the BMW's engine. A mountain stillness descended around him. He looked across the road and up the slope of the ancient crumbling terraces. This mountain land had not been farmed for generations. Perhaps for longer than that. Here the bare bones of the land showed through the flesh of soil and greenery. It had an austere, threatening kind of beauty.

From the saddlebag he took a Walther PPK. He retracted the slide and let it snap a round into the chamber. Then he slipped the weapon into his waistband over his right kidney and began to climb the rockfall.

He climbed for six minutes, steadily, with intent purpose. Far below he could see Villa Stefano, with Zachary's old wreck now parked outside the garage that housed Mary's Porsche Targa. He could see Zachary moving Megan's rented Alfa out of the driveway. He took out his binoculars and looked at the house. From here one could see well into the broad windows Zachary had built in the kitchen.

He turned and climbed higher still, until he had almost reached the shale shelf. Here he paused and took the PPK from his waistband. He slid himself over the shale ridge silently, weapon ready.

Nothing.

He pursed his lips, put the pistol away, and began to search the ground carefully. After a time he found a shredded cigarette end and farther down the backside of the hill a crumpled empty pack of Winstons. When he smoothed it, he saw that it carried a German Customs stamp.

He held it in his palm for a time and then crumpled it again and sailed it down the hill.

Here he stood almost on the same level as the pass, but on the shoulder of the mountain that bore it. He could see a long way to the east and north. Here and there the tarmac of the road from Santo Stefano to Malvista, the next village beyond the pass, could be seen.

He raised his glasses and studied the visible sections of road. He was not disappointed. A very dusty Mercedes saloon bearing Rome plates was racing northeastward. He memorized the number and then slowly made his way back to the road and down to the wide verge where he had left his motorbike.

Ten minutes later he was in a *trattoria* in the village buying a package of his favorite Swiss Virginia Number Five cigarettes. He asked the proprietor where the local policeman might be and was told that Carabinieri Constable Malatesta had ridden down the mountain on his bicycle last evening to investigate the theft of a sheep. He would be back perhaps at midafternoon, perhaps not. It was difficult to say. The Constable, alas, was ambitious and hard-working, but nothing ever happened in Santo Stefano.

"Far better so," David said.

Five minutes after that he was riding the BMW back between the gateposts of Villa Stefano.

13. ROME

The top story of the old building on Via Palestro had once housed a ballet school. The loft still contained rows of wooden lockers, with doors vandalized and splintered, a practice bar that ran the length of the long room, and a wall of mirrors.

The mirrors gave the place a kind of nightmare population of images that was many times the number of real persons living there. The silver nitrate had peeled from many of the panels. In other places it had yellowed. In still others the glass was cracked and crazed, so the images seemed to jump from one reality to another like spirit figures leaping from heaven to hell and back again, endlessly duplicated, fractured, tortured, and from time to time conjured to a temporary normality as the room's occupants passed a mirror panel that had, by some miracle of indolence, been ignored by the passing vandals who had, until recently, used the old loft as a shelter and a place to smoke hash and shoot harder drugs.

But the old ballet school had been taken over by more permanent residents. The outside walls had been heavily backed and reinforced with sandbags and cast-concrete bricks. Sandbags had also been stacked around the head of the stairs and in the space between the foot of the stairs and the street entrance. The door, heavy and ornate when it was hung at the turn of the century, had been faced with steel plates front and back, the plating secured by heavy carriage bolts.

There was a narrow hallway between the stairs and the brick wall behind which the lower story was divided into small rooms. Here there were more sandbags, and in the first room stacks of unfilled bags and a pile of coarse sand stolen from a construction site.

The second room was a storeroom and contained a dozen crates of canned food, a galvanized tub of not-so-clean but potable water, a camp stove, several ten-gallon containers of gasoline, a case of empty bottles, and a pile of rags, and another case filled with charged gasoline bombs ready for use.

The last room in the row, the one at the rear, was the ammunition storage and final redoubt. It was fully lined with sandbags and concrete bricks. Outside the doorway and commanding the hallway to the armored door stood a Soviet RPG-7 rocket-propelled grenade launcher, a 1960s weapon of dubious value against tanks (its original prey), but still highly effective against civilian and police targets. Propped against the walls of the sandbag revetment surrounding the RPG were three rounds still not cleansed of the cosmoline in which they began their journey to Rome from Damascus.

The last redoubt was intended to serve also as an aid station, though the facilities were few. A half-dozen Soviet infantryman's battle kits lay there in their original packings. There were some ampoules of morphine, stolen years ago from Syrian military warehouses, where medical supplies had spent almost two decades.

The more lethal matériel was plentiful. There were several cases of 9mm ammunition, a stand of six spare AK-47 Soviet assault rifles, a stand of American M-16s captured half a world away and long ago, when the victorious North Vietnamese Army marched into the military supply depots of the defeated Army of the Republic of Vietnam.

While Americans were still scrambling onto their helicopters atop the United States Embassy in Saigon, these weapons were beginning the long journey that ended here, on Via Palestro.

In the far corner of the room, behind the bunker containing the RPG-7, stood a wooden crate, open side down. From it ran wires that vanished into the walls or were stapled to the door frames to disappear into the flooring above. The crate protected the battery-powered detonator that was connected by its wire spider web to thirty-one two-kilogram charges of French plastic explosive placed strategically about the old building.

On the wall above the concealed detonator a slogan had been spray-painted with an aerosol can—a slogan and an admonition: IN EXTREMIS REMEMBER THAT THE PURPOSE OF TERRORISM IS TO TERRORIZE. With academic nicety, the putative author of the statement was credited: *Mikhail Aleksandrovich Bakunin*, a nihilist so violent that even his fellow revolutionaries in the upheavals of 1848 disowned him. Of Bakunin it was said: "On the first day of a revolution he is a treasure; on the second he ought to be shot."

The young terrorist who had inscribed the slogan on the wall to give himself courage *in extremis* was insufficiently educated to know that Bakunin's anarchism earned him Karl Marx's odium and expulsion from the society of early Communists. The unit commander, however, was a professor of political science at the University of Milan and knew all about Bakunin. He had, in fact, taken him as tutelary deity of the newly organized Palmiro Togliatti Unit of the Red Brigades, and an example of what all terrorists should try to be.

The Togliatti Unit was manned by a mix of recruits and veterans and survivors of other operations. Total strength varied between fifteen and thirty "fighters," depending on the state of discontent among the young hooligans of Italy's political left.

The command cadre was well trained in the theory and practice of urban irregular warfare; the "troops," far less so. In attitude and devotion, the low-ranking members of the Togliatti Unit were expected to aspire to emulate the fedayeen of the Islamic terror movements. "Fedayeen" had many meanings, but its primary import was "men of sacrifice." To a Bakuninite urban guerrilla leader, the fedayeen were the ideal soldiers.

Gianbattista Calvo, the founding commander of the Togliatti Unit, was a young man with a profound sense of history and an absolute conviction that it mattered not an iota if the "new society" to which he and his movement were committed came in this decade or this century. He was convinced that he would not live long enough to see the new world, and he worked hard to ensure that society's enemies—namely, the Americanized, uncultured bourgeois who dominated Italy and the rest of Western Europe—would not survive to see it either.

Calvo intended that when the history of the new socialist order was written, the names Gianbattista Calvo and Palmiro Togliatti Unit would be central to the story of the new Europe. It was a grandiose ambition, he knew, there being so many bourgeois enemies and so few young men and women in the Togliatti Unit. But he was convinced that both he and his people, his fedayeen, would prevail.

Despite his taste for political violence, he was an academic at heart. While on sabbatical from the university, he had attended the school for Shiite Muslim terrorists in Lebanon's Bekaa Valley. There he had been selected for leadership training by the Spetsial Nasnacheniye—the Soviet Army special forces. His Spetsnaz instructors graduated him with special honors and the recommendation that he form and be given command of a shock unit of the Red Brigades in his native Milan.

The Red Brigades coordinating council had taken more than a year to respond to the suggestions made by the Soviet brothers, but eventually Calvo had been given the charter he desired and felt he deserved. He was ordered to gather a flexible strike force able to operate in Rome. Milan was not selected as his base of operations because at least one of his Soviet instructors had appended a secret protocol to his recommendation. The protocol estimated Calvo's survival as an urban guerrilla at less than six months. "Make certain," the faceless man had written to his superiors, "that the *brigatista* command places only expendable fighters at his disposal. He appears able to inspire fear and anger in his followers. He will be uniquely useful in situations requiring extreme violence of short duration."

So that he could devote his time to political murder and destruction, he took a leave of absence from his teaching post. He told his superiors that he was going to spend a second sabbatical year researching a doctoral thesis on the Paris Commune of 1848. He found it amusing to write postcards to his former colleagues from time to time detailing his imagined progress.

In the brief lifetime of the Togliatti Unit, only two "short-duration" actions had so far been undertaken. One had been an attack on an isolated Carabinieri station in the Roman slums. A force of three policemen had been attacked by a dozen of the terrorists armed with AK-47s and grenades. The carabinieri had been killed almost at once, and two bystanders had also died in the hail of gunfire. Two others had been seriously wounded. No terrorists had been casualties. Calvo had been enormously pleased. He told Mariella, his second-in-command, that he wished he could write a thesis on urban guerrilla war, and that perhaps one day he would do exactly that. Mariella, the dour eighteen-year-old daughter of urban Italian poverty, had not been amused. She was contemptuous of Gianbattista for being an overeducated, overprivileged son of the very bourgeoisie he so despised.

The second action had been less successful. It was an attempt to dynamite a power station in the Dolomites. This target had been guarded by the military as well as the national police, and Calvo's troops had been bloodied. Two Neapolitan members of the unit had been literally shot to pieces by the Italian Army. Three others, two boys and a girl from Milan—original members of the unit—had been brought down by gunfire from a police helicopter as they were retreating from the power station. Calvo had executed the girl, when she could no longer travel. It had been a difficult thing to do, but he had managed it for the good of the unit.

He had complained bitterly to the council about the choice of target. His unit was manned by city people, not clodhoppers—farmers and peasants. The Togliatti Unit was intended to operate in Rome, not out in the mountains where only goats and peasants were comfortable.

Replacements had come from the north, some from the far north. Seven Swedes had arrived in the month of inactivity after the failed power-station attack. Two of the gaunt young men were students, and of bourgeois background. Three were from the slums of Stockholm, and the other two were petty criminals recently released from a government halfway house. Mariella, a harsh disciplinarian, had already warned them that the use of any drugs harder than marijuana would have dire consequences.

Peculiarly enough, Calvo noted, the Swedes—whose country had not indulged in international thuggery since the days of Charles XII—had a genuine talent for violence. In the games they played among themselves and with the other members of the unit, they often shed blood. Lars, the oldest of the Swedes, nineteen, had offered to rape Hanalore, the best trained of the urban guerrillas from Germany, the very day they moved into the ballet school. He had discovered, to his shame and humiliation, when he managed to throw Hanalore to one of the dirty mattresses scattered about the building, the point of a razor-sharp knife held against his genitals as the slender German girl coldly offered to unman him.

She would have done it, too, Calvo thought with a grim smile. Lars had no way of knowing that Hanalore was a lesbian, or that she had served for three years with the remnant of the Baader-Meinhof terrorist group and had personally executed at least three enemies of the people. She had brought with her Erich and Dieter, experienced fighters from Cologne.

Mariella regarded the contingent with speculative caution. "It is true they are comrades," she told Calvo. "But they are also *tedeschi*, Germans." Mariella's grandfather had died doing forced labor for the Nazis, and her mother had told the story again and again to her twelve children.

Hanalore had only just returned to the ballet school after spending three days in the company of the Frenchman. The assassin was in the employ of the Soviets. His identity had been

78

vouched for by no less a personage than Tikhonov, who, Calvo was certain, was KGB Resident in Rome. When money came to the Togliatti Unit, it was almost always delivered by Tikhonov, a large, silent man with the look of a pork butcher.

Three other members of the Togliatti Unit, two of them Hanalore's German comrades, had now taken over custody of the American hostage. They had established themselves, at the Frenchman's instructions, in a building on Via Nardi. Hanalore had brought the Frenchman's instructions that the hostage keepers be rotated every third day, until more prisoners were delivered by the Frenchman to the ballet school. The operation grew vague at that point—deliberately so, Calvo suspected.

The unit had never worked with the Frenchman before, but apparently the Resident had spoken well of them to him, because the assassin had not hesitated to use the manpower they made available.

Before dawn, Calvo had received a telephone call from the three fighters who had been sent to the Abruzzi to report on the activities at the house of the Quinn woman.

Mario had called from the village of Santo Stefano. Following the Frenchman's instructions, a watch had been kept on the Quinn villa until the American woman appeared. Under no circumstances, the Frenchman had said, were the fighters of the Togliatti Unit to allow themselves to be seen, nor were they to begin their action against the Quinn house until ordered to do so.

Calvo disliked taking orders from a stranger, but the Frenchman was a particular sort of stranger. He was a designated killer from the First Chief Directorate. The Togliatti Unit should be proud, Tikhonov had said, to be associated with an agent of the Frenchman's experience and reputation. Even the fabled Carlos, dead of cancer several years ago, had worked willingly with the Frenchman.

Fighters drifted into the ballet school most days. But there was some difficulty recruiting Roman *brigatisti*. The antiterrorist forces were watching central Italy. The attack on the police post and the abortive attempt to destroy the power station in the Dolomites had stirred up a hornet's nest of searches and investigations.

With Mariella, Calvo prowled the building, inspecting the precautions against attack and noting the condition of his troops. He indulged himself in the conceit of using military terminology and refused to entertain the notion put forth by detractors that

79

the *brigatisti* were not soldiers, but common criminals. In this he knew that he challenged the ghost of his ideal revolutionary. Mikhail Bakunin loathed and feared armies. Military organizations were, by their very nature, rigidly structured. And to Bakunin, social structure was the plague that destroyed all freedom. The anodyne was death, and he had always been willing to dispense it. With that conclusion, Calvo sincerely agreed, and he resumed his cloak of devotion to Bakunin.

Last night he and Mariella had sat late in the redoubt talking politics. He had tried hard to make her grasp the purity of Bakunin's view of society as oppressor. From her surly refusal to concur, he concluded that she hadn't the intelligence to understand him fully.

He stood at the head of the stairs and studied the disposition of people and weapons. His Spetsnaz instructors had been lavish in their bestowal of information on the construction of antipersonnel bombs and the methods of infiltrating airport security systems while armed. But what faced him now was a straightforward problem of infantry warfare. He had, at the moment, twelve fighters—thirteen, including himself. This was not really an adequate force to hold such a large building as the ballet school. It was unlikely, however, that the operation would deteriorate into an assault on the building by the authorities, and it was even more unlikely that in any such assault the government would use heavy weapons. The thirteen in the building now could at least count on that.

But the inadequate force could hold the school for no more than an hour or two. Plainly—though it remained as yet unsaid—the intent was that any hostages held here would be killed in an attack by the police.

It was a sobering thought. And as Calvo inspected his troops and his fortress, he wondered if, at last, his time had come.

Because the thought was peculiarly disturbing, he looked at Mariella with more warmth than he really felt. She was slender, with a plain face pocked with acne scars. She wore dirty American-label jeans and an Italian Army field jacket. She customarily went barefooted, but today she was wearing a tattered pair of Adidas running shoes. Her long, greasy hair was caught at the nape of her neck in a ponytail. There were times—and this was one of them—when Calvo found her sexually stimulating. Some depravity in his nature, he suspected, was attracted by the girl's poor hygiene and by her consequent slightly fetid body odor.

Mariella—her name had been Sophia Pasquino, but she had not heard it since she was thirteen—was not one of Calvo's upper-middle-class students. She had spent the first two-thirds of her life in the slums of Ostia. The last third belonged, body and soul, to the Red Brigades. Before coming to the Togliatti Unit, she had participated in the cold-blooded murder of a provincial mayor marked for liquidation by the Red Brigades. It had sickened her, and she seldom spoke of it. But it was an act of faith for her. She did not understand the theory of dialectical materialism or world historical imperatives or the garrulous dicta of Mikhail Bakunin that so entranced Gianbattista. She knew only that the Red Brigades were her family, the only family she was ever likely to have, and that when the time came to die for them she would do so. Bravely, she hoped—though having seen death at close range she was unsure about her courage. But bravely or gibbering with fright, she would die among comrades, taking with her as many enemies as she could possibly manage.

Life had always been simple for Mariella. Dirty, brutal, ugly, and almost certainly short—but simple. She hoped with all her heart that death would be the same.

"Mariella," Calvo said.

The girl knew that tone of voice. She had heard it from men since puberty.

She regarded him unblinkingly. Her eyes were her best feature. They were like polished bits of black glass.

"Last night—"

"I didn't understand any of it," Mariella said. "I don't understand your way of talking."

Ignorant bitch, Calvo thought. Why is it, he wondered, that when I think of death and killing, my loins fill and I act like an ape in rut?

"Are you uneasy?" That was not what he wished to say either, but, Goddamn it, how could he beg such a slut?

She judged him more acutely than he could judge himself.

"Afraid. *You* are afraid."

"Certainly not."

She looked at him calmly. "It is natural to be afraid. It has nothing to do with how one fights. You will feel better if you tell the truth."

Calvo looked at their images in the crazed mirrors lining the room. There were half a hundred Mariellas, or parts of her. Heads separated from bodies. Blue jeans stuffed with nubile thighs. Black sweaters and dirty khaki jackets by the score, all stretched by large soft breasts. Faces and parts of faces framed by black hair and spangled with eyes like windows into interplanetary space. Where am *I*, Calvo wondered suddenly. Where are *my* images? They were there, all around the room, but he had trouble defining them. It was as though the walls contained only Mariella.

And Hanalore. Suddenly she appeared in the reflections, standing at the end of the long room looking at him. Evaluating. Judging.

He turned away from the ruined mirrors and said, "Let's go downstairs."

Hanalore smiled and returned to the work she was doing, field-stripping her AK-47 for cleaning. There were others in the room, some dozing on mattresses, one reading a paperback novel, another drinking from a can of Diet Pepsi. The incredible banality of it was dismaying, Calvo thought. Those who make history should not be so vulgar.

Mariella—who was there in the building more vulgar than she?—said, "If you want."

Want? Calvo's erection filled the crotch of his trousers. He would gladly have killed for a woman. Any woman. *This* woman.

He caught Mariella's grimy little paw in his hand, and together they went down the stairs, stepped over sleeping bodies on mattresses in the hallway, and went past the sandbagged RPG-7 into the redoubt.

Dieter was there, tinkering with the detonator.

"Get out," Calvo said.

The big German looked insolent. He glanced at Calvo's stretched trousers and grinned. "At your command, comrade," he said with mock discipline, fist raised. He lumbered out into the hallway. There was no door.

Calvo pulled Mariella to the grimy mattress in the corner of the room. She regarded him with cold, impassive pity. She disliked him. He was afraid, she thought, and as time went on, he would be terrified. Her instinct told her that what was to come would be very bad.

But he *was* a comrade. What did it cost to ease a comrade's pain?

She kicked off the running shoes, unbuttoned the waistband of her jeans, and pushed them down her thighs. Her belly was rounded, furry with black down. Her mons was pronounced, thickly bushed. She took off her jacket and pulled the black sweater over her head. Her pale breasts rolled free, dark nipples nested in a tracery of tiny fine veins.

Calvo peeled off his clothing in a frantic rush. His penis stood out of his forest of black curly hair. He snatched at Mariella, smearing her mouth with saliva, breathing in the smell of her unwashed body.

"Easy," Mariella said. "Not so fast."

They were on their knees on the mattress. She reached for his penis and lowered her head. Calvo let her go for a few moments and then pulled away from her, spread her legs, and drove into her once, twice, a third time, and then spewed himself inside her.

He rested on his knees, gasping for breath. Her breasts were larger than he had imagined. They sagged to either side of her narrow chest, pale-skinned, unbelievably vulnerable and naked. With the tip of his penis he could feel the wet labia hidden in the fur of her mons. Her knees rested against his flanks, slippery with sweat and sexual fluids.

He tried to enter her again, and failed. The flesh was slimy, pungent. He backed away, making a sound that she interpreted as—what?—distaste?

Probably it was, she thought. The comrade's pain was soothed, his hunger slaked. Now she revolted him. Men were like that.

"Mariella—"

"Don't give it a thought," she said coldly. "I used to do this for a bowl of fish-head stew when I was twelve. I came from Ostia, you know. It's a fishermen's town. I got no money for it until I was fourteen."

She moved out from under him and began to dress.

He watched her, shaken, ashamed, wondering what diseases she might carry, worried that he had compromised his position of command.

She read him clearly. What a posturing fool he is! She thought. He will kill us all in the end.

PART TWO

FIRST PRELUDE

1962

Underneath the surface of Today
Lies Yesterday, and what we call
The Past.

—Eugene Lee-Hamilton,
  "Roman Baths"

14. THE WALL, BERLIN, JANUARY 1962

Feliks Plakhanov stood on a bridge over the Spree, looking across the frozen river to the new wall. The thing was an abomination, a constant reminder to the socialist world that a barrier was needed to prevent the East Germans from fleeing to the West.

How like the Germans to put the USSR in such a position! They were a people without shame and without honor.

All except Peter. He had to go on believing that. Betrayal by Peter Arendt would be too much to bear.

The bridge lay in the dead zone between the Wall and the minefields. The *Volkspolizei*—the East German People's Police—had shown their Teutonic efficiency by bulldozing an area of a hundred meters between the Wall and the river. They had then set up watchtowers and gun positions with a clear field of fire into the dead ground.

It had not stopped escapes from the East. There were already tunnels and trickery every day as Easterners struggled to get out of the Democratic Republic to indulge their greed for the luxuries they saw every day on the television broadcasts from West Berlin and West Germany.

One thing had certainly been accomplished, Plakhanov thought as he walked slowly through the new dusting of snow. They have taken a place of riparian grace and beauty and turned it into the annex of a prison yard, barren, cold, ugly.

On the western side of the Wall there were graffiti and displays of protest. The eastern side was naked of any human touch except for the wreaths and bouquets of flowers hung over it by

West Berliners to memorialize the Easterners periodically gunned down by the Vopos while trying to cross the border.

Thank God they were becoming more sophisticated, Plakhanov thought. Perhaps in time they would learn to cope. Every time some German zealot shot a countryman trying to escape to the West, the reputation of the Soviet Motherland suffered.

Someone—Plakhanov could not remember who it was—had once said to the Germans that they never made small mistakes, only great ones. He thought of this and of Peter Arendt at the same moment and shuddered.

He stood for a time on the bridge. The snow was unbroken there. A mantle of virgin white covered the road and dusted the steel bones of the cantilever span. In the center of the river the ice was broken, exposing the swiftly moving black water. Elsewhere the river was frozen solid. In a few places, reeds protruded through the ice like images on a Japanese screen.

This should have been a good time. On Monday last, Plakhanov had received notification of his promotion from captain to major. The occasion had been celebrated in style, with caviar and vodka, at the Soviet Mission. Peter, however, had been absent. And that had been cause for some concern.

Plakhanov remained uneasy about Peter's competence as a field agent. He was too young, too vulnerable, too trusting. In any normal situation, Plakhanov would never have chosen him to run a network on the far side of the Wall.

But there was no other way to keep Peter by his side, no other way to protect him from the snoops of Special Service II, who had noticed him first when he sought employment with the East German secret service. Plakhanov had often wondered what had possessed Peter to imagine that he could ever be a successful intelligence officer. The boy did things in innocence. Plakhanov had warned him that the work was dangerous and should be approached with great caution.

Yet he had incorporated Peter into his operations in West Berlin. He would have preferred to keep him on this side of the Wall, perhaps working at some office task. But there was always talk, and talk could destroy a man in Plakhanov's position.

Twenty-four hours ago, Hans Kleiner, Peter's courier, had sought out Plakhanov. Kleiner's appearance was disturbing, because Peter was under strict injunction never to use him unless it was a dire emergency.

Interrogation had produced little information—only that Peter was distressed and needed a personal meeting. Kleiner did confirm that one of Peter's agents had been arrested, effectively crippling still another West Berlin network.

Networks were always expendable. That was a given. But Peter was not. A softness there, Plakhanov admitted. He had never been able to put the boy in mortal danger.

He had ordered the Vopos to watch for Peter at the Spree-brücke crossing point. It was a track through one of the ruined buildings that had been incorporated into the Wall. Some tunnel diggers from the West had broken through and released an East Berlin family. No one on the other side knew that the breach was under surveillance. There were a dozen machine guns pointing at the gap in the Wall. It made Plakhanov edgy that Peter had chosen to come through the breach, rather than risk a crossing at Checkpoint Charlie, where his counterfeit Western credentials might be closely examined.

Now Plakhanov began to move toward the center of the span. The cold struck through his fur-collared greatcoat, with the new epaulets. His boots made a crusty sound on the snow. The sky was almost the same stark white as the road and the frozen banks of the river.

Squinting against the glare, he looked for some depth in the sky. A few flakes touched his face and melted there. It was beginning to snow again, gently, the flakes spinning and falling slowly out of the white sky toward the white earth.

He felt an uneasy tightness in his chest. Yet he was not given to useless speculation, having learned that from listening to his father. Ivan Plakhanov was forever surrendering to the drama of his speculations. Awash in wartime vodka, he would lament his "probable fate": "*If* the Germans come . . ."; "*If* I am captured . . ."; "*If* I am sent behind the lines . . ."

NKVD man Ivan Plakhanov had lived in a constant maelstrom of fears and furies. Some of his tantrums and lamentations were about the sluts he brought home. Some about his slender, silent son.

Did it matter? Ivan Plakhanov was no longer a live bully. He was a dead hero. And his son stood on the Spree bridge waiting for a pretty German boy Ivan would have shot on sight. Memories were distasteful. What use was it to dwell on what was mercifully finished and forgotten?

He watched the gray cold shape that was the Wall. This was not the sort of meeting he enjoyed. The last had been in Leipzig. Before that in Magdeburg. Once even in Prague. Risky. But

Peter was a network controller, and it was reasonable that he should meet often with an officer of the Soviet Mission.

The tryst in Magdeburg had been especially sweet. Peter Arendt was a fresh slate, upon which could be written whatever Feliks Plakhanov wished. The war had kept the boy ignorant, but his mind was quick, and he learned with a new lover's eager willingness.

Russian poetry moved him, confounded him, made him weep. He was especially affected by V. I. Ivanov's verses.

> *Snow, snow, it is all snow. . . . And dark, dark night*
> *Will never end nor yield to dawn's bright light.*
>
> *Russia is dust. And silence—crisp and clear.*
> *What if all that Russia is is fear?*

He had understood the poet in some deep and primal way. He had listened to the Russian words and then Plakhanov's careful German translation, and had reached into the soul of the poem and made some vital voice he heard there his own.

Then he had smiled, with still-damp eyes, and said: "German mind, Russian heart, Feli."

Plakhanov looked away from the empty white sky and past the black bones of the bridge, and he was there, walking innocently along the abandoned road, leaving a long trail of footprints in the snow.

The flakes whirled and fell more thickly now, and Peter resembled one of those figures in a glass globe surrounded by snow that fell and swirled in miniature.

Plakhanov shivered. At this time of year on the wintry North German plain, it was almost as cold as in Moscow. For some odd reason, he recalled that when he and Peter had last met he had promised to take the boy to the Crimea, to sun and sand and sea. It was a promise made with love, as ephemeral as a snowflake. He had told himself many times that he had meant it. He meant it now. Yet the journey seemed as far off as a journey to the moon.

Peter had begun to run through the deep, ice-crusted pack on the road. Plakhanov could see that he was bareheaded, the snowflakes melting in his thick golden hair. He was like young Baldur, slim as a wand of mistletoe, his face bright as sunlight.

Plakhanov could not see the Wall now. Its mass was hidden

in the winter mist, but it was there, a shadowless, ominous presence.

How I hate the Germans! he thought. Though they freed me of my father. Though they bred Peter Arendt and gave him to me. But, though the day is white and without form, they are *there*, unseen, brooding about disloyal countrymen intent on committing *Republikflucht*. For some seconds Plakhanov had an empty moment of doubt. What sort of people could invent a crime and give it the name "flight from the republic"?

But they were there, the Germans, behind the curtain of white, in their gun towers, watching with Teutonic intensity the beautiful young man running through the snow on the bridge across the Spree.

Peter wore a dark-green loden coat with the collar turned up. He had bought it in the West. No such garment was available in the GDR. His breath condensed in white puffs. His face shone with high color. He was not as tall as Plakhanov, but he moved like a dancer. His boots made almost no sound on the crusty snow. Plakhanov could hear clearly the gurgle of the river's black current beneath its thin sheath of ice.

Peter's blue eyes were bright with the pleasure of seeing Plakhanov. He gripped the older man's gloved hands. "*Gruss Gott*, thank you for coming alone, Feli. I was afraid you wouldn't be able to."

A small, cold knot formed in Plakhanov's belly. "Has something happened?" It was a flaccid, unmanly way of phrasing the question. Anyone but Peter would have been ordered to report at once the reason for demanding an extraordinary meeting.

Peter hugged himself, rubbing his arms and shivering. Plakhanov took a silver flask of schnapps from his pocket, uncapped it, and handed it to him.

The young man accepted it gratefully. He drank a mouthful for the cold, then another because he was frightened.

"Tell me what has happened," Plakhanov said again, still gently.

Peter returned the flask before replying. Then he leaned on the iron railing and stared down at the frozen Spree. "Paladin," he said. "It is Paladin."

Paladin was the KGB code name for a new arrival in West Berlin, a CIA officer named John Wells. It had been reported that Wells's specialty was the discovery and subversion of penetration agents. Moscow Center had dispatched an advisory about him.

"Are you certain?" It was customary for inexperienced agents to attribute failures of organization, execution, or security to agents of the opposition. Life was not usually so simple, as he had explained to Peter early on. "The main enemy, *glavny vrag*"—he had used the Russian words that, in the language of Soviet Intelligence since the days of the Cheka, meant the United States—"the main enemy is not made up of geniuses. They do not plan every one of our misfortunes. Sometimes we fail because we are men, and fallible."

But Peter shook his head. "Yes, Feli. This is truly Paladin." He glanced sidelong at the taller man beside him at the bridge rail. "I met with him, Feli."

"You did *what*?"

"Please, don't be angry. I had no choice. He knew all about us."

Plakhanov's world tottered sickeningly. "*What* does he know?"

"Everything, Feli. I don't know how or why. He knows about Leipzig and Magdeburg. And Prague, Feli. He even knows about *Prague*."

It seemed suddenly very much colder. Plakhanov had to hold himself rigid to keep from shivering. A great latitude was allowed members of the Soviet elite, the *nomenklatura*. As with any ruling class, the sins of its members were held in confidence. Since the death of Stalin, the servants of the Soviet state no longer paid with their lives for every mistake. But there were mistakes and mistakes. Love between men outraged Soviet puritanism. For an officer of the KGB to be exposed as a homosexual meant, at the very least, a term in a psychiatric hospital and years in the gulag for the crime of perversion. There could be no mitigating factor.

Peter asked plaintively, "How could he have found out?"

Numb with cold and apprehension he had not known since his father died, Plakhanov said, "What does it matter? Tell me what he said to you."

"He took one or two of my people in and then sent me a message that he wanted to talk. I assumed he might be willing to exchange them. Was I wrong to think that, Feli?"

Wrong? Completely, stupidly wrong, Peter, Plakhanov thought. Who had given Peter the impression that any of his agents were worth trading for? What could the boy have been thinking?

But he said only "Go on, Peter."

94

"He didn't want to talk about my agents."

"No."

"I was a fool, wasn't I, Feli?"

Plakhanov said in a dead voice, "You are very young."

Peter seemed to take comfort from this ambiguity. He said, "I met him in a restaurant, Feli. An ordinary restaurant on the Ku-damm. I was terrified, but I kept the appointment, and there he was, sitting at a window table drinking schnapps. He knew me by sight. I had no idea they could be so well informed, Feli."

Plakhanov gripped the rail with both gloved hands.

"He is a handsome man, Feli. Bigger than you, but no taller. He wears wonderful clothes. I think he is rich."

"*Damn* it. Tell me what he *said* to you."

"I'm sorry, Feli. I thought you would want to know about him."

"I do, Peter. But tell me what he said."

"I sat down with him, and he told me who he was. He said he worked for the American government. He didn't say CIA, but I knew, of course. He was so pleasant, Feli. We talked just like friends. I didn't tell him anything I should not have. But he didn't ask me about our operations in West Berlin. He was more interested in you, Feli. He asked me many questions about you. What you liked and disliked. The music you enjoyed. What you liked to eat and drink. How long I had known you. He even knew you had just been promoted to major. He said I was to congratulate you."

Plakhanov closed his eyes. He was in a frozen nether level of hell, in the grip of a nightmare.

"Then he ordered a meal, and we sat there eating. He bought wine. He gave me cigarettes. He never asked me anything at all about what we were doing in West Berlin. Nothing. It was as though he didn't really care about that."

Plakhanov said, "He cares about other things."

Peter looked at the river and bobbed his head like a pupil being interrogated by a schoolmaster. "Yes." The boy turned his head and looked at Plakhanov with the eyes of an innocent. "He gave me a message for you."

Yes, Plakhanov thought. It would come to that, of course. He looked for the far bank of the river. It was still lost in the mist and falling snow.

"He said: 'Take this message to Feliks Plakhanov. Tell him that we see things differently in the West. Tell him that you and he can be safe with us. We don't put men in prison for loving other men.' Did he mean that, Feliks? Could it really be so?''

Well, it has come at last, Plakhanov thought. What the Spanish call ''the moment of truth''—the instant when the matador must reach over the horns of the bull to make the kill.

He tried to imagine himself a defector. He tried to piece together from the shards of this life that other life Paladin offered.

Peter said softly, ''If you say no, I can't go back, can I? They will arrest me, won't they?''

''Yes. If I say no, they probably will.''

''I don't know if I could bear that, Feli. I am not really very strong or very brave.''

The thought of Peter Arendt in a cell until his youth was gone was devastating.

Plakhanov touched Peter's face with a gloved hand. It was an instinctive, tender gesture. ''Don't be afraid, my dear.''

''I can't help it, Feli. The thought of going to prison terrifies me.''

''I will never let them arrest you.''

''What shall I do?''

Now I shall know grief, Plakhanov thought. ''Go back,'' he said. ''Tell Paladin—yes.''

Peter regarded Plakhanov with shining eyes. ''You mean that, Feli? You truly mean that?''

Plakhanov nodded. His face felt frozen.

''Are they really like that in the West? We can just be together?''

Damn you, Paladin, for a cheat and a liar. Damn you for charming an innocent.

Peter said doubtfully, ''Are you certain, Feli? I could just stay here, on this side of the Wall.''

But you cannot, Plakhanov thought. You cannot stay. You cannot return.

''Tell him I said yes. When do you see him again?''

''Tonight. At nine.''

''Then tell him.'' How my father would sneer at me now, Plakhanov thought. He would laugh and say to his whore, ''You see? I was right about Feliks all along. I should have dressed him in skirts and had him learn ballet.''

He looked away from the frozen river. The snow was spinning and swirling among the girders of the iron bridge. The air felt even colder than before. God, he thought, how I shall hate winter. How I shall despise the sight of ice and snow. In his imagination Paladin was a vast pale figure of ice, sculptured by the polar winds.

"Are you certain about this, Feli?" Peter asked once more.

Plakhanov placed his hands on the young man's shoulders. He pressed his cheek against Peter's, once, again. "Go," he said. "Quickly. Before I change my mind."

Peter asked, "Will we be happy in America?"

Is that what he was told? Is that what Paladin promised? Plakhanov's thoughts seemed to struggle against a tide of anger and despair that was focusing into hatred for the seducer.

"Go, Peter. Go!"

Peter recoiled from his anger, turned obediently, and began to retrace his trail in the snow. He looked back.

Plakhanov lifted a hand in salute. It was all he could manage. Peter vanished into the mist.

Plakhanov closed his eyes and gritted his teeth against the pain in his chest. It was a palpable wound, agonizing and draining.

There was another poem Peter Arendt had loved, one he had found himself in *lieber* Feli's book of Russian verse.

> *We won't be asked then: Did you sin?*
> *We'll only be asked: Did you love?*
> *And without raising up our heads,*
> *We'll say bitterly: Yes, alas.*
> *We loved . . . oh, how we loved.*

He stood on the bridge, a stiff figure in a crystal globe, the snow falling all around him. Paladin, he thought, I promise to see you in hell one day.

One minute passed. Five. Then, like a man in pain, he took a hand-held radio from the pocket of his greatcoat. In German he said, very slowly: "The man who crossed at the Spreebrücke is returning. He is to be stopped."

Plakhanov had almost reached the end of the bridge when he heard the machine guns. He had thought they would wait until Peter was farther from the meetingplace, but they were Germans, he thought bitterly. They spare me nothing.

He turned and tried to see through the falling snow, but there were only moving shadows on the killing ground. Another burst of fire battered its way across the frozen river, and a shout. *"Er ist Todt! Nichts mehr davon!"*

His orderly mind translated before he could close it off: "He

97

is dead! No more of that!'' The last wild burst of shooting had apparently endangered one of the Vopos and he was angry.

Plakhanov smashed the radio down on the iron railing of the bridge. Again and again, until it was a twisted tangle of bent metal, wires, shattered transistors. He cut his heavy glove and the flesh beneath it before dropping the radio into the Spree. Then he thrust his bleeding hand in its tattered glove into the pocket of his greatcoat. And at last he began to walk back to his car—stiff-legged and with great effort, in the way of all the walking wounded.

SECOND PRELUDE

1972

Into a land of mirrors
without time or space,
And all they had to strike
now was the human face.

—W. H. Auden,
 "Diaspora"

15. SAIGON, FEBRUARY 1972

She had come to Saigon almost on a dare. She was still that young.

The moment she had stepped off the airplane at Tan Son Nhut, moving, in a half-dozen steps, from the air-conditioned cool of the 747 into the humid, rain-soaked ninety-degree heat of the Vietnamese capital, she had begun to regret it.

The problem was Uncle Jack. His worship of her dead parents had become, over time, more of a burden than she could carry. The final argument had ostensibly been political. Actually, she regarded it as a break for freedom—a word her friends used often and somehow could never define. Uncle Jack never used the word. He always spoke of her "responsibility," instead.

Well, he was like that. In times of thoughtful assessment of her life as pseudo daughter to John Wells, she understood that he had been young himself once upon a time; that he had adored his elder brother; that he had been, most probably, in love with his brother's wife—in a stiff and secretive way, of course, because even as a young man he must have had all the makings of the spook he had become.

"Spook" was not a word Megan used often. But her radicalized friends at Stanford, students and teachers alike, used it, with real contempt in their voices. At first she had felt disloyal for listening. But as the war in Southeast Asia went on and on, and the casualty lists grew longer, she began to wonder if they were not right. The war was called "immoral." In the first two years of the 1970s, there was an enormous volume of talk about what was and was not moral. And about compassion. And relevancy. And, finally, about outrage.

It was outrage that had driven the students to destroy the Computer Center and to burn the ROTC building. Outrage and, of course, morality. In Washington, during spring break, Uncle Jack had made an effort to be home and be family. But it had been a mistake. His timing had been faulty. There were too many memories of holidays at European boarding schools with the mistresses, because the other pupils had gone home, too many summers spent in the bleak and half-empty country house where the de Lattres, her grandparents, still lived their austere, lonely lives. There had been trouble that spring because Megan fell into the trap of presenting ideas not her own to a soldier of the Cold War.

She thought it was through the Department of Political Science that she was given a student internship with the Agency for International Development. She was wrong. A contrite Uncle Jack had arranged it, and she had marched off to the other side of the world to see for herself the evil her country was doing.

For the first month, she hated Saigon. She hated the weather, the confusion, the strangeness. She had spent much of her childhood in Europe, but this was strangeness of a different order.

She saw one of the last of the burning priests. The yellow-robed Buddhist knelt calmly and deliberately at a street corner, parting the crowds with his body. Then he arranged his robes with care, doused himself with gasoline, and set himself alight.

From the second story of the U.S. Embassy, where she happened to be, Megan, unbelieving, saw the flames leap skyward and watched horrified while the yellow robes turned to charcoal and the silent martyr crisped and charred and melted into the bubbling tarmac.

The death of the last of the self-immolators drew almost no press attention. The television reporters and cameramen had been caught unawares, unwarned of a newsworthy pictorial event, and so arrived long after the ARVN military police had cleaned up the site.

Mary Quinn, hard-bitten and cynical, said, "It's too late for burning monks. Madame Nhu is in Paris. Diem is ashes in a jar. Tiger cages are the thing now. Tiger cages and Peace Talks."

Megan had been drawn, almost at once, to Mary Quinn. Mary was what Megan thought she herself had always wanted to be: competent, skeptical, and brave. Mary wrote her stories in the field, where the troops were, not in the bar of the Continental Hotel, where the press talked to one another and bad-mouthed the army.

The work at AID turned out to be undemanding. In a nation at war, aid for civilian "development" tended to be rudimentary. Often during her first few weeks in Saigon, Megan had been tempted to give it up and return to school. The reality of the war seemed to have little in common with the heated academic disputations in surroundings both comfortable and rakishly bohemian that had formed so many of her political opinions.

Being by nature a fair-minded person, she found herself wondering how she could apologize to Uncle Jack without totally compromising her principles. She had very nearly decided to write an apologetic letter when, quite by accident, she discovered that her precious internship with AID had come not through Stanford, but as a special favor from the Director, who was repaying a debt to an old friend, the Deputy Director of Operations of the Central Intelligence Agency—John Wells.

The discovery enraged Megan. She was a person of considerable sensitivity and had flashes of real insight about the people with whom she dealt. There was more than a single, simple reason for Uncle Jack's clandestine assistance. In another setting, she might have realized it immediately. But what she did recognize—and at once—was the Jack Wells touch. His longstanding desire to oversee her life, to protect, to guide, if necessary to interfere, in the name of family love and responsibility—responsibility above all else. Megan was the last of the Wellses, and the daughter of Matt and Denise, the two people Uncle Jack had most nearly idolized. Megan, pale with fury, told herself: He means to keep the bloodline safe—and pure.

She was being unfair. Her lonely childhood made it impossible for her not to be unfair.

What neither she, nor Uncle Jack, nor the de Lattres had ever taken the time to consider was that Megan had grown into an attractive, inquisitive, and passionate woman. The two people who might have foreseen what would happen to her were Matt and Denise—both, alas, not there to see.

Megan was an intelligent but woefully inexperienced young person. She was also courageous to the point of foolhardiness, easily hurt or angered or both, and given to intense enthusiasms and loyalties.

And on the eve of the first day of her second month in Saigon, she met the correspondent of *L'Humanité* and a half-dozen other small leftist French-language journals.

She met Jean Thierry.

* * *

103

La Marianne. In every French colonial city in the world there must be a café known as La Marianne. This one was a houseboat on the river, and to see it, Megan thought, no one would ever imagine that the Republic of Vietnam was at war.

Colored lanterns lit the open deck where couples danced. There were candles on the tables and white tablecloths and champagne icing in pewter buckets. A four-piece band of draft-age Vietnamese, long-haired, dressed in American clothes, played for the largely foreign crowd.

Megan was surprised when Jean Thierry took her there. He had been so explicit about his dislike for Americans. "Don't be offended," he had said. "I do not think highly of the French, either."

She had heard the story that his father had been a French officer killed at Dien Bien Phu. The mathematics didn't seem quite right. He had told her that he was almost forty years old.

They waited while a Vietnamese waiter poured their wine. Jean offered her a cigarette. It wounded her pride a bit that he could never seem to remember that she did not smoke. Mary scoffed and said, "Does it on purpose, the horny bastard." But Mary disliked Jean. It was obvious in everything she said and did. To be fair, she didn't gossip about him the way the others around the U.S. Mission did.

Charlie Blaisdell said straight out that he was a Communist sympathizer, just because he wrote for *L'Humanité*. That was Blaisdell's brand of the vaunted American fairness. The problem with him was that he had been in Southeast Asia too long. That was not just Megan's opinion. It was a consensus.

When she and Jean were together, they spoke French. Mary said the other Mission women were envious, but that they didn't have much sense. Mary's way was always to give a little and take a little away. She did agree that Jean was a damned attractive male—not handsome; attractive.

Megan was happy to hear the older woman's confirmation. She had met Jean at a reception at the Japanese Embassy, and had found herself in his bed less than a week after that. She still didn't understand how it could have happened so quickly. She had thought of herself as experienced, but the schoolboys with whom she had performed her adolescent experiments did not belong on the same planet with Jean Thierry.

Was it love? She hesitated even to ask herself, there were so many obstacles to overcome.

First of all, Jean. She looked at him in the café. His strong, almost coarse features were burned brown by the sun. He was a photojournalist, and always worked alone. Some of his photographs were spectacular, shots that had to have been taken in the very center of fire fights and ambushes. There was a story going around the Military Assistance Command that patrols with Thierry were to be avoided.

"He draws NVA like horseshit draws flies, beggin' your pardon, miss," Major Collie, the Marine Public Information Officer, had told her at the last embassy gathering. Collie had been drunk and resentful of the media people present, who had, he said, "made a separate peace" with the enemy after the Tet offensive. But what he said about Jean was apparently true. When he went into the field, he came back with both pictures and reportage. He was so good, in fact, that some people wondered why it was he made no effort to catch on with one of the networks. Journalistic reputations were being made in Vietnam. A three-minute segment of atrocities committed by the ARVN or of U.S. Marines taking casualties in some useless rice paddy was worth a bid from the news department of one of the three major networks.

But Jean didn't give a damn about that. He came into town. He entertained Megan. He fucked her. (She used the vulgarism freely for the first time in her life and felt defiantly liberated.) Then he was gone again, into the field, alone, to get his stories.

He had a thick torso and a broad chest with gray hair between the flat, hard pectorals. Somewhere, somehow, he had trained his body well. He was formidable.

He wore what all the other correspondents wore, the journalistic uniform: bush jacket, washed to softness, loosely belted or not belted at all, with sleeves rolled or pushed above the elbows; khaki trousers; jungle jump boots. When he went into the field, he carried three tape recorders, two Nikons and an Olympus with a 300mm lens, rations, a canteen of whisky and one of water, and three black-market military first-aid kits.

Except for his field gear, his outfit at the café was what he wore at work. Jean did not believe in dressing up, even for La Marianne, which the girls at AID had told Megan was very grand.

She did not think it so grand. She was thinking of something else entirely. She had missed two periods. It was difficult to believe that in this day and age a girl could get caught as simply as that. But she had. There was no doubt about it. This morning she had awakened with a queasy stomach and all the other minor, but damning, symptoms a gravid female was supposed to feel.

It was so unbelievably gauche. She had simply forgotten to take her pill for a day, and suddenly there she was, about to become a breeder.

She had spent most of the day trying to decide what to do. It made her blood run cold to think of informing Uncle Jack that she was pregnant. And by a man he would be certain to dislike; a man she had known for a few days less than two months. One she was not even sure *she* liked very much. Except when they were in bed together. Uncle Jack would be ''delighted'' to hear any part of that report. The de Lattres would also be ''so pleased'' to have the news about their *petite fille* being knocked up.

She was being foolish, she knew. Abortions were no longer the great sin they had once been. She could probably have one at the military hospital at Da Nang, if it came to that. Or, if she wanted to keep it from Uncle Jack, she could pay for one herself. There were civilian doctors around, dozens of them.

But there was a problem, and it had been troubling her more and more as the days went by: She did not want to abort the child growing inside her.

She had never imagined she would have this kind of problem. She had been raised a nominal Catholic because Uncle Jack said Denise would have wanted it and because it pleased the two old people at Villa de Lattre. But religious scruples were not what troubled her.

The life inside her was precious.

In some other place, where one could not hear the guns late at night or see the dead and wounded being taken from the helicopters flying in every day from the jungle, she might have destroyed her baby without a second thought.

But this was a land in the throes of self-immolation. Life had grown incredibly cheap here—and incredibly dear. She saw it in the taut, tired faces of the military doctors and nurses at the Officers' Club, in the corridors of the hospitals at Nha Trang and Da Nang. She was discovering that she could not easily destroy still another human life, no matter how unknowing and unaware it was.

Jean said, ''You are very quiet tonight.''

Tell him now, she thought. See what he says. ''Yes,'' she said. But nothing more. The moment did not seem right. He had been away for ten days, and she could feel the sexual hunger he radiated. That was one of the strange things about him. His emotions seemed to surround him like an aura. Sometimes it was so sensual it made her knees tremble. At other times it was so black, so menacing, that she wanted to run from him as she would from a venomous snake or a predator.

Adolescent images, overdramatized, she knew. But then, how many nineteen-year-old girls from California ever met a man like Jean Thierry?

Beyond Jean she could see the glitter of lights on the Saigon River. The river was navigable well past the city, and there were freighters moored in the stream. There were also the remains of ships sunk early in the war by Vietcong frogmen, their masts and superstructures still above water, crusted with rust.

A full moon was high. Yesterday it had rained, but tonight the sky was clear, and stars seemed to vie with the moon for place. A thick smell of mud and algae and other, less attractive, things rose from the water under the houseboat. Megan had been in the country for less than ninety days, but she was growing accustomed to the smells and the sounds of Saigon.

"A quoi pense-tu?" Jean's French had an Asian sibilance. One of the stories about him was that he had had a Vietnamese mother. It might be true, though a Eurasian connection, if it existed, probably lay farther back than a single generation.

Of course she was thinking of him, but dared not say so. She was, in fact, considering what the tiny globe of cells that had taken root in her womb might—if she let it live—one day become.

A boy. Yes. With Jean's masculinity surrounding her like a cloak, she could not even entertain the idea that their child might be a female. A boy, with Jean's dark eyes and black hair. A boy with a gift for languages and adventure and such bravery that she would spend her old age in delicious terror as he ranged the world. She suppressed a smile. What would Jean make of that?

He poured more wine and stretched out his legs. He was tired; the strain of a long and difficult trip upcountry showed in his face. He had got as far as Pakse, in Laos, and had obtained— God knew how—an interview with a Pathet Lao district chairman. "Perfect," he said, "for the comrades at *L'Humanité*."

She had yet to see anything by him in print, but he explained that it took time. Mary Quinn's thick eyebrows arched into her bangs when Megan spoke of Jean's journalism. The U.S. newspeople said he was a "flake," whatever that meant.

She studied his face in the candlelight. It was like a rock

carving, with strong, well-developed proportions, but somehow brutal. She shivered slightly. What was she thinking of to use a word like that to describe Jean?

The father of her unborn—perhaps to be born?—child.

Jean said, "Have you written to your uncle about us?"

Megan shook her head. There was a strange streak of perversity in Jean. Surely he knew who her uncle was and what he did. It seemed to her that everyone in Saigon knew she was the niece of the CIA's Deputy Director of Operations. She hated it, but there was nothing that could be done. Saigon was a maelstrom of loose talk, much of it true.

Jean showed his teeth in a smile. Sometimes he looked feral when he did that. "What would he think?"

He probably already knows, she thought, feeling pressed. Uncle Jack didn't lack for sources of information in Saigon, of all places. Blaisdell boasted of being Jack Wells's man in Saigon. That was hard to believe, Megan thought. The men were as dissimilar as chalk and cheese. But one thing *was* true: Blaisdell and Uncle Jack had been recruited into the Agency the same year. But now, mainly it came to this: Jack Wells gave orders; Charlie Blaisdell took them.

"Charles le Gros" was what Jean called him. There was no denying it. Blaisdell was worn out, overweight, crude, and rumpled. At embassy functions he liked to corner Megan and talk half-drunkenly about what she suspected had been a very tenuous connection with Uncle Jack. As often as not he would get onto the subject of Jean, whom he seemed to hate with a visceral passion. And she would listen, angry, but trapped by her sympathetic nature. Blaisdell had his reasons for being as he was. Mary had explained them. Yes, he was overweight and overage in grade and embittered. He might have been good a long time ago, but now he was simply putting in the time he needed for his pension. Others in his class—Uncle Jack, for one, Megan thought—went to Europe or to one of the satellites, or even to the USSR, and got on the fast track to promotion. But Charlie Blaisdell was an Indochina specialist, and the whole peninsula— Vietnam, Laos, Cambodia, even Thailand—was going down, slowly, but surely. The war the French had started to lose had been handed over to the Americans, and they were losing it, too.

Megan wondered if this was true or was merely Mary's way of expressing the prejudices of the Saigon press corps. It was so difficult to make any political sense of the crazy way the war was being fought.

But, Mary said, Charlie knew what was coming. The hill tribesmen he had helped recruit and train in the early days, when the war was still secret and belonged to President Kennedy, were going to be abandoned, and he knew it. He had worked mostly in Laos and along the Thai border, and he knew the Khmer Rouge as well as anyone in the country. He knew exactly what they would do when the Americans were gone. It haunted him.

The war was being lost, at home, in the press, in the Congress. And Charlie was about to become surplus, Mary said.

"What are you thinking?" Jean asked again.

Megan gave a Gallic shrug. "Charles le Gros," she said.

Again that feral smile. "You waste time thinking about idiots like that one."

"I have time," she said, "for people who will talk to me. Mary says Blaisdell thinks we are losing the war."

"He is right about that," Jean said. "You *are* losing the war. The little men in sandals are beating you to your knees."

"Doesn't it bother you? It was your war once."

"Never."

Jean was no Blaisdell. And he wasn't a fool. He listened to the talk. He knew exactly who she was. So when he asked about Uncle Jack, what was it he wanted? Some crazy assignment from the CIA? It wasn't possible. His attitude toward the U.S. officials in the city was openly derisive. Of course, there was not that much difference between his attitude and that of the rest of the press corps. They particularly despised MAC-V, the Military Assistance Command there.

The orchestra of young, draft-evading Viets was playing a ballad. That was rare in this incredibly noisy city, where hard rock was the musical standard. Megan was suddenly filled with a petulant, despairing anger. She looked across the table at Jean.

She wanted to be loved. She wanted to be loved and to make love with the father of her child.

"Dance with me, Jean," she said. "Hold me."

For Jean, dancing was not an act of love, but of dominance. He held her tight against him, and she could smell the masculine scent of him. Even fresh from the bath, he smelled like a man.

She felt an overpowering urge to confess, to share the secret in her belly. After all, it was not hers alone.

Jean let his hand slip down to her buttock, he held it like he would a melon, pressing his fingers into the cleavage between the cheeks. The thin layers of silk between her skin and his fingers made her feel naked, and it made her feel uneasy to be handled this way in public. But no one at La Marianne seemed to notice, and his searching hand sent sexual chills down her spine.

An American officer danced by with an expensive bar girl. Megan knew him by sight. He glanced at her, at what Jean was doing, and looked away. Megan felt her cheek burn.

"Jean—"

His hand left her buttock and moved upward. Her sundress was bare to the waist in the back. Jean let his hand rest on bare skin for a moment and then slipped it under the silk and under her arm so that his fingers touched the soft swell of her breast. Her knees felt watery.

It wasn't love, she thought. Love wasn't like this. Strangely, as the lust in her rose, so did a sadness. She had expected something else. What? she asked herself. Silver knights and blushing maidens? She pulled back so that she could look at Jean. For a moment, she had the strange notion that he had no face, no face at all.

A trick of the light. Only that. The music stopped, and the musicians left the tiny stage. The houseboat moved under her feet, rising and falling so slightly that it was a movement sensed rather than felt. The tide of the South China Sea did not reach this far up the Saigon River.

"Jean, listen to me," she said desperately, the words thick in her throat. *"Je suis enceinte."*

His eyes caught the light from the lanterns. Megan hugged her bare arms. How could she have been so damned stupid? How could she have just blurted it out that way? What in God's name had she done?

Jean had stepped away from her, his look unreadable. What was he thinking? Did he believe her?

He dropped a sheaf of piasters on the table, took her arm, and led her up the wooden planking to the dock, where rickshaw-bicycles were waiting.

He gave the address of his rooms in Cholon.

"Jean—"

He cut her off with a sharp shake of the head. She sat beside him feeling young, vulnerable, foolish. She watched the narrow back of the rickshaw boy as he maneuvered them through the littered streets.

Why did I come here, she wondered. What am I doing in this

terrible, strange place with a man almost twenty years older than I am?

They climbed the outside stairs. He held her arm as they walked around the verandah to the riverside. Megan could hear the sound of Chinese voices and music. Cholon was populated mostly by Tonkin Chinese, the aliens who had come across the northern border two centuries ago and dominated the commerce of all Indochina. "The Jews of Asia," Jean had once called them.

Jean opened his door and, still holding her arm, walked into the darkness. He lit a single light before he released her. Then he stood looking at her with shadowed eyes, still unreadable.

He said, "Your shoes. Take them off."

Obediently, Megan did as she was told. She kicked off her sandals and stood barefoot.

"The dress."

She crossed her arms over her breast instinctively.

"Take the dress off," he said, not moving.

Megan felt herself tremble. She slipped the halter and reluctantly let the dress fall from her bare breasts.

Jean stood still, fully clothed—a figure in armor. "*A nu,*" he said.

She hooked her thumbs in the waistband and slipped the dress and briefs down over her thighs. She was aware that her body was glistening with sweat, though the air in the room felt cold. She tried inadequately to cover her nakedness with her bare arms. Her skin felt slick.

She had lain in bed with Jean a dozen times by now and yet at this moment she felt more completely exposed than she had ever been in her life.

He stepped forward and grasped her shoulders. He was smiling that frightening feral smile. "Now tell me again," he said.

"I am pregnant."

He began to laugh. It was terrifying. He let his hands fall to her waist. He guided her to the bed, and took her without undressing, without regard for her pleasure, or, she suspected, for his own. Ritual rape.

But he was still smiling when he rolled over and, looking at the ceiling, said, "We will marry. The civil authorities will do."

16. KADENA AIR FORCE BASE, OKINAWA, MARCH 1972

The rain fell in torrents, with a sound like a river rushing through a gorge. The wind battered against the windows of the operations building, found its way through open passageways and past closed doors. The papers on the bulletin boards rustled restlessly, and from the snack bar down the corridor Blaisdell could hear the shouting and laughing of young voices.

It had been almost a year since he had been away from Vietnam, longer than that since he had been to Kadena. Here the young airmen seemed curiously detached from the war. They had the relaxed manner of men who knew their worth and needed no outside assurances.

Two sorts of aircraft flew from Kadena. One was the great black jets of the Strategic Air Command that pulverized targets in North Vietnam and, sometimes on command, just outside the wire of camps under attack. Blaisdell had been in a camp at Chon Do one night when the camp commander, a twenty-two-year-old Special Forces second lieutenant, had called in a B-52 "Searchlight" strike. A North Vietnamese Army battalion had massed just outside the concertina wire and seemed intent on overrunning the Montagnard troops holding the perimeter.

Blaisdell had heard nothing, not a sound. Then the Green Beret communications officer had looked up from his radio and said quietly, "Searchlight on the way. Now."

The bombers had crossed the camp unheard at an altitude of forty-nine thousand feet. A single three-ship element of the ancient Boeings had bombed from ten miles up in the stratosphere, and the bombs had struck within a dozen meters of the concertina, one thousand-pounder for each ten square meters of ground occupied by the NVA. The shock, noise, and concussion had been incredible.

In the morning, the ground around the camp looked as though it had been churned. Six hundred enemy soldiers had occupied that ground, and the camp garrison found not one single body, only burned and shattered bits of steel, wood, cloth, and meat.

God damn, Blaisdell now thought, huddling his bulk against a steam-heat radiator for warmth. We could kill like that and we were still losing the fucking war. How was it possible?

The second kind of aircraft flying out of Kadena was the Blackbirds, with which Blaisdell had a relationship, once or twice removed.

The futuristic black Lockheeds were not based at Kadena, but flew there from Beale Air Force Base in California. In Okinawa they were refueled and "rearmed" with film for their fantastic cameras. When the target was too small or too nonstrategic to require the repositioning of a KH-13 satellite, it was the Blackbirds who got the pictures.

Blaisdell had seen this sort of "product" for most of his career in the field. We're so damned good, he thought, looking miserably at the rain-swept air base. Why *are* we losing the damn fucking war?

"Mr. Grenier?" The baby-faced airman wore the stripes of a master sergeant.

"Yes?"

"I was asked to tell you when General Bolton's airplane entered Kadena Traffic Control Area. They'll be on final approach in six minutes."

"In this weather?" The storm had worsened since Blaisdell's arrival at dawn in a Navy A-7 Intruder.

The kid grinned. "Magic, Mr. Grenier. Wild Blue Magic."

He was only trying to be pleasant, but Blaisdell felt like hitting out. Life wasn't the way this child saw it. The B-52s killed people. The Blackbirds helped kill others. Airplanes crashed in rainstorms. If that was what he called "Wild Blue Magic," he should read the combat-loss reports being filed by the squadrons operating over North Vietnam.

And for what? To hit "political" targets while letting real ones that might help win the war go untouched. He had begged Langley to recommend that the dikes in the north be hit, flooding the rice fields that supplied the 150,000 North Vietnamese troops operating in the south. But no, not a chance of that. Henry Kissinger, the man who invented détente, was discussing the shape of tables in Paris. The world, at least the part of it Blaisdell inhabited, seemed to have gone mad.

113

And then this order: "Get to Kadena and meet the DDO. Do it now."

Well, here he was, after one of the roughest, most miserable flights of his life. In a damn-all Navy attack plane too damaged to be returned to its carrier and being flown instead to Okinawa for repairs.

One thing at least, he thought as he stood to stare out the window at the seemingly solid curtain of rain, the order had been marked SECRET and it had been *kept* secret. Other than Blaisdell, not one person at MAC-V knew that Jack Wells was in this part of the world.

It had to do with the girl. Blaisdell was certain of it. The girl and that Communist French bastard. My God, what could she have been thinking of? The man was a Soviet agent. He couldn't prove it, but it was so. He knew it—and so did Jack Wells. Why else was he here?

Blaisdell succumbed to a surfeit of mingled admiration and envy. Wells was traveling as a civilian member of Bolton's inspection party. Bolton was Air Inspector General for the Military Airlift Command. He was forever on the move, snooping at one thing and another. Without breathing hard, Wells had perfect cover for a trip to the war zone. He would go from here to Thailand and then on to Europe, and no one in Washington (except those he wished to know) would be aware that he had ever left the United States.

Did he remember Charlie Blaisdell? He must, Blaisdell thought. Why else would I be here—"Mr. Grenier, of AID," waiting for one of Bolton's bureaucrats?

There was a gleam of light out in the dark-gray storm. It was one in the afternoon, and every light on the base was on. Okinawa was experiencing a series of equinoctial rainstorms.

The young sergeant reappeared. "They've just touched down, sir. General Bolton's aide says you are to bring your gear and get aboard at once. They want to clear for Bangkok before the weather gets really bad."

"*Before* it gets bad?"

"Wild Blue Magic, Mr. Grenier."

"My bag is in the BOQ Sergeant."

"I'll send a man for it. Generals hate to be kept waiting, sir."

To say nothing of generals' anonymous companions, Blaisdell thought.

Now he could see the silver, gray, and white Starlifter taxiing up the fueling ramp. Strobes flashed on wing tips and tail. It bore a red flag with two stars. But was Bolton even on board? This was Jack Wells's trip.

Because of Megan Wells.

Correction, Blaisdell thought: Because of Megan Wells Thierry. If that was the bastard's real name. He surely was a KGB hood.

One last great move, Charlie, he told himself. One real coup before retirement.

If he was right about Jean Thierry, there was a chance for one last grab at the brass ring.

He saw an airman in a streaming poncho running across the ramp carrying his canvas valpak.

He unfolded his plastic slicker and put it on over his wrinkled seersucker jacket. Then he made his way down the stairs to the field level of the ops building and out the door into the rain, jogging heavily in the direction of the great droopy-winged airplane parked on the concrete ramp.

17. CHOLON, MAY 1972

There was no change of seasons. The weather grew wet and then less wet and then wet again. The threat of the monsoon lay like a sweaty hand on the city.

Megan lay listlessly on the bed leafing through a two-week-old copy of *Time*. The cover story was about the end of still another bombing pause, this one of long duration. Nixon's February trip to China was being trumpeted by the administration as a great success, but on April 16, B-52s had bombed Hanoi and mined Haiphong harbor. Within hours, a fury of controversy had erupted in the United States Senate.

The North Vietnamese Army had captured the "northern capital," Hué. There were ugly rumors about a massacre of civilians, but not in *Time*. The South Vietnamese Army commander whose responsibility it had been to protect the north was facing a court-martial. The U.S. Marines were preparing to retake the city.

Megan closed her eyes and dropped the magazine on the floor beside the bed. She felt vaguely ill. She sat up, parted the wrapper she was wearing, and stared at her belly. It should have been big as a mountain, but it was not. Only a small bulge between waist and mons. So small a cause for so many mornings of vomiting and retching. It didn't seem fair.

She could hear the neighbors shouting at one another in Chinese. She had tried to learn some Mandarin, but it was hopeless. The inhabitants of Cholon spoke a dozen dialects, all of them flavored with a Vietnamese accent. It was obvious that she was never destined to tell the neighbors, in their own language, to be quiet.

The room was thick with the odor of cooking. Every family in the building prepared food in its rooms, and there were no chimneys, no flues. The threat of fire from an overturned brazier was ever-present. All Cholon smelled of burning, frying, and the river. Always the river. Very different, she thought, from the filtered, distilled, and cooled air of the offices where she worked.

Where she *used* to work.

She liked to think she had resigned her job. Her parting from the Agency for International Development was rather more ambiguous. Jeremy Taylor, the Director of Personnel, was trying to solve what he saw as a bureaucratic dilemma. Megan Wells had come with powerful recommendations. But she was now the wife of a foreign national. Taylor had put her on indefinite leave of absence—without pay—while he searched the rule books for guidance.

How much of the difficulty, she wondered, was because Jean's politics were suspect?

In any event, the job was actually gone. There had been an immediate offer of a priority to fly home on one of the carriers chartered to the military. Megan had rejected the idea. Damn them, she thought. I am four months pregnant.

Of course, they did not know that. She had not been near any of the physicians attached to either the military or AID. Somehow she had the feeling that they would only have to look at her to know. And that they would then immediately report back to Uncle Jack.

She was not ready yet to tell him any of this.

Mary Quinn was the only one of her associates who came to visit her in Cholon. The others were wary—of Cholon; of me, perhaps, she thought. Lightweights, the lot of them. She did not miss them.

She thought if she never again had to hear one of Blaisdell's stories about life in the mountains with the Meo, or about attending leadership classes at Langley with Uncle Jack, it would be fine with her.

But she was lonely.

Jean spent more and more time in the field as the year went on. The manifestations of her pregnancy seemed to disgust him. She told herself she imagined that.

But he would arrive in Cholon from the north travel-stained and laden with recorder tapes and rolls of film—most of which the censors at MAC-V confiscated. He never seemed really to care. It only made him more contemptuous of the ARVN and the American military.

At home there would be a few nights of not very satisfactory sex. He would say only, "Do not concern yourself. You will learn." She would flush with humiliation, not at all certain that the fault lay with her.

The woman-pleasing Frenchman had vanished the day they had left the Municipal Registery as husband and wife. If sex was no more than a function to Jean, then why had he married her? Not because of the child, certainly. He was not so old-fashioned and chivalrous as that.

The question was never answered. Never even asked. Two, sometimes three days after appearing in Cholon, he would gather his gear and be gone.

Mary said he traveled in the north, into Cambodia and even Laos, going where the U.S. press never went.

Once every fourth day, Megan would stop by the U.S. Mission and collect her mail. Every three days there would be a short, affectionate letter from Uncle Jack. It was typed, and, Megan thought bleakly, quite possibly written by his secretary at Langley. There was never a Langley, Virginia, postmark, and the return address embossed on the envelopes was Uncle Jack's apartment in Washington.

Uncle Jack (or his secretary) never seemed genuinely to understand why she had left Stanford and run off to Saigon, and he was too controlled a man ever simply to ask. Megan felt certain that Jack Wells would never allow his life to be untracked by the doings of a teen-aged girl.

She answered the letters. It took an effort each time to dissemble, but she did it. Yet she had to chastise herself for her lack of courage, for being unwilling—yet—to tell him that she had married . . .

A man nearer his age than hers . . .
A man her aristocratic grandparents would despise . . .
A man she, herself, did not really understand . . .
A man with whom she was curiously ill at ease . . .
A man *whose baby she carried*.

She rose from the bed and walked across the room to the pier glass at the wardrobe. She studied herself, frowning at the swollen eyes, the pallor, the dull half-auburn, half-nothing hair, the ribs showing beneath her swelling breasts, the knife blades of her pelvis. You were supposed to get plump and beautiful when you were pregnant. No wonder Jean was uninterested.

She looked closely at her face and imagined she saw wrinkles forming there. She thought, How can that mirror person be me? I'm only nineteen.

She had almost finished dressing, intending to hire a rickshaw to take her to the Mission to collect her mail, when her visitors arrived.

Jean had left a week ago. He seldom said where he was going. But he had mentioned that he was reasonably certain that U.S. Green Berets were operating illegally inside Cambodia, acting as death squads and assassinating Khmer Rouge cadres. He was always pleased when on the trail of Yankee crimes.

The thought had left Megan in a bad temper since he departed. She was growing weary of his never-ending attacks on her country.

Last night again she had slept poorly. She had been sick just after dawn—not once, but several times. She was worried about Mary Quinn, who had gone north to Hué and had not yet surfaced in the wreckage of the ARVN defeat.

And now, suddenly, at her door stood James Dunnivan, who worked for the Second Secretary at the embassy, and Kay Carey, an officious AID secretary who had been unpleasant to Megan the whole time she had worked for the agency.

Dunnivan affected the diffident air of the career civil servant. "Ms. Wells—" he began.

"Mrs. Thierry," Megan corrected him, more irritably than she intended. The unannounced appearance at her door of two near-strangers had shaken her. Only bad news was delivered this way.

Kay glared at Dunnivan reprovingly. It was a "woman's look." It meant: Don't be abrupt, you foolish man. Be sensitive. Be feminine.

Dunnivan tried again. "Mrs. Thierry, Colonel Collingwood, one of the military aides, would like to see you."

Megan felt a needle of fear under her heart.

"Why?"

"Please. I am not authorized to discuss this. Would you mind just coming with us? We have a car downstairs."

Megan had the wild fantasy that she was about to be abducted. That these were two CIA agents, who would kidnap her, put her on a plane, and have her back in Washington before she could prevent it.

"Dunnivan, you idiot, you're frightening her," Kay said. "Really, Meg, he can't talk about it here."

I hate being called Meg, Megan said to herself, meaning she hated it when anyone but those she cared about used the nickname.

Kay's look hardened, but she said, "Actually, it's the Second Secretary who wants to talk to you. Why don't you put your sandals on and come with us. We'll drive you back afterward."

Megan's first thought was: Something has happened to Uncle Jack.

She never thought of Jean. Jean was indestructible. Jean was made of stone.

The embassy car was a Chevrolet. The air inside it was so cold that Megan was taken by a fit of shivering. Dunnivan shouted at the Vietnamese driver to turn down the air conditioner. He sat on one side of Megan, fidgeting as the car moved through Saigon traffic. Kay simply sat and stared at the throngs of people, the shoals of scooters, the goods displayed at stands on the street.

Megan still thought about Uncle Jack. Had she sulked herself out of the last days of his life? Was it possible that he had crossed one bridge too many, flown across his last ocean, fought his final Cold War battle? The thought made her feel sicker. The cold air seemed to blow through her, as though she were without substance.

At the embassy, an army colonel met them. He introduced himself to Megan as George Collingwood. They had met, she now remembered. He was one of the briefing officers from MAC-V, part of the crew the press laughed at and accused of lying. He was a burly young man with a thick Mississippi accent.

Megan had another thought. "Is it Mary?"

"Mary Quinn?" The Colonel looked perplexed. "Oh, I see.

I used to be a press information officer and you thought . . . No, I work for Secretary Lowell now, thank God. Miss Quinn is perfectly all right. She got out of Hué in plenty of time. We have sent helos to airlift the press back to Saigon. Miss Quinn is just fine.''

"Then why am I here?''

Just then the Second Secretary's office door opened. A gaunt man in a white suit said to Dunnivan and the Colonel, ''Thank you both. You can stand down now. Please come in, Mrs. Thierry. Kay, will you stand by, please?''

He closed the heavy door behind Megan and led her to a deep leather sofa facing a coffee table. There was a silver tea set there, by no means government issue. It was monogrammed JTL. The nameplate on the wide desk read JOSIAH TALBOT LOWELL. Megan had the mad impulse to giggle. Men like the Second Secretary were selected for the foreign service because they resembled President Lincoln (which Lowell did), because they owned family silver with crest or monogram (which Lowell also did), and because they had the gift of delivering horrid news gently but firmly. She felt a tear run down her face. It *was* Uncle Jack. It had to be.

"Are you unwell, Mrs. Thierry?''

"No.''

"Then may I give you tea? It is hot and fresh.''

Megan shook her head, unable to speak.

Lowell's accent was New England, his age indeterminate, his manner suave. "Mrs. Thierry,'' he said, "have you received any communication from your husband within the last week?''

Jean?

She said slowly, "Jean never writes when he's upcountry. Never.''

"No. I should think not.''

Megan said in a whisper, "What's happened?''

Lowell's pale-brown eyes fixed themselves on her. His skin was very pale, almost white. His hair was thin, every strand in place. "I regret to have to tell you this, Mrs. Thierry. But your husband was killed in a fire fight three days ago. It happened on the Thai-Cambodian border. He was with a company of Khmer Rouge guerrillas. They were trapped by a company of the Thai Army. I am very sorry.''

The office seemed to flicker and fade. Emotions appeared to have jammed inside her. What Megan felt was nothing like what

120

she had always imagined she would feel when presented with a personal loss.

"Mrs. Thierry?" Lowell was at her side, a glass of whisky in his pallid, long-fingered hand. "Have some of this," he said. "Drink it down."

The liquor made her gag, and she turned her face away. Her fingers gripped the arms of the chair. She imagined she could see *through* them, as though the flesh had dropped away, leaving only bone and tendon and livid unlacquered nails.

"Mrs. Thierry?"

"I am all right," she said. Then, with an effort: "How did it happen? Where?"

"The fire fight took place inside Thailand, I'm afraid, Mrs. Thierry. The Thais were within their rights. Of course, they could not have known there was a journalist with the Khmer. Mr. Blaisdell has the details. Would you like to speak with him about it?"

Megan shuddered. "No." She sucked in a deep shuddering breath. "Where is he?"

"Mr. Blaisdell is just outside."

"No, no," she said. "I mean where—where is Jean?"

Lowell looked uncomfortable. "I regret to say that the Khmer Rouge removed his body. The Thais had to leave them temporarily in command of the battlefield. And they do that, you know. Remove their dead. So that the enemy can't compute the casualties."

"Jean is no Khmer Rouge."

"No, of course not, Mrs. Thierry. He was a French national with full press credentials. Doing his job." Lowell sounded uncomfortable, too, and suddenly Megan despised him. "And very good he was at it, too. I understand that he was popular with his colleagues."

Megan glanced up at the gaunt American. He looked like death in a white linen suit. To hear him speak of Jean Thierry was like listening to the sound of wind in a cave—senseless noise.

Lowell said, "I offer my sincerest condolences. I wish there was something more I could say."

Megan felt hollow. There was an ache in her belly and the taste of old brass in the back of her throat.

"Mr. Blaisdell has just returned from Thailand. Are you quite certain you don't want to speak with him?"

"He is the last person on earth I want to speak with."

Her reply troubled Lowell. He took refuge behind his desk, near the stand of flags, and said carefully, "I am really most terribly sorry for your loss, Mrs. Thierry. If there is anything I can do—anything at all . . ."

Megan whispered, "I want to go home. Oh, God, I just want to go home."

18. BUNG KAN PRISON, OCTOBER 1972

At first, Thierry's rage had sustained him, despite his fear. On the long trek through the forest, arms wired behind his back, breath hissing in his broken nose, eyes swollen almost shut by the indifferent, routine cruelty of the soldiers, he had sustained himself by imagining that he was performing unspeakable tortures on the American.

But as he grew weaker in the sullen heat, as the Thais lacerated his buttocks with their bayonets and beat him with their rifle butts, and as he was forced at last to accept his situation, he began to lose heart. Nothing the Russian spy masters had taught him had prepared him for the reality of capture.

They drove him—it could not be called marching—from Lumphat, where the Thai Marines had ambushed the Khmer band, two hundred kilometers, to Bung Kan.

The fire fight had taken place on the muddy shore of the Srepok River, and it had been a short one. The Marines had been in company strength. The Khmer Rouge band with whom he had been traveling had numbered fewer than fifty. He suspected that they were all now dead. Most of the Thais wore at least one bloody ear, some as many as three, on strings around their necks.

He had fought, but when the Khmer tried to run, he could not keep up. He had been prepared to die then. But it had not happened. Instead, Charlie Blaisdell had appeared, sweat-soaked, in jungle fatigues.

He could have saved me, he thought. With a word. One word.

Then, swiftly, horrid understanding had come. The Thais had stripped their single captive naked there by the Srepok, and the mosquitoes had swarmed and covered him like a living blanket while they exchanged cheers and toasts with Blaisdell.

Even then, he had thought that Blaisdell was only punishing him for past slights and would speak for him to the Thais. But when the anonymous black Air America helicopter had arrived in midafternoon, Blaisdell had collected the bullet-shattered pieces of the cameras and recorders, climbed aboard, and flown away.

Then, he had understood that it was Blaisdell who had gathered the intelligence, co-opted the Thais, set the ambush. The American had penetrated the operation and preempted it. Stupid, foolish Charlie Blaisdell had outflanked Plakhanov.

It was a long journey from Lumphat, with feet bleeding, face swollen, teeth broken. Finally there was a junction with the upper Mekong and another trek along the muddy river to Bung Kan prison, where the world ended.

He woke from fitful sleep, slimy with his own sweat. There were purple bruises on his thighs and calves. Thick blood was lumped under his skin. Boring insects pierced his bruises and laid their eggs in his clotted blood. Sometimes, driven beyond endurance by the things creeping under his skin, he would claw with broken fingernails until the blood ran down his legs.

He estimated that he had been at Bung Kan for two months, quite probably more; it was impossible to be sure. One lost track. All the training he had received, all the doctrine he had so carefully memorized through the years, appeared to have leached out of his flesh in sweat and watery feces. His ribs had begun to show; the flesh seemed wasted from his once muscular arms.

Every day there were hours of despair. What was Plakhanov doing to obtain his release? Or did he even suspect that the Frenchman was still alive, dying little by little in this terrible place?

The jailers were worse than the Marines had been. The Marines had mistreated him out of their contempt for the white man. The jailers enjoyed inflicting pain. They pretended to speak no French. They smiled that stupid Asiatic grin when they slashed at him with their scourges.

For a time, he tried to sustain himself with tales he had been told as a child about the Communist heroes of the French Resistance who fell into the hands of the fascists. He regarded the stories now with skepticism and disbelief.

It was terrible to fear interrogation. It was worse to be forgotten. Bung Kan was a rotting oubliette, the modern equivalent of the terrible cells beneath the floors of the château of Chillon, where medieval prisoners had been entombed until their bones turned to chalk.

That was the horror. There was no point of reference. He could be in Bung Kan a thousand days or ten thousand. He could live like this for years, or he could die tomorrow of a capricious beating, of malnutrition, of the bite of an insect.

Bung Kan was a midden of murderers, thieves, rapists, drug runners, and smugglers. Though he had been kept apart from the prison population, he had tried to find other politicals. There were none. Guerrillas captured in the field were generally executed on the spot. The Thais had no reluctance about killing Communists.

The northeastern border of the country was protected by Royal Thai Marines, men whose politics were as simple as a bullet or a bayonet could make them. It was to these, Thierry thought bitterly, that Blaisdell had delivered him.

Did Plakhanov have any idea of what had happened to him? The Russian had cocked and aimed him like a weapon, straight at the Deputy Director of Operations of the CIA. The weapon had performed according to specifications. But the plan had misfired badly. Perhaps Plakhanov didn't want to know that.

The land immediately outside the pink concrete walls was bare, a wilderness of dead trees and leached earth. The defoliants sprayed on the Ho Chin Minh Trail by the Americans drifted westward on the prevailing winds, across the mountains of the Chaîne Annamamitique, across the Laotian panhandle, finally to fall here, poisoning the earth.

When Thierry had enough strength to climb upon the cement shelf that served him as a bed and lift himself to the high, narrow window so that he could look out, he had just a glimpse of the river.

When he had arrived at Bung Kan, the Mekong was high with runoff of the equinoctial storms in the highlands. Now the monsoon had come and gone, and the river was twenty feet below the earth dike built to contain it. The air was heavy with the smell of rotting vegetation.

Prisoners more privileged than the Frenchman were sometimes allowed outside the walls to repair the dikes or to fill the prison's water jars. Others were taken outside to form the human chain that lifted the jars to the cistern on the roof. Standing for months at a time in a great galvanized tank on the roof of the main cellblock, the water was always warm from the heat of the sun and the living things that swarmed in the dark interior of the tank. Thierry's drinking water tasted of chlorine, so he could comfort himself with the thought that someone wanted him to live.

The burial ground on the river wasteland was mounded with the graves of prisoners who had succumbed to dysentery, hepatitis, or flukes of an almost limitless variety. Bung Kan had been a research station for the study of the indigenous diseases of Southeast Asia before the government of Thailand decided that expensively educated physicians were wasted at a place so far from Bangkok.

Even so, as long as his strength lasted he would hang from the narrow barred window to feast his eyes on the barren scene between the prison and the river. On the other side of the unseen water lay Communist Laos.

But Thierry was never permitted to join in outside work. When he asked his jailer, a lean scarecrow of a man named Bok, for permission to join a work party, the reply came in the form of blows to the face and a scourging.

Thierry's cell measured six feet by twelve. There was a trough running the length of it. Into this went urine and feces. Once a day Bok would appear with a bucket half filled with green water. Thierry was required to use this to clean the floor of his cell and flush the trench, which flowed out through a four-inch hole in the wall at floor level.

The walls were cement covered with flaking plaster and an ancient coat of whitewash. If a prisoner defaced them in any way, he was beaten. Scorpions and spiders were common, the spiders of a swift variety able to race up the walls and across the ceiling with astonishing speed. The scorpions were small, yellow, and virulent. Fortunately, they were not aggressive.

The shelf on which Thierry slept was approximately five and a half feet long, but only twenty-four inches wide. This made it impossible for him to turn over in sleep without falling to the floor. For covering, he had an unhemmed piece of thick canvas once used to cover the back of a military truck.

The air near the river stank of mud and decomposing plants. Bok stank of spoiled fish. And the cell reeked of sweat, urine, and shit. There was nothing to do, nothing to expect, except a lash across the buttocks with the split bamboo. Thierry hunkered down on his bed, his back against the wall, and slipped, each day, closer to insanity.

Night at Bung Kan was a time of screams. Unseen prisoners shrieked and blubbered for mercy, for freedom, for whatever they could not have.

Thierry, too, begged and yelled in the night.

There were dreams. Sometimes the dreams were of his American wife. In his night visions she was nothing like his memories of her when awake. He saw her swollen, ripe with a man-devouring fecundity, like some ancient Cretan goddess, her breasts painted and huge, with golden tips. The woman of his nights in Bung Kan reveled in his helplessness. She was a consuming, horribly erotic image.

One night, while the prison sweltered in the wet heat of a threatening rainstorm, and the air rumbled to the echoes of thunder in the Laotian mountains to the east, Bok looked through the spy hole in the door to discover Thierry, half-awake, his erect penis in his hand, masturbating madly after one of his dark dream encounters.

The little Thai burst into the cell in a fury and repeatedly slashed Thierry across the genitals with his bamboo. Thierry had never known such pain. Bok shrieked at him in mingled Thai and French, excoriating him for lewdness and perversion. At Bung Kan, any pleasure, no matter how degraded, was forbidden.

After that, Thierry no longer dreamed of having sex with his bloated Cretan goddess, but of killing her.

Thierry was a man without many inner resources. He had never been religious and he had no gift for or appreciation of music or literature. He was not imaginative or thoughtful. His greatest talent was for killing; his second greatest was for dissembling and intrigue.

In his Bung Kan dreams, he killed many times. The victims varied. Sometimes they even included Plakhanov. The Russians had taught him to be an assassin. In Bung Kan he learned to relish murder.

His half-Vietnamese mother, Nicole Beauclerc, lived hopelessly and died when Thierry was a young man. Only occasionally did he dream of finding her with some man in the tumbled bedclothes that always seemed to smell of spring flowers. Then he punished her with swift death and a child's tears. But Charles le Gros Blaisdell he tortured until he died, and then was revived to die again.

Better still were the horrors he inflicted on his father. Thierry had never actually known Captain Paul-Claude Thierry. There had been a photograph of him on his mother's dresser in the house they once rented in Châlons. He remembered that he and his mother lived the life of the petite bourgeoisie on a small allowance from that soldier in the photograph.

But when Paul-Claude Thierry died in his native village, Thierry-sur-Saône, his entire estate—not large, but comfortable—went to his legal wife and three legitimate daughters. For Nicole and her son there was a settlement of two thousand francs and a letter from a lawyer telling her that she was no longer to use the surname Thierry. She did not tell her son about the injunction. He discovered it among her papers.

Until her death, in 1956, Nicole labored to pay her son's fees at the Sorbonne. A Soviet scholarship to Moscow University had come as an enormous windfall. But Nicole died while Jean was in Moscow. It cost all he had saved to bury her.

On holiday, he traveled to Thierry-sur-Saône and spent a week there, making anonymous threatening and obscene telephone calls to Paul-Claude's widow, his own half-sisters, and his aged grandparents. Before returning to Moscow, he entered the parish churchyard and desecrated his father's grave.

Bok was a northern Thai of indeterminate age. He dressed in an ill-fitting cotton uniform and sandals made from the carcass of a discarded automobile tire. He fit in perfectly at Bung Kan prison.

When the Thai Marines had delivered Thierry, Bok greeted him with a terrible smile. Thierry learned to dread that gap-toothed grimace. Thierry feared Bok, and Bok despised Thierry. Their relationship was as fixed as the orbit of two planets.

Bok had a dismaying habit of dragging his split-bamboo scourge along the walls of the outside walkway, so that he could be heard approaching. The sound of the bamboo rattling on the walls made Thierry's sphincter tighten and his bladder ache to discharge. Bok was an artist at causing terror and inflicting pain.

Thierry heard Bok approaching. The scorpions clacked across the floor of the cell, scuttling for the safety of the shit trough.

A pale dawn was troubling the high window. The air was still, heavy with moisture, warm enough for a naked man to drip sweat.

The door exploded inward, at it always did when Bok wished to impress on his prisoner that the occasion was an important one.

Thierry lowered himself from the bed to the floor and bowed to Bok as he had been taught to do. Bok pointed with his scourge and screamed at the top of his voice: *"You come!"*

Bok looped a noose of wire around Thierry's neck and pushed him toward the door with the bamboo. No sooner had Thierry begun to move down the dim walkway than Bok pulled on the choking wire and slashed him across the buttocks with the bamboo. The stinging pain made Thierry gasp, and the gasp seemed to enrage Bok, who rewarded him with a shower of blows to the face and head.

Bok seized Thierry's shoulder and thrust him onward. *"Go! Gogogogo!"*

Thierry stumbled on. When he saw that they were going to the interrogation room, urine spurted from him. He had suffered agonies in that room. Soon after his arrival in Bung Kan, and daily for two weeks thereafter, he had been marched to the dirt-floored room (dirt, he soon discovered, absorbed the by-products of torture better than did concrete), where he was savagely beaten, cut, twisted, and broken while Thai officials took turns asking questions about military matters he neither knew about nor understood. Because he had been with the Khmer Rouge when he was taken, they seemed to have assumed he knew something about the Khmer's strength. It was absurd. He had not been trained for military duties. To ask an active-measures assassin about howitzers and shoulder-fired antiaircraft missiles was useless. They eventually realized it. Not because he had remained silent. Far from it. He had screamed answers. But he could invent nothing they could believe. They sent him back to his scorpions and feces.

Bok saw the wet splashes on the floor and made disgusted sounds. He slashed the backs of Thierry's thighs. Bok loathed the French, as many Indochinese did.

The door stood open. Bok pushed with the sharp end of the bundled scourges and screamed, *"Stand straight! Look from door!"*

Thierry stood. Urine still wet the inside of his thighs. His stomach ached. His beard crawled with lice. A single light bulb hung from the cement ceiling. Insects battered against it, moths and great tiger beetles with hard black wing casings.

Thierry looked sidelong, without moving his head, at the

bench to which one was strapped when they wished to beat the soles of the feet.

A rattan chair with a tattered fan back stood on the packed earth floor. A wrinkled seersucker sleeve could be seen. Thierry shifted his position and drew an immediate slash across the legs from Bok. *"No look! Stand straight!"* Thierry's knees trembled.

A voice said in English—American English: "Bring another chair."

Bok shouted, *"Prisoner stand. Prisoner no sit."*

Charlie Blaisdell turned to look at Bok. The rattan chair creaked. "I said bring a chair, you little shit. *Do it!*"

Bok scurried away. Thierry closed his eyes in mingled hope and hatred. He put his hand in front of his naked genitals. For the first time in months he became conscious of his nudity.

"Jesus!" Blaisdell said. "You look like a pile of shit. It suits you. Stand over here where I can look at you."

Thierry stood before the rattan chair, the rattan throne. The wire noose hung down his back. He tried to stand at attention with his hands against his thighs.

Blaisdell was more gross than ever. The flesh of his face was red, wet, and unhealthy-looking. His eyes were hidden behind aviator's sunglasses. Thierry could make out a huge gun in a shoulder holster under the damp seersucker coat.

Bok appeared with a wooden stool. Blaisdell grinned without humor. "Making a point, are you, you little shit? All right. Out. Wait. Take the noose off him."

"Comment?"

"You understand English. Do as you're told."

Bok glared his hatred first at Blaisdell and then at Thierry. He could deal with Thierry. Thierry bent his head so the noose could be removed.

Blaisdell said, "Out. *Allez.* Close the door."

Bok departed, still glaring at Thierry.

Blaisdell said, "Sit down, boy-o."

Thierry did as he was told.

"Jesus, you stink." There was a shaving rash on Blaisdell's throat. He wore a sweat-soaked shirt and loosened tie. He looked tired; his flesh was loose, soft, as though it were beginning to melt away.

Thierry said hoarsely. "Charlie—"

"Mr. Blaisdell to you, you Commie bastard. Christ, I leave you for a few weeks and look at you. You're a mess. But this isn't exactly Saigon, is it, lover boy?'' He pushed the goggles to his forehead and left them there, like a fat, soggy, ugly starlet. He was showing his yellowish teeth in a grin.

"Charlie,'' Thierry said again. In French, he said, "I don't know why you did this, Charlie, but it is enough now. Please. Get me out of this place.''

"Talk American, you bastard.''

"I'm going crazy in this place, Charlie. I beg you, get me out.''

"So you can join up with your Khmer Rouge buddies?''

"I was only traveling with them,'' Thierry said desperately. "I am a journalist—''

"You are an active-measures hood. A lousy Moscow gunman. Did you think we didn't know?''

Thierry shook his head, unable to speak.

"I had you dialed in the day you arrived in Saigon. You had KGB written all over you.'' He ran a hand through his sparse damp hair. "Who was running you, lover?''

"Charlie, no, listen to me—''

"Was it Kalganin? Metrikov?''

"Please listen to me, Charlie. Please?''

"You do look like a piece of shit, boy-o. For chrissake cover that tiny prick, will you? It's disgusting.''

Thierry huddled, squeezing his thighs together.

"You'd sure knock 'em dead at the Continental Hotel bar.'' Blaisdell shifted his weight again, and the rattan squeaked and rustled. "It was Plakhanov, wasn't it? Of course. Feliks the Faggot.''

"No. Please.''

"What the hell do you mean, 'no.' You're a Moscow hood, and Plakhanov was running you.'' He leaned back in the creaking chair and started to laugh. It was a broken, jagged sound, but the laughter was genuine. "I should have known. I should have known at Kadena.''

"I don't know what you mean, Charlie.''

"You may figure it out. In time. But no more of this journalist crap. If you're a journalist, I am the fucking King of Siam. Now you *talk* to me.''

"I was only with the Khmer because—''

"You haven't learned a thing. Maybe it's just too soon. A few more years, maybe.'' He leaned forward and made as if to rise from the chair.

Thierry screamed, *"No, Charlie! God, no! Don't leave me here!"*

Blaisdell sank back in the chair. "Then talk to me."

"What? What do you want from me?"

"It may hurt your feelings, boy-o, but right now you aren't worth much. For a pound of lard and two pounds of pig meat, I could have you with bells on." The sunken bloodshot eyes glistened. "Plakhanov. Right?"

"Yes. *Yes.*"

"He pointed you at the girl? At Megan Wells?"

"Yes." Thierry could feel the sweat rolling down his ribs. He held his hands folded tightly over his crotch. Lice moved in his hair.

Blaisdell grinned. "Clever Feliks. But it didn't work, did it?"

"No."

"He underestimated Jack Wells."

"He gave no orders about Wells."

"He would have, boy-o. You can bet your ass on it. In fact, you did bet your ass on it. And you lost."

"Charlie, get me out of here. Please. I beg you."

"The Frenchman begs fat old Charlie the joke? The has-been? What did you call me? Charles le Gros. That was *funny*, wasn't it, boy-o? Here comes old Charlie the clown. Happy hour at the Continental bar, with Thierry the Frenchie leading the cheers."

Thierry's hands had begun to shake. "Charlie," he said through clenched teeth. "Please. Don't do this. I have never done anything to you to deserve—"

Blaisdell reached across the intervening space and slapped Thierry sharply across the face. "Don't tell me about what you've done. I know exactly what you've done. How many and where. So shut up about what you deserve."

Thierry began to weep. His shoulders shook. Tears made dirty rivulets down his bearded cheeks.

"What did you think the spook business was, boy-o? Hump a college girl and if she's the *right* college girl you get the Order of Lenin? Is that what Feliks told you?"

"I have to get out of here, Charlie."

Blaisdell looked at floor, walls, and ceiling. "I bet you do. It's not the Crillon, is it?"

"You don't know."

"But I do, I do. I picked it for you. The back of beyond, boy-o. You can rot here for thirty years and no one would miss you."

"Megan—"

Blaisdell slapped him again, making his head rock. "I'd forget that name if I were you. I mean that. She's gone, by the way. Flown away to the World, where they have real seasons and they fight the war on television every night at six."

Thierry stared at the earth beneath his feet. So she was gone. Gone with not a second thought. Bourgeois bitch.

Blaisdell regarded him with strange intensity. "I heard she was pregnant. If that's true, boy-o, I may have to let nature take its course here."

The threat chilled him, but the implication that there was another option meant far more. He sat as still as he could manage.

"That bothers you, does it?"

"No. She means nothing to me."

"That I believe, boy-o. But I'll still have to think about things."

"What things?"

"Business. Only business."

"I'll do anything you say. *Anything.*"

"Of course you will. But what you do isn't worth thinking about. It's what Plakhanov is willing to do. I will have to give it some thought."

"Charlie, I promise you—"

Blaisdell slapped him again. This time with all his strength. Thierry sprawled on the dirt floor.

"Don't promise me anything," Blaisdell said. "In fact, don't even talk to me. There is nothing you can possibly say that I am interested in hearing."

He lurched to his feet and stood looking down at Thierry with a frown. "Plakhanov is in Hanoi. I don't suppose you knew that." He took a half-pack of Winstons from his jacket pocket and a book of damp paper matches. He dropped them on the floor and walked to the door and thumped on it to be let out.

"Get me out, Charlie."

Blaisdell hunched his thick shoulders under the wet seersucker and left the room.

In order that a visit from the American Big Nose and his treatment of a prison guard should not give the prisoner an inflated sense of his own importance, Bok took the Frenchman back to his cell and had him lean over his bed while he stripped the almost healed skin off his buttocks with the bamboo. "Like child," he said in French, "you must learn good manners."

He then expropriated the cigarettes the Big Nose had left. All but one, which he lit and handed ceremoniously to the prisoner. It was always best to be politic. It was remotely possible that the Frenchman might be more important now than he was before the American's visit.

When he closed the door to Thierry's cell and looked through the spy hole, Bok was gratified to see that the prisoner was smoking the cigarette he had given him, and weeping like a woman.

19. BUNG KAN PRISON
DECEMBER 1972

Days became weeks and then months, but Thierry had no wish to chronicle the passage of time any longer. Charlie Blaisdell had raised expectations that had come to nothing. Life in Bung Kan went on as it always had: days during which the passage of the hours was measured by the slant of the hot sun through the narrow window above the prisoner's head, nights so black the very air seemed to congeal, and the ever-casual, ever-present cruelty of the guards was the only reality.

Thierry no longer thought of freedom. He thought almost exclusively of killing.

The year he completed his training, he had been given a Lebanese Arab to kill. He had tracked him through the streets of Beirut, a city often likened to Paris, and he had found him alone at last in the Christian quarter. The actual killing had been almost ludicrously simple. He could have used a knife or the heavy Makarov automatic pistol given him by the local PLO chieftain. But instead, he chose a blow, a simple upward, stiff-armed hit with the heel of the hand under the nose.

His instructor had assured him that it was indeed a killing blow, that the fragile arch of the nose almost invariably shattered into splinters, which were driven under the sinus cavities and into the brain. Thierry had been enormously curious to know whether or not this was so.

The startled victim, a plump merchant supplier of Christian militiamen, turned at his call and never saw the blow coming. He fell like a bullock struck with a poleax and lay trembling, with scrambled reflexes, on the pavement of the deserted alley where he had walked his last twenty paces.

Thierry had watched with fascination as the open eyes had pooled with blood, as though the dead man were weeping scarlet tears.

He had killed twice more, at Major Plakhanov's command, but never again with such a sense of wonder and enjoyment.

In his Bung Kan dreams he now killed Charlie Blaisdell with that blow, again and again and again.

The rains began. The dead land around the prison was impervious to the flood. The leafless trees stood in a red sea of mud. The dike oozed as the water rose, and prisoners—not Thierry—were set to work repairing the earthen barrier. The Mekong could be heard day and night, swollen with the mountain runoff as it rushed headlong toward the distant delta and the South China Sea.

Thierry's face healed into a gross caricature of his former brutal good looks. His broken teeth ached and decayed. His hair became streaked with gray. But he had struck bottom and he was still alive. He began to force himself to eat the repulsive stuff he was fed. He started to exercise. He refused to accept final defeat. Hate kept him alive.

Then, on a winter day when the sun shone briefly and set the red land to steaming and crusting around the prison, Bok appeared, smoking an American cigarette.

Thierry stared, red-eyed, at the white cylinder between Bok's betel-stained teeth.

Charlie Blaisdell had returned.

Bok threw a pair of tattered cotton trousers and a shirt at him. "You dress," he said. He did not scream. He carried his scourge, but he did not offer to use it. Nor did he wire Thierry's neck when they left the cell.

Blaisdell was in the interrogation room, sitting on the rattan throne as though he had never left it. Bok shoved Thierry inside and slammed the door behind him.

"Take a pew, comrade," Blaisdell said thinly. There was a wooden chair facing the rattan throne. A chair, Thierry noted, not a stool.

He sat down and looked at Blaisdell. Charles le Gros looked ill. He had grown thinner; his flesh hung on him. His seersucker suit was wrinkled and damp, as always. There were dark wet circles under his arms. The enormous automatic bulged beneath his coat.

Blaisdell said, "So you are still alive. They trained you pretty good, your Russki friends. Did they tell you to eat bugs and worms for protein? They say you can develop a real taste for them."

Thierry stared at Blaisdell mutely, not daring to interpret his return to Bung Kan.

"I've been to Vientiane," Blaisdell said. "To meet Feliks the Faggot. It took some doing. He's cautious, no mistake." The American's speech was swifter than Thierry remembered it. Edged, nervous. "This fucking war is almost over," he continued with deep bitterness. "Nixon blows McGovern out of the water and he still wants to bug out. We're a peculiar lot, we Americans, boy-o."

Thierry said carefully. "We don't talk about politics here."

Blaisdell began to laugh. The laughter degenerated into a fit of coughing that turned his already sunburned face redder still. When he stopped, he lit a cigarette and sucked smoke into his lungs. The smell tantalized Thierry, but this time Blaisdell did not offer the pack.

"You know what Henry Kissinger told the press last month? He said, 'Peace is at hand.' Peace is at fucking hand. Isn't that just wonderful?"

Thierry watched, waited. He scarcely dared to breathe.

"Your side is fucking winning, asshole. We're down to twenty-four thousand troops in-country. We're cutting our losses. That make you feel good, boy-o?"

"I don't know anything about that, Charlie." Thierry spoke as calmly as he could. He was terrified that something he said might cause Blaisdell to vanish again, perhaps forever. He wondered desperately if Blaisdell had actually met with Plakhanov, or if what he had said was some interrogator's trick.

Blaisdell seemed to be staring at something in the far distance.

"The NVA are coming straight on down the road. The ARVN can't stop them. Congress has cut them off. The airplanes can't fly. The guns can't shoot. They're dying in the hospitals for lack of dressings. You know what our press says? It's corruption. Vietnamese selling American medical supplies on the black market. It's marvelous, boy-o. After all these years Uncle Ho is picking up the marbles, one by one." He glared suddenly at Thierry. "Wouldn't you like to march into Saigon with your comrades? Damn right you would. Goosestepping in like a Kremlin Guardsman with a red flag in your hand?"

The approaching collapse of the imperialist war effort had Blaisdell on the brink of the abyss.

It was the first political thought Thierry had had for months.

Then he thought: Has he come back to murder me? To get me out of the way?

Blaisdell said. "I bring you tidings of great joy. It is early Christmas."

"Charlie, don't. Please."

"Didn't you hear what I said? I've seen Plakhanov. And you are my golden boy."

Thierry stared mutely. Then he whispered hoarsely, "Don't play with me."

"Hear me, you piece of dreck," Blaisdell said violently. "They have lost my fucking war for me, so I am going into business for myself. That's known as capitalism, boy-o." He reached into a sagging pocket and produced a pint bottle of Vietnamese brandy. Only a third of it remained. Blaisdell drank half and passed the bottle to Thierry. "Drink up, you Hero of the Revolution. Drink to the day of liberation."

Thierry held the open bottle but lacked the courage to lift it to his mouth.

Blaisdell unholstered his gun and pulled back the Colt's slide, levering a bullet into the chamber. The metallic clack was loud. Blaisdell leveled the pistol at Thierry's face.

Thierry screamed and dropped the bottle.

Blaisdell pulled the trigger. The sound was like the world ending. The bottle between Thierry's bare feet exploded into shards and slivers. Thierry felt the glass bits embedding in his legs, and the burning cold of the liquor.

Blaisdell leered at him like a skull.

The door was flung open. Bok and other guards peered in, saw what had taken place, and erupted into hysterical laughter.

Blaisdell looked at them. They stopped laughing. The door closed swiftly.

Thierry was weak with terror. He had soiled himself.

Blaisdell put the pistol back in its holster. He looked gray. His breath came hard. He said, "You are shit, Thierry. I wish I could afford to blow you away, but I can't. You are worth money. There are still people in the world who love shit so much they buy it. Can you believe that?'' He sat for a moment in breathy silence. Beads of sweat rolled down his red, raw face. "I've never been a shit merchant before. But it doesn't matter. They've lost my war for me. They've broken all the promises I made. So what's left? Answer me, you piece of shit. What's left? And who cares?''

He lurched to his feet and stood, a wasteland of a man, swaying over Thierry. "*You* care, don't you, boy-o? Fucking right you care."

"Charlie—"

"Oh, shut your mouth," Blaisdell said wearily. "Shut your fucking mouth." Stiffly, like a man whose movements caused great pain, he walked to the door. Thierry remembered that he had always moved lightly, with peculiar grace. He moved that way no longer.

The next evening, as the light of a rainy twilight faded over the dike beside the river, a smiling Bok exchanged cigarettes with members of a patrol of Pathet Lao. Then he surrendered his prisoner to the Laotians, who had come down from the mountains to collect a man who, they had been told, was a great soldier of the revolution.

As a trembling Thierry climbed into the rubber boat for the trip across the Mekong, Bok, with hands together before his face, bowed and gave *namaste*. "Buddha," declared the little Thai with ineffable satisfaction, "is merciful. Buddha is love."

Thierry's last vision of Bung Kan was of Bok standing on the dike under the darkening sky, his palms together in token of benediction and farewell.

PART THREE

March 15

the fourth day . . .

Blow the cobwebs from the mirror
See yourself at last.

—W. H. Auden,
  "Songs and Other Musical Pieces, X"

20. WILLIAMSBURG, VIRGINIA

Hillary Traina heard the telephone ringing in the dark. It was the one with the shrill bell tone, the Important One. Ever since she had married Frank, she had lived with important telephones ringing in the night. She was an expert at responding to them, no matter how deeply asleep she might have been seconds before the first demanding ring.

She opened her eyes and looked at the red numbers of the digital clock on her nightstand. Three-twenty-two. Barely Sunday. She could hear rain falling in the garden. The air was moist and still.

The girls were away at school. The *au pair* was asleep in the quarters over the garage. The red and green lights on the security control glowed steadily, reassuringly. Somewhere out there along the fence line the three men assigned by Internal Security were watching.

All was well at the Traina house. All except for the shrill, insistent ringing of the hot line that tied her husband more firmly to his job than to any other thing, probably including his family.

She raised herself on one elbow. Frank slept like a stone. If the Trainas ever began to sleep apart, the Agency would have to connect a siren to what Frank sometimes called the "right-now-God-damn-it" phone.

She shook her husband's shoulder. He was sleeping the sleep of the exhausted. Something had happened that had the Agency in a dreadful flap. It concerned Jack Wells. Frank didn't bring the office home, but she had been his wife long enough to know that someone, somewhere, had dropped a clanger. (Hillary was

British, an RAF officer's daughter, and still used some jargon she had grown up with.)

"Frank, Frank, wake up."

Half-waking, her husband put a hand between her legs.

"Frank, you dreadful man, *telephone*."

Traina sighed and sat up. He lifted the phone and said, "Yes?"

"Duty officer, sir. One minute for the Director."

Frank squinted at the nightstand clock. A hand seemed to be tightening its grip on his stomach. There was one thing of which he could be certain: However bad things were at six last evening, when he left the Langley compound, they must be worse now.

He swung his legs over the edge of the bed. Hillary, long experienced, was on her feet, putting a wrapper over the micro-mini bit of silk she contended was a nightgown. With regret he watched her barely covered pudenda vanish.

"I'll make breakfast whilst you dress," she said. That, too, was long experience in action. Frank had received calls like this in London, Bonn, Ankara, Cairo, and now in Williamsburg. This was the last stop before retirement, she thought as she walked barefoot through the silent house. What will he do when the calls stop coming?

She could not imagine Frank doing what her retired group-captain father did—spend six hours every day on the golf course, complaining about the deplorable condition of the seventh fair-way and the eleventh green. Perhaps when the time came, they could retire to Maui. She rather fancied herself in a bikini. More to the point, so did Frank.

Daniel Street's voice sounded alert and fresh. Traina wondered if the man ever slept.

"Good morning, Director."

"That is rather a matter of opinion, Frank," the Judge said.

"Problem, Judge?"

"We have just completed a computer run on the projects Wells ran when he was a case officer and then DDO. Eight years' worth of clandestine operations. The man was indefatigable."

Only Judge Street, Traina thought, would use a word like that. What did he mean exactly? Tireless, inexhaustible, endless, un-limited, boundless? Yes, Wells was indeed indefatigable. A man to have working with you rather than against you. He was bright, hard-edged. And, under some conditions, absolutely ruthless. Traina suspected that having a favorite grandniece the victim of a political kidnapping qualified as one of those conditions.

144

"Can you come in right away, Frank?"

"Of course, Judge."

Traina wished he could be certain whether he was dealing with an innocent who should not stand anywhere near the helm of the Central Intelligence Agency or a shrewd manipulator whose skills had been honed in the labyrinth of the judicial system.

"I do appreciate your coming in on a Sunday morning."

"Don't you ever sleep, Judge?" Traina could not help asking.

"One doesn't, you know, when one has the President of the United States asking, 'Where the hell is my Secretary-of-State-to-be?' "

"I'll be in right away, Judge."

"Thank you, Frank. There are things about this computer run I want to discuss with you."

Traina replaced the telephone and walked into the kitchen. "Just coffee, Hilly. I have to go in right away."

Hillary shook her head in familiar commiseration.

"I'll warm a Danish at least. Go take your shower."

They said intelligence officers should not marry, Traina thought as he stepped into the shower. But without Hillary to make some sense out of the way I've lived, I'd be selling used cars by now.

Jack Wells, he thought, gave me my first promotion, and he was once Deputy Director of Operations, and better at the job than I can ever be. He had run interference for a hick from Wyoming, all the way, almost to the top of the pyramid.

If you were the kind of man Frank Traina was, you didn't forget. Loyalty mattered. It mattered almost more than anything else in the shadow world of intelligence work.

He drove into the compound at Langley at ten minutes to five. The sky was dark, the rain falling steadily but without much enthusiasm. Spring was ready to burden Washington with its first wave of tourists.

The parking lot was largely empty. Only the duty crews were on hand at this hour. He drove straight across the lot and into the supergrades' tunnel. His space was almost directly across from the elevator. Only the Judge's stall was closer. The Judge disliked using government limos. That came from his days as a graft-hunter in New York. His space held his three-year-old Oldsmobile. He disliked having to have Internal Security people with him, but the President had put his foot down. "Frugal is fine if you are running for office, Judge," he had said in Traina's hearing. "You aren't." So a limousine full of bodyguards followed wherever Judge Street drove his Olds.

Wasn't the Olds supposed to be the "doctor's car" years ago? Traina tried to remember. Not too fancy, but not too cheap either? No, it was the Buick. It came back to him as he strode past the Judge's wheels and into the private elevator.

Even though he used his own key, Traina had been under scrutiny since he approached the tunnel. The lessons of the Marines' fate in Beirut had been costly, and they had had to be learned again when the Hezbollah fanatics blew up the embassy. But now there were metal roadblocks buried in the concrete roadbed, steel barriers that would spring out and up at any suspicious vehicle's approach. The elevator's television cameras, secure behind armored glass, remained fixed on the occupant of the steel box so that a security guard could be ready at any time to order the release of either a peculiarly nasty variety of CS gas, to incapacitate, or a derivative of Sarin, to disconnect all synapses and produce death in convulsions in under eight seconds, if that was what was required.

At least at Langley, Traina thought, the odd terrorist or KGB assassin could expect an unfriendly greeting.

The question was: What good did it do if the same sort of people could snatch your citizens off the streets of any foreign capital—or the streets of Washington, for that matter—with no fear of capture or reprisal?

At the upper foyer, Traina checked in with the duty officer and asked the Director's whereabouts.

"In Theater One, sir."

Looking at what, Traina wondered. Well, he would soon know. Street was being pressured by the President. That meant the word on Wells's disappearance was getting around. It was impossible to keep a secret in this town, Traina thought grimly. By eight o'clock there would be a critical article in the *Washington Post* and an angry one in the *Washington Times*. Jack Wells was too well known not to have his sudden absence from the Washington scene arouse speculation.

If the speculation became too colorful, the Senate Foreign Relations Committee would begin to react.

Traina walked swiftly down the featureless hallway to Theater One. The red CONFERENCE IN PROGRESS light was on above the door. He slid his card-key through the slot of the sensor and waited.

Walter Tannenbaum, from Internal Security, opened the door and said, "He's waiting for you." Tannenbaum was one of the most senior members of the security staff. It was unusual to find him working as fuzz.

There were only three other men in the room. Judge Street, a young man from Records named Thomas Gunderson, running the projector, and Emryn Wilson, the deputy chief of the Presidential Secret Service Detachment. When the Judge had said he had the President on his back, it hadn't been just a figure of speech. Wilson, a man who looked like a retired NFL linebacker, was wearing a very sour expression. It was his troops who had arrived at both Jack's and Megan Wells's doors just a bit too late. Traina did not need to imagine what the President's reaction to that report had been.

"Judge. Emryn."

The Secret Service man said, "I've seen all I need to see, Judge. Frank. I am reassured that there was nothing we could have done to keep Wells protected. Not when he insisted on doing things his way."

Traina looked at Street but said nothing.

Street said, "You are welcome to stay, Emryn. You might learn something useful."

"No. I have an appointment at Treasury. I'll be gone now, Judge."

When he had left, Traina said, "I'd hate to swim up to a lifeboat with Emryn in it."

The Judge shrugged. "Let's get on with it, Gunderson," he said.

Traina asked, "Have you been up all night, Judge?"

"Almost. But no matter. I think we may have some viable information."

Traina winced inwardly. Judge Street was learning to speak pure inside-the-Beltway jargon. A few more years in the federal government and he would be completely unintelligible to his former colleagues and associates who had stayed in the real world.

"Sit down, Frank." To Gunderson, he said, "All right, hit the light and let's go again."

Traina gave his attention to the rolled-down screen in the pit of the theater. Identifiers scrolled past, *secret* classifications, complete with threats and warnings. Then young Gunderson began to narrate.

"We started a complete run on Mr. Wells's service at seven

147

last night. We concentrated on two theaters of operations: Germany and Southeast Asia."

Traina frowned. "Jack never operated in Asia. By the time we had our tit in the wringer in Vietnam he was too senior to be screwing around in the field."

"Patience, Frank," the Director said.

"Mr. Wells organized an operation while he was in West Berlin. It was called File–Hausemartin—"

For many years CIA had been assigning two-part nonsense code names to operations. It still did.

"You remember File–Hausemartin, Frank?" the Judge asked. "Wells ran it while you were deputy chief of station in West Berlin."

"Barely," Traina said. It was a long time ago. And it had failed. As Hillary might put it, it was one of Jack's few clangers. After it was closed down, he never spoke of it; Frank had no need to know.

The camera whirred, and a strip of black-and-white film, obviously taken surreptitiously, appeared on the screen. A street, a German street. The Kurfürstendamm—familiarly known to natives and Americans alike as the Ku-damm—as it had been in the early sixties.

The traffic was not so heavy as it later became; the shops were not quite so glitzy. But the "economic miracle" was already well under way. There were more Mercedeses than Opels, and there was a plethora of American-owned cars with fishtails and too much chrome. The camera was on the window of a restaurant across the Ku-damm. At a conspicuous table sat a much younger Jack Wells, sharing a meal with a man younger still. A boy, really, with finely molded features, white-blond hair, and a smile so innocent, so ingenuous, that it could scarcely be believed. Despite the sunshine pouring through the window, the boy wore a heavy loden coat.

"The man with Mr. Wells is Hausemartin," Gunderson said.

"Name, Peter Arendt," the Judge said. "Age when that was taken, nineteen years two months. Birthplace, Leipzig. Served two weeks in the German Volkssturm at the age of six. Yes, they were that hard up in 1945. Pretty lad, wasn't he?"

Frank said, "It's coming back to me—some of it. Jack never told me who File was. A Russian target. He did say he was Russian. KGB. And that if it had come off, it would have been a real coup. But File never came over."

148

"Quite so," Street said. "It was an ambitious undertaking. File was Feliks Ivanovich Plakhanov."

Traina was stunned. "The same Plakhanov who now runs the First Chief Directorate?"

Judge Street said, "Oddly enough, it appears that it might have worked out as Wells intended if Hausemartin had not been a very bad spy."

"Counterintelligence had him identified from the first day he appeared in West Berlin," Gunderson said.

The figures on the screen finished their meal and sat drinking wine. Hausemartin looked very intense and more than a little frightened.

Traina said, "Jack did speak about Hausemartin. He said he had never seen such a pretty young man." He frowned, trying to remember events more than two decades old. "Hausemartin was killed east of the Wall. The Vopos shot him. They said he was trying to defect." His frown grew deeper. "Can that be right?"

"Mr. Wells wrote an action report at the time," Gunderson offered. "He said he thought he had convinced Hausemartin to carry a message to File. File had just been promoted to major, and Mr. Wells wanted him badly. Hausemartin was just a messenger."

Traina remembered talk he had heard about Plakhanov. Gossip.

"Something, Frank?" the Judge asked.

"Yes, I think so."

"Significant?"

"You tell me. People said Hausemartin was Plakhanov's lover."

"Any hard evidence to back that up?"

"No, but there were stories about Plakhanov when I was in Ankara in the seventies. The Turks didn't think anything of it, but we had people in Ankara Station who thought we could use it against him. It seemed to me that if there was anything to it he would have been reeled in years ago. Or shot. Brezhnev wasn't a tolerant man. Not about homosexuals in the KGB. Apparently 1972 was not my year for intuition."

"Did you say 1972, sir?" Gunderson asked brightly.

Traina turned.

"We had two resignations from the Humint Section in 1972."

"So?"

"One was Mr. Wells himself. He said he was tired, wanted

149

to practice law. And his niece had just been widowed. She married a French journalist who was killed—''

''Yes, we know about Thierry,'' the Judge said hastily. Clearly, Gunderson did not know about the NSA intercept of the Soviet wiretap with Thierry's voice on the tape.

''He was not a really suitable person for John Wells's niece,'' Street continued, ''but I understand he was a competent war correspondent. Though not always on our side. Still, that was the way the media people were then.''

''The other 1972 resignation was Charles Blaisdell.'' Gunderson turned to Traina. ''How well do you know Blaisdell, Mr. Traina?''

Was counterintelligence on a fishing expedition? The hunt for moles had gone out of style with the retirement of James Jesus Angleton, but one could never be sure.

''I know him slightly. He's not exactly everyone's choice for all-American.''

''In March of '72, Blaisdell took an unauthorized trip from Saigon to Kadena. He met someone there. But there is no record of who it was.''

''Charlie was operating pretty much on his own in Saigon then,'' Traina said. ''By '72 we were not doing anything significant in Vietnam. We were down to working with the Fifth Special Forces Group on jobs like Omega. Charlie was a specialist. He started back in the New Frontier days working with the Laotian Meo.'' He looked at Gunderson. ''You were still in short pants, sonny, but that is the way it all started, with Kennedy telling people how we might have to fight to hold the Plain of Jars in *Lay*-ose. He couldn't pronounce it, but he was willing to fight to defend it.''

''There's no point in lecturing Gunderson, Frank.''

''No, I suppose not. I just find myself remembering.''

The Judge said, ''You made a telephone call to Charlie Blaisdell Friday night. You asked the duty officer not to log it. Did you intend to keep that off the record?''

''Did the duty officer report that the call did not go through?''

''Yes.''

''Now what? The polygraph?'' Traina was growing angry.

''Of course not. But I would like to know why you think Wells might have gone to see Blaisdell. That is why you tried to reach him, isn't it?''

Traina looked at Gunderson. ''Out,'' he said.

''I was only doing my job, Mr. Traina.''

"It's all right, Gunderson," Street said. "Mr. Traina knows who ordered the investigation."

When the door closed, Traina said, "Didn't you order it?"

"I would have, but the word came from on high."

"The President?"

"He is *very* upset, Frank. John Wells is practically our next Secretary of State. There is a summit coming up in a matter of months. The Russians are coming again, Frank. Try to see his point of view. Blaisdell is rather a disreputable character. The President wants to know what connection there is between his almost-secretary and Blaisdell."

"Poor Charlie, the remittance man," Traina said. "It was before your time, Judge, but the Company is responsible for Blaisdell being a burnout. We used him up and threw him away."

"That isn't quite fair, Frank. The government tries to do the right thing."

"I'm sorry, Judge, but, with respect, you're full of shit. Intelligence agencies aren't in business to 'do the right thing.' We throw away men and women like used Kleenex. Charlie was one of the chosen when we were working with the mountain tribes. He fought with the Meo. He loved them, I suppose. But there came a day when operations in the Laotian hills were no longer 'cost effective.' That was the totem, Judge. Some bureaucrat decided it was time to pack up and get out of the Laotian highlands because the rest of the war was going down the toilet on campus and in Washington.

"So there was old Charlie sitting in Saigon with nothing more to do, reading the Pathet Lao intercepts about how many of his old friends were being butchered, accepting the fading radio messages from the hills begging for weapons, first, then food, please, and, finally, medical supplies. By the time the radios went quiet, I guess old Charlie wasn't a very lovable guy in Saigon."

"He wrote a report in early April 1972," Street said. "Then he buried it here. I think he made sure it got lost in Records when everything was computerized."

"I didn't know him when he was active. But what I've heard of him doesn't suggest a report writer."

Street smiled grimly. "I rather formed the same opinion. But the report was quite enlightening—if you knew what went before, what Blaisdell left out of the report."

Traina said carefully, "He was in Saigon when Megan Wells was there. Is that part of it?"

"Implicitly. Not explicitly."

"Charlie is not a complex man, Judge. Devious, but not complex."

"Complex enough to have been witness somehow to the death of Megan Wells's husband, the French journalist."

"You sure about that, Judge?"

"It is in the report. The report was endorsed by the Second Secretary in the Saigon embassy. One Josiah Lowell. Unimpeachable. He just retired after a double tour as ambassador to Burundi. Solid sterling."

"But?"

"I don't know, Frank. We heard Thierry on our tape of a Soviet telephone tap last Thursday. So did Wells. We saw to that, didn't we? Now he's gone. Where?"

"Blaisdell's?"

"I'm not born to this work, Frank, but wouldn't you say that was a good guess?"

"I sure as hell would, Judge."

"You were planning to go over there and look for yourself, weren't you?"

"How did you know?"

"Instinct. I think we can get you a priority-one flight, Frank. You won't have to scrounge from the Air Force."

"But we had better notify Swiss Intelligence, Judge."

"Not yet," Street said. "Let's keep it in the family as long as we can.

"You think Wells is dangerous?" he asked. Suddenly the intelligence innocent was back and the shrewd manipulator had vanished.

"I *know* Jack is dangerous, Judge. Particularly if he thinks Charlie is mixed up in anything that will harm his two girls."

"I think you'd better get moving. Have you ever ridden in an F-15?"

"I'm afraid that by tonight the answer to that will be 'yes.' "

21. VILLA STEFANO

David Ashburn prowled the house silently. For a time he stood on the piazza looking up at the northeastern sky. The stars were brilliant here in the mountains. He could see the spilling dipper of Ursa Major in the sparse star fields of the north. It reminded him of watching the sky from the deck of a freighter en route from Long Beach, California, to Rotterdam when he was a child. His parents had been adventurers. He had lived in a half-dozen countries before he was eighteen.

Behind him, the villa was quiet. He glanced at his watch. It was 0510. Soon it would begin to grow light. He had slept again during the day yesterday, because he planned to spend the night guarding the house against the return of the watcher whose presence he had discovered in the rocks near the pass. Perhaps he would not return. But there was no way to be certain. Better to watch and wait.

He had sat up late with Mary and Zachary. He suspected that both were happy to have him in the house, though they would have denied it if asked. Individually and as a couple, the Quinns made a fetish of independence. David understood. His parents had been the same way. Valuable remnants from another age, a nonrelativistic time when moral choices were clear. The Quinns were gallant holdovers from another time, and it was for that, as much as for anything else, that David valued them.

But he had not come to Villa Stefano to indulge his quixotic affection for Mary and Zachary, but to protect—insofar as it was possible—the niece of a political person whose services were desired by the President of the United States.

He left the piazza, went inside, and stood for a moment, still as a cat, listening to the silence of the house.

Long ago, the Villa Stefano had been a stone farmhouse. During the mountain battles around Rome in 1944, it had been a German strongpoint, then an American outpost. But long years before that it had sheltered generations of Abruzzi peasants,

153

who had scratched a precarious living out of the thin skin of dirt held in place on the mountains by terraces. The terraces were vanishing, because the ground had been sucked dry of the ability to produce any growing thing, and the people who had built them and tilled the soil were gone. They were being replaced by Roman businessmen searching for a bit of mountain cool in summer, and by intellectuals and artists who had discovered they could afford to live here, though unable to live in the more fashionable places such as Positano, Rapallo, and Santa Margherita.

Instead of the Med, there was the harsh beauty of the Gran Sasso here, compounded of rock, steep mountain, and sky. David vaguely remembered places like Santo Stefano in his own country. The Sierra Nevada were far more impressive mountains, but stone and sky were much the same anywhere.

It had been four years since he had last been in California. Oddly enough, being with the Quinns, convinced expatriates both, made him think of home.

He walked into the hallway and stood looking up the shadowed stairs toward Megan's room. When Herrick had handed him this job, he had not welcomed it. He had denigrated it as "baby-sitting." Now, having seen Megan again after all these years, he was still unsure of his feelings. He had been more ill at ease with the idea of seeing her than disgruntled by the task.

In law school they had been friends, then nearly but not quite lovers. He had been almost in love with her. But she had closed the door on him. As though she was afraid of her feelings, or perhaps simply unwilling to be diverted from the life she was planning for herself. He never knew.

He did know something of her background. He knew about her parents and her uncle. He even knew that she had been briefly married.

It had come as a surprise, but not a shock, when she told him, one summer afternoon under the oaks at Zot's, that she had a daughter.

"We're adults," he had said with feeling. "We aren't virgins." That, he remembered, had earned him a strange, covert look. Now that he knew *who* it was she had married out there in 'Nam, he understood.

For years, he'd thought it was his decision to join the Agency that had killed their relationship. When he went east to Langley, Megan never wrote, never answered his letters, chilled him when he called on the telephone.

And there, he thought, was an end to it. Until now.

He went quietly up the stairs and stood before her open door in the darkness. Megan lay awake, softly weeping for her endangered child. It had to be that, he thought. What else could it be?

"Meg," he said quietly.

There was no reply, but he knew she was listening to him.

"May I come in?"

"What do you want, David?"

"I want to talk. All right?"

She drew a deep, shuddering sigh. "I wish you hadn't come here," she said.

"I had no choice." He stood in the doorway, speaking softly to the darkness. "Is it all right if I come in? We don't want to wake the Quinns."

"All right. Yes."

He walked carefully into the dark room, closed the door, and sat on the foot of her bed.

He said, half smiling, "A feather bed."

"Are Zach and Mary frightened?" she asked.

"Zach doesn't frighten easily," he answered. "And Mary is always ready for a fight."

"I saw you from the window. What did you find up there in the rocks near the pass?"

I should have known, he thought. She had not simply gone up and fallen asleep.

"There was someone up there. Or there had been. Just watching."

"Then they know *you* are here, David."

"They would assume that anyway, Meg. They know who you are, they know who your friends are likely to be."

"My *friends*?" she said bitterly.

"Yes, your friends. The order to watch over you came from Washington. You may not like it, but you have friends in high places."

"If you know, then Uncle Jack knows."

"Yes."

"Where is he?"

"In Italy. That's all we know. That's the truth, Meg."

He heard her sitting up, felt the movement of her feet under the feather bed. "Tell me what *you* know," she said.

"I know what we can expect at the Sword and Scabbard."

She sucked in her breath. Anger mixed with fear. He was experienced enough to know how well the two mingled.

"It's a drop, Meg. He won't be there. Only a message."

"How can you be sure?"

Dare he tell her? Yes, damn it. She had the right to know. "Jean Thierry is a Soviet agent. He has been for a long time. I'm sorry, Meg. That's a fact."

"He has my daughter." The tone of her voice rose up the scale toward hysteria. But it stopped short.

"A week ago," she said, tightly controlled, "you would have been certain that Jean Thierry was years dead. That was what your friends told me in Saigon. They said he was traveling with the Khmer Rouge, and the Thais killed him."

"What can I say?"

"The truth. If that isn't asking too much."

"The Agency thought Thierry died in 1972. They still are not sure the man who called you isn't an imposter."

"Why didn't they ask me?"

"Because by the time they thought of it you were gone," he said quietly.

"I was following instructions."

"All right. So am I. So are we all."

"Damn you, David. I want my daughter back."

"We are going to find her."

"I wish I were so confident. But she isn't your daughter. It's easy for you."

He made no reply.

"Oh, God, that was an awful thing to say."

"A bit. But no one blames you. We have to work together. That's why they sent *me*. They had some idea it might be easier for you to have me, rather than a stranger. I'm sorry if it isn't working out that way."

He felt her hand on his knee in the darkness.

"I should be sorry, not you," she said bitterly. "If I'd had any idea what he would do one day, I'd have killed him myself. God help me, but that's the truth."

He rested his hand on hers, waiting to see if she would let it stay. She did.

"You may not be very happy to have me here, Meg," he said quietly. "But I am glad to *be* here. I used to think we had something going for us." How inarticulate we are, he thought. I'm trying to tell her I once was in love with her, and listen to how I say it.

"You wanted Uncle Jack's life more," she said in a whisper.

"Maybe. I'm not so sure now. But I knew you could do without me."

"Oh, God, David. I wish I could talk about it."

"To me?"

"Yes, to you. You were—"

"What was I?"

"The only man I wanted—after I was over Jean."

His hand turned, enclosed hers.

"Did he mean so much to you? You would never talk about it."

"I wanted him until he got me. Do you understand how that can be? From the first time we made love, it was like living in a wasteland. When they told me he had been killed, I was shocked. But by the time Denny was born, I knew I would never have shared her with him. I would have been frightened of what she might become."

He reached out and held her. "We'll find her," he said. "I promise." An empty, hollow promise?

He stroked her hair and kissed her. Even if she took it only as a gesture of comfort, it needed doing.

Her lips parted under his.

"God," she breathed softly, "I do need to be loved."

He cupped her breasts and kissed the erect nipples. She made room for him under the cover. Why did her actions seem so unpracticed? She was a mature woman, not a girl.

Then it came to him—a revelation. Her time with Thierry had savaged her sexuality, left her frightened and celibate. That was the rejection he had sensed in her all those years ago.

If he had been a man, instead of a boy, he might have known it, known how to deal with it.

He stripped swiftly and lay for a time simply holding her, warming her cold body with his own. Her arms went around him. She was trembling.

I have been lucky, he told himself. I have stumbled into a reprise. And this must be the most unprofessional thing I have ever done.

22. AIRBORNE, LUFTHANSA

There was a direct Aeroflot connection between Moscow and Rome, and ordinarily General Plakhanov would have used it. But this trip was special. He had ordered Ekimov to book Aeroflot only as far as Vienna; from there he had chosen that they travel by Lufthansa. It was a small precaution, but one worth taking, with the Frenchman in the field.

Minutes after sunrise, the aircraft had been over the Adriatic coast at Trieste. The land below was still shrouded in darkness, but the sky to the east, clearly seen from the portside windows of the tourist-class cabin, in which the Russians were riding, was brightening minute by minute.

The northern Adriatic was hidden under a solid cloud deck, but as the aircraft flew to the southwest, the undercast thinned, exposing a blue sea streaked with the white wakes of boats. Mariners had been making the crossing in these waters since men first built boats. The sea was ultramarine in places, the color of turquoise in the shallows. Ekimov fidgeted in his seat and stared down at this European sea.

Plakhanov regarded his aide critically. It was true that he was a handsome man, but civilian clothes did not really become him. He wore a suit as though it were a peasant's smock. It was all right, but on this occasion Plakhanov would have wished it otherwise.

He himself was vaguely uncomfortable out of uniform. He missed the way a uniform held one's body, firmly armored in heavy cloth, crested buttons, and gold bullion. Without the golden sheaves of wheat that decorated a Soviet general officer's tunic collar, he felt unclothed.

The stewardess, a buxom German girl with hair the color of those same wheat sheaves he missed, made her way down the aisle serving the drinks for which she had earlier collected money. And at this hour of the morning! Plakhanov thought disgustedly. The breakfast of rolls, fruit jam, and coffee, however, had been excellent. Half the passengers—mostly Central European businessmen—had accepted the breakfast. The other half, Ekimov among them (to his discredit), had ordered drinks. In fact, it seemed to Plakhanov that Ekimov was far more nervous traveling abroad than was proper in an officer of the KGB, but he hadn't the time or the inclination to investigate the Captain's psyche now.

Most of his thoughts were with Paladin. Was it so strange that for all these many years since Peter Arendt died, he had thought of John Wells as Paladin?

Such were the rewards of patience, he thought. There had been a half-dozen occasions in the last twenty-five years when he could have sent assassins after Paladin. They might even have succeeded, though as Paladin became grander and more important the success of an ordinary team of killers grew less and less likely.

And surely there had been almost as many times since he had rescued the Frenchman from his Thai prison that Thierry must have thought of abandoning his assignments and going off on a private hunt. But Plakhanov had, many times, warned him that a target such as Paladin could be struck only once, and that it must be done with great stealth and elegance. The latter was a strange word to apply to an act of murder. But no other would do.

Ekimov watched the General's thin, ascetic face warily. It was the face of a saint, a face like those in the ikons in state museums that used to be churches.

Saints could kill with a glance. The old *babushka* who swept the floors of Number 2 Dzerzhinsky Square once told him that. She believed it. She almost made him believe it, too.

And what would this particular saint do when he discovered, as he almost certainly would, that his aide, Comrade Captain Ekimov, who should have been grateful as well as loyal, was spying on him for Kalganin?

He thought of his Yelena Petrovna and the children, still at the river dacha and able to remain there at the special dispensation of General Plakhanov. What would she think of the act of disloyalty he was committing?

Probably nothing at all, Ekimov thought miserably, since it was to cover her foolish, greedy, stupid father's transgressions that he had agreed to be Kalganin's agent.

On the other hand, he thought, looking down at the blue of the Adriatic, if one was elected cat's-paw, wasn't it best, after all, to be the cat's-paw of the most powerful man in one's service?

Chairman of the KGB Kalganin was certainly that. And, as he had so generously explained, what he sought to protect was the image of the General Secretary as a man of peace, disarmament, and détente.

Could any faithful son of the Soviet Motherland find fault with that?

23. LEONARDO DA VINCI AIRPORT, ROME

Rico Milgrazie thought of himself as a youthful sprig of an ancient tree. The tree was the street people of Rome, and it was three thousand years old. There had been poor Romans when the SENATVS POPVLVSQUE ROMANVS ruled the city, and there were poor Romans still. The duty of every root and branch of the Roman tree was to prosper, to use one's wits and grow rich. In some ways, he thought, it was an advantage to have been born, as he was, without a name, home, or occupation. One could always invent one's own name. He had, taking Milgrazie from the thanks he had received from a tourist whose traveler's checks and passport he had returned—after helping himself to the cash in the wallet. Rewarded, he had rushed to a flea market to buy a camera and some film. For years he had seen the paparazzi, the independent street photographers, swarming around the celebrities who populated Cinecittà, or around the Grand Prix drivers of Ferraris and Mercedeses who had all the girls they wanted, or around the sleek rich folk who lived in guarded villas in the suburbs. He followed the men who followed the celebrities, learning their noisy, brash craft.

By the time he was eighteen years old, he was selling photographs to *Oggi* and some of the racier tabloids.

At the age of twenty he was a successful papparazzo: inventive, alert, and, despite having accumulated many possessions, still a Roman street urchin at heart, greedy to his fingertips.

This Sunday morning he was hard at work. Many of his colleagues declined to labor on Sunday. Some out of religious scruples, but most because they pretended to believe that the rich and powerful—the street photographer's natural prey—disliked traveling on weekends.

Some had evolved theories about this. Milgrazie's favorite was one propounded by Tomasino Vano (his most talented competitor). Vano contended that the rich and powerful preferred to travel while common folk worked, both as a mark of their social superiority and out of a desire to avoid mixing with plebes. It was an ingenious theory, Milgrazie conceded, except that it was absolute nonsense. Vano was famous for his social theories. But the fact was that the rich traveled on any damn day they chose, on Sunday as often as any other day. And for that reason Milgrazie now found himself at the end of the Lufthansa bay awaiting the arrival of Flight 28 from Vienna.

It was Milgrazie's practice to meet arriving aircraft in rotation. Though he did not know that his memory was eidetic, he did know that he seldom, if ever, forgot a face. By spending much of his free time at the international terminals at Leonardo da Vinci, he was often able to be the first free-lance photographer to catch a picture of an arriving celebrity. And on more than a few occasions, it was Rico Milgrazie who produced the photograph that unleashed a flurry of gossip and scandal. *"What film star arrived incognito without her husband but with her lesbian Finnish tennis-star lover . . . ?"*

There were Italian actresses who made the sign of the horns when they saw Milgrazie. He loved it, and he loved even more being well paid for skill with his evil-eyed camera.

But his talent was not fixed exclusively on movie stars and world-class athletes. He had other interests and curiosities.

On this Sunday morning he had been intrigued to see, among the few Romans in the Lufthansa bay, two familiar faces that most definitely did not belong to the world of sports or the arts.

Because Milgrazie also made a practice of monitoring the arrival of Aeroflot's thrice-weekly flights from Moscow and Leningrad, the faces of the Soviet security teams had become familiar. There was Fat Ivan, a balloon of a man who resembled a youthful Nikita Khruschev; Boris the Bear, an older thug who limped; Kiril, who fancied himself a womanizer (Milgrazie had an interesting file of photographs chronicling Kiril's doings in

161

Trastevere); Andrei, who could lose himself in a crowd, he was so ordinary to look at; and Ubriaco, who had earned his Italian alias by appearing never to be quite sober.

Milgrazie had assigned the names. They were part of his personal filing system. His surveillance of the Soviet Embassy security men produced a tidy profit from the sale of photographs of newly arrived Russians to the French, the British, and the Americans.

This morning, as he lurked near the entrance to the Lufthansa bay awaiting the arrival of the flight from Vienna, he was startled—and pleased—to see Fat Ivan and Ubriaco making common cause with the airport security men guarding the head of the bay: sharing American cigarettes and friendly pleasantries.

Neither Ubriaco nor Fat Ivan was a likable man, thought Milgrazie. It was unlikely that they had drifted down the concourse to the German airline to spend their time exchanging tobacco and small talk with the Italian teen-agers assigned to guard the passengers arriving from Austria.

He sauntered closer to the entrance of the bay. A pair of German flight attendants, blonde and pink and delicious-looking, smiled at him. He returned the salute, as his countrymen liked to say, *con brio*.

Milgrazie was particularly pleased with his appearance this Sunday morning. In Friday's mail he had received the long-awaited package from the American store Hammacher-Schlemmer, and at long last his outfit was complete. To go with his Reebok running shoes and his prized genuine Levi's, he now had a Hammacher-Schlemmer photographer's jacket. This was a marsupial garment of waterproof material consisting mostly of pockets and Velcro closures. It had cost him 180 American dollars, but it was certain to set a standard of elegance and usefulness among all the *pappas* of Rome.

He had filled the pockets with his second and third cameras, a light meter, a set of filters, long and medium lenses for each of his cameras, and a dozen canisters of 35mm film. The jacket was a Chinese puzzle box of pockets within pockets. There was even room for a carefully wrapped provolone sandwich and a bar of Swiss chocolate. Milgrazie had been hungry many times while growing up on the streets of Rome, and now he was never without emergency rations. He did not realize it, and his weapon was the camera, but his attitude was that of an urban guerrilla. He had chosen sides long ago. Not for any of the high-sounding ideals the politicians talked about so freely, but because he believed that what he earned was his, and no one else's.

The German flight attendants were still looking at him with intense, frankly sexual interest. He returned their scrutiny with a flashing white smile and regretfully moved on. This was business. The fact that Fat Ivan and Ubriaco were at work this morning convinced him that there was money to be made.

He sequestered himself in the alcove of the shut snack bar facing the Lufthansa bay and unlimbered his Maxxum 7000 and attached his new 300mm lens. He glanced at the telescreen set in the wall above the entrance to the bay. Flight 28 was exactly on time. Which was only to be expected, Milgrazie thought. What would happen to the world if the Germans began to run their airline unpunctually? The sky would fall, and Frenchmen would become humble.

In one of the most secret inner pockets of his sartorial wonder, he carried a thick wad of lira. This was a fund to be used to bribe the airport security people if there should be trouble about his use of a camera. Italy was supposed to be a free country, and for the most part it was. Except when some acne-scarred rock star's bodyguard took it upon himself to thrash a *pappa*. Then, the assistance of the security people was needed and available—at a price. That, Milgrazie thought, was the way of the world. Those who have get more. And those who know who to bribe cannot be thrashed. *That* was the way of Milgrazie.

He measured the ambient light with a meter and loaded his Maxxum with 1000 ISO film. The measurements were mainly for the benefit of the two waiting flight attendants, but they had begun to lose interest in him. They sat on a bench, flight bags at their feet, chattering animatedly. About their dates last night, Milgrazie thought broodingly. About their depraved sexual adventures in the Eternal City on a March Saturday night. Lurid adventures to carry home to Bremen or Limburg or some other place named for a sausage or a cheese.

On the lower level of the concourse, the passengers from an American Airlines flight from Los Angeles trooped out of Customs toward the taxi and bus ranks. Milgrazie dreamed of going to Los Angeles. His heart was there, where there were golden stars in the sidewalks, and famous film actors and actresses were to be seen every day in the supermarkets. He loved supermarkets. He divided his free time between the cinema and the glorious temples of American-style consumption.

The public-address system announced the arrival of Lufthansa

163

28 from Vienna. A few people, not many, drifted down the concourse and into the bay where the aircraft would deplane its passengers. The announcement was made in three languages: first in English—Milgrazie could imagine how that displeased Fat Ivan and Ubriaco—then in Italian, which was only polite, after all, and last in German. How circumspect the Germans had become, he thought. Remarkable what a lost war and forty years of prosperity could do to improve a nation's manners. He remembered a line from an old movie, a classic. An Italian officer, a prisoner of war, complains of the Germans to an Englishman: "How can a nation that belches understand a nation that sings?" And he marches away singing Verdi.

Milgrazie leveled his camera at the line of deplaning passengers appearing out of the tunnel at the end of the bay. He studied the scene through his telephoto with interest. Fat Ivan was watching the Vienna passengers anxiously. Milgrazie triggered the auto-wind as he ran off three quick shots of the pudgy Russian. Ubriaco was on his feet, which was unusual. The man much preferred to meet life's challenges in a seated position. Preferably with a glass of vodka in his fist. Milgrazie chided himself for lack of charity. Probably, if he had been born and raised in a country like the Soviet Union, he, too, would have opted to be a drunk instead of a papparazzo.

Was there someone on the airplane important enough to keep Ubriaco on his feet this early on a Sunday morning? Holy Virgin, Milgrazie thought, send me an important fish, and I will light you a candle. All right, two. But he must be an important enough fish for Signor Drayton. A shark, please?

Out of the tunnel came the last few passengers. Fat Ivan pushed forward through the waiting crowd. Milgrazie watched Ubriaco. Not until the second man's attention was commanded did he react. Then he aimed the Maxxum at two men, one young, one not young, but gray and slender as a sword, with a cold, cruel face. He let the Maxxum snap picture after picture. Either Drayton would pay or he would not. But for some reason, Milgrazie felt sure that he would, and gladly. The old man now walking between the two protective KGB men had presence. He walked as though he was important, like a prince, perhaps even a pope.

Who are you, old man, Milgrazie wondered. It was one of the never-changing ironies of life that he would supply Drayton with pictures and Drayton would supply him with lira, and he would never know whether he was being paid for accomplishment or for hope of something better in the future. He continued to shoot pictures as the Soviets swept past him. He found it interesting that the rest of the passengers from Flight 28 had been herded by security into the passport control area, but not the princely gray Russian. He *was* Russian, of course. A brute as arrogant as Fat Ivan would never show such servility to anyone not beloved of the Motherland and entitled to suckle on her capacious teats.

Just after the party passed the alcove, where Milgrazie was now unloading his camera, Ubriaco frowned and glared back at him. Milgrazie jammed the Maxxum into a pocket and departed at a trot. He had gone a third of the way to the main terminal when he took the time to look back.

What he saw dismayed him. Ubriaco and the young man who had deplaned with the grayhead were walking swiftly along behind him.

Without a moment's hesitation, Milgrazie broke into a run. Experience had taught him that a fleeing papparazzo lost only dignity, while a caught papparazzo lost teeth. The heavily loaded jacket bounced against his slender frame. He found the wadded roll of lira as he rounded into the main concourse and trotted up to the policeman on duty at the information kiosk.

He slipped the roll of notes into the man's hand and said, "There are two unfriendly persons, just there. Can you help me?"

The money vanished, and the corporal looked down the concourse. Milgrazie was surprised to see Ubriaco actually reaching into his coat pocket. For a weapon?

The new arrival saw the carabiniere and put a hand on Ubriaco's arm. But was it really possible that Ubriaco was going to take out a weapon? Was it that important? Milgrazie began to reprice the roll of film in his pocket. After all, Drayton was a rich American, and if whatever he had captured on film was important enough to tempt Ubriaco into an act of foolishness in the main concourse of Leonardo da Vinci, Drayton would gladly pay a few dollars more.

24. ROME

The voice of Anne Barringer, Reuben Herrick's first assistant, came through the intercom. "It's Mr. Ashburn, Mr. Herrick. He's calling from Santo Stefano."

"And about time," Herrick muttered. "Put him on."

"Line nine, sir."

"What's happening there, David?" Herrick demanded.

"I have Megan Wells's permission to go with her when she makes contact."

Herrick stared at the receiver. Ashburn had Megan Wells's *permission*? What, in the name of all that was holy, was that supposed to mean? Ashburn had not been sent to Santo Stefano to ask anyone's permission.

"I have a request, Reuben," Ashburn said.

"What?" Herrick was suddenly angry. This whole affair had gone badly from the beginning. Traina had made a mistake in telling Jack Wells that his niece and grandniece were at risk. He should have waited at least until the Company had had a chance to bring things under control.

But he had not done that. More of the old-boy network functioning there. "Trust me, we went to Exeter together." Or Choate or wherever. Great! See where it got the Brits when they behaved that way.

But Wells was no sweet old boy. He was a hard-bitten spook of the old school. One able to remember the glory days, when what a Company man did was take action, and whoever didn't like it could screw the pooch.

Because Rome Station had been careless—Herrick had to admit that—Wells was loose, and everyone would have to go damned carefully until he was found and got under control.

Jack Wells had used his tradecraft to drop off the edge of the world. As anyone with any experience at all would expect him to do.

Telling all this to Judge Street had not been a good experience for Herrick, nor had he been delighted to discover that Frank Traina must by now be in either southern Switzerland or northern Italy, on the hunt himself.

The Swiss were going to become broody, as they always did when they thought someone was running an operation in their country. That meant that when all this was over, they were going to be damned difficult to live with. *More* difficult to live with.

And now, Herrick thought, Ashburn was beginning to act as though he was allowing himself to become personally involved. Well, damn it, everyone *was* involved. State was involved, the Agency was involved and, for Christ's sake, the *White House* was involved. This was no time for Ashburn to start acting like a schoolboy.

Of *course* everyone was concerned about the safety of the young Wells girl. But she was peripheral, not central.

"Reuben?"

"What is it?"

"I want your permission to go in after Thierry and the girl."

Herrick suppressed his anger. Ashburn was one of the best. What had happened to him in the last twenty-four hours to make him ask permission to behave like an amateur?

"That is out of the question, David," he said. "We stick to the plan. The girl goes where Thierry wants to take her. There isn't time for anything fancier than that."

"What if something happens to her?"

"For Christ's sake, David. Since when did you start a mission with 'what if'? That's my department, not yours."

There was a distant humming of telephone lines. Herrick could imagine what Ashburn was thinking. The damn guy used to lust after Megan Wells. He had been given this assignment precisely for that reason. Now it appeared that he still lusted after her, and no lover was ever reliable. Herrick momentarily considered relieving Ashburn. But there wasn't time. And there was no assurance he would obey any such order.

"We stick to the game plan, David."

"We don't really have a game plan. We are just prodding and hoping."

"More than that. The girl *is* Wells's grandniece."

"Meg wants to know where her uncle is."

"He took a flight to Rome, but he deplaned in Geneva Saturday."

Herrick heard a murmured conversation on the other end of the line. "Are you sharing all this with the press?" He meant

Mary Quinn. Despite her having become a full-time writer of books, to Herrick she was, and always would be, a member of the media, and not to be trusted completely.

"Mary and Zach have been damn helpful. And kind to Meg."

What happened last night, Herrick wondered. An hour or two in bed and now this?

Unfair. He realized it. In ordinary circumstances he would have given his congratulations and best wishes, transferred Ashburn back to a desk at Langley, and gone about his business.

But Jack Wells was politics. And to the Agency, politics was bad news.

Ashburn said, "I want some protection up here for the Quinns. There was a bogy up in the rocks. He ran before I could get up there, but I think he'll be back."

"Did you actually see anyone?"

"I saw someone."

"One person?"

"And a big Merc running like hell."

"I'll speak to Tevera."

"Better yet," Ashburn said. General della Tevera was the commander of the Italian Army's antiterrorist battalion.

"It will take time, David. They're stretched. There have been quite a few reports of Red Brigades people slipping in from Germany."

"No arrests?"

"For what? Crossing a border? It's a free country. We saw to that."

Silence. Well, what could he say? What he was being told was true. After the Second World War, the United States made its enemies into liberal democracies. It was never intended that they become battlegrounds for the sort of gutter wars that were being fought from the Middle East to Northern Ireland.

Ashburn said, "We'll be here for the rest of today. If you hear anything more about Wells—"

"Certainly, David. Assure Miss Wells that we will keep her informed."

When he had broken the connection, he sat for a long moment, deep in thought. It seemed to him that there was something disturbing about Jack Wells's having begun his crazy trip in Switzerland, rather than in Italy, where his grandniece was being held. It had an odor of duplicity, of cover-up. Langley had supplied Herrick with a dossier on Charles Blaisdell, but there was certainly more than the bare record showed.

According to Langley, Wells had never met with Blaisdell. Blaisdell used to claim they were classmates, but that was bluster. Officially, the men were strangers.

And then there were the grapevine and the rumor mills. Wells had resigned in 1972. Blaisdell had resigned in 1972. Megan Wells had made a violently unsuitable marriage in Saigon that year. Jean Thierry had died in an ambush that year. Blaisdell had been the CIA officer tasked with dealing with Thai anti-Communist border actions that same year, because he had made a study of both the Pathet Lao and the Khmer Rouge.

And Blaisdell—a very sick man, according to the dossier— lived in retirement in Switzerland.

Now why, Herrick wondered—and he knew that by now a number of people must also be wondering—was Wells making ready to pay Blaisdell a visit? To investigate a breach of contract?

Herrick did not envy the man who would have to explain all this to the President of the United States.

The intercom on his desk pinged imperiously. He touched the switch and said, "Yes, Anne?"

"Mr. Drayton is on line three, sir."

Parker Drayton dealt with the local civilians. A slickly handsome man of thirty-five, product of Groton and Dartmouth, he seemed an odd choice to be the point-man in negotiations with taxi drivers, Vice Squad policemen, pimps and whores, tabloid-newspaper people, and papparazzi. The truth was, Drayton enjoyed dealing with street people at the lower levels. These people worked for money, and he understood this and approved.

Herrick punched button three on his console and said testily, "Yes, Parker?"

"I am in the photo lab, sir. We have something here that should interest you."

"What is it?" Drayton's most irritating habit was a tendency to fatten, as they said in the theater, his part. He was social, rich, well connected—and ambitious.

"I have to show you, sir. Shall I come up?"

"Damn it, Parker. Stop blowing smoke and tell me what the hell you think you have."

Drayton was imperturbable. "One of my *pappas* left me a roll of film. Pictures he took at Leonardo da Vinci of a man who got off the Lufthansa flight from Vienna this morning. I ordered a computer ID scan. There was no need, but I wanted to be sure—"

"The point, Parker, the point?"

"Of course. The commander of the First Chief Directorate appears to be paying us a visit. General Feliks Plakhanov is in Rome."

25. PORZA-LUGANO, SWITZERLAND

Valetta Rossano awoke with the late sunshine pouring through the window of the garden apartment she shared with two of the other medical secretaries at the Municipal Medical Clinic of Lugano.

Faustina was on holiday—in Venice, no less—and Claudia was visiting her mother in Geneva. Valetta had the day, and the apartment, to herself.

She had only one task to perform. Dr. Caravello, the oncologist to whom she was assigned, had become concerned about his American patient. It was known that Signor Blaisdell lived alone up on the mountainside, and he had missed his last appointment for radiation treatment of his worsening leukemia. The man was difficult, to be sure, but that was understandable. His affliction had been in remission for a number of years, but had recently become once again active. "The leukemia is terminal," Caravello had dictated into his notes. "But the patient has a determined attitude and, with treatment, may survive for between eighteen and twenty months. Perhaps more."

Valetta liked to think that all of Caravello's patients would survive indefinitely. The doctor reminded her of her father, who had never, insofar as she could remember, been wrong.

But Blaisdell would not survive a month without his treatments, and to have him miss an appointment offended both the doctor's and Valetta's Swiss sense of order.

When the clinic closed on Friday evening and Blaisdell had not appeared, Dr. Caravello had asked Valetta to look in on the patient during the weekend and to remind him that his treatment schedule must be adhered to strictly. "Explain, also, that patients must be charged for missed appointments," Caravello said severely.

As she woke, Valetta had remembered this with some feelings of guilt. Yesterday, Saturday, she had ridden to Locarno on the pillion of Robertino's Vespa. They had toured the lake on the steamer, eaten lunch at an out-of-the-way *trattoria* in Brissago, and had then spent the afternoon making love in a mountain meadow. Robertino was a fine strong lover and not promiscuous. One had to be so careful these days.

He was constantly asking to use the apartment for their trysts, but that was out of the question. Even with her roommates absent, Valetta had a strong sense of the properties. She could not imagine bringing Robertino, who worked as an auto mechanic at Alfa Romeo, into this frilly nest of women. The grassy meadows were better.

She glanced now at the clock on the nightstand and saw that it was already ten in the morning. Robertino was due to collect her at ten-thirty. She had resolved to have him drive her up the mountain to Porza, where she could discharge her errand for Dr. Caravello. From there they could descend to the border crossing at Chiasso and a day at Lake Como. It was important that Robertino not lose sight of the fact that life and courtship were not all rolling nude in the grass. A young lady must be wooed.

She dressed quickly, listening to music on her portable Taiwanese radio. For breakfast, she had only a croissant and chocolate. Lately she had noticed a definite tendency to plumpness when she stood critically before her wardrobe mirror. So far she was only voluptuous. If she was not careful, she would become fat.

But she loved sweets. It was an odd thing, but she connected sweets with Signor Blaisdell. The American was eccentric, even perverse, in his dealings with the clinic staff. The last time but one he had kept his appointment, he had brought her a great 750-gram slab of Tobler's *chocolat avec noisettes*, her particular favorite. Was it possible, she wondered as she dressed and looked at herself in the glass, that the old gentleman had a fondness for her? What would it be like to be the wife of a retired American civil servant? The idea was amusing, but not absurd. Thoughts of marriage were never absurd to a daughter of the Rossano family. Valetta had four sisters, only one of whom had thus far managed to catch a husband.

She finished dressing by squeezing herself into tight spandex-

and-denim trousers, a heavy cablestitch sweater, and ankle boots. The trousers were so tight she could wear nothing under them, and after thirty minutes on the Vespa her buttocks would be numb. But sacrifices had to be made for the sake of fashion.

She had just finished straightening her bed when she heard the piping horn of the Vespa in the street below. She looked out and waved at Robertino, who replied with another thrilling toot on the scooter's horn.

Valetta snatched up her shoulder bag and ran down the two flights of stairs to the street. The morning was clear, the sky pale blue. The air was crisp with a promise of spring. There was a scent of blossoms in the air. Spring came early and easily in this canton.

Robertino was wearing his favorite "distressed leather" jacket, styled after the jackets worn by American airmen in the Second World War. The Americans' jackets had been issued by their army. The new ones cost three hundred U.S. dollars. Robertino could never afford such luxuries without the extra money he earned as a smuggler of Swiss cigarettes into Italy. Petty smuggling was an old and honored tradition among the Ticinese. There was even a smuggler's museum on the road to Saint Moritz, where relics of the trade were proudly displayed.

On Valetta's first visit there with Robertino, she had seen a home-made submarine used on the lakes to smuggle sausages into Italy from Switzerland during the war.

"Where shall it be today, Valetta?" he asked. "I have food and a bottle of wine in the saddlebags." Yesterday's outing had been expensive. Today's would not be. Valetta understood and approved.

"We can decide that later," Valetta said. "First, take me to Porza."

Standing astraddle the Vespa, Robertino frowned. Porza was not far, but it was only a mountain village, the dullest of the dull. "Why Porza?" he asked.

"A request by Dr. Caravello," Valetta said, seating herself on the pillion. "I must look in on a patient."

Robertino was of Italian descent, as were most of the inhabitants of the canton of Ticino, but he was Swiss in all things that mattered—including his sense of hierarchy.

"Va bene." He kick-started the Vespa and waited until Valetta reported her readiness. Then he accelerated away from the apartment with all the speed the scooter could muster, zigzagging through the light Sunday traffic to the north.

172

The church bells were ringing in all the villages surrounding Lugano when the laboring Vespa reached the center of Porza.

"Where now?" Robertino asked.

"To the right there. And then down the path toward the pines."

When the bells ceased to toll, they left a ringing emptiness in the air. The pines were tall and dark against the sky. Robertino reached the head of the path and stopped the Vespa.

"Wait here," Valetta said. "I won't be long."

Robertino studied the grove of pines and decided that possibly there were suitable secluded places among them for lovemaking. He wished with all his heart that Valetta had not worn her spandex trousers. They were so tight it was almost impossible to remove them. But they did display her buttocks in a most provocative way.

"I'll come with you," he said.

"Come, then," Valetta said, and took his hand.

They went slowly, with much sexual byplay as they sauntered along. Robertino put his hand under her sweater and kneaded her full breast.

"Enough," she said, and covered herself. Laughing, they trotted down the pathway, past the grove, and then beyond, to the silent cottage with the ruined garden.

"He cannot be a rich man," Robertino said.

"I did not say he was rich. Only that he is American."

Robertino wrinkled his nose. "What is that smell?"

Valetta paused. There was a slight fetor in the air. "Something dead in the pine grove," she said.

She stepped to the door and rapped on the stained-glass insert. There was no reply.

"Look," Robertino said. "The lock is broken."

Valetta knocked again on the colored-glass panels. *"Signor Blaisdell? Ecco Valetta Rossano del clinico. Signor?"*

"He's gone away," Robertino said, grinning. "He has run off without paying his bill at the clinic."

"Never," Valetta said. "Dr. Caravello would never treat a patient who would do something so dishonest."

"Then where is he?" Robertino pushed on the door. It opened.

"Roberto! You mustn't," Valetta whispered.

"I already have," Robertino said. "Ugh, Valetta, smell!"

The fetid odor permeated the air inside the house. It terrified

173

Valetta. She snatched at Robertino's jacket sleeve and said, "Let's leave."

Her fear challenged him. Robertino said, "Wait," and stepped inside.

There were brown-black stains on the floor. A line of moving ants connected the stains with the baseboard.

"He's not very tidy, your American," Robertino said faintly.

"Please," Valetta said. "I don't like it here. I don't like this terrible smell."

There was a heavy chest against a wall. Robertino was taken with an insane urge to clown, to make black-humored jokes about Valetta's sudden fear, and his own.

"It looks like a coffin," he said.

"*Stop it!* It isn't funny."

Robertino stepped forward and reached for the chest's lid. He was appalled to see that it, too, was swarming with black ants.

"*Don't touch it, Roberto!*"

The air was suddenly filled with great hollow clangor. The bell in the church tower just up the hill had struck the quarter-hour, and the single resonating tone made the cottage tremble.

Valetta whimpered.

Robertino, revolted by the ants, reached out and flung back the lid of the chest.

Charlie Blaisdell looked out at them with crawling eyes.

Frank Traina heard the girl screaming. The Swiss agents ran down the path like a battalion of infantry. But from the stench in the air, Traina knew what they would find. The question was: Who had done it? It would take forensic tests to be certain, and Traina did not envy the autopsy surgeon his work.

A thousand yards farther up the mountain, Jack Wells studied the scene through binoculars. He recognized Traina the moment he left his car in the village square. Rather remarkable, that, he thought. Traina was still a man who reacted swiftly when his instinct was aroused. Another might still be sitting at his desk in Langley waiting for confirmation from the Swiss.

Wells looked gray, like a man carved from a single block of granite. His eyes were pale and empty of compassion. He thought: The French bastard saved me the trouble. If he had not done murder, I would have done it myself.

He had told himself he had come to Lugano only for infor-mation. But that was a lie, and he knew it. He had come because

Blaisdell had deceived him, and in so doing had put at risk the only two people in the world he loved.

It was too late to drag anything useful from Blaisdell now. Thierry had been here. Here, and how many other places?

For the first time he could remember, Wells felt old.

He replaced the binoculars in their case, reassured himself that the Glock 17 he carried was secure, and headed back to the stone turnout where he had parked the rented Mercedes.

Let Traina do what he had come to do—clean up the mess and keep secret the involvement of a secretary of state–designate.

I am not the man the President believes I am, he thought as he started the car. I am not the shrewd, contained, reasoned individual I have pretended to be. Quite the reverse. I am racked by emotion, tortured by love, moved by beauty and memory. Megan and Denny are the family that might have been mine if I had not loved my brother's wife.

As he drove quietly by the massed Swiss police cars in the Porza village square, he thought of a line in an Auden poem. One he had thought, even earlier, profound:

> Blow the cobwebs from the mirror
> See yourself at last.

26. ROME

The thought that Gianbattista Calvo was going to lead the Togliatti Unit to its death was one that Mariella, the unit's second-in-command, could not dismiss from her mind.

It was not that she was not prepared to die for the revolution. Her eighteen years of life had not been so delightful that she was unwilling to part with them. And she believed, with all her being, that the only hope for a decent society tomorrow was through ample bloodshed today. People were too stupid to understand anything less impressive than bombs and blood.

But Mariella was a practical woman. She knew that there were prices to be paid for all things. It worried her that she might have to pay the price, not for the revolution, but for Calvo's bourgeois adventurism.

Calvo had been a teacher. This automatically made him suspect to Mariella. In her experience, teachers taught because they could not *do*. There had been many academics in the movement. There was something about the life of ivy-clad, cloistered comfort men led on college campuses that made them hungry for the trappings of militancy.

Mariella had known a young teacher of European history from American University in Beirut who had been a veritable tiger when there was talk of attacking the imperialists. But when the time had actually come, he had frozen with fear and endangered the team of saboteurs with whom he had crossed the border into Israel.

The mission had been aborted, and the stragglers were driven back into Lebanon—without the young instructor who had spoken so eloquently about the need to rid the Palestinian homeland of "the Zionist entity."

Very likely the man was still alive in an Israeli jail, and no doubt he regaled his prison comrades with the tale of his moment as a man of sacrifice, a member of the fedayeen.

Calvo was not so bad as that, Mariella conceded, but he was a young man dangerously in the grip of his fantasies. One could live with that if one must. After all, the idea of a few hundred thousand of the revolutionary faithful overturning all of Western civilization was, in itself, a formidable flight into fancy.

But Calvo, she suspected, would, in the end, be found lacking. He believed in the movement with his head, not with his gut. And when it was time to stand on the barricade and fight, or drop one's weapon and run, the rule of the head was insufficient. It took *pancia*—belly—and a great deal of it.

Calvo's absurd display of sexuality in the redoubt had stripped him naked to Mariella's coldly critical eye. He had wanted her enough to behave recklessly, foolishly. Very well, there were worse things in a commander. But once having had her, his bourgeois structures had collapsed on his head like this rotten old building in which she now stood. He was ashamed to have wanted a woman like her at all. And, having taken her, he was terrified of the consequences. Lars, whose fascination with matters sexual was limitless, had rushed to tell Mariella that their brave commander was afraid she might have given him AIDS.

Calvo had laughed when Hanalore had offered to castrate Lars,

176

and the Swede was unlikely to forget it. Calvo did not attract loyalty.

To go into battle against the forces of the Italian state with such a clown as Calvo at the head of the column was an invitation to disaster. Yet Mariella was too disciplined a comrade to consider mutiny. What would be would be.

The Russians were due to be sent back to the residency, but one was still on duty at the so-called safe house where the American girl was confined.

Calvo had requested that the Russians remain, but the Soviet paymaster had refused to allow it. By tomorrow they would be gone.

The building was as disreputable as the ballet school, but smaller and less well fortified. It made Mariella uneasy that Calvo had chosen to keep the hostage hidden away from the main strength of the unit. She, though unschooled, had the sort of mind to which military considerations came easily. She would have made a talented commander of troops in any time or place. She sensed that she was far more clever at tactical dispositions than Calvo, and it seemed to her that he was committing a cardinal military sin by dividing his strength. The American girl was a military asset, as were the fighters assigned to guard her. They should be at the ballet school, and not in the disintegrating tenement.

Unless, she thought suspiciously, the Soviets had plans for the hostage they chose not to share with the people who would be doing the fighting—and the dying.

"Ask Ivan why she is being kept in a closet," she ordered Lars, who was on duty there. Mariella thought of all Russians as "Ivan." To her, they lacked names and individuality. Calvo compared them to the imperialists with what he thought was gallows humor. "They are dollarless Americans," he would say when he wished to camouflage his dependency. He had learned a few things from the Ivans, but not their skill at the art of dissembling. Mariella had brought that ability with her from her mother's womb.

Some of the *brigatisti* found it difficult to dislike the Americans. After all, they wore American clothes, listened to American music, envied American possessions.

Mariella was made of sterner stuff. She had been introduced to sex by American GIs and made to covet the power they seemed to enjoy in the poorer districts of Ostia, where she grew up. Not all Americans had treated her badly, but she could afford no gratitude. Americans were fat and rich. They had what she intended, someday, to have. That was enough to make them targets for bombs and bullets.

She had a certain cold curiosity now about the American girl. She had never seen one her own age. Not in these circumstances.

To Lars she said, "Tell Ivan I want to see the American."

The Russian, one of the original two who had abducted the girl, spoke in fractured Italian: "I very well speak. From Moscow University I studied."

"Tell him," Mariella said to Lars. "In *his* language."

Offended, Ivan opened the door of the closet where Denny Wells had been confined for three days.

Mariella smelled the urine that had soaked into the thin mattress. She scowled at the girl's nakedness and at the bandages over her eyes.

Denny, her lips pale, her face drawn, responded to the sound of the opening door. She was frightened, weakened by her ordeal, humiliated by her nudity among strangers. And she was angry. Mariella saw that at once. She read it in the tautness of neck and belly muscles, in the tensely clutched fists wired behind her back. Terror and fury were battling for dominance.

"She is tough, this one," Mariella said. "I wonder how tough she will be with a bullet in her."

"You aren't going to shoot her!" Lars said, shocked. "She is bait for a bigger fish."

Mariella looked at the miserable prisoner and felt herself consumed with angry envy. Why has she lived a soft life while mine has been so hard?

"Close her up," she said. When the time comes, she thought—and it would—she would take care of this bourgeois flower herself.

27. MOSCOW

For many men, Gregor Borisovich Kalganin thought, even those as highly placed in the *nomenklatura* as he was, a night visit to the Kremlin would be a fearsome thing.

Kalganin's own special KGB guards had been replaced with soldiers chosen from the Kremlin Guards Regiment, the most loyal of the loyal. Big men, well trained, and probably as intimidating a body of troops as existed in the world.

It was all very impressive, but one tended sometimes to forget that the General Secretary was, in fact, a colonel general in the KGB, that his sponsor, the last General Secretary but one, had been the chairman of the KGB, and that the officers commanding all the troops in residence in the Kremlin were, every one, picked commanders of the KGB.

For a number of years, *glasnost* had created atmospherics that put the Americans and West Europeans in a self-deluding mood, but a man who was born, so to speak, to the purple (or should that be "red," Kalganin wondered) understood precisely who it was who ruled the Soviet Union and by what instrumentality.

The General Secretary knew it and so did Kalganin. And perhaps Kalganin knew it even a bit better than the General Secretary, who had, over the years, been forced to associate so much with imperialists that his revolutionary convictions might no longer be as strong as they once were.

The long black Mercedes, cruising at high speed in the center lane reserved for important people, rolled down 25 October Street, past the Historical Museum and up to the Mausoleum Gate in the Kremlin wall.

It both amused and irritated Kalganin to be riding in a new Mercedes built in the Soviet Union. The co-production agreement was two years old, and it still was wedged in the Americans' throats like a chicken bone. His irritation was caused by the honey smoothness of the ride and the praise, profuse to the point of fulsomeness, lavished on the car by his squad of drivers.

Warrant Officer Rochenko, the bullet-headed man presently at the wheel, had had the bad manners to ask Kalganin if it would be possible for him to attend the Mercedes maintenance school in Stuttgart.

Kalganin had also heard him say to a fellow veteran of the war in Afghanistan that if the armored forces had driven West German Panthers, instead of Soviet-built T-80 tanks, it might have been safe to venture out of Kabul from time to time.

People like Rochenko failed to understand the purpose of the war in Afghanistan, which was to train and blood the army and to give the officer corps the experience it would need when the time came to invade Western Europe. But he would learn, perhaps, when he was returned to face the Mujahedeen for a second tour. The withdrawal of Soviet troops from Afghanistan was *far* behind schedule.

The security check at the gate was brief but thorough. The General Secretary had developed the open life-style of an imperialist politician, but his accessibility was an illusion. The way to his side was fraught with checks, examinations, and weapons in the hands of experts. Kalganin, who intended to be the next general secretary, would not have it any other way.

The new steel-and-glass administration building recently constructed in the park area near the Moscow River wall was incongruous amid the ancient stonework and the golden onion domes of the Kremlin. What would Great Peter think of that glittering abomination, Kalganin wondered. Or Catherine the German nymphomaniac. Or Ivan the Terrible. Or even poor ludicrous Nicholas.

The new tsars in the Kremlin were a different breed, but, except for that, nothing really Russian changed.

Flanked by two Kremlin aides, Kalganin made his way into the glass building. It was like being inside a diamond. The lights on the Kremlin walls and towers reflected from every angle inside the foyer. The dome covering the reception complex was geodesic, designed by a Japanese architect in the service of the Moscow City Planning Collective. Through the tinted glass could be seen the underside of the low clouds hanging over the city. There had been intermittent snow and rain for weeks now. Muscovites longed for the advent of spring. When it came they would crowd into the parks, the men shirtless, the women in sleeveless dresses, their flesh fat and winter white. I wish I could do that myself, thought Kalganin as he marched along a glass-paneled corridor toward the elevator that could descend five levels, to the shelter below. As he marched, he could see himself reflected in the hall of mirrors: tall, immensely fat, heavily muscled. No wonder they call me the General Secretary's Dancing Bear, he thought.

They have the animal right, he told himself, but there is some question about the ownership.

The General Secretary's personal assistant, a pale young man, met him at the elevator door.

"Please follow me, Comrade Kalganin," he said. "The General Secretary is in the computer room."

Kalganin hated the computer room. He hated all the technocratic paraphernalia that had stolen through the walls of Slavic primitivism to engulf the heart of the Soviet Motherland.

When I govern here, he thought, things will be very different.

The aide ushered him into a vast, brightly lighted room. The doorway was of heavy steel, fashioned to withstand a nearby nuclear blast, and it opened to a steel-and-glass mezzanine overlooking an acre of computers aligned in row after gleaming row.

The computers were all Japanese, and obtaining them had, paradoxically, been one of Kalganin's early triumphs as chairman of the KGB. There were sixty of them in the Kremlin center, another twenty in KGB headquarters at Teplyy Stan, and another twenty-five in the Defense Ministry's deep shelter. All were connected, to form a network. Two-thirds of each day's computer time was devoted to military matters—war games and searching for ways to neutralize the military power of the West. Two-thirds of what remained was dedicated to matters of concern to the Committee for State Security.

Kalganin regarded the rows of metal boxes with distrust. The massed computing power of the state—and there was no computing power not controlled by the state—could not match the power of a single U.S. Super-Cray computer. The Americans were up to their asses in computers, he thought. They even designed yachts with them. On this level, we simply cannot compete. But there are others. By the hairy ass of God, there are others.

"Impressive, are they not?" The General Secretary had appeared behind him, moving soundlessly, as he always seemed to.

"They are only machines, Comrade General Secretary," Kalganin said.

"Thanks to you we have them."

"There are better machines. There are *always* better machines."

The General Secretary smiled thinly and ran a hand across his nearly naked scalp in a characteristic gesture.

"Your views on technology are well known, Gregor Borisovich. I didn't ask you to come here to discuss them. What I want to know about is Plakhanov. What is he doing? The Foreign Ministry received word from the embassy in Rome. General Plakhanov has suddenly materialized there. Why?"

Careful now, Kalganin thought. He is quite capable of ordering Feliks Plakhanov straight back to Moscow, and that would not do. An enemy of the USSR was about to be liquidated at absolutely no cost to the KGB or the Motherland. Plakhanov was given his orders and he had chosen to disobey them. If he had ever had a chance to continue up the ladder of promotion and preferment, that chance was gone—or soon would be. Losing a homosexual general was a small price to pay for the removal from the political chessboard of so formidable a piece as John Wells.

"It is complicated, Comrade General Secretary. But hear me out."

"Has this anything to do with that mad scheme of his you presented? What was it—Operation Paladin?" It was said in certain circles that the General Secretary had a pleasant smile, but behind the smile were steel teeth.

"John Wells has always been a formidable opponent," Kalganin said.

"That is no secret, Gregor Borisovich. There are men I would rather see as secretary of state. But—" he shrugged—"*nichevo*. It can't be helped."

Kalganin decided on boldness as the best path to approval. "He can be neutralized."

The General Secretary's eyes glittered coldly at his subordinate's tone. "We agreed that Operation Paladin was too risky."

"We did agree, comrade. We *do*. But suppose a means could be found simply to discredit the American, rather than run the risks of an assassination, which might be disclosed?"

The man was timid enough to accept the offer being made, Kalganin thought. He put on a great show of leadership, but when killing was called for, he had a tendency to hesitate, as his predecessors would never have done.

If he could be brought to acceptance now, the rest would fall into place almost without further effort on Kalganin's part. The key had been Plakhanov's decision to go to Rome. And it appeared that Kalganin need not have worried. Plakhanov was obsessed with Wells—to the point of madness.

Item: Operation Paladin had been disapproved by the General Secretary. Kalganin had presented it almost exactly as Plakhanov had conceived it, and it had been rejected.

Item: The urge to murder was so strong in Plakhanov that he chose to disregard the rejection and carry on with Paladin. The only thing that troubled Kalganin was that he did not understand why Plakhanov, a man of the KGB, was willing to risk himself and the reputation of his country to kill one American. It was known that Wells had once been an American spy. But beyond that there was nothing in the files of the KGB, the GRU, or those of the socialist intelligence services. Plakhanov had purged the files, all of them—Kalganin was sure of it. But the opportunity was too good to ignore.

Item: Plakhanov's favorite assassin, the Frenchman, was at the point of Operation Paladin. Without a doubt, the Frenchman, too, had some personal stake in the elimination of Wells. Kalganin had studied the Frenchman's dossier, but it, too, had been tampered with. There were gaps. Where, for example, were the debriefing reports he must have made to the Pathet Lao when he escaped from Bung Kan prison? For that matter, *had* he escaped? Was it possible he had been turned? Made into a deep-cover agent of the imperialists? The time factor and the undoubted successes he had scored in the field since then argued against that, but how could one ever be sure? The world of intelligence, espionage, and assassination was one of shredded records and shattered fragments that reflected, not the truth, but a thousand versions of the truth—all of them false. No truly sane man could make sense of it. None tried.

Item: What mattered to Chairman Kalganin was that Feliks Plakhanov, a potent rival, was about to take himself out of the game. When it happened, all hell would break loose. If incriminated, the USSR would have to accept humiliation. Even war was a possibility. That meant that the General Secretary would have to make amends, tacitly accept responsibility, retreat. When *that* happened, the General Secretary would be standing in Nikita Kruschev's boots, and very near to the old peasant's fate.

As a result of Operation Paladin, Kalganin thought, I stand closer to supreme power in the state than ever before.

Very carefully, and with omissions, he began to brief the General Secretary.

28. VILLA STEFANO

"He slept with her last night, and he's in there again with her now," Zachary said. "It's outrageous."

Mary suppressed a smile, thankful for the bedroom darkness. Ever since Megan's appearance at Villa Stefano, Zachary had been acting the heavy father. There was a quality in Meg that brought out protectiveness in men, she thought. It had always been like that. Even so unlikely a father figure as Charlie Blaisdell had reacted to her presence by attempting to protect, in his own crude way, Megan's vulnerability.

Zachary did not really dislike David Ashburn, who was not an inherently dislikable man. He was jealous. David was everything Zachary had been long ago: brave, active, a risk-taker, and, above all, a true believer.

Because times had changed so much, the two men sometimes thought they believed different things, but Mary knew they did not. They both valued loyalty, courage, and integrity. What rankled, Mary suspected, was that the character of the battle had changed, and that Zachary was no longer young and on the barricades.

It had come as a surprise to her that David shared Zachary's romantic nature. Don Quixote seemed oddly out of context in the 1980s. She had watched him with Megan through the day, and had found herself touched. Was it really possible to find a knight in running shoes, Levi's, and fisherman's sweater—and carrying a CIA identification folder? Or was it that David simply lacked judgment where a woman like Megan was concerned? Was love the spy's ultimate hazard?

Megan and David belonged to a generation that had cut its eyeteeth on "love." There had been "make love not war," and "the summer of love," and even—ultimate adolescent arrogance—"the love generation." Perhaps Zachary resented that a little, too. She knew that she did.

When *we* spoke of love it was of free love, she thought, and when we indulged in it, there was a price, a delicious price, to be paid. And then later, when it became clear the fascists would be satisfied with nothing less than everything, we spoke of love of country and love of freedom. We quickly discovered we could not have all that and be loyal Marxists, too.

No wonder Zachary was jealous and disapproving. Why, the old bohemian was furious because suddenly Megan (everyone's daughter) and David (Zachary reborn?) were in love "apolitically." We never had that option, Mary thought wryly. It was enough to make anyone envious.

"Megan is frightened, old man," she said. She turned her head on the pillow to look at Zachary's craggy profile. She had not been celibate during the years away from him. But she had never *loved* another. Old bohemians, she thought again. Yes, that's what we are, and it hasn't been so bad.

She said, "She's terrified for Denny. Don't begrudge her what comfort she can get from David."

"He belongs to Reuben Herrick," Zachary said.

Mary pulled the feather bed up around her neck. The nights were still sharp and cold in the Abruzzi at this time of year. "David doesn't belong to anyone," she said.

"He's a company man."

"Is that what's bothering you, old man?"

"He's taking advantage, Irish. Her defenses are down."

"How do you know Megan isn't buying him?"

"How do you mean that?"

"Oh, come along, Zach. You know exactly what I mean. Megan needs someone to fight for her. You're too old and I'm too fat. A fine young man will perform some remarkable feats for a good piece of ass."

"That," said Zachary icily, "is disgusting."

Mary kissed her husband's stubbled cheek. "Try not to think about it, old man. You'll do us both an injury."

Megan whispered, "I can't get her out of my mind. I'm terrified about what he may do to her."

David held her against him in the darkness and thought, This is not what Herrick intended, not at all. He meant me to be a loyal Company man and nothing more. He meant me to keep Megan safe, but occupied, while the police and the Italian Army dealt with Thierry. A sanitary operation, clean and as swift as could be contrived. And if the girl paid a price, well, that was a pity, but the important thing was to keep Jack Wells out of the headlines.

Herrick thought he could actually do such a thing. What did that say about Herrick and the organization he and Herrick worked for?

Too harsh a judgment, he thought. Nothing skewed the sense like a woman one loved weeping in the dark for her child.

He said, "He'll do nothing more than he already has, Meg. He doesn't dare. It's you he wants, and your uncle, I think. Denny is only the bait to lure you both." He cradled her head against him and said, "I promise you. We'll get her back."

"No soldiers, David. No police. I know him. If we don't do exactly what he said, he'll harm her—"

"She's his own daughter, Meg."

"Don't say that! I don't want to hear that!"

"It's true, Meg. Until you face that, nothing's real."

She pressed her cheek against his naked chest. "I think I'm going crazy, David. Why is he doing this?"

"That doesn't matter. Tomorrow we drive to Rome. Tuesday you pick up his message at the Sword and Scabbard exactly according to instructions. Then we'll see."

"I want my daughter back."

David said firmly, "And we will get her back, Meg. No matter what it costs." He wished, as he spoke, that he could be as confident as he was trying to sound. The record for recovered hostages was not good.

March 16
the fifth day . . .

Hast thou found me, O mine enemy?

—I Kings 21:20

29. ROME

"What I did not need, Frank," said Herrick, "was a visit from the Director of Operations." His eyes, pale-brown and stony, were fixed on the man sitting on the other side of the littered desk.

"I didn't come to interfere with your station, Reuben. And I'm not spying on you," Traina said. "Langley has confidence in you, or you wouldn't have a plum assignment like this. You know the Judge."

"Then why the hell *are* you here, Frank?" Herrick demanded, unconvinced. "I get a hot rock dropped in my lap and the next thing I know here's the Director of Operations breathing on me." He glanced at the twenty-four-hour wall clock above the banked television sets. It was three minutes past seven in Rome, 1:03 A.M. in Langley. The hour set for the conference call due in two minutes gave an indication of its importance to the Director.

Traina ran a hand over his stubbled cheek and frowned in irritation. Even a man as good at his job as Herrick had to fight for his turf. Traina understood that. But it would go down better if the quarrel weren't at the end of a harrowing flight across the Atlantic and half of Europe in an Air Force F-15, followed by an anticlimactic clattering ride across the top half of the Italian boot in a Swiss helicopter after the revolting discovery in the mountain cottage in Porza-Lugano. Charlie Blaisdell had been dead for at least four days. The smell had been sickening, and the ants the last disgusting straw.

What Traina did not need now was a turf battle with the Rome Station chief.

He said sharply, "I'm here because Wells is here, armed and looking for his grandniece. If it were anyone but Wells, I wouldn't have come. The Judge is damn worried. Aren't you? There's a summit brewing. Wells could kill it."

"Of course I'm worried. Christ, you're talking about the man the President wants for secretary of state. It's only that I don't like the idea of tight coverage. If the Judge didn't think I could handle the situation, why didn't he say so up front?"

"No one doubts your ability, Reuben. But everybody is very agitated about all this. If Wells weren't one of us, it would be different." He stood and walked to the window. He could look down into the embassy parking lot and across the new security wall and its armored television cameras to the corner of Via Boncompagnie and Via Veneto. It was still too early for most of the tourists, but there were some, he noted, already on the prowl, covetous of the items to be had in the fancy shops along Rome's version of Rodeo Drive.

Traina said, "We have to find Wells, Reuben. And we have to hold on to Megan Wells. Agreed? I mean, no matter what. Does Ashburn understand that?"

"Yes."

"You're certain."

"We went over it before I sent him to the Quinns' place."

"We don't want to lose the hostage. But there are worse things that could happen. It is understood, then: We don't *let* them happen." A compromised Secretary of State, Traina thought; if there was something worse than that, it was hard to imagine it. But would Megan Wells see it that way? Would Jack? Or Ashburn?"

A telephone rang amid the papers on Herrick's desk.

"Herrick." A pause, then, "All right. Put it through. And tape it." He hung up the phone and said, "On the center monitor, Frank."

"Where are the cameras?"

Herrick indicated all four walls. Traina could not detect the wall apertures, but knew they were there.

The monitor came alight, and the two men were looking at the Director of Central Intelligence. He was not alone and he was not in his own familiar office. There seemed to be others off camera. Both Traina and Herrick frowned at that.

Judge Street said, "You are taping, Herrick. Turn off the recorders. We will handle it here."

Herrick shot Traina a "subordinates together" glance. Both men were surprised by Street's tense curtness. It was true that the Judge was not an old boy, not an intelligence professional.

But, for all of that, he had been a good DCI, certainly the best the Agency was likely to get at this time. Tension and stress tended to bond men like Herrick and Traina; it set Daniel Street apart.

The Judge began without preamble. "Is there any word on Wells?"

Traina said, "We think he wanted to talk to Blaisdell."

Street's expression suggested that he had never heard of anyone named Blaisdell. Herrick found that very disturbing. So did Traina. Why the charade? For whoever was in the room with him?

"Blaisdell is dead, Judge. He was killed and stuffed in a trunk," Traina said. He was deliberately blunt. Street had to level with his troops or nothing would get done.

Herrick shook his head minutely and said, "I thought you might have heard from Bern Station by now, Judge."

Street looked shaken.

Well, it was time, Traina thought with sudden bitterness, that Daniel Street learned that people died on the Company's business. Sometimes a long while after they thought they were safe.

The Judge looked somewhere off camera to his right.

"I spoke to the Swiss authorities. They will keep us informed," Traina said. "Two confederate people and the cantonal police were with me when we checked Blaisdell's house. They can have no complaint, Judge. Except maybe against Charlie, for getting himself greased on their turf."

"There is no need to be coarse about it, Frank. Particularly if the man was a friend."

Herrick frowned at Traina. Both were thinking: What was *that* about? They knew that Street was something of a prig, but it took more than priggishness to produce so fatuous a remark. Something was making the DCI extremely uncomfortable.

"Quite right, Judge," Traina said tightly. Frowning, he began to fondle his pipe. Herrick doodled on a pad. He let the sheet deliberately fall to the floor. Traina retrieved it. On it Herrick had written: "The President is with him." The word "President" had been underlined three times.

Valentin Ekimov awoke in a cold sweat in his narrow bed under the mansard of the Soviet Embassy in Rome. He had been dreaming about Chairman Kalganin, who had somehow taken the shape of a gigantic bird of prey, too vast to be contained by Ekimov's vision, too gross to do more than waddle obscenely

191

across an empty space with his eyes fixed hungrily upon the dreamer.

But who *was* the bird in his dream, he wondered. It must have been Kalganin. Who else could it have been?

Ekimov's mother, Natalya Ekimova, had liked to whisper mysteriously to her children of her part-gypsy origin. It had driven her husband, Ilarion, to distraction. She seemed incapable of understanding that, although there was no racial prejudice in the Soviet Union—indeed, it was specifically made illegal by the Soviet constitution—no Russian civil servant would be well served by stories of a gypsy wife.

As a little child, Ekimov had been delighted with his mother's gypsy fantasies. But after he had joined the Young Pioneers, the rumor that he was half-gypsy (which was, in fact, absurd) cost him the leadership of the machine-gun unit, one of the proudest and most highly decorated Young Pioneer squads in his age group.

From time to time the old rumor surfaced, even all these years after Natalya Ekimova's death, and each time they did, her son lost some coveted assignment.

He rose shivering from his bed. The heat was iniquitously distributed in the embassy of the workers' state. Juniors, whether military or civilian, were given cold accommodations. The Ambassador, a survivor from Yuri Andropov's regime (and a fellow former KGB general), was convinced that sleeping cold built character.

Ekimov dressed quickly and shaved at the tiny basin in his narrow room. The face in the mirror looked gray. It was the face of a stranger. Yelena Petrovna would not recognize those pallid-blue eyes, or the shadows under them, caused by several days and nights with too little sleep.

The General had been furious that some scruffy Italian papparazzo had photographed him at the airport. He had complained bitterly to Tikhonov, the Resident, about careless security. Colonel Tikhonov had replied sulkily that Italian street photographers were impossible to control. "We are not at home, Comrade General," he had foolishly said. Plakhanov's eyes had gone hard as pebbles, but he had made no direct reply.

Ekimov wondered if the incident of the Italian *pappa* was one of the things he was expected to report directly to Kalganin. He had the uncomfortable feeling that Kalganin had not been frank with him at Teplyy Stan. There had to be more to his work for the Chairman than merely spying on the man he worked for.

General Plakhanov's state of mind made Ekimov apprehensive, and to have been forced into betraying him by the need to protect his own father-in-law's bourgeois greed filled him with angry despair. More was coming from Kalganin, he was sure. He felt like a man in the path of a juggernaut.

Kalganin was already being mentioned as a future general secretary. What could be so important to General Plakhanov that he would defy such a powerful rival?

Though he was, at home, a heavy sleeper, Ekimov was already accustomed to Plakhanov's ascetic work habits, and he made it a point to report early to the office Tikhonov had assigned to the General. He was dismayed to be told by a secretary that the Comrade General had already spent a half hour in the office familiarizing himself with maps of the city, and had gone. No, he'd left no instructions for the Captain, nor did he say at what hour he planned to return to the embassy.

Ekimov felt a combination of guilt, apprehension, and relief. If he was not with the General, he could not spy on him. If he could not spy on him, he did not risk incurring his displeasure. But if he did neither, Kalganin lurked in the shadows, marking down in his black book of sins all of Ekimov's failings.

He tried to think of what he could do at this moment that would improve his situation. He could think of nothing except to wait for General Plakhanov's return.

He located the duty officer's office and stepped inside. He was relieved to discover that the man on standby there was, like himself, a captain.

"Ekimov, comrade," he introduced himself. "From Number 2 Dzerzhinsky." All the junior KGB officers who worked at Dzerzhinsky Square identified themselves that way. There was a touch of insouciant arrogance about it that rather appealed to Ekimov.

The duty officer, a ruddy-faced young man with thinning reddish hair and pale eyes, said, "You came in with General Plakhanov yesterday—the man who made such a stink about the Italian photographers. I'm Kadogin, from Codes and Ciphers." He extended a cold and slightly damp hand.

Ekimov felt constrained to defend Plakhanov. "I have never before been in a place where deplaning Soviet intelligence officers are greeted by free-lance photographers, Comrade Kadogin."

The young man grinned unexpectedly. "*Glasnost*, Ekimov. *Glasnost*."

"General Plakhanov seems to have bolted into the city without me, Kadogin," he said. "Would you have any idea where he might have gone?"

"Goodness no. I'm only a cipher clerk. I don't get to travel about on civilian airliners with generals in mufti." His grin had vanished, and he was now regarding Ekimov with suspicion. He appeared to have assumed that Ekimov was engaged in some sort of head game for his general, perhaps snooping into the attitudes of the men at the Rome Residency.

"I think I will do some sightseeing of my own, then," Ekimov said mysteriously. "Please sign me out until one this afternoon."

"Of course, Comrade Captain. But before you go, there was a message for you from Teplyy Stan. A verbal order from Colonel Malinkovsky." Ekimov had never met Malinkovsky, and he had no idea what his position with the KGB headquarters hierarchy might be.

"You are to report to Major Yevgeny Chebrin before you do anything else. At once, in fact," Kadogin said.

Ekimov felt a chill traveling down his back. "And Comrade Chebrin is . . . ?"

"Our weapons man, comrade. One goes to Chebrin to be equipped with the latest and deadliest. He is *very* good at his job."

Judge Street said, "I am going to assume that you made a personal identification of the person who was murdered in Porza, Frank."

Traina stared straight at the monitor and said flatly, "Yes." The phrase "personal identification" did not begin to describe what it was like to view the corpse of a man killed the way Charlie Blaisdell had been killed and left to ripen from Thursday to Sunday.

"Then there is no doubt whatever that he is a former employee of ours."

"None."

The Judge conferred with someone off camera. Traina wondered if the President was really there. Or was Herrick getting paranoid?

Street said suddenly, "I want all of our people, including you, Frank, to drop this case. Right now."

"*What?*"

"The Agency has no further interest in the case of John Wells,

194

Frank. From this moment, you are to consider it a police matter and stay out of it.''

Traina stared at Herrick, who said nothing, but whose expression spoke volumes.

"Am I to assume that suddenly the government doesn't care about Wells's whereabouts or intentions?'' he asked. "What the hell am I doing here then, Judge?''

"We have been doing some searching here, Frank. I have decided it was a mistake to send you to Rome. I suggest you take the next available flight back to Dulles.'' There was another murmured conference. "Better still, why don't you telephone Hillary and have her join you for a week or ten days in Paris or London. You need a vacation, Frank.''

While Traina digested that improbable message, Judge Street addressed himself to the station chief. "I suggest you retrieve your man Ashburn, Herrick.''

"Just a damned minute, Judge,'' Herrick protested. "Do we have evidence an American girl is being held hostage here or don't we?''

"I said before, it is a police matter.''

Traina refused to accept the shocking turnabout without explanation. He was, after all, the Director of Operations. Either he was trusted or he was not. If the answer was "not,'' his resignation was in order.

"I'm sorry, Judge,'' he said. "It isn't that simple. We owe Jack Wells more than a bug-out. Our people are involved. One of them has been offed in a peculiarly dirty way. I don't hold any particular brief for Blaisdell, but I think we need to know what happened to him and why.''

"Frank, I am ordering you to—''

The Judge was interrupted by the appearance of a familiar image. Herrick had been right. It was the President of the United States. He was in pajamas and dressing gown. The loop must originate in the White House Situation Room, Traina realized.

"Mr. Traina, Mr. Herrick, do you recognize me?''

"Yes, Mr. President,'' both said.

"I am going to instruct Judge Street to give you information that, strictly speaking, you have no need to know. And I am going to confide in you gentlemen a decision I have just taken. A painful decision, I will tell you, since it involves my administration and a close personal friend.''

The photogenic face and the familiar rasping voice were those of a man born for the politics of the late twentieth century.

"It can be no secret to either of you that I hoped to have John Wells as my secretary of state. I regret that this is no longer possible." He smiled charmingly, ruefully. "He has, as our Mexican neighbors put it, *demasiado cola*—too much tail to step on. So there's an end to it." He addressed himself to the Director of Central Intelligence. "Tell them what your people have turned up, Judge. I'm going to bed."

The President of the United States had just delivered a lesson in politics. Faced with the choice of a smooth summit with the Soviets or the well-being of a friend, he had unhesitatingly made the politician's choice.

Forty minutes later, the men in Rome sat before the now gray television monitors and regarded one another warily.

"Who the hell is Gunderson?" Herrick asked.

"A ferret. The Judge thinks highly of him."

"Is his stuff to be trusted?"

"Afraid so, Reuben. He's like a computer."

After the President's intervention, Street had called into the conference the Internal Security man, who had brought all the records he had unearthed from the innards of the Cray.

It sounded as though this time he had been instructed to take an adversarial position in his search of any records dealing with Wells, with Blaisdell, and with the French journalist Megan Wells was known to have married in Saigon in 1972.

"I instructed Gunderson," the Judge had said in his frosty way, "to search the records as though he were the staff counsel for a Senate select committee. He did so."

"First, Blaisdell," Gunderson said eagerly. "We discovered that he met with the then Deputy Director of Operations, Mr. Wells, at Kadena Air Base in Okinawa and flew with him on an Air Force plane to Bangkok. As far as we have been able to ascertain, that was the only time the two men ever met face to face. But the timing is significant. Within three weeks of that odd meeting, Jean Thierry was ambushed and killed by soldiers of the Royal Thai Army."

His youthful face had been flushed with the excitement of the paper chase. He would never operate in the field, but the basement lair of the Super-Cray computer at Langley was hunting ground enough for him.

"I uncovered at least eight significant reports about Thierry. They cover the time from his graduation from the Sorbonne until his death. Two accuse him of sympathy with the Vietcong and the North Vietnamese. Two others suggest that he be denied a visa for travel to the United States—though as far as I know he never asked for such a visa. One signal came from French Military Intelligence. It suggested that he might have been with the Viet Minh at Dien Bien Phu—which was almost impossible. He was in Paris at the Sorbonne in the fifties. But the other three reports were solid stuff. They came from Republic of Vietnam counterintelligence and they accused Thierry of being an agent—not of the North Viets, but of the Soviets. They definitely placed him in Department V of the First Chief Directorate. The name of his controller was Feliks Plakhanov.'' The bright young face was suffused with the pleasure it gave him to announce that name. ''You remember our show-and-tell of Friday night, Mr. Traina? The connection between File and Hausemartin? That almost closes the circle, sir. Mr. Wells tried to turn Plakhanov through Peter Arendt. And Arendt died trying to recross the Wall. A few years later, an agent run by Plakhanov appears in Saigon and romances Mr. Wells's niece off her feet.

''I don't know Mr. Wells's personally, of course, but I know his reputation and his record when he was with the Agency. I think Plakhanov and Thierry made a serious mistake. They didn't think Wells would act so quickly. But he did. I think he gave Blaisdell his orders on that flight between Kadena and Bangkok.'' The ferret shrugged and smiled, probably at the damned deviousness of his fellow man, Traina thought grimly. Judging by his expression, Herrick agreed.

''But Blaisdell was the linchpin of the operation, and he'd gone rotten, I think. He'd been in Southeast Asia too long. He'd made too many promises that were never kept. I think he went into business for himself. I don't believe Thierry was ever in any danger of being killed in that ambush—if it ever really took place. I think Blaisdell and the Thais threw Thierry in prison and then sold him back to Plakhanov.

''I have no idea how long it took or what Blaisdell got for Thierry, but he knew the Russians. If they can get one of their people back, they will, no matter what it costs.'' He smiled thinly. ''Rather admirable, actually, loyalty like that. But I think it was more than that. I think it went back to File–Hausemartin. Plakhanov thought Mr. Wells was responsible for Arendt's death. I suppose maybe he was. But Plakhanov hadn't forgotten it. And you know what, Mr. Traina? I think he hasn't forgotten it yet.

''Jean Thierry is the Frenchman, of course. And Mr. Wells knows it. Plakhanov and Thierry are going to kill Wells, Mr.

Traina, or he is going to kill them. And I am probably out of line to say so, but that is why Mr. Wells has gone from almost being our next secretary of state to being a political liability.''

Judge Street had interrupted harshly with the statement that no one was interested in Gunderson's political opinions.

Yet what the ferret had said was no more than the truth, and both Traina and Herrick knew it. They had, in fact, known beforehand most of what they had been told. It needed only, as Gunderson had said, the closing of the circle.

When the Judge was back on the circuit, Herrick had demanded, ''This is all very well, sir. But we have a hostage situation on our hands here. What are we to do about it?''

''You are to do nothing whatever. As I said before. It is a police matter. An *Italian* police matter. The Department of State is in touch with the Italian authorities.''

''*State?*''

''That is correct. The subject is no longer open for discussion.''

After the Washington loop was broken, Herrick had asked about Gunderson, and the two men fell silent for a few minutes. Then Herrick said, ''I wouldn't have believed it of him.''

''Street?''

''The President.''

Traina said dryly, ''Politicians who let friendship come before politics don't get to be president. He's thinking about the next election and the party.''

''I think it stinks.''

''You'll never be president,'' Traina said. ''You better talk to Ashburn, hadn't you? And let him know the game has been canceled?''

Herrick dialed the number of the Quinns' villa. But it was too late. Zachary Quinn informed him coldly that Megan Wells and David Ashburn had left early and were driving to Rome.

Herrick looked at Traina. ''Now what do I do? Call the police and have them arrested?''

''Watch and wait, Reuben,'' Traina said. ''That's all we can do until State has its say.''

''State. *Shit!*'' Herrick said. ''What are you going to do?''

''You heard the Judge. I'm going to take a vacation,'' Traina said, standing. ''But I don't think I'll call Hilly just yet.''

Dressed in well-cut gray suit and topcoat, General Feliks Plakhanov appeared to be an early-morning stroller on the Piazza di Monte Savello. With a regular but unhurried pace he crossed the piazza and turned south along the river. The trees lining the bank were not yet in leaf, and they made stark dark patterns against the gray March sky. As he approached the Ponte Palatino, the rush of the Tiber's current against the freestanding arch of the Ponte Rotto—the Broken Bridge—made a sound that could be heard even above the rumbles of Rome's early traffic.

Plakhanov reached the Palatino and stood for a moment looking at the river and the ancient remnant standing in the stream. There was something intensely satisfying about a culture that cared so much about its past that it went to such lengths to preserve its ruins.

That was a very *Russian* thought, he told himself. Though hardly a Soviet one. Not for the first time in these ancient and grand surroundings, he thought about Peter Arendt. Peter had loved old things, fine things, impractical things. He had had a wonderfully self-effacing sense of humor about it, however. He had once obtained for "Lieber Feli" a copy of a book written during the Nazi times about Hitler's vast and grandiose plans for rebuilding the Third Reich once the war was won. The sketches of public buildings far surpassed in monstrous taste even the socialist-modernist excesses perpetrated in the Soviet Union on behalf of Joseph Stalin.

Plakhanov gazed at the flowing Tiber and half smiled in memory. Peter knew that his Feli was a Stalinist. "But politically only, surely, Feli? You couldn't possibly admire the Premier's taste?" And then, translating, he read to Plakhanov the "National Socialist theory of ruins," a philosophy that was to have been applied to all Nazi civic construction, so that in five thousand years, or ten, the ruins of the public buildings of Nazi Germany would delight the eye more completely than the Parthenon, the Colosseum, and Karnak did today.

Remembering, Plakhanov felt his eyes grow moist. To have been responsible for the murder of such a young man as Peter Arendt was a great crime—one that cried out to be avenged.

He looked beyond the traffic on the bridge and saw the Frenchman approaching, his half-ruined face partially hidden behind mirror glasses. It was said that the eyes were the mirrors of the soul. What did those insectile horrors conceal?

He waited to speak until the Frenchman was face to face with him.

"Paladin is in Rome," he said.

"I expected him to be," the assassin replied.

There's a stench of death about this man, Plakhanov thought suddenly. I have put it there. I have guided him, used him. What would Peter think of him?

The answer to that was not difficult to guess. Peter Arendt would have been horrified by Jean Thierry. What may have begun well had become a power of evil.

The man had had his own daughter abducted. If he had ever troubled himself about right and wrong, that day was long gone. Perhaps he left the ability to make such fine judgments in Bung Kan prison.

The Frenchman leaned on the stone parapet of the bridge and with a slow smile pointed to an opening in the stonework by the riverside. "Do you know what that is, Comrade General?"

Plakhanov shook his head. Somehow, over the years, he had come to speak less and less with the Frenchman. What needed to be said was said, but since Thierry's Bung Kan adventure, the two men had "conversed" little.

"It's fitting we meet here. That is the opening of the Cloaca Massima. Through that flowed most of the *merde* of ancient Rome."

Plakhanov felt flustered and disgusted by the implication.

"That is interesting, I am sure. But now tell me how you plan to deal with Paladin?"

Plakhanov stared at his own distorted images in the mirror eyeglasses. Behind them, he realized, was a madness to match his own.

The Frenchman's scarred lips formed a smile of sorts. "Simply, Comrade General, very simply. Today I plan to trap him. Tomorrow I plan to kill him."

30. THE ABRUZZI

It rained that morning in the Gran Sasso, a spring rain, more mist than storm, but cold and windy in the mountain valleys.

They left early, before first light, in Megan's rented Alfetta. Both Zachary and Mary had risen to see them off. David told

Zachary what he had seen near the pass above the villa. "They might not be back, but you can't be sure. I'd call the police. Or maybe some of your hired hands."

Zachary said, "I can handle it."

Probably he could, David thought. But he could not forget that Zachary's last fire fight had taken place near Saragossa in 1938.

"Zach," he said, "call in some law. The *brigatisti* have a bounty out on Mary."

Zachary turned away and stood with his arm around Mary's waist. We two, he was saying to David, are a team. We can take care of ourselves.

Right, David thought. So never advise old warriors. End of story. Megan kissed Mary's cheek and got into the car. David followed and started the engine.

North of L'Aquila the road was under heavy repair, so David turned onto the secondary highway through Tornimparte. Megan had been silent since leaving the Villa Stefano. David thought she might have dozed. She looked exhausted, and he felt a stab of guilt. What sort of man took advantage of a grieving woman's need for support to seduce her?

One who loved her, he told himself. Not nobly, like some "parfit knight" out of Malory, but selfishly, like the twentieth-century man he was.

Megan *had* been sleeping fitfully, and when she woke the sun was shining in a water-blue sky. The mountain stream beside the road fell in a spring torrent over steps of granite and shale. The mist caught the sunlight and made a brilliant rainbow that shifted and vanished, only to reappear each time they changed direction.

"What happened to the rain?" she asked wearily.

"We're back in the old Papal States. It can't rain here without a dispensation."

She essayed a thin smile. "You're irreverent. Isn't that against Company regulations?"

"You're confusing the Company with the Boy Scouts."

"Not likely," she said. She took a comb from her parka pocket and began to pull it through her auburn hair.

"How do you feel?" David asked.

"Better. I can't think why. Maybe it's because we're doing something at last."

"You can't rush these things, Meg." The trouble was that even those who presumed to write the book on handling terrorist-

201

hostage situations, the Israelis, had no really clear idea of how to deal with them. Some terrorists were frauds, ready to collapse at the first sign of resistance. Others were martyrs in the making, eager to die in any number of gruesomely appropriate ways for their beliefs. And there was an infinity of variations between those extremes.

To some of the deep thinkers at the Rome Station, the fact that the person who planned this was the hostage's father suggested that the plan was designed to prevent the girl's being harmed. David was not so sanguine. His gut instinct told him that the reverse was true: that any man who would have his daughter—no matter how unfamiliar to him—taken hostage in a Cold War game would also be willing to see her killed.

What David sensed was a step-by-step capture of the Wells clan. One took the easiest mark and used her to entice the next easiest, which was Megan, so that finally, somehow, the old Cold Warrior dropped into the pit almost willingly.

But what was the purpose? Simply to discredit Wells would be a Cold War victory, but he was no longer in the front line of battle. He had not been for many years. Was it possible that the opposition, gross as it often was, had become so inept as to believe that Wells could be turned? That kind of thinking had gone out in the fifties.

"What time at the Sword and Scabbard?"

David hated testing her. But he had to know she would hold nothing back. He had known the time and place of the Tuesday meeting ever since Herrick's Italian burglars had brought back the film they had exposed in the Sword and Scabbard. But she knew nothing about that.

"Tomorrow. At ten," Megan said. Her voice was scarcely more than a whisper. "He actually laughed, David. He laughed and said, 'At ten, when the neighborhood is asleep.' "

"All right," he said. "We are in plenty of time. Try to get some more sleep."

She rested her head against the seat and closed her eyes. And David thought bitterly: What a wonderful thing a man's love is! By badgering my way into her bed, I've made her too tired to lie to me.

Megan slept fitfully for a few minutes and then awoke with a start.

"It will be all right, Meg," David said.

She regarded him bleakly. "Will it, David? He has my daughter."

"We'll get her back. We'll have all the help we need from the Italians, and we have the Company, Meg. I know you don't want to hear it, but you are one of us. We don't abandon our own."

Megan showed a thin smile. "Uncle Jack speaking."

"D. Ashburn speaking, Meg."

"He recruited you, didn't he?"

"Yes."

"Why did you do it, David?"

"I thought it was important. I still do."

She stared out the window at the mountains. "I hate it."

"You always made that clear enough."

She looked at him with an expression of perplexity. "I don't understand, David. I never understood Uncle Jack, either."

David flexed his hands on the steering wheel. How could you explain color to a blind person. Worse still, to a *blinded* person, one who had been used, taken advantage of, battered, by an enemy not, unfortunately, too different from those who claimed to be her friends.

But there was a level beyond the personal, and it was there that one reached out to protect the abstractions that made life in the West what it was.

"No intelligence service is perfect. No intelligence officer is a saint," he said.

"Don't tell me about ends and means, David. It is *my* daughter Jean's taken."

"I'm sorry, Meg. But it's just too easy to make judgments that way, claiming that the end justifies the means or that it never does. Sometimes the ends *do* justify the means. One has to make adjustments. That's part of being human."

"You sound like Uncle Jack," she said bitterly.

"Do I? I'm glad of that."

Anger flared in her eyes. "Are you? Do you have any idea of what it was like growing up as John Wells's niece? As Matt and Denise Wells's daughter? I don't remember what they looked like, but they were there, with me, every day of my life. Uncle Jack never let me forget who I was. I was the daughter of a hero and a heroine." She looked away, at the steep mountainside. "Why do you suppose I went to Saigon? I was trying to live up to my breeding, like a mare on the racecourse."

She ran a hand through her hair and shook her head. "God, that isn't right, either. It was just another box."

"Box?"

"That's the way I lived my life, David. In one pretty box after another. Uncle Jack started it, and I never discovered how to make things different. First, there was the special box Uncle Jack made for me when I was a child. I was in a box labeled 'Matt and Denise's little girl.' Uncle Jack spent as much time with me as he could. It wasn't much, but he was wonderful to me when he could be. I almost believed I was *his* daughter. But he never allowed that. He loved me. I never doubted that. But I belonged to the family ghosts and I had to live up to *them*.

"Then there was the school box. I went to school in Lausanne. Everyone treated me well. I was a rich American's child, but I was foreign, of course. I spoke French as well as I spoke English, but that didn't matter.

"When the other girls went home for holidays, I went to my grandparents'. Another box. A huge, quiet old house. Grand-mère still grieves for her Denise. She will until she dies. I remember going to Mass with her, but since I couldn't remember Matt and Denise I could never share what she felt. Grand-père was wounded in the war, and I was expected to understand that and be very still. He had had a regiment in the Caserne Maginot. He's almost ninety now. When he could have me back for holidays, Uncle Jack always did. But most of my holidays were spent in Normandy with the de Lattres. A box, you see?"

"It sounds lonely," David said.

"I didn't know that's what it was. Until one summer I went home with a school friend. Her name was Zibby Neville. Zibby for Elizabeth. The family, English Catholics, lived in Surrey. There's nothing very remarkable about Surrey. But families live there. Zibby had three sisters and two brothers. Mr. Neville ran an automobile dealership, Mrs. Neville ran the house, the family, the children. She was very special to me." Megan leaned against the seat back and closed her eyes momentarily. "Uncle Jack had them investigated!" She shook her head in disbelief. "I don't know how they found out. But they did, and Zibby told me about it when we went back to Lausanne. I was humiliated. One can be very prickly at age eleven, David.

"I thought when I went to Stanford that everything would be different, but nothing important had changed. I was still in a box. I don't know what happened, but there was a political-science professor there who seemed able to get all sorts of secret information. He was short, about my height, and had a beard and long hair. He always wore jeans and work shirts. He set the students to raiding the Computer Center and trashing the Medical Center. And he made me his special project because Uncle Jack worked for the CIA.

"When Uncle Jack found out, he wanted to take me out of Stanford and find a place for me in the East. I said no, that I wouldn't stand for it. I was trying to climb out of my 'Meg the Student' box, and he wouldn't have that. So I declared my independence, or so I thought. I dropped out of school and applied for work with AID." She smiled ruefully. "I got the job, of course. Uncle Jack pulled some wires in Washington. He had another box ready for me."

She looked steadily at David as he drove. "You have never asked me how I came to marry Jean Thierry. You want to know, don't you?"

"I want to know everything, anything, about you."

"I was nineteen. I'd never had a man before. Nothing but fumbling boys. That's one of the worst boxes of all—knowing almost nothing about men, so that when one chooses *you*, you are certain that it's for love."

David said, "I thought it might be something like that."

"Exactly like that."

"I wish I had known."

"I should have told you, but you frightened me."

"Frightened you?"

"You were a man, and I thought I saw Uncle Jack and Thierry in you. You did go your way, after all."

David lit a cigarette. Megan put a hand on his thigh and said, "You shouldn't do that, you know." The bleak smile returned. "God, isn't that ridiculous? To say that to someone with a job like yours."

He held her hand.

She said, "What happened to the *autostrada*?"

"We'll be back on it soon."

"I keep forgetting you live here."

"Near enough. In Trastevere."

"Across-the-Tiber. What's it like?"

"Like the Left Bank in Paris. With a Roman flavor."

Megan removed her hand. "I should have asked before this. Did you ever get married, David?"

"Yes."

"What happened?"

"It didn't work out."

"Why?"

He smiled. "She wasn't bred for the racecourse."

205

"Oh, David." She breathed wearily and rested her forehead against his shoulder.

"There are boxes enough for everyone, Meg. Even for the likes of me."

"Not you. Never you."

"Me. You were over there. You saw it. Parts of it, at least. I enlisted because I thought it was the thing one should do. When Kennedy said we would bear any burden, I believed him. I bought it, and I wanted to do what was right. Then when the war was lost, when the men I served with were frittered away like low-denomination poker chips in a backroom game, I was angry. But I still believed in what the country had tried to do in Vietnam. That was the box I came home in. That's where I was when I met you. I didn't care that much about being a lawyer, Meg. In my mind I was still driving my Huey gunship. Well, it might have been the wrong battle in the wrong place, and it was sure as hell run badly, but it was my battle, and it is still going on. It is going to keep going on until the Soviets understand that we won't quit, that we won't accept their sort of world.

"And that's why I am what I am. That's why I think there are things that need doing. I wish we were perfect, but we aren't. We just have to do the best we can." He brushed her forehead with his lips and then asked, "What ever became of Zibby?"

Megan smiled bleakly. "She's married to her third husband. I saw her when she came to California on her last honeymoon. All she asked about was what had become of my marvelous, mysterious uncle."

"Boxes," David said, and for a long while they rode in silence.

Near Leofreni, David stopped to get fuel for the Alfetta.

Megan went to the roadside store and returned with prosciutto, fresh bread, and a bottle of Chianti. "We'll eat on the way," she said.

A full mile up the road, a dusty Mercedes saloon waited on the grassy verge. When the Alfetta resumed its journey toward Carsoli and the entrance to the *autostrada*, the Mercedes, too, moved out.

In the distance could be seen the wide concrete ribbon of the new expressway to Rome, but where they were the road wound through small meadowed valleys and empty fields. The sun was thin in the rain-washed air, but bright with the pallid brilliance of advancing spring.

"Let's stop," Megan said.

David recognized and understood the uncertainty of one who approaches an unknown battle, the doubt, reluctance, anxiety. At such moments, one surrendered, if wise, to the frailties of simply being human.

He pulled the Alfetta into a grove of willows overlooking a tiny tributary of the Turano River. The sun was high, and the light was dappled under the willows. High overhead a hawk wheeled and soared in the mountain thermals.

"What a lovely spot!" Megan said as they got out of the car. "Where is everyone?"

"There was a farmhouse back there."

"If this is farmland, where are the farmers?"

"It won't be planted until the end of April. There's a shorter growing season up here than down nearer the coast."

"I didn't remember you were a farmer, David."

"My family came from Nebraska," he said with a grin. "But I won't deceive you. Most of what I know about the Italian countryside I learned from reading Company papers. National Technical Means. That lets us snoop on everyone's harvest from four hundred miles up there."

Megan looked at the pale, bright sky and shuddered.

"Can they see us?"

"They could if they were looking. Does that bother you?"

"I think it does. What ever happened to our right to be private?"

"When we are challenged," he said, "then we fight. It is the best we can do."

"Horrible," Megan said.

She *is* a public defender, David thought. Love her, love it all. Her quirks, her ideals, her concerns. Her daughter, too.

In a sunny clearing in the meadow, a quarter-mile from where they had left the Alfetta, they lunched on sun-dried ham, warm fresh bread, and light red wine. There was almost no traffic on the road so near the *autostrada*.

They ate and drank in a deepening silence. Megan looked closely at David's face. Pleasant features, regular and unremarkable enough to get lost in a crowd. But the eyes and the firm set of the mouth she recognized. He had the inner stillness of a man at home in the shadows, a man who could find his way through the maze in the hall of mirrors.

Megan knew those qualities well. She had grown up in houses filled with such young men, drawn there by the brilliance of

207

Uncle Jack. And perhaps, too, by the romance of his precursors, Matthew Wells and Denise de Lattre.

She thought about Jean Thierry. At first with anger, fear, and loathing. But then some inner stillness of her own allowed her to see him as he was, as he had always been. I need not have married him, she thought. I was not really so ignorant of what he was. Mary warned me. As did others. Even old Charlie Blaisdell cautioned me about him. And yet . . . And yet . . .

Was it really so? Was there a need in the blood? Did secret men touch some wellspring in her?

David said, caressingly, "Meg, look at me."

She accepted him as protection against despair. He leaned forward and kissed her.

"David . . ."

He touched her cheek with his fingertips. "There's time," he said. He kissed her again.

"Oh, why?" she whispered.

"I don't know. Do I have to explain it?" His hands rested on her shoulders. "Tell me to stop and I will."

For answer she put her arms about him and drew him down into the grass. I'm not like this, she thought. I can't simply stop thinking and *feel*.

But she could. She must. There was a void in her that needed desperately to be filled. She needed to be needed. She had always yearned to reach for love wherever it was to be found. Had Denise de Lattre been like this, snatching at love wherever and whenever it was offered, no matter the dangers? Uncle Jack had often told her how her father and mother had met in the Resistance movement during the war. Had they made love in the rainy, misty forest while Nazi soldiers hunted them?

David's mouth opened on hers, and she searched with her tongue. She felt his hands on the nakedness between her sweater and the band of her jeans. She sat up and pulled the sweater over her head, unfastened her jeans, and slipped them off. She sat naked in the grass, her breasts hard, her mons damp.

She had never been like this, naked under the open sky. The breeze made her aware of her most intimate flesh. She was half-frightened, half-delighted. David was upon her, searching, kissing.

She spread her thighs and felt him enter her. This was more than it had been at the villa. This was elemental, an act of lust and passion that was needed to overcome her doubts and her fear. She wrapped her legs around him and cried out savagely.

Un coup de foudre, the French called it, this sudden explosion of desire. It was the right name, she thought, for this heedless, headlong surge of passion. Uncle Jack was right, after all. I am my mother's daughter.

From a turn in the road on the hillside above, Lars, the Swedish would-be rapist of the lesbian Hanalore, watched the Americans making love. His erection, thick and painful, thrust against his tight denim trousers. Angrily and enviously, he held the binoculars with one hand and masturbated with the other. After he ejaculated, he had nothing with which to clean himself, so he used pages from a book Calvo had given him to read and which he did not understand: *The Letters of Mikhail Alexandrovich Bakunin*.

31. MOSCOW

An early twilight was descending on the white birch forest of Gorky Park. A flight of ravens circled in the blue-gray heights above the treetops. Kalganin raised his eyes and squinted at them. There was something infinitely sad about ravens, he thought. They were like the black spirits of disappointed men endlessly scanning the earth for their lost opportunities.

He walked briskly over the still nearly frozen ground, feeling the firm strike of his boot heels against the cold, solid earth. At a distance, his black Mercedes followed him, rolling with Teutonic silence and smoothness along the tarred surface of the narrow road.

There was a curfew in Gorky Park these days. *Glasnost* had turned Moscow's parks into centers of hooliganism. Kalganin had solved the problem, temporarily, to be sure, by closing the parks at 6:00 P.M. This ensured good order during the hours of darkness and had the additional benefit of leaving the parks free for the enjoyment of persons who appreciated them.

Kalganin was considering Captain Ekimov, at present far from the disciplined atmosphere of Number 2 Dzerzhinsky Square and Teplyy Stan. He considered that he was using Ekimov as a poker—to stir a fire. An interesting fire. It was always pleasing to see a potential rival burning himself to cinders. Soon there would be only ashes left of Feliks Ivanovich Plakhanov.

The man was resolved to carry out his Paladin plan. Kalganin had been certain he would defy orders, and he had. Whatever fed Plakhanov's obsession was a mystery. But it was powerful, deadly, self-destructive. Paladin was almost certainly an operation years in the making. But it was, somehow, overbalanced. Yes, that was the word that seemed best to describe it.

John Wells had been a thorn in the ribs of the Soviet Union for years. He had been used time and again as a negotiator in situations in which the Americans wished only to obstruct, complain, and protest.

The man was implacable. At Geneva he had been a black tower of anti-Sovietism. Without him, the Soviet negotiators would have produced more for the Motherland, and with considerably less effort.

It had been Wells who was sent by the American side to visit the Krasnoyarsk battle-management radar and the nuclear-weapons testing grounds at Semipalatinsk.

The man, Kalganin thought grimly, would have made a good Soviet citizen.

Plainly it was to the advantage of the USSR that Wells should not become Secretary of State. Yet Plakhanov's zeal to prevent it seemed excessive.

Killing members of the ruling class was always risky, but the attempt, years ago, on Pope John Paul II had set a kind of grisly standard.

Common sense had led every thinking investigator past the Bulgarians straight to the KGB. But common sense did not give the enemies of socialism the answer to the vital question: Do we really want to know that the security service of a state armed with twenty-five thousand nuclear warheads would be so rash?

The lesson had not been lost on Andropov's successors, nor on Gregor Borisovich Kalganin. If the killing was rash enough, the West—indeed, the world—would ignore it.

Kalganin turned and marched swiftly back to his German limousine. To his new driver he gave the order: "To Teplyy Stan. Use the lights and siren."

Within minutes the black Mercedes with the flaming-sword-and-shield badge on its grille was racing through the streets of Moscow toward the ring road and the special expressway north.

Deep inside the Kremlin, the General Secretary paused in his perusal of the papers on his *fin-de-siècle* desk, listened to the faint sound of a siren, wondered briefly, and returned to work.

32. ROME

In the Soviet Embassy in Rome, as in Soviet diplomatic missions all over the world, the intelligence officers customarily took their meals apart from other members of the staff. And in an embassy where security had a particularly high priority, officers above the grade of colonel dined with the Resident and his chief deputies in a special room on the floor above that in which the *krestianin*—the peasants—were fed.

At the stroke of seven, Feliks Plakhanov, in full uniform, was shown to his table by a steward. Valentin Ekimov, much distressed by having been at loose ends all day and upset by the instructions he had received from Teplyy Stan and from the formidable weapons expert in the subbasement, followed Plakhanov into the senior officers' dining room.

Whatever had happened to the General today, Ekimov thought, it seemed to have done wonders for his disposition. Plakhanov took his place at his table, spread the starched white napkin over his well-tailored legs, and ordered a bottle of Valpolicella.

Ekimov was unaccustomed to seeing his dour chief in a joyous mood.

Ekimov's own spirits were sagging badly. He did not have the temperament for intrigue. At this moment he wished for nothing more than to be in his Moscow apartment, in bed with a naked Yelena Petrovna, drinking vodka and listening to sentimental music.

But it was Yelena Petrovna's idiot father and his peculations that had put him into his current situation. When all this was finished, he was never going to allow Petrov Orlov to forget what his son-in-law had done for him.

"Have you a problem, Ekimov?"

211

Startled, Ekimov was certain he must look hangdog and guilty. "Problem, Comrade General? I have no problem."

"What a fortunate man you are then," Plakhanov said. "Most mere mortals have more problems than they can handle."

He waited while the steward opened the wine. After sniffing the cork, he signaled for the wine to be poured. He lifted his glass and looked at the light through the red liquid.

"Look before you taste it, Ekimov."

Mystified, Ekimov did as he was told. To him, wine was wine, and, frankly, he preferred stronger stuff.

Plakhanov said quietly, "It is too thin for blood. It is more like river water with blood in it." Did blood run into the Spree that wintry day?

"Sir?"

Plakhanov lifted the glass to his lips and drank. Only after he had drained the glass did he reply, "Yes? What is it?"

"I didn't quite understand what you said, Comrade General. About the Spree? Is that the river in Germany?"

Plakhanov's pale eyes turned cold as winter. "I said nothing about any river, Comrade Captain."

Ekimov flushed. "I misunderstood the Comrade General. I ask your pardon."

Plakhanov made a dismissive gesture with his long, slender hand. He asked, "Did Tikhonov keep you busy today?"

"No, sir. I did not see the Resident."

"Then did you use your time to advantage?"

"Sir?"

"This is a historic city. Corrupt, but ancient, and filled with significant things. Who knows when you may see it again."

I hope I never see it again, Ekimov thought miserably. Oh, for a transfer back to the Sluzhba and away from these people of the elite who thought strange thoughts, spoke oddly, and scared the shit out of a simple man.

Colonel Tikhonov strode heavily into the room in civilian clothes. The shiny Italian suit made him resemble a corpse, Plakhanov thought suddenly, like a bloated body in one of the black plastic sheets the army used to wrap the mutilated dead in Afghanistan for shipment back to the military crematories.

Tikhonov made his way through the dining room until he stood before Plakhanov.

"Comrade General, I had intended to ask you to dine with me and my wife, but I could not find you until now." He gave

Ekimov a withering glance, as though the General's elusiveness was the Captain's fault.

"My regrets," Plakhanov said shortly. "But I am here unofficially, Comrade Colonel. I should have had to decline."

Tikhonov regarded his superior with what he had hoped was a respectful expression. Actually, he was uncomfortable about the rumors he had heard for years about Plakhanov, and now that the man was before him, he found that he loathed and feared him.

"I have received a call from Teplyy Stan, Comrade General. I think perhaps we should discuss it." Once again he looked coldly at Ekimov.

"I think the Colonel would feel more confident, Comrade Captain, if you would leave us alone. Go have your meal with the junior officers. Take the wine with you. Tell the steward."

Ekimov stood, drew himself to attention, clicked his heels, and rushed out of the dining room, forgetting the wine.

Tikhonov held himself rigidly as he addressed Plakhanov. Their relationship had got off on a bad footing the moment the General had deplaned from the Lufthansa flight. Next had come the cryptic message from the Chairman for Ekimov. Tikhonov, despite being Resident, had been specifically excluded from its distribution—a highly unusual procedure. Moreover, Plakhanov was not even to be told that the message had been received.

And now here was another message from Chairman Kalganin. This one was to be delivered to Plakhanov verbally, by the Resident. Such instructions made Tikhonov uneasy. To be the only sharer of verbal messages could be dangerous.

He said, "May I sit down, Comrade General?"

Plakhanov nodded.

Tikhonov took Ekimov's abandoned chair. "We have just had the signal from Teplyy Stan, Comrade General."

Plakhanov said, "Deliver it, Comrade Colonel."

"Here?"

"Your establishment is secure?"

"Of course."

"Then deliver your message."

Tikhonov's face reddened.

"I am to tell you that 'Paladin' has been re-evaluated and may proceed. I am not familiar with any operation of that name. However, I am also instructed to make available to you whatever resources you need. The Chairman suggests that you 'may wish to consider a diversion.' Since I am not privy to Paladin, Comrade General, I do not know what assets you will require or when. Would you care to enlighten me?''

Plakhanov felt his heartbeat quickening. He had been resolved to sacrifice his career—or what remained of it—to Operation Paladin. Was it possible that the Politburo had reversed the General Secretary? What else could account for this radical change?

''What forces does the Italian Army have in the city?'' he asked.

''Very few. Italians are still sensitive about too many uniforms in Rome,'' Tikhonov answered.

''But the antiterrorist battalion. Where is it stationed?''

''For the last few months at Ostia.''

''Numbers?''

''Six hundred men.''

Plakhanov sat with an inner stillness his enemies would have recognized. Presently he asked, ''What assets have we? For overt action?''

Like many Soviets, Colonel Tikhonov was a hoarder by nature. At home in Moscow, his storage rooms were filled with Western food and trinkets he had collected over the years and saved ''for leaner times.'' ''Most of our finances have gone into equipping the Red Brigades,'' he said.

''I know what passes for a commando in the Brigades, Comrade Colonel. I have developed a mission for the Palmiro Togliatti Unit in Operation Paladin.''

Tikhonov was growing distinctly uncomfortable. He was being kept in ignorance in his own residency. ''May I at least know what the purpose of Paladin is?''

''It will be better if you do not know, Comrade Colonel. This is a First Chief Directorate staff operation.''

''I understand,'' Tikhonov said.

You do not, Plakhanov thought, but it doesn't matter. The idea that had come to mind at the first mention of ''diversion'' seemed to mature almost instantaneously.

''That woman who wrote the book about the Bulgarians and the Pope. She lives nearby?''

''Yes. In Santo Stefano.''

''Good.'' Plakhanov paused, considering, then said, ''I wish to visit the Palmiro Togliatti Unit.''

Tikhonov bridled. The Americans had an expression he thought useful to any bureaucrat intent on protecting his rear. They said: ''Not on my watch, you don't.''

"Comrade General, I must protest. If something were to go wrong and a general of the KGB was discovered among a gang of *brigatista* hooligans, we could have a disaster on our hands."

To Tikhonov's surprise, Plakhanov raised no objection. "Very well, Comrade Colonel. Have the unit commander brought here to me before midnight. I will have instructions for him." He stood. "I seem to have lost my appetite for dinner. Give the order and then join me in my quarters. I have a bottle of vodka and a tin of caviar." Then he added the bait he was certain would bring the gross man to heel. "I will tell you the origin of Operation Paladin."

Tikhonov said grudgingly, "May I at least know one thing, Comrade General?"

"You may ask."

"When does Paladin run?"

"Tomorrow, Comrade Tikhonov."

March 17

the last day . . .

For among my people
are found wicked men:
they lay wait,
as he that setteth snares;
they set a trap,
they catch men.

—Jeremiah 5:26

33. THE ABRUZZI/
SANTO STEFANO

Hanalore, the German comrade, rode in the back of the Mercedes with the weapons, her handsome, masculine face somber and perplexed.

She had never regarded herself as a thinker or planner. The philosophical arguments for the things done first by the Baader-Meinhof and now by the Red Brigades had never been of interest to her. For her, it sufficed that the organizations to which she had devoted five of her twenty-two years of life were dedicated to the destruction of a society she loathed. It was all very well to play with Marxist catchphrases and paramilitary posturings, but she felt it was enough that she could repay the sneers and dirty whisperings of her schoolmates with bombs and bullets.

Nothing in her short life had given her much pleasure. Before she discovered that her preference was for members of her own sex, it had been apparent to others. She had been sent home from boarding school, escorted by a provost. What the bitch had told her pretentious parents had been enough to humiliate them. Other schools, less permissive, had followed. Twice again she had been sent home as "odd" and a troublemaker. By that time, she understood the nature of her "oddity."

Her parents, well off and embarrassed by an obviously—and increasingly defiant—lesbian daughter, then made the cataclysmically inappropriate decision to try to engage her to the son of a dependent family.

Hanalore, at seventeen, had stood five feet ten inches and had a physique well suited to an Olympic sprinter. She was strong, increasingly less feminine as she grew more mature, and in the process of discovering that she could enjoy her lesbianism.

219

It was this girl that the bribed suitor decided could be "made right" by a night of sexual intercourse with a proper man—himself, of course.

She left him bleeding in the bathroom of his Munich flat, his lips lacerated, several teeth missing, a wrist broken, and genitalia so battered it took almost three months for him to sit without pain.

Hanalore, already recruited by the Munich Baader-Meinhof, began her Marxist adventure while her would-be seducer was in the hospital. Her parents, undoubtedly much relieved, disowned her. She did not see either of them again until the afternoon when, hiding in a crowd, she saw her mother's corpse, with a half-dozen others, on the floor of the central station of her native Munich after an attack by a unit of her own Baader-Meinhof remnant.

She felt nothing. No sorrow, no compassion, no remorse. Only a cold and dispassionate sense of the fitness of her mother's end.

Though Hanalore had little intellect and no fear, she had developed what she considered a talent for making things "fit," as she had that day in Munich.

And that was what was troubling her now.

In the late hours of last evening, Gianbattista Calvo had been summoned to meet with a mysterious Russian at the Soviet Embassy. When he returned at midnight, he had seemed agitated and displeased.

He had assembled the group on the top story of the ballet school to pass on the orders he had been given. The unit had had its role expanded in the coming action, he'd said. Lars's request for information as to what, exactly, they were supposed to accomplish in Rome had been met with a cold, Italianate stare.

All *brigatisti*, Calvo had said, had to be aware of the presence in Italy of the woman Mary Quinn, the journalist who had, before all the world, accused the Red Brigades of being in the pay of, and under the control of, the Soviet Union. It had been Quinn, he reminded his troops, who had accused the Bulgarians of complicity in the attempted assassination of the Pope—an accusation that by inference put the responsibility for the act at the doorstep of the KGB.

"Let no one doubt that the woman Quinn is an enemy of peace," he'd said. "Therefore—"

And with the "therefore" had come the orders he had received from his controller at the Soviet Embassy. The Togliatti Unit, already divided, was to be split again. Six comrades were to be dispatched today to the village of Santo Stefano. From there they were to deploy and wait until noon, at which time they were to attack the villa where the Quinn woman and her husband lived. They were to press the attack home as strongly as the attack against the power station that had blooded the unit. They were to kill Quinn and her husband between the hours of twelve and one.

Mariella had frowned at the new orders. "It is a diversion," she said. "What does the main unit do?"

"We stand by to deal with a hostage," Calvo had said.

"The American girl?"

He'd shaken his head. "One of you—either you, Mariella, or you, Hanalore—will go to the girl early tomorrow morning and liquidate her. She has served her purpose and is of no further value."

Hanalore had felt an odd twist of pleasure in her belly, a delight that was almost sexual. She, unlike Mariella, had had no dealings with Denny Wells. But the thought of killing her was a thing to be savored. It appealed to her sense of the fitness of things. It was she the Frenchman had used on the telephone to reach the girl's mother in San Francisco. It seemed right to be in at the death.

But Mariella had said immediately, "I'll do it. Hanalore can go with Lars and the rest to Santo Stefano."

It was arranged that way. A soldier of the revolution rose above disappointments and did not begrudge a comrade's role, but she hated thinking of the dirty Italian street urchin as a comrade. Especially as a superior. But there it was. The girl, she had to admit, had an animal cleverness.

Lars, Erich, Paolo, Hussein, and Julio crowded the Mercedes. They were all carrying AK-47 assault rifles and six spare clips of ammunition. Hussein, who had been trained in Lebanon, had wanted to take one of the mortars, or the RPG-7. But it could not be allowed. The rocket-propelled grenade launcher was needed for the defense of the ballet school, and there also had not been room for it. Calvo had forbidden the stealing of another vehicle, for fear it might be spotted on the road by the police.

Outside, a gray light drained the colors from the countryside. It had begun to rain. The right-hand windshield wiper made a muddy smear on the glass. Hanalore glanced at the large aviator's wristwatch she wore. It was nearly eight. At eight o'clock, Mariella was supposed to be cleaning up the safe house where the American girl was hidden. She closed her eyes and smiled as she imagined the report of Mariella's pistol shot.

Hussein, who was without battle experience, said worriedly, "What is it, comrade? Are you all right?"

"Don't be afraid, little man," she said, still smiling. "Hanalore is with you."

From the open window of Mary Quinn's room came the rattling clack of her battered portable typewriter. Zachary paused for a moment in his labor of clearing a drainage ditch flanking the broken-stone road from the gate to the house and listened.

Each time he heard Mary working, he felt both admiration and a touch of envy. When they were young, he had imagined that eventually it would be the name of Zachary Quinn that would be known, that his writings would be the instruments of political change, that he would, in fact, become the voice (well, *a* voice) of their generation.

He had gone to Spain to fight the fascists and right the wrongs of a world that seemed paralyzed in the face of the Brown Shirt threat. In the following years, he had discovered many things, not least that the political system he had been so sure would save the world was resolved to enslave it. No Marxist could see it so, of course, and it had taken Zachary most of a lifetime to grasp the murky truth that either the citizen or the state could rule— not both.

Mary had accepted it sooner, and she had been gifted with the intellect and talent to say so in a manner millions of people could understand. Mary had been, to him, a star in her chosen field of journalism long before she wrote her "breakthrough" book about the attempt to murder the Pope.

Damn it, Irish, he thought ruefully, you are so very good. I could never compete with you. I could only stand aside and stand by. But it's been a good life. For a pair of old bohemians, we haven't done so badly.

He wiped his hands on the bib of his overalls, unaware how much he resembled the farmer in a well-known Grant Wood painting. He looked at the house, feeling the morning sun on his face and hearing the familiar, comforting sound of the typewriter coming from Mary's room.

He did not hear the car slow on the road.

Mary stopped typing and appeared in the window. Zachary

heard her scream at the sound of gunfire. It was a rapid burst, far swifter than the old Hispano 6.5mm machine guns he remembered in front of Barcelona.

A bullet struck him in the back and spun him around. More bullets struck the ground around him. He saw a dusty Mercedes rolling by. My God, he thought, I am a soldier again. Irish won't be pleased. Not pleased at all. He tried to reassure her by calling out that he was all right as he fell.

He did not hear her reply or her anguished cry of grief and rage before he saw the broken stone of the roadway beneath his cheek and the bright mountain morning turned dark.

Hanalore shrieked furiously at Julio. "You *stupid* man! Don't orders mean *anything* to you?" To Lars she shouted, "Keep going! *Keep going!*"

Shocked and confused, Lars put the Mercedes's accelerator to the floor, and the dusty saloon hurtled up the steepening unpaved road to the pass above the villa. Erich, usually silent, uttered a grunt.

Hanalore snatched the AK-47 from Julio and slammed it into the seat. "Didn't you *listen* to Gianbattista? What is the use of having a commander if you don't *listen*?"

"What did I do that was so bad?" protested Julio. "I saw the old man. We have to kill him anyway. So I shot him. What's wrong with that?"

"Gianbattista said to attack the house between twelve and one. *Not now.*"

"There are no police up here," Julio said.

Hanalore slapped him hard across the face. "Do you *know* that? *Do* you?" Hussein watched, his eyes wide. He had never seen Hanalore really angry.

Julio's eyes glittered dangerously. He was not accustomed to the ways of the West German movement. He did not like being mistreated by a woman.

"It is done," he said. "There's an end to it."

Hanalore struck him again. "An end to it, is it? An end?" This time she used her fist, and Julio's lip puffed out, burst, and began to bleed.

Julio snatched at her wrist, but with a suddenness that shocked him, he found himself pinned against the door of the car with Hanalore's hard-muscled forearm across his throat.

"Listen to me, you Italian idiot," she hissed in his face. "We were ordered to attack the villa at twelve. Now we have to cut

223

the telephone line and attack at once. Gianbattista and the others won't like it. *I* won't like it. From this moment on, you obey orders. *Or I'll kill you.*" Julio tried to speak, but she cut off his breath with the pressure at his throat. His eyes began to protrude. *"Do you understand? Do you?"*

Julio bobbed his head desperately. In the front seat, Lars, the one-time would-be rapist of this Amazon, grinned knowingly.

"All right," Hanalore said, releasing Julio and ignoring his gasping breaths. "Turn around and go back, Lars. We have to see to it that the old woman does not telephone for help."

34. ROME

There was no lovemaking. They had left that in the meadow on the way to Rome. But Megan had slept poorly, and, she suspected, David not at all.

She had imagined that he would take her to a CIA safe house, but he had not. Instead, they had spent the night in the Cavalieri Hilton, an elegant hotel that was so standardized in character that it could have been in Manila, Cairo, or Kuala Lumpur. The room in which she awoke was one that had been mass-produced from the plans that had created its siblings all across an increasingly Americanized world.

She could hear David in the bath. The water was running and a radio was on with the morning news in Italian.

Last night, when she had asked him why, of all places, they had come to this lair of tourism on Via Cadlolo, he had smiled briefly and answered, "That's exactly why. Because it's a place one is likely to find hundreds of Americans. Harmless ones."

David had been edgy ever since they had entered the capital. She had expected him to report in to his Agency superior at the embassy. But he had not. Instead, he had sat with her, here in this room, through dinner and then a long—oh, so long—night. Denny, she thought, Denny, where are you?

"We will find her today." David stood in the doorway to the

bathroom, bare-chested, his hair tousled and damp from the shower.

Megan held the bedclothes against her breast and said, "How did you know what I was thinking?"

"What else would you be thinking?" He came into the room and sat on the edge of the bed. "We *will* find her, Meg. Believe it."

"Are you going to call Herrick for help?"

"We can use some troops."

"What about Uncle Jack?"

"Ah, yes. What about Uncle Jack? Well, we can't be as sure about him as we can about help from Herrick. He's a wild card, Meg. He's used to making deals at a higher level than ours. We'll just have to hope we can keep him out of the game."

Megan looked at him, gray-faced. "Game?"

He stood and began to dress. "Sorry. That was only a figure of speech."

But it wasn't, Megan thought. With people like David and Uncle Jack, it never was.

She picked up the telephone.

"Who are you going to call?"

"Mary," she said defiantly. "She might like to know we made it to Rome safely."

David said, "Yes." That was all. He had suddenly grown laconic. The lover was gone, the intelligence officer was back. She missed the lover.

The switchboard operator said, "May I help you?"—not *"Prego?"* or *"Pronto?"*—in an accent that would have been at home in Cincinnati.

Megan gave Mary's unlisted telephone number in Santo Stefano. To David she said, "Can we go straight to the Sword and Scabbard?"

He pulled his sweater on and ran a hand through his hair. "Let's wait and see."

Before Megan could reply, the hotel operator returned to the line. "I am sorry. There is some trouble with the line in Santo Stefano. Shall I try again in a half hour?"

Megan felt a strange unease. "What sort of 'trouble'?"

"I do not know. I will inquire if you wish?"

"Thank you, no," Megan said slowly. "Try again later, if you please." She replaced the telephone in its cradle.

"Not there?" David asked.

"Trouble with the line," Megan said.

David frowned, sat on the bed, and picked up the telephone. He gave the operator the number of the U.S. Embassy. When the reception desk answered, he said, "This is Crile. May I please speak with Mr. Dunn in Protocol?"

He looked levelly at Megan through a twenty-second wait. Then Herrick's voice came on the line. "Where the hell have you been?"

"On the way here from the mountains. We were followed, by the way."

"Did you get a look?"

"Not a close one. But he was with us all the way."

Herrick asked, "Did *she* know?"

David looked at Megan and smiled bleakly. "Yes. She knows."

Herrick sounded distracted. "Look. Is this line secure? Where are you?"

"Hell no. We're at the Cavalieri Hilton." He could not resist the impulse to chide his sober chief just a bit. "Not in the best room in the place, but far from the worst," he said.

"Best or worst, it's none of our concern any longer."

"What does that mean?"

"It means that the Home Office called and we are out of it. I mean the *main* Home Office, the one downtown. The Man spoke to us personally."

David's face seemed to harden into stone as Megan watched. She had never imagined he could look so angry or so dangerous.

"Who is 'us personally'?" he asked in a deadly voice.

"Frank. He came in by mil air. And there's me." A long pause, a waiting pause as Herrick tried to guess how committed to this operation Ashburn had become and what he intended to do. When Ashburn said nothing, he asked "Are you still there?"

David sat frigidly, "The President himself gave instructions to let Jack Wells sink or swim?" He caught Megan's hand in his, squeezing it and holding her in the bed.

"*Jesus Christ, man!* You're on an open line!"

"I know what kind of a line I'm on. What I want to know is what kind of a chicken-shit outfit do I work for?"

"David, for God's sake. Is she right there?"

"Yes."

"I know what you're thinking. I know it's politics. Hell, it's all politics. I didn't think you'd want to back off, but understand me: It will have to be a free-lance piece of work. Frank and I are on our own time starting this morning. I was just waiting for you to call.''

"Reuben, don't shit me. I give you fair warning.''

Megan whispered anxiously. "What's happened?''

"Listen, David,'' Herrick said, "don't tell her this. Blaisdell is dead. He was killed sometime last week and left in a trunk. Some Swiss girl who works for the clinic in Lugano found him. Are you listening?''

"Yes.''

"J.W. got off an Alitalia flight in Geneva. The Swiss police think he could have stopped in Lugano to pay Charlie a visit on his way to Rome. It doesn't work their way. The time is all wrong. But he had reason.''

"Go on. I'm listening.''

"Better still, why don't you both come in?''

"Negative. And don't send anyone. I won't cooperate.''

"I wouldn't try to bag you, David.''

"Where is Frank?''

"Trying to find J.W. We need a place to start.''

"I thought you said the Company was out of it.''

"It's the Man's Company. If he says it's out, then it's out. But Frank and I both owe Jack a few turns. I told you we were taking a few days off.''

"What motive?''

Herrick was not rattled by the sudden backward twist of the question. "It is pretty certain that Jack set up an ambush in 'Nam. To get rid of Thierry. Only, Thierry was one of the bad guys, a hood, and worth money. We think Charlie turned entrepreneur. But there were almost two-dozen months inside Bung Kan prison. Charlie got paid back for that, last week. Thierry is looking for Jack, to finish the job. That's why Frank is moonlighting.''

"Then that's all there is?''

"I'll link with the Italian police. That's really all we could have done anyway. We're taking a chance being involved at all after the Man said to cash in.''

"*God damn it*, Reuben. There's a young girl in this.'' Once again he held Megan's hand immobile, painfully, in his grasp.

"Take it easy,'' Herrick said. "That's my fall-back position with the boss.''

"What the hell does the Judge know?'' David asked angrily.

"Wait. A message just came in from Frank. General della Tevera says there has been significant Red Brigades action at the northern border and here in the city. There is a third-stage alert on.''

David said, ''Ask the police to check on Mary and Zach Quinn at Santo Stefano. There was a sniper up there Sunday. And their telephone is out of order now.''

''Why didn't Quinn ask for protection, for Chrissake?''

''Because he's Zach.''

''I'll see if Tevera can send a chopper up there for a look.''

''Yes. Do that.''

''David, I'm sorry. We'll try to help. We'll do what we can.''

''That's comforting,'' David said, and broke the connection.

Megan asked, ''What is it?''

''We're on our own,'' David said. ''It's better this way.''

Jack Wells regarded the blue-and-white placard affixed high on the wall of the building. It read Via Sforzesca. Italian over-statement, he thought sardonically. The *via* was an alley between two only slightly broader streets. This was not a morning neighborhood. In other districts of Rome, the overhead balconies would already be bright with drying wash or airing blankets, but not here. The buildings on either side of Via Sforzesca were shut and sullen. Only a narrow strip of sky could be seen overhead, and from that one could assume that there would be rain before the day was over.

He studied the steel-shuttered windows overlooking the street. Was it possible, he wondered, that Thierry had hidden Denny in one of these blind warrens? It wasn't likely. Too close to the message drop, too many chances for unplanned encounters.

I should be telling myself that I am too old for this kind of thing, he thought. But, God help me, I feel more alive than I have for years. A man my age should be afraid of his own limitations. But I feel like a warrior again. How did one account for such a thing?

He started down the street toward Number 17, the *trattoria* named the Sword and Scabbard. Closed and shuttered, of course, at this hour. There were places like it all over the poorer districts of Rome; there had been for a thousand years. He heard a metallic creak, and his hand closed over the grip of the Glock in his trench-coat pocket. But the creak was from an opening shutter overhead. Two women's faces appeared, one above the other. He heard laughter inside the room. Someone called, ''*E mattutino, bel 'uomo.* It's too early, handsome fellow. Come back later.''

"There is a message here for me," Wells said, and held up a five-thousand-lira note.

"*Aspetta, signore.*" Not a woman's voice this time.

Wells turned and once again studied the shuttered windows overlooking Via Sforzesca. There were walkers and three-wheeled vans on the distant cross streets, but none on this narrow alley. The sidewalk on which he stood was little more than a broad curb, a foot and a half wide, no more.

The metal shutters protecting the door to Number 17 were pulled up with a clatter. Beyond them the door opened six inches, and a man looked out suspiciously. "What name?"

"Wells."

"I was told to expect a woman by that name."

Wells held up the five-thousand-lira note. "You were told wrong."

The narrow face and pinched mouth made the man look like a weasel. The shiny black eyes followed every movement of the money.

"The message," Wells said.

The man took a rumpled envelope from his waistband. It was unsealed.

"I didn't do that," he said. "It was that way when he gave it to me."

Wells held the envelope and tried to imagine what Thierry looked like now. He had never seen him, but in 1972 he had been familiar enough with his photographs, his writings, his history. What had the intervening years done to him? All the years Wells had thought him safely dead, he had been growing older. Still working for the Soviets? Was it possible?

Plakhanov was a fading memory, but there had been a German boy, a sweet-faced creature who was killed crossing the Wall.

"I delivered the message," the sharp-eyed man said.

Wells handed him the money, and he retreated into the dark interior of the *trattoria*. The shutter rattled down, and the door closed. The window overhead was closed as well.

Wells took a single sheet of paper from the envelope. It read: "North entrance Vatican Museums. 2200 3/17. We will talk."

Talk about what? About what price Thierry would ask for Denny's life? Megan's? Not likely. No. Jean Thierry had carried a debt with him for almost two decades. Once it was known that he was alive, that Blaisdell had failed to do his job, the price was obvious. Thierry had murdered Blaisdell for revenge, but it had been like brushing aside a fly. What he really wanted was the man who had connived to have him killed, and, failing that, was responsible for whatever came after.

What Thierry wanted was John Wells—his life. Nothing less.

35. SANTO STEFANO

For Vittorio Emanuele Malatesta, now completing his second year as a probationer in the forces of the Carabinieri, volunteering for duty in the mountain village of Santo Stefano had been a calculated risk.

He came from a family that had produced three generations of policemen. His grandfather had worn the praetorian uniform of the King's police in Rome when Mussolini was still writing fiery editorials for *Giovinezza*. Malatesta's father had served as a motorcycle policeman for three years before being crushed to death by a truck driven by a drunk on the Torino-Genova *autostrada*. His son Vittorio, named for Italian kings, with a grand sense of duty and honor, was following a family tradition.

As soon as Vittorio had completed the barest educational requirements, he had taken himself to Rome, to the police station, to enroll as a probationer, a *questore-candidato*. He had absorbed the training easily, as though a talent for police work was a natural attribute. As indeed it was, according to his mother. The Malatesta home in Milano was filled with photographs of carabiniere Malatestas, and there were cases full of police memorabilia dating back eighty years.

Vittorio was a tall, slender young man with soft-brown eyes that were more attractive to women than they were intimidating to criminals. He wore his uniform with what his mother and sisters thought of as "a Milanese flair." For a man of modest means, he had style, even elegance. His mother claimed that the Malatestas of Milano were descendants of the dukes of Ravenna. There was no evidence to support this claim, and Vittorio knew it, but if it made his female relations happy, who was he to deny it?

He had asked for the posting to Santo Stefano when he learned that Mary Quinn, the famous American journalist, had bought the villa above the village. He had read the Italian edition of her book about the attempt by the Reds on the Holy Father and everything else he could find by her on the subject of international terrorism. He became convinced that Signora Quinn had placed herself in mortal danger.

His natural affinity led him to read heavily about the Mafia, the Sicilian Black Hand, and American gangsters of the 1920s. The new breed of lawbreakers, he lamented, had none of the heroic blackguardism of the lawbreakers of Italy's past. The Palestine Liberation Organization, Black September, Baader-Meinhof, the Red Army Faction, and, above all, the indigenous Red Brigades all claimed to be "political" organizations. To a young man so steeped in the tradition of law enforcement, the very idea of politically motivated lawbreaking was repulsive. No member of Malatesta's family for three generations had ever been able to understand the concept of political dissent. Political terrorism was an attack on the very foundation of civilization. It hardly needed saying that the foundation of civilization was "Law and Order."

Malatesta had volunteered to be the single policeman in Santo Stefano because he was certain that one day the creatures that Mary Quinn exposed in her books and articles would come to punish her. When that day came, he intended to be on hand to do what policemen bearing the name Malatesta had been doing since the 1920s.

It was self-serving to a degree. He accepted that. But doing one's duty was always, to some degree, self-serving. How could it be otherwise? And it was not as though he neglected his less glamorous duties. He was as willing to pedal down the mountain in search of a stolen farm animal (and perform the tedious climb back to Santo Stefano) as to pause and pass a pleasant ten minutes with Signor Quinn or, if fortune smiled on him, with the famous author.

On this March morning, Malatesta found himself faced with the necessity of riding his bicycle down the mountain to obtain the signature of a farmer on a Report of Mysterious Disappearance or Possible Theft relating to the missing sheep. He had telephoned the district police station at L'Aquila to inform the officer on duty there that he would be absent from his post for most of the day. There was nothing more to be done. He locked away his automatic pistol—a weapon he had not fired since

231

training days—drew on his waterproof cape in case of a sudden spring shower, and rolled out his bicycle.

He did sometimes envy the highway police and their gleaming red-and-black MotoGuzzis capable of two hundred kilometers per hour. But given the way his father had met his death, his mother would never have tolerated his asking for such duty. Besides, he told himself often, what he did here in Santo Stefano was important. Thankless, to be sure, but work of value to Italy. To NATO, even.

Still, on such a morning as this, to ride a sleek and powerful motorcycle . . . It was one more dream of many for young Vittorio Malatesta.

He stepped out onto the narrow, deserted street and pulled on his gauntlets. There had been a young man, an American, staying with the Quinns. Then a young woman had arrived, driving a handsome new Alfetta. The man had arrived on a beautiful shaft-driven BMW 750cc bike. And he had left early Monday in the Alfetta with the woman. A carabiniere needed to be very observant, and Malatesta was interested in everything that went on in Santo Stefano and its environs.

That meant that the BMW must still be at Villa Stefano. It would be a delight to inspect such a machine at close range. He was certain that Signor Quinn would have no objections. A small pleasure before an unpleasant duty. Surely a tiny indulgence?

He mounted and started pedaling up the slope toward the villa. Farm women from below—there were no farms above the village, since soil had long ago gone to stones and shale—had begun to drift in twos and threes toward church. The deacon, in shabby black vestments and with heavy work boots on his feet, was making his way from the shed in the churchyard to ring the bell.

"Buona mattina, Diacono," Malatesta said as he rolled by.

"Buona mattina, Candidato."

Malatesta sighed. The old deacon never failed to address him as "Candidate," never as "Constable."

He was a mile from the village when he heard the alarming ripping sound of gunfire. He did not recognize it at first. It was nothing at all like the sound of the shotguns and antique *lupi*, the heavy-caliber wolf guns, still fired in these ancient mountains. He had heard such a sound only in training camp in Sicily. It was the open roar of a modern military weapon firing on full automatic.

He spun his bicycle in a tight turn and pumped with all his

232

might back to the tiny police station, scattering churchgoers as he went. Crashing through the locked door, he unlocked the rack holding his machine pistol, discarded his cape, and searched desperately for his flak vest, which he had allowed to fall behind his narrow cot. He finally found it and put it on. Then he snatched at the telephone. The line was dead.

He pounded on the door of the house next door, but the neighbors were devout: she for the church, he for the early opening *trattoria* in Via Marco Aurelio. He slung his weapon and mounted his bicycle again.

As he raced back through the square, he was appalled to hear the sudden clangor of the church bells. The noise they made drowned out his alarms.

By the time he had passed through the medieval town gate, he felt a dismaying certainty that none of the early risers in Santo Stefano, not one, had heard his shouted warnings.

When Mary saw Zach go down by the roadside ditch, she felt a mingled pain and fury she had not imagined possible. Ever since embarking on her late career as an investigative journalist specializing in terrorism, she had known she or Zach might come under attack. But the reality of it was more violent and surprising than she could have imagined. She had never really *believed* it would happen. But she was not a timid woman. She left the window at a run, stopped only long enough to pick up Zach's 12-gauge shotgun from its place with his other hunting guns, and rushed through the house and down the piazza stairs to the road.

The Mercedes from which the shots were fired had vanished up the road toward the pass in a cloud of dust. She did not believe for a moment that it would not return.

Zach lay face down near the drainage ditch he had been working to clear. Mary dropped the shotgun and rolled him over. His face was white. There was blood on his chest, on his left arm, on his legs. She put her face close to his and discovered he was breathing. His breath came in shallow gasps, but it came. "You're alive, old man," she whispered.

Zach's eyes made an attempt to open. "Irish?"

She held him against her. "They tried to kill you."

"Came close. Bastards." He tried to move and could not. "Drag me," he whispered. "Back to the house."

"Let me get help."

This time he managed to open his eyes and keep them open.

He remembered the dying on the field before Barcelona. He said, "Need cover. First."

Mary heard a car coming toward the villa from the direction of the pass. It was the Mercedes.

"They're back," she said.

"Gun?"

"I brought the shotgun." She had never fired it. She disliked hunting. Zach had tried to teach her to shoot. She had accepted a little instruction after the threats began to arrive, but she had never taken it seriously.

Now there was no one but the two of them, and Zach might be dying.

Zach said, "The ditch."

She dragged him. "Am I hurting you, old man?"

Through gritted teeth he said, "I don't feel a thing."

"Liar," she said. "Old liar." Tears were coursing down her cheeks. She had not wept for many years.

"Keep your head down." The voice sounded thinner.

Mary gripped the shotgun awkwardly. The Mercedes was at the stone gates now. The left rear door opened, and a young woman and two men stepped out. Mary raised the 12-gauge out of the ditch and fired. The shotgun's magazine was loaded with the buckshot Zach used on vermin. Each shell contained a half-dozen lead slugs. Two smashed through the car's hood and destroyed the fuel injectors. One struck Hussein and sent him sprawling. The others passed harmlessly over Hanalore's cropped blond head.

Lars, startled by the resistance and by the sudden stopping of the engine, shouted for Julio, Erich, and Paolo to take cover on the far side of the Mercedes. Only Hanalore took immediate action. Her return fire scattered the shards of shale all around Mary. One fragment struck her on the cheek and drew blood. She could feel Zach feebly trying to pull her into the ditch.

From down the road came another sound, one like that of tearing canvas. The windshield of the Mercedes vanished into flying bits. Paolo turned in panic to see where this new resistance came from. He wanted to shout at Lars and Hanalore that it wasn't supposed to be like this.

Malatesta, having flung himself from his bicycle and onto the road before firing, rolled into a depression on the verge before essaying another burst with his Belgian machine pistol. He had only three magazines in his flak vest, and at the pistol's rate of fire that meant six bursts of three seconds each. The radio he carried was useless, because there was no one to respond back at the station. Like the magazines, it was part of the gear always kept with the flak vest.

The important thing was that the terrorists—he had no doubt about whom he was fighting—had not yet been able to murder the Quinns. A 12-gauge load of buckshot had surprised the killers and had thrown their timing badly off. The situation was hazardous. He had no idea how many he was fighting. But between himself and the wielder of the shotgun, they had the attackers flanked. It was just as it had been taught in training.

He saw some movement and shouted, "Signor Quinn! Behind the automobile!"

A gray head came up, and the shotgun boomed twice. A semiautomatic shotgun held a half-dozen shells, no more. Possibly even fewer. Some owners' guns carried a plug to reduce the number of shells in order to make hunting a more sporting proposition. He hoped that Quinn's was not one of those.

The gray head rose again, and Malatesta was appalled to see that it was not Signor Quinn, but Signora Quinn who was using the shotgun.

From behind the car came more gunfire. The shotgun boomed again. Two things happened simultaneously. The shotgun went flying, its wooden stock in splinters. And the fuel tank of the Mercedes erupted into flames, sending a pillar of oily black smoke into the morning air.

Hanalore, Lars, and Erich were well clear of the Mercedes. But Paolo was not. He was showered with burning gasoline and he dropped his weapon and screamed as he ran toward Malatesta. He threw himself to the ground and began to twist and arch his back like a beached fish, all the while uttering cries that became progressively less human.

The others began firing again. Hanalore and Lars at the Quinns. Erich fired at Paolo until his shrieking stopped.

Malatesta raised his machine pistol and fired at the place where he thought the shots that killed the burning man had come from. It was not possible to know if he had struck anything, and he had reduced his store of ammunition by a third.

He rolled onto his back, inserted a magazine in his weapon, and shouted, "Signora Quinn! Are you injured?"

"My husband needs a doctor!"

The young policeman heard a thumping sound rising from the valley. It grew steadily louder. He shielded his eyes against the glare of the white sky and saw a helicopter. It bore army markings.

He was flooded with relief—and then with anger. As the helicopter flew low over him, he raised himself and shook his fist at the soldiers making ready to land. *"Bastardi! Bastardi spudorati!"* he shouted indignantly. "Where were you when you were needed here?"

36. ROME

Jean Thierry, seated in the back of a Fiat taxicab, drove slowly past the building on the Via Palestro. Even from the street it was possible, if one was searching for signs, to see that the Togliatti Unit had fortified the ballet school quite well. The steel shutters on the top story were folded back, but the trained eye could see the tops of rows of sandbags on the windowsills and what appeared to be steel plates fastened to the shutters to strengthen them.

He turned his attention to the buildings around the ballet school. About half of them appeared to be empty, which was bad. Thierry's specialty had always been single actions—"one on one," as the Americans put it. But he was sufficiently knowledgeable about urban warfare to know that uninvolved civilians in a battle zone were customarily used to shield the active forces. Just as the Iranians used battalions of unarmed boys to clear Iraqi minefields, so urban guerrillas used bystanders to inhibit the violence of the authorities' response.

The unit could have placed itself in a less decrepit area, one that the Italians would be less likely to level at need.

But, to be fair, he thought, as the taxi rolled slowly by, the Red Brigades had not exactly been forewarned about the coming battle of Via Palestro.

He smiled grimly and told the driver to go on.

"Where to, *signor*?"

"Find me a French restaurant. Something good; not an Italian imitation."

236

The driver's good humor vanished. This man was unpleasant, he concluded, and impolite as well. He recommended the most expensive French restaurant he knew.

"The *signor* will enjoy Chez Ducasse, in Trastevere."

"I don't know it."

"It is excellent. I have eaten there myself," the driver said, and headed for Ponte Regina Margherita. This route would take them well out of the way, on what amounted to a tour of a number of the city's scenic places, none of which the fare had evidenced the slightest desire to see. Retribution, the driver thought with satisfaction, was a finely construed art in the Eternal City. His principles prevented him from recommending a bad restaurant, but not an overpriced one.

Midday traffic made the trip a slow one. The Fiat, swerving in and out of traffic in the Roman manner, circled the Borghese Gardens and the Piazza del Popolo. There was a short traffic tie-up at the bridge. They waited there for five minutes while Roman drivers displayed their impatience by blowing their horns repeatedly. Thierry sat smoking a Gauloise. He had all the time in the world, and everything was running on rails. He allowed himself only a brief instant of satisfaction that a plan so many years in the making was coming to fruition on this day.

He wondered if it meant as much to Plakhanov. It seemed to. From what he had said at the bridge yesterday, the old nance was looking to retirement after this operation. Russians tended to think in terms of honors and medals—yes, how the bastards loved medals. He even had some Soviet baubles himself, because they thought everyone liked them, too. But Plakhanov had said nothing about awards for this Paladin thing. Could it be that Plakhanov's reasons for this action were as personal as his own? That would be a remarkable thing.

The taxi began to move again, across the bridge, then along the turbid Tiber past Castel Sant'Angelo, around the bend, and along the tree-lined avenue of the Lungotevere Gianicolense.

"It was here that the Roman Republic was formed," the driver said. "The last Roman king, Tarquinius Superbus, behaved badly and the people rebelled against him." The man watched Thierry in the rear-view mirror. "Tarquinius once killed a man by kicking him down the Curia steps. Or so they say. But no matter. It was here that the Roman Republic first drew breath. We Italians are democrats," he declared proudly.

"Claretta Petacci would be surprised to hear it," Thierry said laconically.

"Who?"

What a marvelous thing the passage of time was, Thierry thought. It allows this young lout to forget Benito Mussolini and his mistress ever existed. It allows Plakhanov to scratch some chronic itch. And it allows me to pay off my good and faithful wife and the ghostly ever-present Wells. And the girl? Is she really my daughter? And if she is, what does it matter? She, at least, is a stranger to me.

As the Fiat passed the great, ugly façade of a building outside which tenscore women and children waited in the street, the driver said, "That is the prison Regina Coeli. A place for—how do you say it?—soft criminals. The wives and families gather here each Monday to be allowed inside. It is very enlightened."

Thierry allowed himself a grim smile. Everything in the West was "very enlightened." Otherwise, people like him could not do the work they did.

It was nearly one when he was deposited on the doorstep of Chez Ducasse on Via della Scala. He was greeted effusively as a foreigner and charged accordingly. But the driver had been right: The food was excellent. Thierry indulged himself, knowing that tomorrow's meals would be hurried and eaten on the run.

He ordered *filet aux herbes de Provence*, fresh vegetables, salad, and a bottle of Bordeaux. He ate slowly and with relish. After lunch, he drank several cognacs. For many years it had been his practice to eat and drink well before an action. He could not remember ever having been drunk. From time to time, as he sipped the brandy, he would have flashbacks to the way Blaisdell's cheap brandy had tasted in the interrogation room of Bung Kan prison. On this lingering Roman afternoon, he thought about Blaisdell and smiled.

It was nearly four when he paid and left the restaurant. He walked slowly back to the river and then upstream to the Regina Coeli. He stood for a moment before the prison. There were still some families in the street, though not many. Most had come and gone. A boy called up to a window, and a prisoner waved back. The boy passed a message about a meeting with a lawyer. The prisoner shouted back agreement. No, Thierry thought, not at all like Bung Kan.

He walked slowly across the Ponte Mazzini and then down to the Piazza Farnese. There was a telephone kiosk in the produce market. He dropped coins in the slot, dialed, and waited.

When a masculine voice answered with *"Pronto?"* he said deliberately, "Listen carefully. I am going to say this only once." He knew the message was being recorded. "You are under a third-stage alert. I will tell you the reason. A unit of the Red Brigades is in a building at Number 10 Via Palestro. They are preparing to attack the U.S. Embassy. They have a hostage. They are heavily armed. Did you get that?"

"Who is this?"

"A friend of democracy," Thierry said dryly, and hung up. He left the kiosk and strolled patiently among the flower and produce stalls of the Campo dei Fiori.

It was all done now. The rest was only routine.

At 6:30 it began to rain. It had been threatening all day. And now the streets were slick and wet, and the temperature was dropping.

Gianbattista Calvo disliked the unsettled manners of the Roman spring. He stood at an open shutter on the top story of the building on the Via Palestro, increasingly uneasy about the next few hours. The slender old Russian at the residency had warned him that the Palmiro Togliatti Unit must be ready for whatever duties the Soviet paymasters assigned. "The Frenchman will use you as needed, and you will follow his orders exactly."

But the Frenchman had given no orders, not since instructing Calvo to liquidate the American girl. On his own, Calvo had chosen to wait almost until dark before dispatching Mariella to do the work. The street girl still made him shudder when he remembered his shocking lack of precautions on Saturday. But he also felt a tightness in his loins when he looked at her legs. He wondered why they should arouse him. He had always been more aware of breasts and buttocks than the back of a pair of fat knees exposed by a denim miniskirt.

Calvo had heard nothing from the detachment he had been commanded to send to Santo Stefano to deal with the Quinn woman and confuse the antiterrorist brigade. The lack of information made him uneasy.

The need to guard the American girl and the dispatch of six fighters to the Abruzzi had reduced the strength of the unit from thirty to twenty-two. And the assignment of Mariella to execute the American would reduce the strength further.

The risk of this, thought Calvo, was unknown. If the Frenchman was able to deliver his prisoners without bringing the authorities down on the ballet school, all would be well. If not

. . . But a soldier of the revolution could not think in terms of "if."

He began to prowl. The broken wall mirrors reflected images of a wild and fragmented world filled with odd angular movements, scattered shards of light and shadow, strange and unfamiliar representations of his face and body.

A half-dozen of the German comrades were watching a rock show from Cinecittà on a portable television set. They were eating bread and canned meat and drinking Diet Pepsi.

At the head of the stairs, Aldo, one of the long-timers in the Brigades—but unfortunately not a tower of strength when shooting began—was field-stripping his weapon of choice, an American Armalite M-16.

Calvo spoke briefly to him and passed on down the stairs, looking for Mariella. It was time for her to leave, and he wanted to give her instructions.

In the lower hallway, on a mattress under the stairs, Guido and Marta, a sixteen-year-old of surpassing ugliness, were engaged in sexual games. The sight irritated Calvo. How could the movement ever be taken seriously if it was populated with fornicating children?

He again remembered Saturday, with Mariella, in that doorless room, and had the grace to look away from the pair under the stairs.

He entered the room fortified as a redoubt, the place where, theoretically, the commander of the Palmiro Togliatti Unit would fight his last battle against the forces of reaction. It made him distinctly uncomfortable. And the bombastic graffito on the wall, the exhortation from Mikhail Bakunin, seemed somehow hollow. For a moment, he felt a flash of real fear. This was not a game. People died resisting authority. He had seen it happen. He felt a deep chill, an inner cold.

Mariella appeared behind him. She was dressed as always, in her miniskirt, sweater, and shabby field jacket.

"I will go now," she said.

The pocket of the field jacket sagged with the weight of a pistol.

"What will you use?"

Mariella showed him a 9mm Makarov. Her black eyes glittered. "I don't see any reason why they shouldn't get the blame."

She loathed Americans and she hated Russians. In fact, she had more than enough hatred to go around. It made Calvo feel even colder to realize that, although she hated most men, she *despised* him. What had she said? "I used to do this for a bowl of fish-head stew when I was twelve."

"Who is watching her?" she asked.

Calvo had to think. That was bad. A commander should have everything at his fingertips. Or so he believed. "Giorgio and Umberto," he said. "I want you all back here the moment it's done."

Mariella stared at him. Was he really the fool he appeared to be? If he was, and if the authorities found the unit, they were all dead.

She wondered if the American girl ever thought of such things. It did not seem possible. Mariella was still fascinated by the girl, who was so privileged, or so doomed.

"What time is it?"

Calvo looked at his Japanese digital watch. He kept it in the twenty-four-hour mode. That was more military.

"Eighteen forty," he said.

"I will go now," Mariella said.

Frank Traina left the Questura at seven. A previous acquaintanceship with both Colonel Guindani of the Roman city police and General Emiliano della Tevera, the current commander of the antiterrorist brigade of the Italian Army, had allowed him to stay in the Records Office of police headquarters while the entire organization suffered a convulsion.

Della Tevera, a rotund man whose appearance belied his rather remarkable savagery when in action, had been entertaining Traina when the telephone call was reported. Traina had been, as he might have put it to Hilly, on a roll. In his name, Herrick had passed on Ashburn's concern for Mary and Zachary Quinn, and della Tevera, with an uncharacteristic willingness to act, had dispatched to Santo Stefano a helicopter and a reinforced company of his antiterrorist commandos.

About six hours later, Zachary Quinn was in the intensive-care unit of the military hospital at L'Aquila, and Mary Quinn was at his side. A serious international incident had taken place, della Tevera had declared, and a far more serious one had been averted.

"A young carabiniere is a hero, and we have five dead terrorists and one being questioned. A young woman. A very manly young woman," della Tevera had said. "We shall make her available to you for interrogation, of course. Professional courtesy."

Ever since the *Achille Lauro* incident some years back that

241

had ended with the Italian authorities allowing Abou Abbas to escape after having been brought to earth in Sicily by the U.S. Navy, Italian antiterrorist officers had been anxious to keep relations on a friendly level. "Of course, we have first try at her," he said with a grim smile. "We shall see what Italian charm can do. The young lady is a West German national, but I foresee no complications."

Della Tevera had been in an excellent mood as the reports came in from Santo Stefano and L'Aquila. All things considered, he had a right to be.

And then had come the telephone tip.

The headquarters had exploded into action. General della Tevera had left his CIA guest in the hands of the duty colonel. When he reappeared, in battle dress—black-and-green coveralls, flak vest, weapons, black beret, and antireflective paint— the plump officer had looked suddenly formidable.

"It is conceivable," della Tevera said, "that the guerrillas in the Via Palestro are in some way involved with your missing girl. We have no way of knowing. You may come along if you choose. But it must be with the understanding that you take no direct part in whatever action ensues. The government is growing very touchy about matters of protocol and precedence."

Traina looked out the window at the courtyard. A line of armored personnel carriers waited, engines rumbling. Behind them were trucks filling with men, and, beyond them, a line of vehicles with crowd-control equipment: lights, barricades, concertina wire. Fully two hundred soldiers and police awaited the word to move out.

A thin rain was falling from a rapidly darkening sky. The lights of the city reflected on the undersides of clouds that formed a low, solid overcast.

Traina wondered if the police and the Italian Army were aware that General Feliks Plakhanov, chief of the KGB's First Chief Directorate, had arrived in Rome on Sunday.

Somewhere out there in the darkening city were Jack Wells and, almost certainly, Thierry, alias the Frenchman, stalking one another.

Under the circumstances, Traina chose to preserve his freedom of action. He bid General della Tevera good night and left the building.

The President of the United States might be ready to jettison his choice for secretary of state, but would he be as ready to see

242

a close friend killed by a Soviet assassin? Traina had decided that since he was now—on specific orders from the Director of Central Intelligence—on vacation, he had better not lose his independence.

He stood on the narrow sidewalk by the gate of the Questura and watched the cars, trucks, and APCs roll swiftly out into the rainy night.

"Very impressive," said an American voice.

Traina spun and gripped a thin, but rock-hard, arm.

"Jesus Christ! Jack! Thank God."

"Decide which, Frank. Then we'll talk."

37. ROME

Herrick took Traina's telephone call with misgivings. The Rome Station chief had suffered through many second thoughts since the call from Judge Street and the President. He had found himself comparing his career with Frank's. He was not, he had concluded, a cowboy like Frank. Far from it. He planned on a few more years and then an honorable retirement. Maybe even a Medal of Freedom for the library wall, if all went right. Now this.

Herrick was not a naïve man, but the finality with which the President had discarded his almost lifelong friend and his concerns still shocked and dismayed him. It was absurd, he knew, because things had changed for the Company in the last few years. But there was once a time, he told himself, when the Agency would have gone hard and far to be loyal to an old spook. And a veteran could remember the halcyon days when the President of the United States believed that the CIA was the nation's secret army, the troops who fought, and sometimes died, in the war that never ended—his cloaked praetorians, who were owed his allegiance in return for their own.

But a surfeit of morality had overtaken the government of the United States, and this was the result. Jack Wells out in the cold, and a touch of that same cold struck Herrick when he heard Traina's voice on the telephone—Traina, who regarded Herrick as a co-conspirator.

"Frank," he said, "did you know there's going to be a damn war in about thirty minutes? Someone blew the whistle on a commando of Red Brigades. Della Tevera's gone ballistic."

"Scramble this, I'm in a public phone box," Traina said.

Herrick keyed in a scrambler circuit and at the same time deactivated the modem connecting his outside lines with the station computer. The security program would note that he had taken himself off line, of course. But he would worry about that when he had to.

"I know about the tip to della Tevera. That can wait. I have just encountered a friend who wants to talk to you," Traina said.

Three days ago I would have given a month's pay to hear Wells's voice, Herrick thought. But now that the President has spoken, I would have given twice that *not* to hear it. Delaying, he asked, "Where are you?"

"Don't bother with a trace. He won't co-operate, and you'll never bring him in. Talk to him, Reuben, for Chrissake."

"All right."

Herrick heard the cultured accent, and it reminded him of all the times he had dealt with John Wells, Washington lawyer, counselor to the President, administration, trouble-shooter, ex-supergrade, potential Cabinet officer.

"Hello, Reuben. I am sorry I haven't had an opportunity to call you before this."

"Wells, come on in with Frank and let the Italian police do their job."

"I can't do that, Reuben. You know that. Or you should. Frank was in Porza, so you know about Blaisdell, of course."

Herrick felt a small sharp flare of alarm. "You couldn't have done that."

"If you mean that the timing is all wrong, you are quite correct. I couldn't have done it. But if I had reached him first, I think I'd have terminated him. He cheated me badly. One day, if the fates permit, I'll tell you how and why."

"I think I know."

"Do you? That's interesting. Then you probably understand why the President did what he did. *He* might not know exactly why, but he has an unerring instinct. That's what makes him such a great politician." There was *approval* in Wells's voice.

"I have a favor to ask, Reuben," Wells said.

"I'll do what I can. As a private citizen. That's all I can say."
Herrick thought about his government-service rating, his pension, Judge Street, the President. He despised himself.

Wells said, "Frank tells me you authorized a black-bag job on a *trattoria* called the Sword and Scabbard, and that you know where and when Thierry is to meet Megan."

"Frank should never have told you that."

"Give me your word that no one from the Company will get within a mile of the place. Thierry is a professional. If he thinks he's being crowded, he'll kill my girls."

"Are you thinking of going in against him alone?"

"I want your promise that you will do exactly what Frank says the Judge and the President told you to do. Which is nothing." There was a long pause on the line. "Do you read me, Reuben? Nothing at all."

"If we alert the cops—"

"Come on, Reuben. You aren't thinking of sending some Italian boy in a funny hat up against a Moscow Center–trained killer. No, our best might *just* be in his league. I'm not at all sure of that, these days. You and the Company keep out of it. From what I saw, della Tevera's people will be busy for the next few hours."

"Did della Tevera guess what you're doing?"

"Of course not." Wells's voice took on an ironic ring. "I have taken the correspondence course. I won't embarrass you or Washington."

Herrick broke out, "How can we be sure of that?"

"You can't be," was the steely reply. "But stay out of it. My daughter and granddaughter—" He broke off, instantly aware of the Freudian slip. Then, more gently, he said, "You see why it has to be me."

Herrick closed his eyes and drew a deep, shuddering breath. "I see why you think it has to be you."

"Consider it carefully. It's me he wants dead. And one thing more. You have a man with my niece. David Ashburn. Take him off."

"He is not very good about calling in."

"Just the same, do it. We have to give Thierry what he wants."

"There's something wrong here. Can't you feel it? We're missing something."

Wells thought: The man's good. He has an instinct. But if he starts thinking about a KGB general, I'll never be free of him.

"This is my operation, Reuben," Wells said. "My niece and

245

grandniece. I know what everything costs and what everyone is willing to pay. Leave it at that.''

"If I don't notify the Italian authorities—''

Wells's voice suddenly snapped with angry authority. "You'll notify *no one*, Reuben. If you mix into this, I will telephone the President and tell him all the things he doesn't want to hear.''

"The driver will take you to Via Palestro. I want you to make a complete evaluation of the ability of the people there to hold out in case they are attacked.'' Plakhanov's gaze was cool and steady. "Make note of what is required to assure that they can occupy the Italians for at least a day.''

Captain Ekimov tried to conceal his dismay. It would be pointless to tell the Comrade General that he, Ekimov, was not really a military man, that his talents lay in the purposeful shuffling of the forms and papers without which the Soviet state could not function.

The General had still not fully explicated the scope and purpose of the operation he called "Paladin.'' Ekimov knew only that it was intended that an American official, an important one, would be held at Via Palestro for an unspecified period of hours or days. Despite Kalganin's instructions, Ekimov had been able to discover very little of what Plakhanov intended.

"The soldiers of the revolution are expecting you,'' Plakhanov said, fastening the buttons of his civilian coat.

Where was he going, Ekimov wondered. And was there any way in which he could avoid his present orders and follow those of the Chairman of the KGB? He could see none.

He started for the door. Plakhanov detained him. His eyes had gone colder than Ekimov had ever seen them. "Take with you the weapon the downstairs armorer issued you,'' he said.

Ekimov's breath caught in his throat. He knows, he thought. He knows I have sold him to Kalganin. And I am a dead man.

When Ekimov was gone, Colonel Tikhonov entered the room. It was a risky game he had chosen to play, but one was either a gambler or one was not. He had betrayed the connection between Plakhanov's aide and the Chairman of the KGB. He risked Lubyanka and a bullet in the neck if Plakhanov lost his power struggle with Kalganin. But a night and a day in deep thought had convinced the KGB Resident that Plakhanov and Kalganin both might damage themselves irretrievably. Tikhonov was high on the list of senior KGB colonels. Nothing was ever gained without risk. And this risk seemed mostly to others.

246

He said, "You frightened him badly with that business about the weapon."

"I suspected Kalganin might have enlisted him against me. I had to be certain."

"We are going to lose the Palmiro Togliatti?"

Plakhanov took a black homburg from the wardrobe and placed it carefully on his head. He picked up a silver-headed cane—a product of the armory in the residency cellar. "Do I look bourgeois enough for Rome?"

"You look like a native, General," Tikhonov said. "I asked you if we were going to lose the Togliatti."

"I fear so, Comrade Colonel," he said, and went out into the gallery leading to the busy Roman street.

Mariella crouched in the stairwell of a basement doorway listening to the movements and the muttered complaints and curses descending into her hiding place from street level.

She had left the ballet school and walked almost the distance to the safe house, where Giorgio and Umberto stood watch over the American girl, when she was appalled to encounter police and uniformed soldiers of the antiterrorist force placing street barricades and concertina wire between buildings. Traffic had already been diverted, and the people who lived and worked in the shabby buildings surrounding Via Palestro were being swiftly and silently evacuated. The worst had happened. The authorities, informed by God knew what mischance or which police spy, were about to come down on the Palmiro Togliatti Unit. And judging from the force she could hear assembling, she was certain that the commando had the choice only of surrender or annihilation. In recent months, the Italian Army's antiterrorist units had shown little inclination to offer other alternatives.

She huddled against the decaying buildings and considered her own situation. It had been an incredible bit of luck that had made Calvo choose this evening to send her out to eliminate the American. It was possible Mariella might survive. She might even do her duty to the revolution and survive, which was really remarkable.

The trouble was in determining where her duty lay. Should she attempt to make it back to the ballet school and warn her comrades of the impending attack? Or was it more fitting for a fighter to go forward, gun in hand, and carry out the orders of her superior? Even so inferior a superior as Calvo.

She listened, her face pressed against the moldering bricks, her thin hands clutching the old field jacket around her body. The rain had settled down to a steady, disheartening drizzle. On the street above she heard the grinding of heavy machinery, and she moved, risking a glance.

An armored personnel carrier, vast, angular, six-wheeled, looking like a huge ugly tortoise, was rolling by on great cleated tires.

Gianbattista, they are going to kill you, she thought. They are going to kill everyone at the ballet school. The bodies will lie broken among the bits of shattered mirrors. Gianbattista, it doesn't matter now that I used to fuck for a bowl of fish-head soup. Whatever disgusting disease you imagine I could have given you will go with you into a pauper's grave. They won't even give your corpse to your slobbering mamma and papa. What do you think of that, you bourgeois bastard?

Mariella clenched her small fist over the bulk of the 9mm Makarov in her pocket. The pistol held six bullets. She hadn't even thought to bring more. Who would have imagined she would need them?

There was more activity in the street above. Distant lights illuminated the falling rain. She heard a police or army radio issuing orders.

"Close the circle, Lieutenant."

"Are the civilians out of Number 20?"

She heard the rumble of diesel exhaust. Some sort of military truck rolled by. Paused.

She heard boots. The metallic sounds weapons make. An officer's voice said, "One squad on each side of the street. Make sure all the civilians are out of the area."

The vehicle rolled on. She breathed a sigh of relief.

She heard a shout: "You! Why are you hiding there? Come out!"

Under the rim of a steel para's helmet, a very young face made every effort to be fierce and official. The soldier carried a machine pistol, and his cheeks had been daubed with camouflage paint.

He gestured with his weapon. "Everyone must leave this area. Everyone. Didn't you hear the orders?"

Mariella huddled on her knees and glared at the enemy.

"Didn't you hear me? Everyone must leave here. Get up." His tone oscillated between entreaty and authority. He was, in fact, only ten months older than Mariella, and this was his first action with the antiterrorists.

Mariella got to her feet. Her legs were cold and wet. She mounted the cement stairs toward him warily. The truck carrying the rest of the soldier's detachment had moved off down the street. Individual soldiers were searching building entrances. The street was strangely deserted, and it was lit by reflections from above. Somewhere a radio was still playing in some apartment not yet flushed out.

The young para said, "What were you doing down there?"

Mariella said nothing. She had learned that silence was always to be desired.

"Answer me. Why were you hiding?" The soldier's tone grew slightly shrill. "What have you got there?"

"Where?"

"In your pocket. Something is weighing it down. Let me see what you have." The muzzle of the machine pistol wavered.

Mariella took the Makarov from her pocket and shot the young soldier in the face with it. He pitched backward; his weapon clattered on the pavement. There were angry shouts from the vehicle down the street, and the sound of running men.

Mariella fled down an alley, across an empty street, down a second alley. She could hear the sounds behind her growing louder. She had never been as frightened as this. Never.

She heard a shout to halt and ignored it.

She darted through a gate, between buildings, into the decrepit entryway of the safe house. This is wrong, she thought. I have led them straight to my comrades. A soldier of the revolution should do better than that, be braver. She fell and skinned both knees. She saw the enemy coming between the buildings.

At this moment she remembered that she hated them, hated the society they protected, a society that had given her nothing, only an ugly life, not even a decent death.

She aimed the Russian pistol and pulled the trigger once, twice, three times. The weapon danced in her hands. For you, American bitch, Mariella thought. For just the fragment of an instant she tried to remember how and why it was that she had so wanted to kill the American. And for almost that long she understood. It was because the American had had so much and she had had so little. That was reason enough to set a world afire.

The street reverberated to the sound of a half-dozen military automatic weapons firing.

In the foul-smelling apartment above, Umberto and Giorgio heard the gunfire. They looked at one another, stunned, and then bolted for the back stairs and a run across the darkening, rainy city.

In the locked closet where Denny Wells was confined, the sounds were dull, but unmistakable. Someone was shooting.

Denny squeezed her eyes shut to hold back any hint of tears. When she heard the shouts and the commands, it took her time to realize that her captors had gone and the building was being searched.

Recklessly and angrily, she began to kick at the walls and the locked door with her bound feet. *"In here! In here, damn it, I'm in here!"*

And three blocks away, on the top story of the ballet school, Gianbattista Calvo paused in the "report" he was giving the nervous young Russian from the KGB.

"What was *that?*"

"What was what?" Ekimov asked edgily.

"It sounded like gunfire."

The façade of the ballet school blazed suddenly with white light. A nightmare stentorian voice, amplified a hundred times, roared up from the street:

"Brigatisti! Your building is surrounded. Throw out your weapons and come out with your hands clasped over your heads! Brigatisti!"

The entire message was repeated in German.

Ekimov moaned.

Calvo, caught by surprise, stared stupidly through the steel shutters at the empty street—until one of the Palmiro Togliatti Unit fighters on the roof, eager to fire his weapon in the crowded city, loosed a burst of AK-47 fire.

The reply was a hail of steel that ripped and chipped and tore at the brick of the ballet school building.

The Battle of the Via Palestro began to convulse the city of Rome.

38. ROME

Herrick sat anxiously in the small office overlooking the floor of the sigint room in Rome Station. The room was a minireplica of a room in Langley, but the maps and screen displays in the pit were devoted to the city of Rome, to Italy, and to the central Mediterranean area.

The room had been built at the time the Agency was suffering nearly terminal attacks of "niceness" (Frank Traina's word), during the Carter administration. In that day, the nation—or at least the Washington establishment—had been convinced that given the CIA's proven tendency toward nastiness, only a complete overturn of the doctrinal balance between humint and sigint—human intelligence and signals intelligence—could save the American soul.

As a junior case officer, Herrick had lived through those days; he thought of them as the Company's own Cultural Revolution. He had seen agents with years of experience and irreplaceable skills fired or urged into retirement so that their human assets could be replaced with artifacts of titanium and plastic peering at the earth from space.

Herrick, wondering darkly where Traina and Wells were at this moment, was being treated to a remarkable enhanced infrared image of the Italian capital. The activity being imaged was taking place under a ground-hugging cloud layer that was dropping rain on the south-central Italian peninsula. To one trained as Herrick was, the developing confrontation in the Via Palestro was clearly discernible. Men showed as points of red light, vehicles as blocks of deeper red. The buildings and streets were painted by the computer's false-color enhancement program in contrasting greens and blues. An expert in urban guerrilla warfare, Herrick thought, would be able to command the battle from a headquarters equipped as this room was.

But the commander was on the scene, and, though Herrick's

frustration would have been eased by action, he thanked God it was General della Tevera and not himself.

He pressed forward against the railing that separated him from the outward-leaning glass and watched the Italian antiterrorist groups closing the ring on the Palmiro Togliatti Unit. Gunfire was a silent flaring of muzzle heat, sensed from four hundred miles in space, zapped across the Atlantic to Washington and back again. There was actually a time-lag while the signals fled at light speed up, across, back, and down again. Marvelous! Herrick thought. If the process were reversed, would all this technology show the limousines gathering at the White House so the heavy hitters could hear that Jack Wells was now a political loose cannon and therefore not an acceptable secretary of state to show the Soviets at still another summit?

On the electronic table below, markers representing the antiterrorist units maneuvered, and the circle grew smaller. Just like an arcade game, Herrick thought grimly. We are reducing human strife to flashing lights and computer-enhanced images.

Yet, for all the technology available to him, Herrick was helpless. He had just about promised Traina that, regardless of instructions from home, he would do as much as he could to help Wells through what must be a horrible time. But what he could actually manage was simply to act as a message drop and information center. Somewhere in the city a young girl was being held—under what conditions, God only knew. Somewhere else—undoubtedly moving in on a rendezvous at the entrance to the Vatican Museums—was Jack Wells. An "old" man. An *armed* old man, Herrick thought, ready to commit murder or any act necessary to recover this girl. And Megan Wells and David Ashburn—where the hell were they? It was like playing chess blindfolded, with the added handicap of not being told to which squares the pieces had been moved.

A light began to flash on the console beside his chair. He regarded it balefully, as though he'd like to uproot all the station's electronic systems. Like many career intelligence officers, he sometimes dreamed of what it would have been like to serve in an earlier time—under Wild Bill Donovan, say, in the London of 1942. Or even as one of Walsingham's lace-collared agents in trunk hose and wrinkled tights, doing the Good Queen's dirty work.

He sighed and picked up the receiver. "Herrick."

"We have a call for you from Colonel Guindani of the Carabinieri, sir."

"Put him on."

The Colonel sounded both pleased and excited, despite the fact that General Della Tevera had left him at headquarters while the army collected Red Brigades' scalps.

"*Pronto*, Reuben?" The Italian always had great difficulty pronouncing Herrick's given name.

"Eustacio. Always nice to hear from you."

"Marvelous news. *We have recovered the Wells girl.*"

Herrick sat bolt upright and began to make plans.

Guindani was making a story, an adventure, out of the recovery. But, God damn it, he was entitled to if they had really rescued Denny Wells from the Red Brigades.

Herrick lifted another handset from the console and said, "Tell the duty officer to report to me here. On the double." To Guindani he said, "Tell me."

"Apparently they were holding her not more than a few blocks from the building on Via Palestro. Outside Della Tevera's perimeter, but not by very much. One of the soldiers flushed out a girl—young, apparently—hiding in a stairwell near the barricades they were putting up before moving in on the terrorists. The soldier, young also, must have suspected her of being one of them, because he tried to stop her, and she shot him. In the face. Killed him, of course. Murdered him.

"The terrorist girl ran. Straight for a safe house. And there she was—Signorina Wells. Her guards heard the shooting in the street and ran away, leaving her unwatched."

"Shooting in the street?"

"The terrorist shot at the soldiers, and they returned her fire. She was killed."

Herrick tried to feel compassion and failed.

"That is good news, Eustacio. Congratulations. Where is the girl now?"

"At the American Hospital. She is not hurt. There is dehydration and a few bruises. I understand she behaved bravely. She wants to speak to a Megan Wells, but we cannot locate her. Is she a sister?"

"Her mother."

"Can you locate her, then?"

"I will. Of course," Herrick said. Of course. Starting where?

"If you would mention the Carabinieri to the Minister of the Interior, Reuben?"

"I will speak to the Ambassador," Herrick said. "It will come better from him."

It was time to disengage himself from this conversation, Herrick thought, and said, "Thank you for calling, Eustacio." He had no wish to tell a colonel of Carabinieri that Megan Wells was with a CIA field agent, and that the Rome chief of station had no idea at all where.

He looked at the clock. It was after nine-thirty. I don't know where they are—only where they *will be*, he thought as he turned to the duty officer.

"We need some muscle. Who's available?"

"Only me, I'm afraid, sir."

"What's your name?" He should know, but faces changed almost daily in the European stations.

"Walter Norton, sir."

Herrick looked at him for the first time. Sandy hair, regular features, soft-brown spaniel's eyes. "How long have you been here?" he asked.

"Eleven days, sir." The young man looked appalled at arousing so much direct interest in the station chief.

"How old are you?"

"Twenty-four, sir." Feeling something more was needed, Norton said, "I was second in my class at Fort Bragg, sir."

"I see. That's good, Norton." Traina, Herrick thought, where in hell are you when I need you? "Can you shoot?"

"Yes, sir. I am qualified in handguns and automatic weapons."

"Good. Draw Uzis for us."

"*Us*, sir?"

"For you and me, boy. And order up a car and a driver. A good one, who knows the city and is at ease with an Uzi."

"Yes, *sir*."

Herrick watched Norton vanish, almost at a run. Well, he thought, you were remembering what it was like yourself not too long ago. Wishing you were one of Donovan's boys. Here's your chance, hero. It's still a war, even if most of the men fighting it are ready for retirement.

Jack Wells, more than most men, would appreciate that.

And so would the Frenchman.

39. VATICAN CITY

David let the Alfetta roll slowly around the Piazza Cavour. The rain fell steadily in a light, uniform haze. The windshield wipers slapped regularly back and forth. It was odd, he thought, that the traffic was so light. But at this time on a rainy night there was little to see on the west bank of the river except the magnificent buildings illuminated against the hazy darkness.

There had been a detachment of police at the far end of the Ponte Cavour. He had been tempted to use them to reestablish contact with Herrick. But the suggestion had distressed Megan so much he'd abandoned the idea. She was adamant about following Thierry's instructions to the letter. Despite all the evidence to the contrary, she seemed to feel that she owed Thierry honest dealing. The closer to the rendezvous she got, the more strongly she appeared to feel this way. To David, it smacked of a kind of madness. He knew the ways of active-measures assassins. Did Megan, on the basis of a single season's marriage a long time ago, imagine she knew better? He hoped not.

He checked his watch. They were less than a mile from the rendezvous, with time in hand. He tried again. "There's a telephone kiosk down there. I want to let our people know where we are."

"He said I must meet him *alone*." Now that the moment was so near, Megan's tone had developed a brittle quality.

"You will be. In a manner of speaking. But Herrick should be told now."

"You promised me." Her voice was strained.

David stopped the car and rolled down the left-hand window. "Listen," he said.

"What is it?"

"Helicopters." He got out and stood in the drizzling rain searching the low overcast to the south. There were soft crackling noises, muffled by distance and the damp air.

Megan heard the sounds, too. Across years a memory came

to her: She stood on the balcony of Jean Thierry's Cholon apartment. The scent of the Saigon River was strong. The air was thick and damp. And in the distance gunfire crackled as the Vietcong attacked isolated units of the South Vietnamese Army.

"Is that what I think it is?" she whispered.

"Heard it before?"

"Yes."

He looked at her upturned face in the car window. Her hair glistened with rain, her cheeks were wet, her eyes were darkly glowing.

He said, "There's a fire fight. A mile or two downriver, as nearly as I can make out. Now we *have* to touch base with Herrick."

"He can't interfere, David."

The moment of truth was coming, he thought. Am I going to lose her yet again?

"*He'll* have to decide that," he said.

Megan opened her door and got out of the car. She started to run across the piazza in the direction of the Via Crescenzio.

"*Megan! Damn it, wait.*" He went after her. She had run almost through the piazza before he caught her, held her arm. "Listen to me. *Listen to me.*"

She turned her face away angrily. "Don't. Don't. *Don't*. What is there to listen to? He has my *daughter*."

"It isn't Denny he wants." David held her by both arms. He drew a breath to start again. I could lose her, he thought, I could lose her right here by saying the wrong thing. "Thierry's never wanted Denny. Or you. It's your uncle he wants. That's what drives him."

"He doesn't even know Uncle Jack," she protested.

"My God, Meg. Are you *still* that naïve?"

"Are you trying to tell me this is some Cold War thing?"

"Your uncle is here in Rome, Meg. He is going to give himself up to Thierry and his friends to get Denny back."

"That's insane. How could Uncle Jack know where to find Jean?"

He drew a deep breath and took the plunge. With Megan's loathing of spooks, there was no telling how she would react, but there was no more time for sanctimonious games.

He said, "The Soviet Consulate in San Francisco has been tapping your telephone for more than a year."

"*What?*"

He studied her face. She had weathered the first shock.

"How do you know that? And why would they do such a thing?" she demanded.

"They started the first time there was a rumor about your uncle becoming Secretary of State."

"The Russians? Tapped my telephone?"

"There are things about Jack Wells they know, but to back them up, they needed to listen to the two of you, or thought they did." The heavy-handed, insensitive Russki, he thought. How could they possibly have known how poorly Megan and Jack Wells communicated? But they should have known. That was part of their job. Now their operation was lumbering along like a tank with a missing tread: heavy, limping, half-controlled. *Inelegant.*

"God. That's *horrible.*"

"Yes, I suppose it is."

She backed away as far as his grip would allow and said, "How do you know all this?"

"An agency in Washington has been inside their computer and communications for a long time. A very long time."

Megan shook off his hands but did not run. "Does that mean that the people I speak with, the things I say . . ." She stared at him, disbelieving. "*Everything* is all tucked away in Washington?"

He nodded.

"Sick. Just sick," she said.

"No, it isn't."

"How can you say that?"

"Come back to the car."

"How?"

"Damn it, don't fight me."

"You think it's all right to have all my private conversations in some Washington data bank just because the government stole the information from the Russians?" Her voice had risen a full octave, driven by outrage.

For the first time, he came near to succumbing to a flash of anger at her attitude. "I don't understand you. It upsets you more that there's a file on you in Washington than that the *Russians* have been spying on you."

"You expect that from the Soviets," she said. "It wouldn't have happened if it weren't for Uncle Jack and your damned Agency. Why can't people just be left alone to live their lives? Why are we manipulated and spied on?"

257

"That's what it's about, Meg. But if you can't understand, I am truly sorry."

"My bloodlines again?"

"There's nothing to be ashamed of in being the daughter of Matt and Denise Wells. Don't pretend there is. What troubles me most is the way you feel about Jack Wells. He isn't an easy person to know. Or even to like. Is there a rule that says he has to be? You say it was tough being Matt and Denise's daughter. He was Matt's younger brother. *That* was really tough.

"Matt Wells came home from the war a hero and a drunk and a psycho—so they say. That's the kind of sacrifices your bloodline is capable of making."

"How awful!"

"It depends, doesn't it, on what is important?"

They walked back to the car through the rain. Megan was silent.

"I may as well say it all," David murmured.

She made no reply.

"I remember now what went wrong with us before," he said. "You told me once how much I reminded you of Uncle Jack."

"Yes, I did."

"I didn't think that was so bad. I still don't." He looked at her in the light from the street lamps ringing Piazza Cavour.

"Have you never realized how much he loves you?" David asked suddenly. "It can't ever have been easy for him. According to people who knew him when he was first thinking about joining the Company—when your parents were still alive—he just worshiped Matt. After Matt and Denise were killed, he must have been lost. But he had you. That must have meant a great deal to him."

"He's a distant man, David," she said.

"You never did anything to reduce the distance between you, did you? You hated his work. I agree you have a right to your opinion. It's politics, you know. That's all that it is. You and your peers don't approve of what the country has been trying to do since the Second World War or how it's trying to do it. Well, that's your privilege. But you're wrong, you know. We aren't perfect, but you don't have a right to expect us to be. Give us a break, Meg, even if it makes you feel pure to think spooks belong under a rock."

He regarded her steadily. "I love you too much to let you get away with that kind of thinking. Just now you were more upset by the file on you in Washington than by the one in Moscow.

For God's sake, *think* about that. You are a wonderful woman. I've never known anyone so quick and bright and better to be around. But when I first met you, you were acting like a child. You were at war with Jack Wells. The same war that got started when you were a little girl, because Matt and Denise were too damaged by what they had been through to be much good as parents. And Jack, for Chrissake, was barely into his twenties.

"When we graduated from law school, I had hopes. I think Jack did, too. And that was the kiss of death for my chances, wasn't it? If *he* liked me, you couldn't possibly take a chance and love me."

David opened the door of the Alfetta and waited until Megan was seated. Then he closed the door silently and walked around to the driver's side.

"Have you had enough of the Ballad of Dreary David?"

Megan shook her head slowly. "Finish," she said. "We may never get another chance."

"There is that," he said gloomily. "All right, I will. I have never been able to understand how you had the sheer *chutzpah* to treat the old man that way."

"He wouldn't thank you for that."

"I suppose not. But try to see it. He loved your parents and he loved you. He took you and did his clumsy best to raise you. He didn't do so damned badly, you know. He educated you, indulged you—yes, that's what I said—indulged. Maybe he didn't behave like a father in 'Mister Rogers' Neighborhood,' but that's never been his style, has it?

"Then what happened? You ran off to 'Nam to impress your sanctimonious friends at school, and when it all went wrong, he did what he had to do to get you back. Then he stayed with you—even though by that time he probably thought you hated him—until you could make it on your own. Only then did he go back to Washington, to politics. That was all he *had*, Meg. What else was there for him?"

Megan regarded him steadily in the dimly reflected light from beyond the rain-dappled windshield. "Where is he now, David?"

"I don't know, my love. But I think if you shouted, he would hear you."

"The Agency told him that Jean called me, didn't they? It must have been Frank Traina."

"The idea was for him to stand still and let other people handle the situation. They were wrong. When he was Deputy

Director of Operations he never handled a black operation that way.''

Megan essayed a faint smile. "I could have told them, if they'd had the sense to ask.''

"They should have done that," David agreed, and cupped her chin with his hand.

"What did Uncle Jack do to Jean Thierry?" she asked. "Why this, after so many years?''

David hesitated before replying. But this is the moment, he thought. If one can face the truth in adversity, half the battle of being human is won.

"Jack tried to have him killed. I think.''

Megan closed her eyes. "Oh, God. Oh, *God*. Because of me.''

"I'm sorry, Meg. But I think so. The Cold War became very personal to your uncle when you married Thierry." David looked at his watch. "We had better get going," he said. "All right?" He touched her cheek with his fingertips.

She said somberly, "There was something more about my parents. What was it?''

"Your father was tortured by the SS. So he drank. He couldn't handle it. And he couldn't shake it after he came home. I think he was flying drunk when he and Denise crashed. I couldn't prove it. I wouldn't want to. But that's what I think.''

Megan whispered, "When you said Uncle Jack loved them both, you really meant he was in love with my mother.''

"I think so, yes.''

"Poor Uncle Jack.''

"Poor Jack, indeed.''

She caught his hand and held it. "Tell me now: What about Jean?''

This time he did not even consider dissembling. "I'm going to call Herrick. And then I am going to take Thierry. It's our only chance.''

She sat huddled against the seat as David drove the Alfetta to the Piazza Adriana.

The Castel Sant'Angelo, illuminated by hidden floodlights, loomed massively against the rainy night. The vast winged iron figure atop the great drumlike structure, more devil than angel in this light, seemed suspended, eerily, against the amber overcast.

David stopped the car. "Are you all right now?" he asked.

She wondered if what he was really asking was whether she trusted him now. I do. I can't. Try to understand me, she thought.

He got out of the car and stood for a moment regarding her with a strange, almost wary expression. The telephone kiosk stood among some trees. It seemed miles away.

As he hesitated, Megan thought he was on the verge of taking the key from the ignition. But in the end he did not do that. Instead, he put something on the car seat. It was a pistol. Megan suppressed an impulse to shrink from it.

"Why, David?"

"Can you use it if you have to?"

"I don't think so."

"Keep it anyway," he said, and turned away.

She watched him walk through the rain and into the park created from the ancient fortifications surrounding the Castel. As he vanished into the trees, she got out of the car and began to walk. Then she began to run, away from the river toward the Piazza del Risorgimento and the Vatican wall. She did not look back. Her breath came in deep, anxious gasps. She could hear her footsteps on the cobblestones.

I am sorry, she thought. But in the end it is I who had to decide. Denny is my daughter. No one else's. Not even Jean's.

The substitute duty officer accepted the call. He had been on for no more than thirty minutes. Norton, in a state of high excitement, had left the building in the company of the chief of station.

When the substitute, even more junior than young Norton, learned that it was David Ashburn on the line, he grew respectful. Ashburn had a reputation among the younger people at Rome Station.

"I'm sorry, Mr. Ashburn. Mr. Herrick left here a half hour ago. He did not say where he was going."

"I need backup."

"I'll try to get Mr. Herrick on the radio, sir."

"Is Frank Traina there?"

"No, sir."

"What's your name?"

"Steinheart, sir."

"All right, Steinheart. I want you to reach General della Tevera—"

"The General's troops are on an operation, sir."

"I know. I can hear them. I want you to tell Tevera that I need

261

a helicopter at the north wall of Vatican City. Outside the entrance to the Vatican Museums. On the double, all right? Tell him the LZ is *hot*."

"Yes, *sir*."

The duty officer almost allowed the connection to be broken before he remembered what it was that had Ashburn so involved: the kidnapping of that American girl last week.

"Sir, sir?"

"What is it?"

"General della Tevera's soldiers found Miss Wells, sir. Some terrorist made a run for it and led them right to her. She's all right. Isn't that great?"

In Piazza Adriana, David suppressed a shout of triumph and hung up the telephone. He broke into a run through the edge of the parkland back to the street where the car waited.

His elation crashed.

He cursed himself for a trusting idiot when he saw the Alfetta parked in the rain with the passenger's door standing open.

40. VIA PALESTRO, ROME

Valentin Ekimov reacted to the sudden flurry of gunfire in the street with absolute horror. He had, on an earlier occasion, heard the sound of guns. As a passenger in a helicopter gunship on a flight between Kabul and Kandahar, he had seen the rocket trail of a heat-seeking missile and he had heard the chatter of the door gunner's machine guns. He had hated every moment of it.

He had been in Afghanistan on a two-week assignment for the Sluzhba, who had used him because his face was not known to the drug dealers in the tank units. But the operation had been a total failure. The soldiers who were clever enough to get rich selling hashish to their mates were far too clever to be caught by a twenty-three-year-old lieutenant from the headquarters of the Second Directorate.

The one thing the tour—arranged, incidentally, by Yelena's father, Petrov Orlov, to fatten Valentin's service record—had proved was that the thing he liked least in the entire world was to be shot at.

The soldiers below fired again, and the steel shutters clanged and reverberated with the impact of bullets. To Gianbattista Calvo, Ekimov said thickly, "Whatever else happens, comrade, I must not be found here. It could create an international incident." He hated the tremulousness of his voice.

Calvo, who was having his own troubles containing his fear, said, "I do not know what happened, Comrade Captain. All of this is premature. We were to have received some hostages before now." He had reacted almost immediately to Ekimov's swift discomfiture. Was it because the man was afraid—which he plainly was—or because he had knowledge that had not been shared with the Palmiro Togliatti Unit?

He wiped his sweaty hands on his trousers. Upstairs on the roof and at the embrasures under the eaves, some of the comrades were keeping up a fairly steady rate of fire. The important thing, he thought, was to prevent a swift rush by the antiterrorist commandos in the street. With time, anything was possible. Even escape. He flushed. The thought was unworthy.

He knelt behind a row of sandbags under the windowsill and pushed gingerly at the steel shutter.

"Why? What are you doing?" Ekimov demanded.

"I need to see what is facing us," Calvo said.

But the moment the shutter moved, there was a roar of gunfire below. Bullets entering between the shutter panels struck the remnants of the wall mirrors, sending shards flying. The wooden floor glistened with millions of tiny fragments.

Two boys, staggering under the weight of their burden, ran from the stairwell with a Browning. It was an almost obsolete weapon, invented during the First World War for use in trench warfare. But copies and equivalents were still used in every army in the world. It required little skill.

The two who set it up were dark, dirty-faced, with eyes that showed the whites. They worked swiftly and with precision. They should have encouraged Ekimov. Instead, they frightened him. To be in battle in the company of such children was an invitation to die.

He had a dreadful premonition of personal disaster. There was a kind of fateful certainty in him that he had been manipulated again by General Plakhanov, who had somehow seen through Ekimov's clumsy spying. His fate had changed when

Orlov decided to betray his trust as a Party official and began to accumulate stolen things and misappropriate money.

It hardly mattered now, except that Kalganin was going to be vexed at the ease with which Plakhanov had avoided the watchdog put upon him. Ekimov thought bleakly that, for all his peculiarities, General Feliks Ivanovich Plakhanov was a cleverer man than Gregor Borisovich Kalganin. At the moment Kalganin ranked Plakhanov, but by this time next year things would be different. Of course, he thought bitterly, Captain Valentin Ilarionovich Ekimov—beloved husband of Yelena Orlova Ekimov and doting father of her children—would be dead. Shot down in the company of Italian terrorists, to the shame and humiliation of the Motherland. And so, damned for all eternity. Or until a different version of *glasnost* became fashionable.

That, he thought shakily, was a remarkably cynical thought for a candidate for the ruling class, for the *nomenklatura*. And mingled in equal parts with the cynicism and his rising terror, Ekimov found a total and absolute desire to survive.

Calvo heard the helicopters circling in the rainy night. The noise brought back the nightmarish hours following the attack on the power station.

He went to the stairs and called up to the people on the roof, "How many of you up there?"

The shouted reply came back swiftly, "Two with the machine gun and five riflemen."

"Two stay with the gun. The rest of you get down here!"

"Why?" Ekimov asked.

"I want the inside barricades manned," Calvo said. His eyes were wide, bulging with excitement.

Ekimov heard the clatter of boots on the stairs, and five armed men raced down from the roof.

"*Madonna*, I wish Hanalore were here," Calvo said. "She's one of the best."

"Where is she?" Ekimov asked stupidly.

"Where your superior had me send her," Calvo answered angrily. "To attack that journalist woman in the Abruzzi. I don't know why!"

Ekimov underwent an epiphany. To divide the forces aligned against us, he thought. None of it was too difficult—as long as one asked only *what* and not *why*.

A girl armed with an M-16 appeared. "The radio says there's a full army brigade out there," she announced.

"You know how they lie," Calvo said.

"Of course. They lie all the time," the girl said.

Calvo's statement appeared to convince her, astonishing Ekimov.

But one of the machine gunners, peering through the gap between the steel shutters, said shrilly, "They've got tanks!"

"Those are armored personnel carriers," Calvo said.

Was that supposed to encourage this ragtag army, Ekimov wondered. He did not believe that the tanks were APCs. He had been in the Crimea when there had been food-price riots. Against traitors one used tanks, not armored personnel carriers. There was neither the need nor the time to allow gentler methods.

There was a whooshing noise and a terrible clang and blast. The steel shutters on one of the windows overlooking the street came off their hinges and spun across the practice floor.

The air stank of explosives. Cathedral bells were ringing in Ekimov's head. Someone below had launched a rocket at the building.

Through the clangor, he heard a thin, shrieking wail. His eyes were filled with dust, and he was, to his astonishment, sitting on the floor. Across the room from him was what appeared to be the stump of a statue driven, somehow, into the hardwood floor. The statue's face was that of the girl Calvo had reassured about the Italian brigade. Her weapon had vanished.

She appeared to be trying to lift herself out of a hole in the floor with her extended arms. Her skin was white with chalk dust. Her eyes had sunk into red-rimmed pits. The sudden transformation from youth to extreme old age was stunning.

He said thickly, "Let me help you."

On his knees, he crossed the floor. The tiny shards of mirror shredded his trousers and became embedded in his bloody knees. He scarcely noticed.

The girl had not stopped wailing, though the sound seemed to have slipped away into some inaudible register of agony.

The hole in the floor from which she protruded was wet and shiny. It was as though she were emerging from a glistening, cluttered pool.

The steel shutter had been blown the length of the practice floor and into the wall. A great smear of blood darkened the floor, a huge disfigurement, as though a vast and massive paintbrush had been used to make a red river there.

The girl stared at Ekimov.

Ekimov stared back witlessly.

She spread her hands, stiffened her arms, and moved.

There was no hole beneath her, only a pool of dust and blood. She raised herself up on her arms, still staring furiously at Ekimov. Then she toppled forward, half a human being, separated from her legs just below the pelvis. As she fell, she managed one last shrill, almost hypersonic scream of protest. *"Noooooooo . . ."*

Ekimov picked himself up off the floor and, without a look at Calvo, who was, with difficulty, doing the same thing, ran, stumbling, down the stairs toward the sandbagged redoubt at the bottom.

41. PONTE MAZZINI

The effects of the rising battle on the Via Palestro were spreading across the city. Unsure of how many terrorists he faced at the ballet school, General della Tevera had decided it would be wise to attack only with overwhelming force. Consequently, he dispatched requests for local reinforcements from the city police auxiliaries and even the highway officers of the Stradale. In order to move these units expeditiously, the city police began to close certain choke points inhibiting the movement of traffic from one bank of the Tiber to the other. Roman police had had two millennia to learn how to paralyze their city. They were good at it and they enjoyed it. It allowed a large number of men an almost unlimited opportunity to exercise authority with the panache suited to their colorful uniforms, the stubbornness of their Mediterranean minds, and their voluble Roman charm.

The taxi in which Frank Traina and Jack Wells were riding reached the Ponte Mazzini, and the driver pulled up, cursing. Ahead was a traffic jam of truly Roman proportions. Beyond the cars could be seen the flashing blue lights of a roadblock.

"What is happening?" Traina asked the driver.

The man spread his hands irritably, "Who can tell, *signor*? It is the mission of the police in this city to prevent traffic from moving." He thrust his head out of the window into the misting rain and shouted, *"Eh, ecco! Nullita! Policia! Che cosa?"*

"I don't think," Traina said, "that we are going to get through here faster by calling the police nonentities." He looked at Wells. The older man's face was still, immobile, eyes hooded. "I think della Tevera's operation is making waves, Jack."

To the driver, Wells said, "Turn around and try the Cavour Bridge."

The driver said, "It will do no good, *signor*. It is the trouble on the Via Palestro. Whenever a nest of red terrorists is found, the police isolate the Vatican. One can emerge, but it is made very difficult to enter. Because of the time the Bulgarians tried to kill the Holy Father, you see." He snapped on the radio. Excited voices were trying to explain to the public what their army's antiterrorist commandos were doing. "You hear, *signor*?"

Wells handed a pair of twenty-dollar bills across the car seat. "Make the attempt," he said.

The driver shrugged and took the bills. "As you command, *signor*. The attempt shall be made." The taxi, a relatively new Fiat, was wrenched out of line and, amid a flurry of shouts, imprecations, and horn blowing, turned to cut across the meander of the Tiber toward the Ponte Cavour.

Traina said, "Jack, shouldn't we bring Reuben in now?"

"The President took Reuben out," Wells said bluntly.

"I think he might come back in."

"I'm sorry, Frank. We can't deal with Thierry as if he were just a kidnapper. It's more complicated than that."

"Because of Megan?"

"Because of *you*," Wells said. "And stop pretending you don't understand."

Wells turned and watched the traffic on the rainy street. As they crossed the Corso Vittorio, the occupants could see, at the river end of the street, near where two bridges crossed the Tiber, a mass of stalled cars and flashing blue and red lights.

The driver looked back and shrugged. Wells signed for him to drive on to the Cavour Bridge.

But when they approached it, the jam was, if anything, even worse than at the other crossings. On the radio, news readers, a man and woman alternating, were describing a street scene downriver, where army commandos "are preparing for a massive, final assault."

"Thierry did that," Wells said.

"Blew a Red Brigades base?"

"It was deliberate. The timing is perfect."

What sort of mind worked that way, Traina wondered. But he knew the answer: the sort we all had once, when we were young and ruthless.

"Stop here," Wells said.

The driver complied, just out of the growing traffic jam.

Wells looked at his watch. "I can't wait any longer," he said and got out. Traina started to follow, but Wells held the door closed. "Go back to the embassy, Frank."

"I'm backup," Traina said through the open rear window.

"You are Director of Operations of Central Intelligence. You don't push into this," Wells said.

"Like hell I don't."

Wells held the large, blunt Glock 17 to Traina's chin.

"You wouldn't."

"Don't make me decide. It's my women Thierry has on a string."

Traina smelled the gun oil. It was convincing. He had never seen a Glock fired. He wondered how well they worked. Probably quite well enough.

Wells tapped the muzzle of the pistol against his old friend's cheek. "I have used up all my time," he said. "And not wisely." He turned to the driver, who had been watching with bulging eyes. *"Avanti,"* he said softly. *"Prego."*

The man turned, raced the Fiat's engine, and pulled away, slipping and sliding on the wet cobbles.

Wells put the pistol in his coat pocket and made his way through the traffic jam in the direction of the bridge.

At their junction, the Via Leone IV and the Viale Vaticano form an oblique angle of more than ninety degrees. A hundred yards west on the Viale Vaticano is a jog in the Vatican wall and a further hundred yards of stonework, pierced by the only entrance to the Vatican Museums from outside the Vatican proper. In the daytime, troops of tourists debouch there from whalelike white omnibuses or arrive in great numbers from the Ottaviano subway stop, five minutes' walk away.

But after nightfall, and in a steady, cold, drizzling rain, the area was deserted. Feliks Plakhanov, sheltering in the lee of the Vatican wall, waited patiently. He had not imagined that when the time finally came to collect the debt owed by Paladin he would be so calm.

He rolled his heavy cane between his gloved fingertips, relishing the antique perfection of it. Any weapon would have done, he thought; he was not such a traditionalist. But it pleased him—and added to the dreamlike quality of the Paladin affair—that the armory of the Rome residency could produce so fine an example of an early-nineteenth-century stiletto. Who would have imagined it? Of course it was the Italian idea of a gentleman's weapon. Perhaps that explained it.

What, he wondered, would his brute of a father have made of a sword cane? Of the entire Paladin affair, for that matter. How the insensitive man would have hooted and shouted at Peter Arendt. "So you are my limp-wristed son's fancy man, are you?" he would have said. And next it would have been "Nazi faggot" or something worse.

It will all be over soon, Peter, he thought. I know you wouldn't wish it so. You were too gentle to live, Peter Arendt.

Revenge, Plakhanov thought dreamily, is never for others. It is for the ease of one's own soul.

Soul? What an un-Soviet concept that was. He looked through the falling rain into emptiness.

He wondered where the Frenchman was. Nearby. Of that he was certain. Plakhanov's spare, ascetic face showed almost no emotion whatever at the thought that the Frenchman had kidnapped and, by this time, quite possibly murdered his own daughter.

That overstated the case, of course. Simple male-female biology could be used to show that this man and that woman produced this child. But a trace on a Mendelian chart was not sufficient to make a relationship. Plakhanov knew it well. His own lack of feeling for the savage who gave him his patronymic was proof enough for that.

The Frenchman had never seen the girl, had never known her. To him, she was related only to John and Megan Wells, and that was enough to make her life forfeit.

Oh, yes. Plakhanov understood very well.

He stood listening to the sound of the rain on the trees and shrubs on the far side of the wall. It was a hushed, soughing sound. It reminded him of the sound of snow falling on the birches in Gorky Park.

Then he became aware of another sound. It was the click of heels on the cobblestones of the Via Leone IV—the sound of a woman running.

42. VIA PALESTRO

The ballet school was burning. Fortunately for the defenders, the army had chosen not to rely heavily on chemical weapons. The one class of matériel the Togliatti Unit lacked was protection from gas: masks and first aid for burns. Two CS grenades had been fired in through the shattered shutters on the practice floor, but that area had been evacuated by everyone. None of the revolutionaries could bring themselves to remain on the same floor as the bifurcated remains of the girl Ekimov had seen die.

For some reason he could not fathom, he found himself asking again and again what her name had been. And strangely, no one appeared to be able to answer him. It was as though her horrid death had shocked the others to the point of selective traumatic amnesia.

Ekimov fought down waves of nausea. He was sickened also by the physical reality of battle. What activity could anyone possibly be engaged in that made such a death meaningful or noble? His fleeting, sanitized view of the war in Afghanistan had been nothing at all like this. When combat soldiers whispered about the things that were done in the field, he had never listened. Now he felt naked and filled with doubts.

He asked himself if such thoughts were a betrayal of the Soviet Motherland and the Communist Party. But the argument would not remain focused inside his skull. It tended to slip free and slide about like a handful of counters in some child's game.

Meanwhile, hidden machine guns in the street chipped away at the stone and brickwork outside; the smell of fire seeped chokingly through the building. The blaze had started on the roof when a concussion grenade had been used to silence the Kalashnikovs there.

The air gradually became heavy with smoke. Ekimov looked to Calvo for guidance, or for some indication that the battle was not being lost by inaction. But the schoolteacher had fallen into a situation beyond his ability to control.

He was afraid, but not yet panicked. Ekimov was closer to that state than the Italian. But panic *would* come, Ekimov thought. It would surely come.

From around the building could be heard the clatter of guns firing. It seemed to Ekimov that any time the Italian Army wished it could overrun the defenders without raising a sweat. He asked Calvo if this were not so.

"Except for this." Calvo lifted the wooden covering of an electrical plenum, a single, massive copper bus that appeared to be the central collection point for masses of twisted wires coming up from between floor and wall, wall and ceiling.

"The building is wired," Calvo said in a shrill voice. "There are nearly one hundred kilograms of *plastique* scattered throughout the building. This detonates all of it."

Ekimov stared at the wire junction in horror. When he had left Moscow with General Plakhanov, he had never imagined himself in a pitched battle. But even in battle he had not imagined himself blown to bloody fragments as an ancient slum building disintegrated into dust and gravel.

"Do you intend to use that?" he demanded.

"*Of course!* When the time comes."

So firm, so sure, Ekimov thought. Except that the voice rings with the cymbal sounds of panic.

A heavy shell struck the building somewhere and shook the entire structure. Ekimov heard the defenders scrabbling about through the wreckage like mice in a trash pile. Plaster dust rolled down the stairs from above and into the redoubt. Ekimov coughed and gagged.

Two guerrillas scrambled down the shattered staircase. One carried two Kalashnikovs, the other a Japanese miniature television set.

"Gianbattista," the one with the assault rifles said, "Giuliano and Federico are dead. So is the last of the *Tedeschi*."

He might have been delivering the football scores, Ekimov thought: Dynamo Moscow has beaten Kiev Red Banner. And, by the way, the field is littered with corpses.

"Look," the one with the television said. "They are broadcasting from out there." His dust-red eyes looked a little mad. "We are famous!"

On the tiny screen was a miniature street war. Floodlights, green APCs, soldiers in combat camouflage. It looked like a documentary Ekimov had once seen, a Gostelradio film about Spetsnaz commandos. But these troops wore red-white-and-green patches on their combat jackets and they were firing at a building that could be seen clearly in the floodlights. *This* building, Ekimov thought with dismay. It was gradually being chewed to bits with small-caliber fire.

The television reporter was a woman. *A woman.* Somehow that was a personal affront to Calvo. It was bad enough that the Palmiro Togliatti Unit was being served to Romans like a circus to be watched over dinner. It was worse still that a plump general in combat gear was being charming to a female Italian television personality and explaining to her that helicopters would be landing teams of commandos on the roof and that the engagement would soon be over. "We deal with terrorists far more severely than we used to do, *signorina*," he said.

The reporter was handed a note. She said, "This just in from Teleradio Centrale. Signor Zachary Quinn, who was seriously wounded in a terrorist attack on the villa of his wife, the journalist Mary Quinn, is said to be improving. He remains at the hospital at L'Aquila."

She turned to the portly officer with her. "General della Tevera, was the attack on the Quinn villa part of a generalized terrorist offensive?"

"It is a possibility, *signorina*. But the day when the Red Brigades could attack whom they pleased whenever they pleased in Italy is now gone."

As if to emphasize his statement, a flare struck the building and exploded into a shower of burning white phosphorus.

Somewhere inside the building, there was a shrill scream as some of that tiny explosion shown on the miniature television screen burned through rubble and found human flesh.

Someone in the hallway shouted, "Gianbattista! They're moving up a tank! *A fucking tank!*"

The thready female voice asked, "Is it true, General della Tevera, that this attack was made possible by an informer?"

"What?" Calvo snatched at the television set. The picture lock tore and left a smear of colors on the screen. But the voices were clear enough.

"We had an anonymous telephone call earlier today."

"What is he saying?" Calvo shouted.

"We believe it was made by a member of the Red Brigades, yes."

Calvo rose to his feet and screamed at the others now concentrating in the reinforced hallway. "Mariella betrayed us! She is a traitor and a whore!"

272

To Ekimov, the scene was rapidly assuming a kind of Dostoevskian madness. What possible difference could it make now if the girl had betrayed her fellows? Somehow, he seriously doubted she had. This chaotic bloodletting had the feel of purpose to it. How completely would an action of this size tie up the law-enforcement and military assets of a city such as Rome? He couldn't be certain, but surely it was having an effect.

And why had Plakhanov dispatched him to the guerrillas exactly when he did? Ekimov, already afraid for his life, suddenly became afraid for his country.

The Dancing Bear had set him to spy on his employer. That was not such a rare thing among the Soviet elite. But had he been entrusted with a larger task than he had imagined? And had he somehow done his job so badly that the Motherland could only be humiliated?

Kalganin had almost given him carte blanche to kill Feliks Plakhanov. Operation Paladin was both individual—which operations must never be—and a potential source of diplomatic disaster for the Soviet Union.

I couldn't have killed him, Ekimov thought, listening to the explosions dismantling the building. Until now, Plakhanov was always moves ahead. Playing chess with him had always been an education. He sent me here like a pawn to Queen's Bishop two—a lamb to the slaughter.

His discipline broke. "I am not staying," he said to Calvo.

"You have no choice. It is for the revolution."

Ekimov stared at the Italian. Though his own discipline had broken, like floes in a river, Calvo's had turned into a solid block of ice. There was terror in his eyes, however.

"You can surrender," Ekimov said.

"Never." He appeared to be looking over Ekimov's shoulder at the wall.

IN EXTREMIS REMEMBER THAT THE PURPOSE OF TERRORISM IS TO TERRORIZE.

Calvo turned and made for the switch box that would detonate the planted explosives.

"No!"

Ekimov found the Makarov issued him by the residency armorer and pointed it at Calvo. He had no intention whatever of firing the weapon. In fact, he was not all that certain that he remembered how.

But the boy with the Kalashnikov knew where his loyalties lay. He swung the wooden stock of the heavy rifle forward in

273

the approved manner and sent the Makarov spinning off into the rubble.

Ekimov shouted in his abominable Italian: "You idiot! He is going to blow all of us into little pieces!" At the same moment, he bolted out into the dusty, noisy hallway.

Behind him he heard the Kalashnikov fire a burst. His sphincter locked, but he was not hit. He pushed his way past a pair of rather dazed terrorists and stumbled toward the door.

The steel panels that had been fixed to the massive oak door were still more or less intact, but the door had been blown slightly ajar. Outside, the noise of electrical generators, an occasional command, as well as gunfire could be heard. The Italians must be making ready at last to assault the building. They would find little resistance. But some guns were still being fired, Ekimov could hear.

He stumbled on toward the door. Behind him he heard someone shout, *"The Russian coward is defecting!"*

He had a wild impulse to give in to hysterical laughter. This was hardly "defecting." It was more nearly "surviving." What would General Plakhanov say about this? But *he* probably counted his former aide as already dead.

He reached the door and threw his weight against it. There was another burst behind him, and hot bullet fragments stung his face. He screamed and drove his weight against the portal. It jammed, then moved.

Ekimov found himself down on the narrow sidewalk. Now the pavement all around him seemed to boil with stone chips, sparks, and flying needles of steel.

Someone behind the brilliant lights shouted, "Cease fire! Cease fire! *Maledetti! Fischiati!* Stop shooting! *Dannati!*"

Ekimov crawled into the street and rose to his feet, ran, fell, crawled toward the armored vehicles. There were no tanks that he could see, but the personnel carriers were threatening enough. He searched his coat pocket and found his passport, which he waved desperately. *"Sono diplomatico! Sono diplomatico!"*

The firing from behind the soldiers' barricades faded into silence, and for a moment the only sounds were the rumble of electrical generators feeding the lights and the noisy helicopters circling overhead.

Cautiously, a large, portly man in combat fatigues signaled for Ekimov to advance.

Calvo readjusted the antenna and watched the scene taking place on the tiny screen of the portable television.

His face was white with plaster dust, but he was unmarked. He could hear the fading cries of the fighter burned by white phosphorus. The young man with the Kalashnikov, frustrated by his failure to kill the defector, had vanished. The owner of the television set held out his hand. "I'm getting out," the boy said.

"You will die."

"Maybe. But if the Russian can go, so can I."

Suddenly it no longer mattered. Calvo surrendered the shiny toy. So typical of the West, he thought. The thousands of man-hours, the precious resources wasted, so that anyone with the price could be amused. While hundreds of thousands starve. While working people are brutalized. While Jews strut like conquerors in the streets of Arab villages . . .

Where is everyone, Calvo wondered. What happened to the Germans? To Hanalore? And what of Mariella? Had she really betrayed her trust? Would anyone ever know? We used to believe history would justify everything we did. What bullshit.

The fire was growing brighter outside. A tongue of flame was working its way down the ancient wooden balustrade. The floor of the loft was burned through, and from moment to moment there were little showers of glistening bits—tiny shards of the long mirrors that had once lined the walls up there.

The fire was quite intense in the stairwell. The quotation from Bakunin was still readable, but the wall was discoloring.

Calvo looked, red-eyed, at the words of the great nihilist. Why was it that he had once lived a life like almost any other's, in the bosom of a loving family? He had even been religious. He had been, if anything, favored with money, a certain amount of privilege. He had intellect, education.

What had so drawn him first to socialism, and then in swift succession to Marxism, to Leninism, to Stalinism, and finally to nihilism?

As the fire crackled about him, he had a momentary insight: I was eager to change the world. Because to do this I would have to wield power. Failing that, there was only emptiness . . .

He imagined that he could hear commandos inside the building. There were none. The fire was too intense by now.

He sat down on the sandbags scattered about the redoubt.

I was a good teacher, he thought. I did make young people think.

Didn't I?

He closed the switch on the detonator, and thunder rolled across the city.

In the hospital at L'Aquila, Zachary Quinn opened his eyes and murmured, "Irish?"

Mary was asleep in a chair by his bed, the earpiece for the wall television still in her ear, the set playing silently.

He looked at his wife. He felt terrible, but no one could feel this way, he concluded, unless he was on the mend. Nor would Mary be sleeping if he were as badly off as he felt.

He turned his attention to the television set. It was a special news report from some Roman street. Police and soldiers were attacking a building with small-arms fire and grenades. Helicopters hovered overhead.

It was unmistakably an army anti-terrorist operation. Get the bastards! Zachary thought. Clean them out.

Mary stirred, but did not wake.

You'd like to be there, wouldn't you, Irish? he thought.

Damn right, she would. And she'd write about it in words people wouldn't forget. She'd tell it with honesty and real power.

Suddenly, the building he was watching appeared to bulge. Jets of fire burst from the windows first, and then from the shattering walls. Concussion struck the television cameras. A nearby church bell began to toll. The screen went blank, and the network logo appeared. A young woman's voice said that there were "technical difficulties" but picture transmission would soon be resumed.

Zachary looked long at the frozen screen. One day, he thought, one day you bastards are really going to do it. You are going to blow up the world. He regarded his wife of many years with tears of love in his eyes. When the end comes, Irish, he thought, I'll wake you up to watch it. It will be the least I can do.

43. LANGLEY, VIRGINIA

Judge Daniel Street was preparing to leave his office when Craig Seymour, on the Italian desk, asked permission to speak with him.

The Judge had been through a difficult week and he had been looking forward to getting home in time to have a meal with his family. Something about Seymour's tone warned him that it was unlikely.

The Italian-desk man was a low-level employee, consigned to gathering routine information about what was happening in Italy and the western Balkans. But like all CIA people, he had personal assets—sources of valuable and not so valuable information about his area of responsibility.

He was a pudgy young man, already losing much of his hair. A shiny scalp gleamed through the few strands that he combed carefully across his head.

"I just got off the fax with Cannon, of NRO, sir," he said. Cannon, the Judge remembered, was an equally unprepossessing young man, who worked for the National Reconnaissance Office, hidden deep in the belly of the Pentagon.

The NRO's primary responsibility was to monitor the real-time images received from the KH-12 and KH-13 satellites. Either of these birds could image objects as small as twenty-four inches across. One ignored KH information at one's peril. It was elint—electronic intelligence—of the highest order.

"KH-12 89A has picked up this from a pass over Rome," Seymour said, spreading a set of prints on the DCI's desk. What appeared to be a full city block of the Italian capital was burning.

"I checked it against Teleradio Italia and got some tape footage from their telecast. The important thing, Judge, is that the Italian Army antiterrorist commandos are apparently mounting a major attack." He regarded the Director with watery blue eyes, vulnerable behind thick eyeglasses. "There's been talk in-house sir. I guess you know that. Of course everyone knows that

Mr. Wells has dropped out of sight. There have been suggestions he's on another one of his trips for the President. But that isn't so, is it, Judge? Mr. Traina went over to look for him. At least, that's what the talk is—"

"Watch what you say, Seymour," Judge Street said.

"I'm sorry, sir," Seymour said humbly. "I am trying to do what I think is right for the Agency."

"Go on."

"I have a friend at the White House."

"And?"

"The story there is that the President watched this on his satellite channel. My friend heard him say to the Press Secretary that maybe he had allowed the Agency too much latitude on the question of Mr. Wells. 'Jack is my friend,' was what he said. But the feeling over there is that the Agency dropped the ball on this one. That we didn't give the best advice. I thought I should speak up. If I have overstepped my authority, I apologize."

"Thank you, Seymour," the Judge said. "You can leave your material with me."

"Yes, sir."

Street sat staring at the closed door of his office for several minutes. Was it possible that Wells had got himself tangled in that Italian holocaust? He shuddered to think what the political opposition would make of it if it was as bad as it looked and a close friend of the President of the United States was involved—as either a perpetrator or a victim.

Having given both Herrick and Traina a direct order to cut his "friend" Wells off, the President, like the politician he was, had had second thoughts. The strange and bitter part of it was that if one were to ask Wells—assuming he was still alive—he would undoubtedly say that a politician was what a president of the United States should be. He touched a call button on his console. "Who is out there?" he asked.

"Joanna Reilly, Director. I'm from the pool."

"Call the White House, please," he said wearily. "Find out if I can see the President tonight."

44. ROME

Traina's taxi had fled a full mile before he could entice the panicky driver to stop. The memory of Wells, ordinarily the most circumspect of men, waving a great ugly Glock at people was something remarkable. Even in his Wild Bill Donovan mode, Wells had never been a gunman. But when one's family was at risk, who could tell?

Traina shouted at the driver that he still wished to go across the river to the Vatican Museums entrance.

"Ah, no, *signor*! Never! Do not think of it. There are the police and there is that insane acquaintance of yours with his pistol. No, no. It is impossible." This declaration was made with arm-waving emphasis. "Now I beseech you. Please get out of my taxi and let me go in peace!"

The car radio was still on. Voices jabbered about the developing battle on the Via Palestro.

"A small white phosphorous shell has been fired by the army . . ."

"There is some return fire from malefactors on the roof of the building . . ."

"Carabinieri headquarters says they are reinforcing the army heavily . . ."

"Please, *signor*, I beg of you. Leave my taxi. I am too old a man to undergo such events. Please. Go."

The man was hopeless, Traina thought, suddenly furious. Another taxi was approaching.

"Damn your eyes, all right. I'm moving on." He opened the rear door and stood on the sidewalk, fishing for his wallet.

But the driver was in no mood to wait for payment. This American was as mad as the one with the gun. He put his Fiat in gear and raced away from the river.

Traina stood in the street and flagged down the other taxi. "I need to get to the Vatican Museums gate," he shouted through the glass.

The driver wound the window down with maddening slowness. "That is very difficult," he said judiciously. "Perhaps at this time it is impossible. The police—idiots every one of them—are blocking the bridges. Presumably so the Red Brigades won't overwhelm the rest of Rome. Actually," he said, "most fares seem to want to go down to watch the battle. Which I think is extremely unwise. But then, people do foolish things, do they not, *signor*?"

"I want to get to the Vatican Museums," Traina said again.

"They are closed," the man said reasonably.

"Of course they're closed, damn it!"

"*Signor*, please. I was merely informing you. There is no need to be rude. You still wish to go there? Even though they are closed?"

"*Si, prego.*"

At that moment there was a crash of distant thunder, and a yellow flare of light against the rain-filled clouds.

Jesus, Traina thought, holy Jesus Christ. Thierry somehow managed all of that as a diversion—a lousy fucking diversion.

He got into the taxi and shouted, "*Avanti! Presto, presto!*"

The driver said, "All in good time, *signor*. All in good time."

45. VATICAN CITY

As she ran, Megan remembered the voice that had begun all this a week ago in San Francisco.

And now she was here. Running through the rain.

"*Megan.*" The accented speech was startlingly familiar. The Gallic stress turned the name of a Welsh female ancestor of Matt Wells into "May-gahn."

The sound brought memories of Cholon, of nights at the Marianne, of her first meeting with a man instead of one more boy. . . .

She stopped abruptly, looking across the street into the trees lining the Vatican wall. The lights were dim here and sparse.

"Here."

"Jean?"

"Come over here," he said in French.

Her hair was wet, a mass of cold ringlets. She shivered as she searched for the source of the voice. She did not find it, and panic clutched at her throat.

There was a shadow among the trees, moving.

"Where, Jean? Where are you?"

The voice was suddenly very near. "Are you alone?"

She turned to face a figure as menacing as the iron archangel atop Castel Sant'Angelo.

"Jean? Is it *you*?"

For a reply, the figure stepped into the light. Megan drew breath in a gasp. It *was* Jean. Or, rather, it had been Jean. There was age, of course. She had expected that. The thick hair was still thick, but no longer black. His hair curled over his raincoat collar just as it had once done when he stood in the Southeast Asian monsoon and smiled at her as though she were the sun breaking through the clouds.

But the face! It was like that of an Adonis vandalized by barbarians. The nose was broadened and broken, the cheeks coarsened and scarred, the eyes sunken and suspicious, the lips thick and inexpressive. It was an old man's face, one that had been physically crushed, and more. All that Jean Thierry had seen and done since the morning he left her in Cholon was there. It terrified her.

"Oh, yes. It is I," he said. Then in a tone of cold contempt he asked, "By the way, *ma pauvrette*, are we still husband and wife? I never thought to ask."

He is lying, Megan thought. He knows everything about me. He knows how I live, my friends, my lovers, my work, everything. He knows every detail about me, and about Denny and about Uncle Jack. Because the Russians have told him.

The horror of it grew. She found herself shaking.

"Where is Denny? What have you done with my daughter?" A cold fury edged her words.

He said, as coldly, "Where is Wells?"

"Uncle Jack isn't part of this," Megan said.

"He is very much a part of this."

Megan reached into the pocket of her raincoat and took out David's German pistol. She held it in both hands and pointed it at Thierry. *"Where is my daughter?"*

The deep cold eyes regarded her speculatively. He looked carefully at the pistol in her hands. It was a Walther PPK. Where, he wondered warily, could she have obtained such a fine weapon? She would have had to pass through metal detectors on her journey to Rome from the United States. Did that mean she had entered into some sort of dramatic plot with her uncle? It did not jibe at all with what he knew to be true of her. Even after all these years, she was essentially the same light-minded, silly American female he had seduced so easily in Saigon.

But he had not expected her to point a weapon at him. And now, if she were to discover that he had ordered Denny disposed of as a needless complication, she might well shoot, possibly even by some foolish female mistake.

The irony of the situation touched his heavy lips with a suggestion of a smile. It had an unexpected effect. She said, "Jean, don't make me do something I don't believe in. Please. I beg you."

"Yes," he said. "You don't believe in violence." Teeth too regular to be real showed in a feral smile. "Give me the gun."

Sounding desperate, she said, "Don't, Jean. I swear I will use it."

As she firmed her grip, he looked at the safety. And simply took the gun from her hand. He was amused at her pretense of pulling the trigger as he did so.

"Drop the gun, Frenchman," Jack Wells spoke quietly but with a voice edged with steel.

Thierry let the Walther fall to the pavement and breathed a deep sigh. "I have delivered him to you, Plakhanov, as promised. Paladin is yours."

At that moment, a prolonged mutter of thunder rolled across Rome.

General Plakhanov stepped from the shadows of the Vatican wall. For a moment Wells thought he might be a passerby somehow trapped in this place by the overzealous police guarding the bridges.

Plakhanov carried his sword cane innocently. It suited his sense of elegance. It was the perfect weapon for a settlement between two old antagonists.

Crossing into the tree line, Plakhanov stopped a dozen feet from Wells, Megan, and the Frenchman. He almost closed his eyes with sweet pleasure as he spoke the words he had been composing ever since receiving the message that "the Frenchman is running."

"Mr. Wells," he said, "put away the pistol."

Wells swung the Glock to cover the newcomer. "Who in hell are you?"

Plakhanov shivered with fury. The gray man before him had injured him as severely as any man could ever do. Yet he had never seen him, up close, face to face. Before this moment, John Wells had been an abstraction. Now, he was real.

The General allowed his attention to encompass Megan Wells. He was not a connoisseur of women, but by any standards this must be a sexually attractive one.

"Mr. Wells, I said put the pistol away. We have the child. There is nothing you can do."

Megan uttered a cry of mingled fear and fury. "Who *is* this, Jean?"

"He is our marriage broker, *ma pauvrette*," he said.

"Don't," Wells said.

"I am not disappointed," Plakhanov said lightly. "Our Paladin is a sensitive man."

Wells responded to the code name. A great ugly bubble of memory surfaced. It was like an eruption liberating poisons trapped at the bottom of a mountain lake.

He stared hard at the slender, ascetic man standing so quietly in the rain. "Plakhanov."

Plakhanov made a slight bow. "We knew one another once. By reputation, at least."

Wells's eyes narrowed. "We had a mutual acquaintance, I think."

Hatred drained the color from Plakhanov's cheeks. Suddenly he looked like a cadaver. Megan glanced anxiously from one man to the other.

"A remarkable pair, are they not?" Thierry asked.

Wells said, still staring at the Russian, "I thought that might be what this was all about. You want a trade."

"Of a sort," Plakhanov said.

"One for one?"

Plakhanov nodded.

"My niece goes free. Now."

Plakhanov looked at the Frenchman and lifted his shoulders in a shrug. It was Peter Arendt at the Wall he was seeking to exorcise, not Jean Thierry's months in Bung Kan prison.

"She goes," Wells said.

Plakhanov said deliberately, "I make you the same promise you made to Peter Arendt."

Wells said thoughtfully, "Yes. I remember now."

"Please give your weapon to my colleague," Plakhanov said.

"Who is this person, Uncle Jack?" Megan asked.

"Forgive me, Meg. I should have said. This is General Feliks Plakhanov, commander of the First Chief Directorate of the Committee for State Security of the USSR. A long time ago, he had to murder his lover because of something I did, and now it appears we all must pay for it. I am sorrier than I can say."

Megan found herself appalled and yet more moved than she had ever been by Uncle Jack. The speech was a farewell; endings echoed in every phrase.

Plakhanov's face grew even paler.

He slipped the stiletto from the cane and stepped into a face-to-face position with Wells.

Wells regarded the slender blade and murmured, "Oh, yes. I understand." He lowered the plastic Glock and said, "Do we have a bargain?"

"Give your pistol to the Frenchman," Plakhanov said.

Wells let the Glock go.

He felt the bite of the stiletto under his ribs and heard Megan scream.

A running man struck Plakhanov, knocked him down, and turned to face Thierry.

"David! Don't!" Megan understood the bargain her uncle had made with the Russian. At the far end of it lay Denny. This was not at all like her half-hearted, *pro forma* attempt to pull the trigger when faced with Jean. This was something different. It was the first time in her life she had faced such a decision. This for that. Positive. Nonrelativistic. A straight choice of this evil in return for that lesser or more acceptable evil. What was important was that in all her life she had never been forced to such choices and now . . . Your uncle in exchange for your daughter. Decide. Don't ponder. Don't discuss. Don't vote. Decide. *Now.*

David was shouting at Megan: "She's all right! The army found her an hour ago."

His shout seemed to reverberate inside her skull, dreamlike, terrifying, liberating. Was it true? Was Denny truly safe? Was this nightmare somehow ending?

The Frenchman closed on David, the Glock held for a gut shot. It went off, and David's right hand went limp and bloody.

Thierry fell into a crouch, steadying down for a second, killing, shot.

Megan felt something against her foot. Her ankle twisted, and she went painfully down on one knee. The object that had tripped her was David's PPK. She took it up, remembering she had not succeeded in firing it before. When she was a child, Uncle Jack sometimes took her shooting. She remembered that now. She pulled the slide back and levered a bullet into the chamber. In one smooth motion, she raised the weapon, pointed it at Jean's midriff, and fired.

The PPK and the Glock fired almost simultaneously. Thierry spun, dropped the plastic pistol, and stared at Megan, disbelieving, unconvinced.

"C'est impossible," he said, and dropped to his face on the muddy cobblestones.

Megan clambered to her feet, visibly trembling.

Wells sat against the base of a tree, holding a fist against a wound below his ribs.

David was on his feet, leaning over Thierry, seeking with one hand to turn him over, off the Glock.

Megan looked around.

The man called Plakhanov was gone. Vanished.

Wells lurched to his feet and spoke to David. "Are you Reuben's man?"

David, trying to wrap his shattered forearm with a handkerchief and a belt, said, "Yes. Ashburn."

"Is it true what you said about Denny?"

"It is. She was kicking the walls down when the army found her. Somewhere near *that*." He indicated the still-bright sky over Via Palestro.

"Thank God," Wells said.

"How badly hurt are you?" David asked.

Megan still stood, half dazed, looking at the Frenchman.

"I'm in no danger," Wells said. "But look after her." He retrieved the Glock pistol.

Megan closed her eyes and tried to keep her trembling from overwhelming her. This was the violence she had always feared. The violence she saw in Uncle Jack, and in the young men who visited the house in Virginia.

Yet she had been suddenly presented with a choice. Two choices. First, between Uncle Jack's life and Denny's. She flushed to remember how easily that choice had been made. That he would understand and support the decision did not make the reality any easier to accept.

And then swiftly, swiftly, had come another choice—one made

285

by people such as David and her uncle often enough to rob them forever of peaceful sleep:

Before your eyes, either David Ashburn or your former husband dies. The instrument of selection is in your hand. *Use it or not.*

The choice was yours, and you chose to kill.

Now live the rest of your life with what you have done. As Uncle Jack does.

She looked around for him, but he was gone. She caught a glimpse of him vanishing down the deserted street in the direction of the Tiber.

David was tottering, blood running in a steady stream from his wounded arm. My God, woman, she told herself. Move. For once in your life see the world as others see it.

She draped David's good arm across her shoulders and said, "The car, where did you leave it?"

"Risorgimento . . ." he said. "Too far. I can't make it."

Behind the Vatican wall, Megan could hear shouts and the sound of men running. With David's weight on her shoulder, she reached the gate and beat on it with her fist. The sound was inaudible.

"*God damn.* Damn. Damn. Damn!" She slipped a wet shoe from her foot and hammered with it on the panels. "Open! We need help here!"

And under the trees across the Viale Vaticano, Jean Thierry, his face set by advancing rigor in an expression of disbelief, scowled at the rainy Roman sky.

46. THE RIVER

His breath came in shallow, agonizing gasps as he ran. He could not remember ever having experienced such pain. The man had exploded from the darkness like a bolt from a crossbow, and he had struck with a karate kick of killing intensity.

The unexpected violence had filled him with a shrieking terror. It had reduced him to what he had been when Ivan Plakhanov used to return from the outer darkness in which he lived to shake and strike a hapless boy who awaited his appearances with helpless horror.

For a lifetime, Feliks Plakhanov had been an important part of an organization whose stock in trade was the infliction of pain and the creation of terror. Yet from the day of the last beating at the hands of his father, Plakhanov had never *experienced* pain—the kind of real physical pain inflicted by one human being upon another. He had never been so low in the chain of command until he had placed himself there to savor the destruction of an old enemy.

Now he ran through the rain, a shocked and gasping man in his sixties—too old for such things under the best of circumstances, but with his aging faculties inflamed by the sudden awakening.

He had created Operation Paladin and he had given it part of his life. Now he was suddenly made aware that there *was* no Operation Paladin, that it had no reality except for what was written in a half-dozen briefing books back in his vault at Number 2 Dzerzhinsky Square.

The madman who had assaulted him had broken his chest. He could feel the grinding anguish of broken bones each time he took a step. Yet he fled toward the river and the Ponte Victor Emanuele because he heard footsteps behind him. Was it Paladin?

Plakhanov paused, holding himself erect against the cold wet metal of a postal kiosk, gasping air into his lacerated lung. He closed his eyes and reached out to Peter in the darkness. Does it surprise you that your Feli is terrified? he thought. Did you think it was his task only to terrify others?

Peter was out of reach, but the memory of that woman killing the Frenchman was not. The combined pain and shock made a monstrous reality. He had crouched on the wet sidewalk like a wounded child and for a terrible moment he had thought that the woman would turn the pistol in his direction. But she had not, and the Frenchman, the skilled killer of dozens, had fallen with only two words of astonished complaint.

Feliks Plakhanov's life had been wrenched, in a single second, out of the pattern of years. A member of the ruling elite was not attacked on the street by men half his age. He was obeyed and respected, not kicked and beaten.

He heard a child sobbing, with fear and rage. He sucked air

into his lungs and screamed at the pain, but the scream was only an agonized moan.

Ivan Plakhanov materialized out of the misty rain, a figure of shadows in his ancient blousy Great Patriotic War uniform.

Plakhanov shied away from him.

There you are, Felushka. Why are you running away?

I'm not running.

I would rather have you a liar than a nance, my son. But you are both. You must be beaten. Better still, you must die, little Feliks. For the honor of the family. For the honor of the Soviet Motherland. There is no place for such as you in the Soviet Union.

Overhead, a low-flying helicopter veered toward the Vatican buildings with a beam of brilliant light, searching.

Ahead Plakhanov could now hear the Tiber flowing between its masonry banks; behind, footsteps.

He began to run again, limping, staggering.

Where did it go wrong, he wondered. Was it because I never understood what really happened in the field? Was Paladin so much better than I?

I want darkness, he thought. I want to hide myself until it can all be made right again. What would Peter think of that?

Gentle Peter.

Oh, God, Plakhanov thought. He had been ready to surrender in 1962, and I killed him.

Run, Feliks. Run.

Who was that speaking to him? It sounded like Ivan Plakhanov. It must be he, because Feliks could hear his dragging footsteps behind, drawing ever closer.

But there, just there, was the river.

He saw Ivan once more. Less distinctly, because the old-fashioned uniform was gone, and instead he wore a civilian suit like his own, and there was a great red patch of blood on the left side. It glistened in the rain.

There could be no question of going back. The very idea brought a wave of horror and disgust.

Plakhanov could feel each individual beat of his heart against his ribs. Thrust upon thrust, and each growing deeper and more deadly.

Is it possible? Plakhanov asked himself. Am I dying?

He had turned, almost by instinct, to the river. As a child he had loved the Moscow and the Volga. In Berlin, before the Wall, before so much pain and loss, there had been the Spree, slow-moving in spring and summer, glazed white in winter. How pure the snow made it!

But here the far bank was brilliant with lights; they spilled over the stone embankments to reflect like molten silver in the dark rain-speckled water flowing under the bridge.

He looked back. Ivan was still there. Calling out in German. Why in German, Feliks wondered. In honor of Peter Arendt?

He stumbled out onto the stone span of the Ponte Victor Emanuele.

Ivan called out: "Give it up, Plakhanov. Your people already know. They are on the way. You have one chance. With us."

Plakhanov stared hard at the phantom. It was not Ivan.

It was Paladin.

I can't manage to stay on my feet much longer, Wells thought. But there he is. *I have him.*

He tried to signal the police to leave Plakhanov alone, not to press him.

Overhead, an Agusta police helicopter swung over the river from the direction of the Vatican. Wells waved desperately for it to stay clear, but instead it illuminated the bridge with its halogen spotlight.

An American voice spoke in Russian through the aircraft public-address horn.

"It is over, General Plakhanov. Give yourself up to the Italian police. Do you understand me?"

Wells almost wailed with despair. "Herrick, damn it, *no*, *no!*"

Plakhanov heard the hated American accent and lost his fear. It was as though Peter had appeared to guide him, and he went easily.

He climbed the stone balustrade, paused for a moment to look at the play of lights on the water below. Then he jumped the thirty feet to the stone pier supporting the arch at midstream. He struck it with a spine-breaking impact, hung for a moment on the stones, and then vanished into the Tiber.

At the instant Plakhanov struck the pier, he saw Peter Arendt very clearly. It seemed almost certain that he was smiling. Plakhanov determined that he would teach dear Peter one more couplet by Ivanov:

How tedious living in this world,
And such a trouble, gentlemen!

And rolling and sprawling through the detritus lining the bottom of the river channel, Feliks Plakhanov made his dark way toward the sea.

PART FOUR

Summit

"The Mock Turtle went on.
'We had the best of educations.
. . . Reeling and Writing,
of course, to begin with . . .
and then the different branches
of Arithmetic—Ambition,
Distraction, Uglification, and
Derision.' "

—Lewis Carroll,
Alice's Adventures in Wonderland

47. THE WHITE HOUSE, OCTOBER 30

She stood in the section reserved for the special guests of the President of the United States. Behind her and the many others gathered on the south lawn, the green fell away in a magnificent sweep to the President's Park. There was no smoke in the clear autumn air from the twenty-one-gun salute. (Shouldn't a General Secretary have had only nineteen?) The wind had blown it away. But Denny could smell the tang of powder mingling with the scent of growing things in the park.

The band of the Old Guard struck up the "Internationale." The President and his shorter, rounder guest stood at attention on the platform. A ceremonial company of the Third Infantry, resplendent in their Revolutionary War uniforms, faced the crowd, still as mannequins.

Denny cast a sidelong glance at her mother. What a great woman! She had always been proud of Megan, but something special had come into their relationship since Rome. Denny allowed herself a slight smile. Come to that, she was rather proud of her own behavior in the events she had come to think of, rather dramatically, as "the Roman affair."

Uncle Jack had said: "I worry more about your mother than I do about you. Be patient with her."

If Uncle Jack only knew how much easier Meg was to live with since Rome. She would explain it to him one of these days. The dear old man had a lot to learn about women.

Jack Wells had almost missed this "ceremony of innocence," as he called it. Denny didn't know why. Perhaps because he was still recuperating from the injuries he had received the night he met the terrorists in Rome. Imagine, she thought with a shiver,

Uncle Jack fought a man with a knife; David Ashburn had been shot; a Russian diplomat had somehow drowned in the Tiber, and another had been shipped back to the Soviet Union in disgrace.

The elements of a spy novel were all around.

Denny had seriously considered changing her major from art and turning to writing, but she had decided reluctantly against it. She said something about it to David while they basked on the foredeck of the *Denise*, and he had laughed and said her career was probably preordained, whatever in the world he had meant by *that*.

David was on medical leave from the CIA. He had spent half the summer sailing the Chesapeake with Megan and Denny and Uncle Jack, and sometimes Frank and Hilly Traina.

Denny decided some months ago that she liked and approved of David Ashburn.

More recently, she had decided she did *not* like or approve of the President of the United States.

He had been very considerate to her family, and that was flattering. But he had promised to make Uncle Jack secretary of state and he had not done it. Uncle Jack and the others accepted that as natural, but not Denny. The steel in her was tempering.

The "Internationale" was very long. Denny regarded the red flag of the USSR snapping in the wind on the White House grounds and grew more thoughtful.

This summer had been unforgettable. There had been the Roman affair, and the publicity that surrounded it. She had appeared on national television, been interviewed by newspapers and magazines. There had even, she thought with a giggle, been a strictly unauthorized version of her experiences as a hostage of the Red Brigades in a check-out-stand tabloid. Debbie and Liz, who had been with her that morning in the Hotel Gregoriana, were green with envy.

But she wondered how envious her friends would be if she told them the truth about those six days in darkness. It had been degrading, humiliating. She remembered the hands in the dark, the stench and pains of captivity. Sometimes—quite often, actually—she remembered Mariella and wondered about her. What made a Mariella? She would have to think about that seriously when there was time.

Uncle Jack told her not to think about it, if she could manage that, and if she couldn't, then to turn to Megan. "People who love you need to be needed, Denny," he said. For some reason, she had wanted to kiss him when he said it, and she had. Her shrink hadn't been much good, and she'd stopped seeing him as soon as possible.

She had the feeling that the media people never quite got things right. They seemed always to have a personal point to make. They never did get straight the events of the week in Rome.

In time, she thought. In time.

The band stopped playing the "Internationale" and took up "The Star-Spangled Banner." Denny stood straighter, and was not surprised to feel a certain catch in her throat. Maybe that was what Uncle Jack meant when he spoke of the "ceremony of innocence."

The breeze riffled her long dark hair and blew the unfamiliar silk dress against her body. She had let her mother select her clothes for today. Megan had loved doing it.

The President moved up to the microphones and began his welcoming speech, while the Soviet General Secretary listened closely to his interpreter.

Denny regarded the President with cool speculation. When it's my generation's turn, she thought, we will do better.

She turned her attention to her mother and David. David's arm was still in a sling. There had been one operation at Bethesda. There would soon be another. Uncle Jack stood straight and tall, despite his long convalescence. He hated all the fanfare, Denny knew. It was an expensive game Jack and David played.

The General Secretary began his response. He mentioned arms control immediately, because that was the excuse for his being here again. Then there were the promises of friendship.

Denny's eyes narrowed. She remembered the Russians who had snatched her from the Roman street, the Soviet weapons in the hands of her keepers. She shivered slightly with anger.

Megan noticed and whispered, "Are you all right?"

She squeezed her mother's arm reassuringly.

David said, "What?"

Denny whispered, "Is he telling the truth?"

"We'll have to see, won't we?"

"Yes," Denny said. "Oh, yes."

She looked away, at the real world, thinking, of all things, of *Alice in Wonderland*.

And as if to show their difference from anything in the world of men and women, the clouds, driven by the brisk breeze, fled across the sky. And the cloud shadows raced over, through, and around the gathering of politicians, soldiers, reporters, bureaucrats, and smiling spectators on the White House lawn, using their fleeting presence to make innocent patterns in the wind.

ABOUT THE AUTHOR

Alfred Coppel was a fighter pilot in the U.S. Air Force. He has been an amateur racing driver, is an accomplished yachtsman and the author of fifteen novels. He lives with his wife in Portola Valley, California.